RUMOURED

RUMOURED

KELLY and KRISTINA MANCARUSO

HEAD
of ZEUS

An Aries Book

First published in the UK in 2025 by Head of Zeus Ltd,
part of Bloomsbury Publishing Plc

9 7 5 3 1 2 4 6 8

A catalogue record for this book is available from the British Library.

ISBN (PB): 9781035910311
ISBN (Export Special Edition PB): 9781035921799
ISBN (ANZ TPB): 9781035912346
ISBN (E): 9781035910328

Cover design: Simon Michele | Head of Zeus

Printed and bound in Great Britain by
CPI Group (UK) Ltd, Croydon, CR0 4YY

MIX
Paper | Supporting
responsible forestry
FSC
www.fsc.org   FSC® C013604

Bloomsbury Publishing Plc
50 Bedford Square, London, WC1B 3DP, UK
Bloomsbury Publishing Ireland Limited,
29 Earlsfort Terrace, Dublin 2, D02 AY28, Ireland

HEAD OF ZEUS LTD
5–8 Hardwick Street
London, EC1R 4RG

To find out more about our authors and books
visit www.headofzeus.com
For product safety related questions contact productsafety@bloomsbury.com

For Mom and Dad,
thanks for always encouraging us
to use our imagination

Authors' Note

This book was born out of a deep love for writing and music, and while some inspiration was taken from real-life musicians, celebrities, and events, our characters are in no way intended to represent any specific person. In fact, Harlow Hayes has been created to exist in the same universe as our favorite stars.

From Bach to The Beatles to Taylor Swift, musicians have been leaving "Easter eggs" in their work for centuries. Searching for these clues and dissecting our favorite artists' music is something that we've always enjoyed—so much so that we were inspired to create a fictional musician and write an entire discography for her so we could leave a trail of clues for a fictional journalist to uncover. We had such a blast doing this that we also decided to layer in our own hidden messages, ranging from fun little Easter eggs to major plot hints for the most eagle-eyed readers.

All will be revealed at the end, but be sure to keep an eye out for clues in the text as you read...

For the glory and fame, I'd do it the same.
Lose myself in this dangerous game.

– Harlow Hayes, from the album *Legacy*

C*LEB NEWS

POP STAR HARLOW HAYES ARRESTED ON SUSPICION OF MURDER

By Joel Casey – *September 24, 2024*

Grammy-winning pop star Harlow Hayes was taken into custody by law enforcement in Nashville, Tennessee early Tuesday morning. She is reportedly wanted by authorities in New York on suspicion of murder.

Ms. Hayes is expected to face a judge in Nashville this afternoon, who will order her extradition across state lines, where she'll be arraigned. Details on the alleged crime and victim have yet to be released.

Born Harlow Eleanor McHayton, the singer-songwriter rose to fame at the age of nineteen following the release of her self-titled album in 2015. She went on to produce multiple platinum-selling hits before sweeping the major pop categories at this year's Grammys with her long-awaited fourth studio album, *Apotheosis*. Released in August 2023, the album marked a notable change in Hayes' music, with the artist moving away from her bubblegum pop roots to a darker, indie sound.

Hayes is due to embark on a world tour later this autumn to promote her most recent album, *Legacy*. The somber follow-up to *Apotheosis* has already garnered millions of sales since its release last month, with its lead single "Garden of Bones" hitting number one on all streaming platforms. However, it looks like Hayes will only be touring courthouses and prisons for the foreseeable future, as sources claim "worrying evidence" led to the starlet's arrest.

While there's no additional information at present, we promise to bring you all the shocking new details as soon as we have them.

Comments:

@KaleighTurnerOfficial: NO. FREAKING. WAY.

@SgtPepper909: Harlow Hayes: coming to a prison near you

@InezWrites22: I called it years ago ya'll – that bitch is crazy!

@SianGilbz: Looks like she's leveled up from writing songs about her enemies to just killing them #mood

@CruelSophieXoXo: Harlow honey, when we said SLAY QUEEN, we did not mean literally… anyway, everyone #StreamLegacy

@HarlowsHarlot94: this is obviously not true, another example of the media exploiting her for clout #freeharlow #harlowisinnocent

@MaxwellsHammer3: Damn, when the girl sang about "Violent Ends" she really meant it

@PerisMum: My bet is she finally snapped and killed Kamryn Hart

@SheSaidEd: As long as she didn't touch my bb Colton Scott, I don't give a shit

@JiminWYlover13: @PerisMum Hope it's that sketchy SB

@LiviaStoneHH: Funny how everyone's reporting on the one bad thing she's ever been accused of, but they fail to report on all her charity work over the years

@summertime_sadness01: @LiviaStoneHH "One bad thing"? Bestie, this is MURDER.

PART I

IDOLS

Interviewer: What's the most common misconception about you?

Harlow Hayes: People think they know what—and who—my songs are about. But they have no idea.

Chapter 1

Risk it! Chance it! Never give up! Dreams really do come true...

Entertainment reporter Naomi Barnes knows it's all bullshit. That chasing dreams is a pointless, dangerous endeavor, despite what stars proclaim again and again in their award speeches.

For most, it ends in tragedy. Sometimes it's quick, like ripping off a Band-Aid—a painful demise before they even get their foot in the first of a million doors. Other times it's slow and depressing, a lifetime spent "never giving up" until one day they realize it's never going to happen, they're never going to be good enough. Never were. All that time wasted. All their potential wasted.

And for the few who do manage to break through? Well, if life has taught Naomi anything, it's that if you fly too close to the sun, you're going to get burned. Or worse.

Over the course of her career, she's covered countless celebrities' rise to the top, only to write up their inevitable crash back to earth the following year. They think they've made it, but then their heels are kicked out (or violently slashed) from under them. Many times, it's their own doing.

Like today's fallen star, Jason Mikaelson, once a fan-favorite reality TV personality, now another body in the morgue. Early this morning, following a very public breakup after his monthslong affair was exposed, Jason's ex-fiancée, actress Lauren Vincent, found him unresponsive in the bathtub, foaming from the mouth.

Naomi is about to break the news about the untimely—and, according to sources, unsurprising—death thanks to a tip from her occasional hook-up at the LA Fire Department who responded to the scene. He spilled all the gory and depressing details, like how Lauren rushed over to Jason's home in the hills after listening to a worrying voicemail from him, only to realize she was hours too late. By the time she arrived, Jason's bloated corpse had turned the water a ripe green as if he'd bathed in his own vomit.

It's a typical Tuesday story for Naomi, who's been at her desk at the West Coast branch of C*Leb News—a popular celebrity news outlet that ranks somewhere between TMZ and E! News on the respectable scale—for two hours already. She came in at seven to give herself enough time to write and publish the Mikaelson piece before she heads over to the courthouse at ten to cover the latest celeb divorce drama. It was silent until a half hour ago, but now the office is slowly coming to life.

Doors swing open, colleagues exchange "Good morning"s—some more enthusiastically than others. Fingers tip-tap on keyboards, the printer roars and clicks, then abruptly stops. Someone sighs and mutters something about paper. Coffee drips loudly from the new machine, the most modern appliance in the room aside from the new intern from UCLA. And then come the "Oh my god"s and gasps of horror. Or is it excitement?

Naomi glances up, still typing. She knows the keys by heart and doesn't need to look at the screen. *The reality star was found unresponsive in the bathtub of his Malibu home by his ex-fiancée, only days after his cheating scandal was made public.*

The C*Leb office is always whirring with chatter, though. Aware of her looming deadline, Naomi ignores the whispers, figuring it's just standard gossip, and turns her attention back to her article.

"Another shining star extinguished too soon," said Mikaelson's longtime producer.

Naomi shakes her head as she types with one hand and grabs her half-eaten granola bar with the other, crumbs falling onto her chest as she bites into it. "Shining star" isn't the phrase she'd personally use; she thinks Jason wanted to punish the actress for breaking up with him after his final gaslighting attempts failed to win her back, and he was willing to hurt himself to traumatize her. He probably didn't even mean to kill himself—just wanted her to feel sorry for him.

It's a harsh, cruel assumption, she knows. But it's a harsh, cruel world.

She refrains from including her disdainful views in the story—she's more professional than that—but she can't quiet her inner cynic after nearly seven years working in the industry and witnessing first-hand how toxic it can be. She's come a long way from the Bambi-eyed new hire, armed with gel pens and a public university degree in journalism, ready to break into the world of glitz and glam. She quickly learned all that glitters isn't gold. That it's all a facade. Lipstick covering the unsightly pig underneath.

When she made the transfer from the New York to LA branch of C*Leb two years ago, she actually thought she'd get to cover more movie premieres and awards shows than overdoses, affairs, and sexual misconduct claims. But the only difference is sunnier skies and prettier people, two things sensitive-skinned Naomi doesn't necessarily appreciate.

"No fucking way."

Naomi looks up again, confused by what could possibly be causing such a commotion among her normally desensitized colleagues. She stops typing when she sees Becky, the social media manager, holding out her phone to Melanie, one of the editorial assistants. They're both tall, blonde, and tanned, wearing similar bright-colored blouses. A contrast to five-foot-three Naomi's all-black attire, accessorized by her favorite lace-up combat boots.

Naomi dusts the crumbs from her top before catching Becky's attention. "What happened?"

"It's Harlow-goddamn-Hayes…" Becky's Carolina twang breaks through her Cali-girl persona, something that only happens when she's overly excited or upset. Naomi often forgets Becky's another East Coaster who fled to the City of Broken Dreams, like herself.

"She's been arrested for murder!" Melanie's eyes are wild with excitement.

Naomi frowns, sure she misheard them. "Harlow Hayes, as in the pop star?" A lump forms in her throat as she speaks the singer's name.

"The world-famous, Grammy-winning singer-songwriter,

yes," Becky confirms. Naomi smiles, knowing that's how her sister would've described Harlow. But her smile quickly fades.

"Wait, which one is she again?" asks Jake, one of the film and TV writers. "She the one who sings that 'Love Story' song?"

"That's Taylor Swift, idiot," Becky responds, aghast. "How do you work here and not know that?"

"How do you live in the world and not know that?" Melanie mutters.

Jake holds his hands up. "Hey, I don't know, all those pop girls look and sound the same to me."

Becky rolls her eyes, grumbling something about his favorite bands sounding the same.

"Harlow's the one who fell down during her performance at the VMAs a few years back, remember?" says Melanie.

"I thought that was Madonna?"

"No, she fell at the BRIT Awards."

"Oh, and then she had that breakdown, right?" A lightbulb seems to spark to life in Jake's mind. "I remember seeing that rehab story."

Becky sighs. "It wasn't a breakdown and it wasn't rehab—the media made it sound a lot worse because she missed a few shows after Colton Scott announced his engagement, like, a month after they broke up—but yeah…"

"You say that like we aren't the media," Jake quips.

Naomi pushes back her chair and stands, weaving through the furniture dotted around the open-plan office to get to Becky. "Let me see."

Brushing her ash-brown hair over her shoulders, Naomi cranes her neck to watch the video looping on Becky's phone from the C*Leb TikTok account, which shows the pop star being ushered into jail. Still looking like her usual demure self, Harlow isn't hiding in a hoodie or staring at the floor like most celebrities do when they're arrested. Instead, she holds her head high and smirks for the cameras.

An eerie feeling washes over Naomi. Crossing her arms, she watches in awe as the footage of the arrest cuts to a photo of Harlow from earlier in her career, when she was dubbed "America's Princess of Pop." Platinum-blonde hair. Dimples. Sparkly green eyes. Thin frame. A complete shift in style to her current, much darker aesthetic. Still, beneath the raven-colored hair, black eyeliner, and thick false lashes, the same magnetic, albeit slightly vulnerable aura encapsulates her.

"This is the article." Melanie pushes her phone toward Naomi.

As she scans the page, her heart races—an uncommon reaction for the jaded twenty-nine-year-old, who's rarely shocked these days.

"Joel published it like five minutes ago," Melanie says, referring to C*Leb's managing editor, who splits his time between the East and West Coast.

"New York always gets the jump on us." Jake tosses a ball of paper into the trash can across the aisle.

As if he's been summoned, Joel Casey's name flashes onto Naomi's now-vibrating Apple Watch. She rushes back to her desk to get to her phone.

"Jo—"

"You see the news?" he says, before she can finish his name.

Joel has been Naomi's boss ever since she first started as his assistant in New York, before working her way up to senior staff writer. He's one of the main reasons Naomi has stayed at C*Leb for so long. Even though he can be brash and borderline offensive at times, he treats his employees well, especially Naomi. He respects her not only as a writer, but also as a person. He was empathetic and understanding when she needed time off after her life came crashing down, then he helped her transfer to LA.

"Yeah. We just saw the video. It's…" Naomi can't find the words to describe it, realizing, for once, she's actually surprised. *Harlow Hayes, of all people…*

If Naomi had to put money on it, she would have bet on Harlow being the victim, if anything. The thought reminds her that there's no mention of one in Joel's article.

"Wait, who'd she kill?"

Chapter 2

Naomi holds her breath as she awaits Joel's response, buzzing with curiosity. *Who the hell did one of the world's biggest pop stars murder?*

She knows the "why" will have to wait, but you can't arrest someone for murder without a dead body. Normally, the identity of the victim is revealed before the suspect.

But this is not a normal case.

"Don't know, it's all very hush-hush, according to my sources. No one is spilling." Joel's frustrated tone is deep but calm. "All I know is she's in Nash now, waiting to get transported to Rikers."

"Rikers?" Naomi blurts, unable to fathom someone as glamorous as Harlow locked up there.

"Well, that *is* where the murderers of New York go."

"I know, but... damn."

Another spectacular fall from grace, she thinks. Although, unlike Jason Mikaelson and all the other B-, C-, or D-listers Naomi usually covers, this is shocking. More shocking than Martha Stewart's arrest, with potential to be as much of a media circus as the O.J. Simpson and Michael Jackson trials. Like them, Harlow Hayes seemed untouchable. Too famous and well-loved to find herself embroiled in something so horrifying. But maybe she's hiding a dark secret too, like those before her. Allegedly.

"Anyway," Joel continues, "we probably won't know any more until she's in front of a judge in New York—earliest tomorrow. They'll have to make her arrest warrant public then. But it's fucking bizarre we don't know the victim yet."

Naomi frowns, wondering who it could be. "Maybe it's some big music industry exec. Gotta be someone powerful for them to keep it so private."

"That's what I was thinking. Or some other hotshot. I have one of my freelancers who used to work in politics asking around, seeing if there are any connections, especially to Washington. But I was hoping you could start looking into everything else."

Naomi's heart pounds. "Me?"

Joel laughs. "Yes, you. How ya feel about heading back to your old stomping ground, finding out what the fuck happened?"

Naomi hesitates, caught off-guard by the request. She moved to LA to get away from the pressure cooker she once called home.

"What about the guys in New York, though?"

Joel groans. "They're all too green. We just lost Eddie to the Post and Macie is on maternity leave. This is obviously going to be a major story over the next couple of weeks, maybe even months if it goes to trial. I want someone I can trust on it, someone with investigative experience and sources, like you. Plus, you're my best writer, on both coasts. In fact, I'm surprised every day you haven't handed in your notice to go work for Vanity Fair or one of those other flashy places that steal all my best writers, so I gotta take advantage of having you while I still can. I know you might not want to go back, though, considering..."

Naomi's stomach twists in knots. *Considering the city is filled with memories of your dead sister*, she imagines him saying.

Naomi's younger sister and best friend Faye died two and a half years ago, after which Naomi moved to LA, choosing to escape rather than cope. Faye died of a drug overdose and smoke inhalation—the coroner apparently couldn't pinpoint which one caused it, the drugs or the house fire— but she idolized Harlow Hayes. The memory of her stirs up an excitement Naomi hasn't felt in years. Genuine intrigue in a story.

Plus, her sister would probably come back to haunt her if she turned it down. *This isn't some D-list celebrity, Naomi. This is Harlow-fucking-Hayes!*

Naomi clears her throat before replying to Joel. "I'd like to cover it, actually. I'll come."

She'll be going to Manhattan, not her depressing hometown upstate, so it'll be fine. In the city, she can reconnect with former colleagues and friends, some of whom still double as sources. She'll be so busy she won't have time to wallow in the past. She starts making a mental list of people to reach out to, people who might have information, like her old college roommate Amelia, who works for a celebrity PR firm, and her friend Jessie, who works for a wpopular music publication and has connections in the industry.

"Really!?" Joel's voice is tinged with relief and elation. "No one's staying at my rental in Greenwich Village. So you can stay there if you want. As long as you need."

If you want. Naomi tilts her head back, wanting to laugh at Joel's nonchalance over his multi-million-dollar brownstone in Greenwich Village. Close to the shopping in SoHo, the clubs in Meatpacking, and a quick walk from the downtown office, it's where Naomi always wanted to live but couldn't afford.

"That would be incredible. Thanks."

"Okay, I'll get Angie to send you the apartment details and book you a flight," Joel says. "Guessing it'll probably be a red-eye tonight, so why don't you finish up whatever you're doing and head home to start packing?"

"What about the Dean Scuttle/Nicole Hare hearing? I'm supposed to be at the courthouse in, like…" she checks her watch, "a half hour to cover it."

"Oh, that?" Naomi imagines Joel scrunching his face and waving his hand on the other end of the phone. "Give that to Jake or someone else."

She cringes, not trusting Jake to cover it fairly since Dean Scuttle is one of his favorite actors. "Can I give it to Melanie? I know she's only an editorial assistant, but I think she's ready to take something like this on."

"Sure, give it to whoever you want so long as I can get you on a plane today."

"Okay." Naomi exhales as she hangs up.

Everyone is silent, staring at her.

She sighs. "Guess I'm going to New York to find out who pissed off Harlow Hayes."

Naomi doesn't make it to her Toluca Lake apartment until 10:30 a.m., even though she left the Culver City office over an hour ago. She laughs at how she used to think New York traffic was bad. Sure, it was a pain, but LA traffic is a fresh sort of hell.

A yellow glow spotlights Naomi as she steps inside her second-floor dwelling. Twice the size of her former Brooklyn abode, the apartment seems bare, like she's only just moved in. In New York, her pull-out futon, coffee table, and bean-bag chair would have been more than enough to fill up the space. But here, the apartment swallows the furniture—and her—whole. Like she's a doll playing house rather than a human living in a home.

She squints as she yanks the curtains shut, blinded by the California sun beaming through the window. While most people love southern California's year-round rays, Naomi misses New York's changing seasons. The pillow-white snow in winter and multicolored leaves of fall, which would be starting to turn by now. She knows not to be fooled by the promise of early autumn leaves, though. New York weather is unpredictable, and she could be sweltering in Indian-summer heat or shivering in icy rain when she arrives, regardless of the forecast. She huffs as she throws her suitcase on the bed, knowing she'll have to pack strategically.

Naomi decides to wear her leather jacket to the airport, but stuffs her waterproof mac and winter coat into her large backpack. The coat makes a hissing noise as she rolls it into a ball and lays on top of it to squeeze the air out. It will come in handy as a makeshift pillow on the flight even if she doesn't end up wearing it. Then she organizes all of her toiletries—a.m. skincare, makeup, shower stuff, p.m. skincare, dental, haircare—into separate travel bags and then carefully places them on top of her shoes, ranging from sandals to boots. She hopes she won't be there for longer than a few days, but she likes to be prepared for every scenario.

Naomi makes a list, crossing off everything she's already packed before analyzing what's left. She walks over to her dresser and opens her jewelry box to select a few pieces, pausing when she sees the silver bracelet inside.

The Christmas after their mom died, when Naomi was twenty-two and her sister Faye twenty, they gifted each other bracelets. They were mostly identical, made of sterling-silver beads with one dangling heart charm. The only difference was the engraving on the charm. Naomi's had an "F," while Faye wore the one with an "N." The gifts had been an exciting upgrade from the frayed friendship bracelets they traded as kids, acting as a symbol of their bond and marking not only a new chapter of just the two of them, but also a shared achievement: Making it out of their hometown.

Only two years apart, Naomi and Faye had always been close. Their dad left when they were toddlers, and their mom wasn't around much, either busy working one of her part-time administrative jobs in the daytime or gigging and partying on the evenings and weekends with one of the bands she sang in. Unable to afford extracurricular activities like their friends, the girls had to entertain each other. They played hide-and-seek, wrote and performed their own plays, and even mapped out treasure hunts for each other in the woods behind their house. When they were older, they smoked weed and drank with friends, before a combination of scholarships and student loans allowed them both to eventually escape to university in New York City, like they'd always planned. A new adventure, together.

Naomi went first, choosing to study journalism, then Faye left two years later, for music. They'd both been obsessed with celebrities since they were little, wondering what it must be like to have anything you wanted, to be revered, fawned over. But while Naomi chose a career path that took her behind the scenes, Faye craved the limelight. Like their mother, she dreamed of seeing her name in lights, her face plastered on the covers of the various magazines at the corner store. Faye's desperation to make it only got stronger after their mom died.

The loss affected Naomi differently, though, which was expected. While Faye admired the ambition of Lucy Marjorie Barnes, the once-beautiful lead singer of a mostly unknown soft rock band, Naomi resented her for it. Sure, she loved her mom and had plenty of happy memories, but their relationship was a complicated one. And she'd never truly forgiven her mom for missing so much of their childhood while chasing a lost hope. For forcing her to lie to Faye in an attempt to shelter her from the truth, telling her sister that their mom missed the talent show because she was off on important music business, when really she was getting drunk and high in the city.

So when the doctors confirmed Lucy had died of a heart attack, most likely from years of alcohol and drug abuse, Naomi accepted it as a long time coming. But Faye rejected their reasoning, convinced it was really a broken heart that had killed her—from not being able to fulfill her dream after trying for so long.

Faye vowed not to end up like Lucy, and for a time

Naomi thought she just might do what their mom couldn't and break through. But her end was even more tragic.

Part of Naomi blamed their mom for Faye's fate, for encouraging her to "Never, ever give up." Naomi would've thought that so much rejection would've jaded their mom, made her salty and pessimistic for her daughter's future, but instead she pushed Faye. Naomi knew she had meant well, for the most part, but she also felt that, deep down, it was a way for Lucy to ignore any regret she felt for having had children in the first place, that maybe her purpose wasn't to be a star, but to raise one. Turns out, it was neither.

Sadness pricks at Naomi as she realizes that she writes about people like her mother and sister now: Tragic dream-chasers who fear failure more than death, turning to drugs and alcohol to numb the pain when they slowly start to realize they might not be among the lucky ones.

Ignoring the stabbing pain in her chest, Naomi stares at a polaroid of her and Faye tucked into the top corner of her dresser mirror. Taken with Faye's retro camera on their annual Thanksgiving road trip down South—a tradition they started following their mom's death—it had always been one of Naomi's favorite photos, from a time when they were closer than ever. In it, the sisters have their heads thrown back in laughter, arms wrapped around each other.

Naomi can't remember the last time she laughed like that.

After she finishes packing and running a few last-minute errands, Naomi orders an Uber to LAX. Within ten minutes, her bags are loaded in the trunk and they're on their way, cruising through streets lined with palm trees and telephone poles. Naomi laughs to herself as they pass a billboard advertising Harlow's latest album. She thinks about the talented young woman, adored by millions for her sweet personality and catchy pop songs. Could she seriously have killed someone? Theft? Sure. Assault? Maybe. Drugs? Meh. But murder?

As an entertainment reporter, Naomi is naturally up-to-date with the big goings-on in the industry—who's dating whom, who cheated on whom, who's feuding, who's canceled—but these accusations have come as a true shock. No indication Harlow was "troubled" or struggling in any way. No rumors of her beefing with anyone. But perhaps that's due to Naomi's own ignorance. She's purposefully avoided anything Harlow-related for the past couple years because it makes her too sad, reminding her of her sister. She scrolled past any photo of or article about Harlow, tried to tune out when anyone talked about her, and turned off the radio whenever she came on. Maybe this wouldn't have come as such a shock if she'd been paying closer attention.

Probably not, though, judging by everyone's reaction in the office this morning.

Naomi sighs, deciding to make up for lost time, and puts her earbuds in before opening Harlow's Spotify page. She hesitates before pressing play on "James Dean," Harlow's debut single. An upbeat pop song that played on the radio constantly when it first came out almost ten years ago, its catchy lyrics still get stuck in Naomi's head from time to time before she forces them out. But now, she allows herself to feel the rush of bittersweet emotions as the song plays, bringing her straight back to when Faye was alive, a teenager screaming the lyrics from the passenger seat.

I want you like James Dean. Fit into my blue jeans. Get under my skin. I want you like him.

Despite the tears stinging her eyes, Naomi smiles at the memory. She's unsure if she'll be able to mentally cope with listening to the whole playlist, but she knows she'll have to get over it if she's going to cover this case. She reminds herself why she said yes to Joel in the first place. How it felt like her sister's ghost was pleading with her to take the story. And how exciting it is to feel close to her again.

She decides that, after she's uncovered the truth, she'll visit Faye's grave upstate, something she hasn't yet had the courage to do. The thought makes her skin hot, overcome with grief and guilt. The last time she stepped into the cemetery at St. Denis' Church was for Faye's funeral, something she barely remembers, aside from that it was a horrific, heart-wrenching, gut-punching fever dream, just like the following days and months. She couldn't bear to visit the gravesite after that, choosing instead to run away to California. But she'll go see her sister soon. Bring her an assortment of wildflowers—her favorite—and tell her all about her beloved Harlow Hayes: The pop star, the icon... the murderer.

Or maybe the wrongly accused. A victim herself.

Naomi doesn't know. Not yet. She'll find out soon enough, though, start researching at the airport, map out her plan of attack for when she lands. The familiar wave of excitement waters down the guilt she felt a moment ago, eager to learn more.

She cautions herself as her thoughts race, imagining all the possibilities. It's important she puts aside any preconceived notions she may have, forgets what she thinks she knows, and waits to make any assumptions until she's done her due diligence. She needs to be focused, unbiased, and logical. Like usual.

But her intuition tells her that might not be so easy this time.

Harlow Hayes

Harlow Eleanor McHayton, professionally known as **Harlow Hayes**, is a multi-Grammy-Award-winning American singer and songwriter. The singer is most widely known for her double-platinum-selling single "Once Upon a Summer" (2017), as well as for her fourth studio album, Apotheosis (August 2023), one of the highest-ranked albums on Metacritic to date.[1] In early 2024, the album won Hayes her first ever Grammy, plus three more to boot, including Song of the Year for the title track "Violent Ends."[2]

Before *Apotheosis*, Hayes' music consisted mostly of upbeat pop tracks and breakup ballads (see Discography). *Apotheosis* signaled a new direction for the singer, drawing comparisons to glamorous sad-girl pop royalty like Lana Del Rey, Halsey, and Billie Eilish.[3]

Hayes was born on July 4, 1996 in Cambridge, Ohio to James and Michelle McHayton, who relocated to New York in 2012 when Hayes turned sixteen so she could pursue a career in music. At the age of eighteen, Hayes signed with Machinist Records.[4] Her self-titled debut album was released a year later, in 2015, to critical acclaim, with the lead single "James Dean" (2015) reaching number three on the Billboard charts. Her highly anticipated sophomore album *One Heart* (2017) gave the singer her first number-one single, as well as multiple nominations at the American Music Awards and Billboard Music Awards (Female Artist). In 2019, Hayes released her third studio album, *Red, White, & Blue*. [5] The album debuted at number one and its title track, "Once Upon a Summer"—rumored to be about actor Colton Scott[6]—is still the singer's bestselling single to date. It was awarded various accolades, including Hot 100 Song at the BBMAs and Song of the Year at the AMAs.

In June 2021, Hayes released "To the Nines" with rapper Mama Money, which was nominated for Top Collaboration at the BBMAs and won Song of the Summer at the MTV Video Music Awards. Hayes performed the song with Mama Money at the VMAs ceremony, where she famously fell down a flight of stairs during the performance.[7][8]

Hayes' next single, pop ballad "Endless Summers," was released in October 2021. The song, which received a lukewarm reception from critics, peaked at number one on the Billboard charts in its first week thanks to the power of Hayes' fandom, but fell twenty spots the following week, with many citing poor marketing and promotion for the surprising decline. This descent made it her worst-performing single on the charts.[9] The remainder of 2021 was also marked by a slew of canceled shows and appearances for the singer and she was rumored to have checked into a wellness facility for health reasons around the holidays.[10][11]

Hayes returned with a vengeance in August 2023 with the long-awaited *Apotheosis*, a marked diversion from her usual sound. [12] It's the first album on which Hayes is credited on every song and her first to be nominated for a Grammy. Overall, the album and its singles earned her five nominations in total and four wins, including Album of the Year, Best Pop Vocal Album, and Best Pop Solo Performance —although many argue the album should have been slotted in the Alternative category.[13]

In August 2024, Hayes released her fifth studio album, *Legacy*, which debuted at number one on the Billboard 200 and remained there for three consecutive weeks. Both singles from the album hit number one on the Hot 100 and Rolling Stone charts, and also maintained the top spot on all streaming platforms for three consecutive days.

Music Journal

HARLOW HAYES SURE TO LEAVE A "LEGACY" WITH HAUNTINGLY BRILLIANT FIFTH STUDIO ALBUM

Building on its Grammy-winning predecessor, Hayes' latest record once again showcases the singer-songwriter's penchant for atmospheric storytelling through music

★ ★ ★ ★ ★

BY KRISTINA VIVIANO   *August 10, 2024*

Almost ten years after Harlow Hayes debuted on the music scene with her young, fun hit "James Dean," she delivers a multifaceted, genre-bending masterpiece with her fifth studio album *Legacy*.

Arguably Hayes' best work yet, *Legacy* is the moody follow-up—a sister record of sorts—to her critically acclaimed *Apotheosis*, the Grammy-Award-winning result of the beloved musician's multiyear reinvention. And what better way to further solidify the rising queen of dark pop's *Apotheosis* by giving life to yet another album that references so much about death?

Each song on the ten-track album adds something special to the final result, creating a mysterious and haunting musical mosaic that lends credence to Hayes' growing fanbase's claims that she's one of the best in the game. But, like *Apotheosis*, Hayes' cryptic lyrics are the spark of much debate. So what do we make of them?

We believe Hayes is expressing an existential crisis from start to finish, something us mere mortals will never have to face—a struggle to live out a human experience despite being treated and worshipped like a god. For example, with lyrics like, "I don't even recognize the real me / That's my legacy," we see Hayes grapple with her "Apotheosis" throughout the album, from the eerie "No Way Back" and "Footsteps in the Snow" to the chillingly vulnerable, devastating piece of songcraft, "Rose-Covered Grave." The middle of the album hides the record's two best songs, the hauntingly brilliant lead single, "Garden of Bones," and the sequel to *Apotheosis*' most popular track, "Violent Ends Part II," which showcases Hayes' underrated vocals as she belts out serrated notes over a powerhouse bass and drumline.

From there, Hayes mimics the beauty and brutality of her experience, warmly singing against a delicate piano on "Melancholy" before her gossamer voice soars over the jagged melodies of "Echo." It's a heart-pulverizing ending that confirms the acceptance of her transformation as she finally finds a way to come to terms with both the darkness and glamor of her persona, admitting, "For the glory and fame, I'd do it the same"—and we're happy to hear it.

Legacy, Harlow Hayes: Track List

No Way Back
Footsteps in the Snow
One Step Ahead
Rose-Covered Grave
Garden of Bones
If You Ever Get Lonely (Yellow Door)
Violent Ends Part II
Endless Loop
Melancholy
Echo

Chapter 3

Naomi lands in New York red-eyed and drowsy from the overnight flight. She hoped to get some rest on the plane, but couldn't sleep. So instead, she paid the extra eight bucks for Wi-Fi and dove back into her Harlow research, wanting to learn everything she could about the singer before she spends the next few days covering her arrest.

She didn't realize how much there was to catch up on, though—Harlow Hayes isn't the basic pop star Naomi once thought she was. Now, she's an iconic enigma, and by the time the plane descended over the foggy dawn of the New York City skyline, Naomi was well and truly down the Harlow Hayes rabbit hole.

After doing the standard Google search and reading a few recent articles, Naomi spent most of her time scrolling through endless #HarlowHayes-related social media posts, reading and watching content ranging from fan edits and tributes sending Harlow "strength," to commentary from D-list influencers chronicling how they could tell she was a psycho from her "dead eyes."

It fascinated Naomi to see how obsessed both fans and critics are. While the harshest critics are celebrating the downfall of Harlow, this person they have never met, super fans—also known as stans—are speaking about her as if they know her personally, referring to her by cute nicknames and defending her with extreme passion, swarming under any post denouncing Harlow with everything from well-intentioned rebuttals to malicious death threats.

These intense reactions don't stun Naomi, though. As a journalist, she knows how powerful online fanbases are and how a bad album review can trigger the wrath of millions. She also knows the disturbing reactions aren't representative of the fandom as a whole, but rather the loud one percent. She wonders if someone from that small percentage took it offline. Took their "devotion" to another level. It doesn't make sense for a stan to frame their idol, but maybe one of them felt slighted by Harlow. Or, conversely, decided to kill in her honor…

In the cigarette-scented cab, Naomi scrolls through a Reddit thread for true crime enthusiasts, surprised by how many are already convinced Harlow is guilty. Citing the copious mentions of blood and death in her more recent lyrics, they make Naomi wonder if she misunderstood the pop star all along. She recites the pre-chorus of Hayes' haunting track "Garden of Bones" in her head as she stares out the dirty window.

A garden of bones, watered with tears. Blood-soaked soil, saturated with fear. No one knows I laid her here. Alongside a part of me buried for years…

In comparison to her earlier albums, there's no denying Harlow's more recent music is much darker. But as a writer, Naomi knows to read between the lines, and instead of taking the lyrics as a confession, she interprets them as a poetic, spiritual metaphor about Hayes burying a part of herself. Plenty of famous musicians make analogies to death and it doesn't mean a thing.

They don't stand accused of murder, though.

A car horn blares and Harlow's eerie song drifts out of Naomi's mind, replaced by the sounds of squeaky brakes, distant sirens, angry drivers, and more honking. And thoughts of Faye.

Naomi was hoping she could hold off on feeling sorry for herself, but everything about the city reminds her of her sister, from the dirty sidewalks they'd stroll down, coffee and bagel in hand, to the bars they'd frequent—or, thanks to Faye, sometimes get kicked out of. It was like trying to ignore someone punching her in the gut over and over again. Impossible.

"Here we are," the driver says, snapping Naomi out of her sad thoughts.

He gets out and pops the trunk of the car to retrieve Naomi's bag. After thanking him and quickly tipping him through the app, she takes a moment to breathe in the familiar yet strange scent of New York City wafting through the air—a combination of car fumes, street meat, marijuana, and burnt coffee, topped with a tinge of urine. It's a unique odor that instantly evokes a mixed bag of pleasant and painful memories.

Naomi's eyes drift up the brick exterior of the tall, thin brownstone, unbelieving it could sell for as much as 20 million dollars. As per Angie's email, she'll be staying in Joel's rental apartment on the fourth floor and is to be mindful of his other tenants in the three apartments below.

Naomi marvels at the intricate carved-glass window in

the front door as she walks up the brick steps and presses the key into the lock. The heavy door creaks loudly as she pushes it open and stumbles inside. Converted from an old home into multiple apartments, the brownstone has no elevator, meaning she'll have to lug her bags up to the fourth floor herself. Feeling more exhausted by the minute, she slowly drags her suitcase up the stairs, cringing each time the wheels clank against the wooden slats. She's sweating by the time she makes it to the door.

Once inside, she breathes a sigh of relief, dropping her bags and kicking off her shoes. As expected, the apartment is gorgeous. The living room is light and bright with beige and black furniture that complements the marble fireplace and colorful abstract art pieces throughout. The same theme is carried through to the guest room, where she'll be staying.

As she continues to make her way through the apartment, it's clear Joel—or his property manager—pays special attention to every detail. Scents of fresh cotton emanate from every plug-in and in every corner, and perfectly kept plants add pops of green all around. She imagines them drooping and dying during her stay, like every other plant she's tried to look after. She'll have to set reminders for herself to water them.

While anyone from California would think the apartment too small, especially for the price, Naomi appreciates its cozy charm. It makes her feel more at home than she's felt in years, in a both comforting and heartbreaking way. It reminds her of her old apartment in Brooklyn, the one she shared with her sister before moving out to live with her now-ex fiancé. Naomi sits on the couch and closes her eyes, noting the momentary silence. Whenever Faye was home, she made her presence known, constantly "banging around," no matter what she was doing. She couldn't even walk quietly. Naomi wishes she could curl up in the plush fur throw blanket, but she doesn't have time. She only has a half hour until she has to leave to meet her friend—and source—Amelia Davies.

Naomi met Amelia during freshman year of college, when they were both studying journalism. Like a lot of their other friends from the course, Amelia pivoted into public relations after graduation, instead of staying in the dying field like Naomi had—not that she regretted it; she'd rather write tabloid fodder any day than be on call 24/7 for demanding clients. Amelia now works as an account director for one of the city's top PR firms, representing some of the world's most famous brands and individuals. Over the years, Amelia has secretly shared insider information—usually about clients she and her co-workers dislike—with Naomi, who writes up articles for C*Leb and thanks Amelia with dinner or cute little gifts in the mail.

Sam Brixton Talent Management, the agency that represents Harlow Hayes, is just one of the companies Amelia's firm works with, so Naomi is hoping her friend will have something to spill.

Naomi quickly showers in the marble and subway-tiled bathroom and then reapplies a basic layer of makeup—a flick of black mascara and an extra-thick layer of concealer under her eyes. She stares back at herself, wondering how she got so thin. When she lived in New York, she used to be curvier, with more rounded cheeks. But the rabbit food of LA, coupled with her general loss of appetite, have caused her to lose the extra layer of body fat. Something she actually misses. She doesn't like seeing her ribs and her cheekbones jutting out. It doesn't suit her. But she doesn't have time to worry about that now.

She checks the weather app, wondering what to wear. While the air earlier this morning was surprisingly chilly, the app predicts the temperature will rise to a high of eighty degrees by this afternoon. Naomi rolls her eyes, but she knows how to dress for this. With layers. She pulls on a pair of black jeans and pairs it with white Vans, a long gray T-shirt, and her leather jacket. At least here, her black-and-gray color palette will blend in rather than stand out. She considers straightening her long, wavy hair, but opts for a side braid—a quicker option that will hold up better in the humidity.

Naomi grabs her phone, keys, wallet, emergency mini umbrella, and notebook and pen, and places them in her over-the-shoulder bag before heading out. Although it's noticeably warmer than it was earlier, a chill runs through her.

She cranes her neck upward, taking stock of the imposing gray city towering above, like a looming darkness trying to trap her in. Unlike LA, which tries to hide its darkness beneath bright colors and starry skies, New York is unapologetically intimidating. She remembers the overwhelming claustrophobia she felt those last few months before she moved. As if the city was trying to consume her, swallow her whole. The feeling isn't overpowering like it was the last time she walked the streets of Manhattan, but it's still there, quietly lingering in the slight buckle of her legs, in the quickening of her pulse. She clears her throat and forces herself to take a deep breath.

Focus. You're here to do a job, she reminds herself, before striding toward the café on the corner.

As she's exiting the coffee shop, two drinks in hand, Naomi's breath catches in her throat. Heart racing, she squints at the man in the navy-blue suit across the street, sure it's Matt, her ex-fiancé. But when the man looks up from his phone, she exhales. Not him.

She wonders what Matt is doing now. The last she heard, he got his happily-ever-after. The one she wouldn't give him. Married with baby number two on the way. Naomi imagines how different her life could have been if she had chosen to stay and get married like they'd planned.

A wave of guilt washes over her as she remembers the argument she had with Faye, when Naomi told her she was going to move in with Matt.

Can't believe you're going to ditch me for a guy.

Faye, he's my fiancé…

Yeah, and I'm your sister.

Naomi will never forget the betrayal in Faye's face before she stormed out of their apartment. She wouldn't meet Naomi's eyes for days after that, only responding when necessary, with one-word answers. If anyone could hold a grudge, it was Faye. Naomi knew she was trying to guilt-trip her, make her change her mind. But they couldn't live together forever. She thought it would be good for Faye to be on her own for a while. Unfortunately, that wasn't the case.

After she died, Naomi felt an immense sense of guilt. She also felt lost and confused, suddenly unsure of what she actually wanted in life. She asked Joel if she could transfer to Los Angeles so she could get away from it all. Start fresh in a new city. Matt had just started his fancy finance job, and was angry Naomi would even ask him to uproot his life like that. He wanted to get married and start trying for a baby that year. "Let's stick to the plan. It'll cheer you up," he said.

And that was when she realized he truly didn't understand her. Because nothing had terrified Naomi more than the thought of bringing children into this horrible world. Everyone she had ever loved had either left her or died. So why set herself up for the inevitable pain?

Baby, there's no such thing as happy endings in a world so violent and cruel.

The line from Harlow Hayes' "Violent Ends" taunts her as she crosses the busy city street.

Chapter 4

Armed with a coffee for herself and a tea for Amelia, Naomi arrives at Washington Square. She takes a seat on a free cement bench and sips on her black, sugarless coffee, musing how her past self would have been enjoying a pumpkin spice latte, getting excited for sweater weather and fall-colored leaves.

But she's a different person now. And that, combined with her recent focus on Harlow's case, has her mind on darker, more ominous things. Like the 20,000-plus bodies buried beneath the park.

She watches people huffing through their morning jogs and scurrying to work, probably unaware of the fun little fact that Washington Square was once a mass pauper's grave, and wonders if they too are hiding sinister secrets.

She imagines Harlow, who spends most of her time in New York, shuffling through the square after committing murder. Sunglasses obscuring her face. A bucket hat hiding the crimson liquid caked in her hair. Balled fists concealing stubborn, dried blood under her acrylic nails. *The carpet was as red as the blood on Harlow Hayes' hands*. Naomi can see the line in one of her articles.

But whose blood? Naomi needs to know who the victim is and how the body was found in order to properly speculate. Hopefully, Amelia will have heard some rumors at work, but if not, Naomi will head over to the courthouse next. She takes out her phone and texts Cameraman Chris, C*Leb's videographer, currently stationed there.

How are things going? Might stop by this morning...

Naomi waits, watching the three dots ripple before his response comes through.

Wouldn't bother. Spokesperson already came out and said they won't be making any comment until tomorrow's press conference after the arraignment.

Naomi perks up, surprised they've already confirmed the arraignment. And that it'll be happening so soon. Joel said it would, but still, in Naomi's experience, these things are usually dragged out. But since it's undoubtedly such a high-profile case, and Harlow has money, power, and connections, her lawyers were probably able to get it expedited. Naomi wonders if this means her team is confident they'll get an acquittal. Or bail, at least.

She's looking down at her phone when she hears a familiar, high-pitched voice call out her name, dragging out the "ee" sound at the end. She smirks when she spots Amelia bounding toward her, dressed stylishly as ever in black jeans, a burgundy sweater—or "jumper," as she calls it—and camel-colored booties that match the trench coat draped over her shoulders. All a perfect complement to her long copper hair and green eyes.

Amelia pulls Naomi in for a hug and kiss. She smells of expensive perfume mixed with fake tan. "You alright?"

Naomi's smile drops, worried she must look a hell of a

lot worse than she thought. She really should have gone heavier on her makeup. "I'm okay. Just exhausted. Why, do I look tired? I took the red-eye—"

"Babe..." Amelia says. "Remember, when a Brit asks if you're alright, it just means 'Hi.' Or 'What's up.' Don't need your life story, do I?"

Naomi covers her face with her hand as she laughs. How could she forget. She made that mistake the first time she got the opportunity to fill in for a red-carpet event and a famous British singer asked if she was "alright." Assuming she was genuinely asking if she was feeling okay, Naomi had rambled on about how this was her first time on the red carpet, how she was filling in for one of the presenters, and how she was so excited to meet her. While confused, the singer had been polite and gone along with it. It wasn't until the next day, when Joel sat her down and explained, that she realized her mistake. But this isn't a red carpet interview with a superstar. It's Amelia.

"Shut up, you know you care," Naomi says, holding out Amelia's tea and a bagged croissant.

"You're right, I do. I actually do." Amelia laughs before thanking her. She takes a seat on the bench and pats it, willing Naomi to sit down and join her.

"Anyway, how are you?" Naomi takes in how put-together Amelia looks, reminiscing on their college days, when Amelia was anything but. When Naomi looks closer, though, she can still see traces of old Amelia peeking through. Like the little loop of ribbon hanging out of her sweater. The stain on her coat. And the chipped nail on her left hand.

"Oh my god," Naomi says before Amelia answers. "Let

me see!" She grabs Amelia's hand, where a large, round-cut princess diamond adorns her ring finger. Naomi knows Amelia and Tom got engaged, but it's the first time she's seen her in person since. "Congratu-freaking-lations!"

Amelia does a little shimmy as she passes over her hand, beaming. "I'm doing fab, as you can see. Tom's amazing. I was absolutely buzzing when I saw it." Amelia pulls her hand back to admire her ring. "You know, Tom has a very handsome single brother, Leo…" She looks back up at Naomi, a devilish grin plastered on her face. "I could set us up on a cheeky double-date while you're here."

Naomi side-eyes Amelia. "I'm not here to date. I'm here for work."

"Did I mention he works for the NYPD? Could be a potential source…" Amelia gives Naomi a challenging look as she takes a bite of her croissant.

Naomi rolls her eyes, but then considers it. The police are unlikely to be forthcoming with information in a high-profile case like this, so he could be her best way in.

"Fine, I'll let you set something up—"

Naomi holds a finger in the air as Amelia squeals in delight. "But first, you have to tell me what you know about Harlow's arrest."

Amelia's eyes light up. She moves her hand in circles as she finishes chewing. "Honestly. It's mad. I still can't believe it. I'm not on the account, but my friend Tabby—she's basically Harlow's publicist—is having a right mare, especially working with Machinist's PR team." She rolls her eyes dramatically. "Tabby's been in constant crisis comms mode, dealing with an insane amount of press enquiries and requests for comment. As you can imagine. And, of course, they're not answering anything yet, as per Harlow's lawyer's request… so nothing juicy there for you."

Even though this is what she expected, Naomi is still disappointed at the lack of information.

"Woah, woah, don't get all downtrodden yet," Amelia says, picking up on Naomi's body language. "Because I have something even better. And you'll be proud of me too, cause I used my little investigative brain to get this intel…"

Naomi eyes her warily.

"I think I know who she offed." Amelia stares at Naomi as the statement lands, watching for her reaction and smirking as the realization hits her.

"Wait, what?" Naomi gasps. "Who?"

Amelia looks around, then pauses dramatically before uttering, "Colton Scott."

Naomi's eyes widen in surprise. "No…"

"Yes," Amelia nods.

Naomi shakes her head, mouth agape in shock. That's not who she expected. Not that she had any expectations, aside from maybe a sleazy old music exec, but definitely not Colton Scott, even if he was one of Harlow's ex-boyfriends. Colton is—was?—one of America's most beloved actors. A perfect specimen of a man. Like Hercules. Invincible. *He's Mr. America, for Christ's sake. How could this happen? And at the hands of bony Harlow Hayes?*

"I…" Naomi shakes her head again, trying to find the words. "So Colton Scott is dead? THE Colton Scott, as in, Mr. America Colton Scott? How do you…?"

"Okay, so I don't have confirmation or anything, and this is going to be a bit long-winded, but just bear with me, K?"

Naomi gestures for Amelia to get on with it, overwhelming curiosity making her antsy.

"So, like Harlow, Colton is managed by Sam Brixton. I don't work on his account either—I used to be jealous of my co-workers who worked with the big celebs while I got all these boring companies to work with, but now I'm pretty bloody grateful, but anyway, I digress... One of the company directors, Max, mentioned last week how Colton didn't show up to this video shoot he was supposed to be doing for a major cologne brand. It was all ready to go and, after months in the making, he just didn't show. He's always had a good rep around the office, so this was out of character. But Max hasn't been able to get a hold of him AT ALL since then, and Sam won't respond to his calls either..."

Naomi furrows her brow in concentration as she considers what Amelia said. "I mean, it's a stretch. But I suppose he did date Harlow on and off for a long time, didn't he? And I guess he's exactly the sort of person—comes from the sort of family—that would be able to keep this so quiet." She thinks about the powerful empire that is the Scott family. An American institution with as much influence as the Kennedys or Rockefellers.

Amelia nods in agreement. "Exactly. Plus, what's that saying—'It's always the boyfriend'? Guess it's the girlfriend this time..."

"But they haven't dated in, what, three years?" Naomi says. "It doesn't make any sense. "Why now? And how?"

Amelia shrugs. "Maybe they had a more recent relationship that flew under the radar. Something that turned really sour this time."

AVANT

The Rising Star of Colton Scott: Hollywood's New Superhero

Scott remains humble as ever, despite landing his biggest role to date in the highly anticipated Mr. America, set to hit screens next summer

BY KELLY PORTER – MAY 14, 2021

Colton Scott is sitting comfortably in a plush gray chair in his favorite Los Angeles restaurant, sipping a coffee, as I walk in to greet him. He gets up as I approach, pressing his hands against his perfectly tailored suit before extending one out to me.

It goes without saying that Scott is the object of many a woman's—and man's—affection. And seeing him in person does not disappoint. With dark brown hair and stubble contrasting against fair skin, kind brown eyes shadowed by thick lashes most women would pay for, and what can only be described as a megawatt smile, he exudes a sort of nostalgic, alluring radiance. He is old and new Hollywood combined into one.

It's not surprising, though, considering Scott comes from one of America's wealthiest families. Descended from a line of oil tycoons on his father's side and a political dynasty on his mother's, Colton Maxwell Scott is a nepo baby of sorts. But you'd never guess he was born into so much wealth and privilege if you didn't know. He's gracious, endearing, and conscientious, treating everyone around him with kindness, even asking the waiters personal questions and helping stack the plates on the table.

Coming off the heels of indie breakout film *Moonbeam*, about a young scientist who discovers something sinister in our skies (a departure from Scott's usual action roles), Scott recently landed the coveted role of the beloved hero "Mr. America," in what is rumored to be Sunrise Studios' most expensive movie to date. Also starring veteran Blaze Butler and Scott's former *Highland Love* (2019) co-star Meghan Rhodes, the action-packed thriller will be brought to the big screen from the mind of legendary Clint Caruso, who previously worked with Scott on *Doomsday* (2017) and *Mojave* (2018).

I congratulate Scott and ask how he feels to be named America's new superhero.

"Frankly, I'm honored," he says, holding his hands up, cheeks flushing red. "But honestly, just to have the amazing opportunity to work on this project with Clint and everyone at Sunrise is all I need. I only hope I can make America proud. It's a big role to live up to."

I ask if there's anything he can tell us about the project, which has remained heavily under wraps until the recent casting announcement.

He rubs his hand over his chin, his cheeky smile adding a boyish charm to his demeanor. "All I can say is that I've been looking for a script like this for a long time, let me tell ya. A powerhouse action film but one with a strong emotional core." He places his elbows on his knees and clasps his hands together. "Between me and you," he winks, "I actually found a few scripts I loved but ultimately the part went to someone else. But it's all gravy. It's all good. Because in the end, I think the universe was telling me those weren't my roles. This was it. Because if I had played those, this one may not have worked out for whatever reason—maybe I would have been shit in those and no one would've ever hired me again. But my character, Jim, he's a fighter. A real fighter. And I know I come from a privileged upbringing for sure, but I've had my struggles too, and just really admire his spirit. How he never gives up. How everything he does is for the one he loves. I really can't wait to bring the script to life and for America—and the world— to fall in love with Jim like I have."

Filming on the first installment of *Mr. America* is due to begin this summer, with a release date slated for 2023.

C*LEB NEWS

PARIS IS FOR LOVERS: HARLOW HAYES AND COLTON SCOTT BOTH SPOTTED IN THE CITY OF LOVE MONTHS AFTER RUMORED BREAKUP

By Sophie Bianca – *December 6, 2021*

It seems Harlow Hayes' new siren song may have guided her leading man back home. Or to Paris, at least…

"I'll be your lighthouse, burning bright across the sea. Baby, endless summers ahead, if only you come back to me." That's what Hayes sings in the chorus of the second-chance love ballad "Endless Summers." When the single was released in October, fans speculated it was an attempt to win longtime on-again, off-again beau Colton Scott back after whatever spat they had around September's VMAs—where Hayes tripped and fell during her "To the Nines" performance with Mama Money.

Hayes, who hasn't released an album since the chart-topping *Red, White, & Blue* (rumored to be about her and Colton's various ups and downs) in 2019, has been in the UK and Europe finally promoting the single to her fans across the pond. And it seems she may have cast her spell over the *Mr.*

America star once again, as he reportedly flew all the way from his film set in Los Angeles to be with his heartbroken songstress.

While many around the world will be devastated to hear Colton might be off the market, at least we can hope for a good breakup song from Harlow once things inevitably go south for the hopeless romantics. Like she sings in her devastating ballad "Through the Wreckage," "something keeps telling me you're not the one, but I ignore it again and again."

Hey, she said it, not us.

NEXT UP: Colton Scott Spotted Getting Cozy with Co-Star Meghan Rhodes

Chapter 5

Back in the apartment, Naomi sits on the L-shaped couch, feet up and laptop open, digging up everything she can on Colton Scott and his relationship with Harlow Hayes. While Naomi was shocked at first by what Amelia said about Colton potentially being the victim, she feels differently now, with her mind battling between disappointment, confusion, and intrigue.

Since Harlow isn't publicly linked to anyone romantically and she doesn't seem to have many enemies, it never crossed Naomi's mind that this could be a straightforward crime of passion. And as horrible as it is to admit, she's a little disappointed by the prospect. Adding to the disappointment is the fact that Colton Scott is extremely likable. Naomi can't recall one bad piece of press about him. And that's saying a lot, since it's literally her job to stay up-to-date on that sort of gossip. He's like Ryan Gosling. Everyone loves him.

Everyone except Harlow Hayes, it seems.

Harlow and Colton were last linked in October 2021, before he quickly moved on to Meghan Rhodes, proposing to her that December. Killing Colton would have made more sense in 2021 if it was a jealousy thing, but three years later seems so random. Especially since Harlow has had her share of romances since then as well, linked to Gloss frontman Johnny Holborne, baseball player Tyler Reid, and even comedian Dave Peterson. So why kill an ex after so many years? Especially at the height of her career?

Naomi browses all the articles covering Harlow and Colton's love affair, ranging from "Harlow and Colton Loved Up in London" to "Harlow's Heartbreak: Colton Scott Engaged to Co-Star Meghan Rhodes." From what she's gathered, Harlow met twenty-five-year-old Colton when she was only nineteen at the premiere of his first blockbuster film, *The Fact of the Matter*, a romantic comedy featuring one of Hayes' hit singles. They were inseparable for a year until they started their pattern of breaking up, dating other people, and getting back together again.

Naomi wonders if their tumultuous dating pattern implied a potentially toxic relationship. Goosebumps prickle atop her arms as she recalls lyrics from one of Harlow's more recent songs.

Who could've known then we'd be the other's demise. Violent ends are all I see for you and me…

Tempted to start writing this up for a rumored-victim article, Naomi dials Joel. He answers after the second ring.

"Hey, how's it going? All settled into the apartment?"

"Yes, it's great, thank you again for letting me stay here." Naomi's shoulders relax as she glances around the room, feeling more at ease than earlier.

"Anything for my star writer. Can't wait to hear what you dig up."

"Actually, the reason I'm calling is because I think I might already have something worth writing about—a possible victim."

"Really? Wow. That was fast. Who?"

Naomi pauses before answering. "Colton Scott."

"Oh shit."

"I have a source in PR who knows people who work with him. And apparently he's been MIA for a week, which is out of character according to her colleagues. Plus, he owns a place here. Splits time between New York and LA, like you, so…"

Joel exhales loudly. "That is interesting, not gonna lie. Damn. Love that guy's movies. What's his connection to Harlow? They dated, right?"

"Yeah, they were on-and-off until a few years ago, but I haven't been able to find anything connecting them or any rumors since 2021."

"Huh, okay."

"Should I write it up?" she asks.

Joel grunts, torn. "You know what… wait. If TMZ hasn't even reported his death, it makes me wonder if maybe he's just in rehab or something. I don't know, don't want to risk breaking this, of all things, if it's not legit. Not trying to get on the Scott family's bad side, especially now that they're pushing his uncle for majority leader of the Senate—they'll be real pissed with any tabloid spec." He exhales, mind made up. "Hold fire for now until you get something a bit more concrete than that. I'll see if any of my sources can confirm or deny too."

Naomi agrees to their plan before hanging up, wondering who he's going to ask. He's always incredibly tight-lipped about his sources. All she knows is that he once told her he didn't mix his professional life with his personal life, and didn't consider any of them "buddies." Unlike Naomi, who is very friendly with a lot of her sources. Sometimes too friendly...

Naomi's face flushes as a text from Amelia appears on the top of her phone screen. *It's a date! Ribalta at 8 p.m.*

With hopes of squeezing out some information on the arrest, Naomi replies with a thumbs-up before letting her mind drift back to Harlow. Did she privately reconnect with Colton? Did they argue over something from the past and she lashed out, accidentally maiming him? Or was it much more depraved than that? Something premeditated?

Naomi's imagination runs wild again, filling with images of red, white, and blue. But what she's picturing is far from the lighthearted nature of Harlow's album of the same name.

Red: Colton's blood, caked under Harlow's long acrylic nails.

White: Flashing lights from Harlow's getaway car.

Blue: Colton's corpse, left to rot by his scorned ex-lover.

Chapter 6

With ample time to kill before she needs to get ready for dinner, Naomi opens TikTok, a subconscious habit she seems to be forming. Her "For You" page used to consist of travel, animal, and beauty videos; now, almost every clip is Harlow-related. But she needs this to get more insight into the pop star, to see her through a different lens.

Naomi doesn't know what she's looking for, so she follows the algorithm, watching whatever it sends her way. In the first video, a group of young women, probably in their mid-twenties, are huddled together, covering their mouths as they watch a livestream of Harlow's *Red, White, & Blue* opening concert. When her hit single "Once Upon a Summer" starts playing and she appears on screen— bedazzling in knee-high red boots and a flowing white dress, a blue guitar in hand—the women lose control. One falls to her knees as two start screaming and hugging, while the fourth stares on in shiny-eyed silence.

Other fan videos are quieter, but still as emotional, with people talking to the camera, simply explaining why they love Harlow and how she has helped them in their lives, from getting over a breakup to overcoming depression or even encouraging them to leave an abusive relationship. Naomi knows some people would roll their eyes at this, thinking Harlow undeserving of such credit. But Naomi has seen first-hand the impact a "silly musical artist" can have on someone.

Her sister was prone to depression, but any time Harlow released a new album or music video, or did anything at all, really, Faye perked up. It provided her with a brief respite from herself, a distraction from her neurotic thoughts when she needed it most. Or for the times when her mind went quiet, filled with "nothing but a sense of doom, like a ticking time bomb," as she'd say, Harlow's music helped bring her back, motivating her to get out of bed and keep hustling. And Naomi would always be thankful to the pop star for that. Although, Faye became increasingly obsessed with Harlow only months before she overdosed, which made Naomi wonder if being such a fan wasn't so great for her sister after all. Just a constant reminder she was still failing to break into the industry.

"My whole life I thought I could do it," Faye said, months before her twenty-fifth birthday. "'You're going to make it,' I tell myself, over and over. 'It's going to happen!' But as I get older, it starts to feel more and more like I probably won't. And it's terrifying. I can't *not* make it, Nay. I can't end up like Mom."

Not long after that conversation, though, Faye had a breakthrough. She'd sold a song to a record label and it seemed like she was finally going to get her chance. And for a few months, it really looked like things were going to work out for her. But then she started acting strangely, became distant and closed-off. And then she was gone.

Maybe that's why she crashed so hard, Naomi thinks. *The higher the climb, the harder the fall.*

As Naomi scrolls through more videos, she wonders if Harlow ever felt a similar desperation or if her rise to the top was easy—a swanky elevator ride as opposed to an impossible rocky ascent.

She pauses on a fan edit—a mashup of various songs according to the caption, including "Violent Ends" from *Apotheosis*, "Winter" from *Red, White, & Blue*, and "Violent Ends Part II" from *Legacy*—and realizes that even if Harlow did have a smooth journey to fame, no one was immune to heartbreak.

> *Can we redo our ending, not just for us*
> *My heart breaks knowing the pain that I caused*
> *But it's too late, it's over and done*
> *There's no going back from the monster I've become*
> ———
> *And you're there with me, spinning me around*
> *Kissing me under the sparkling sky; time's frozen, no sound*
> *But now the sky rains ash, it glitters no more*
> *Ever since you walked out the door*
> ———
> *You meant the world to me*
> *Now I'm dead to you*
> *What was I thinking, what did I do?*

"Yikes," Naomi mutters, studying the lyrics. As much as she doesn't want to admit it, the words spelled out like this in front of her make Harlow seem like a very troubled, heartbroken woman, veering on obsessive. And obsession can lead to motive...

Naomi swipes her screen, hoping for more lyric analysis, but instead she's greeted with someone claiming that Harlow is part of the Illuminati, who have now framed her for murder because she refused to do their bidding. And that if she makes a deal with them, she'll have to continue to kill every three years to retain her place among the elite.

She shakes her head and closes the app, knowing these crazy conspiracy videos aren't a good use of her time. What she needs, desperately, is some fresh air and coffee to keep her going.

After a quick evening walk, Naomi returns to the apartment with a large black coffee, a chocolate-chunk cookie, and two more hours to spare. As tempting as it is to continue to doom-scroll through social again, Naomi decides she'll start the right way this time. With verified Harlow sources. And make her own assumptions.

She resumes the "This Is Harlow Hayes" playlist she's been listening to and brings up the pop star's official website.

Naomi stares at the stunning main image of the pop star. She has one of those scientifically beautiful faces: Large, almond-shaped eyes and full brows framing her perfectly symmetrical face. After comparing it to some of her earlier photos, it's clear Harlow has had some work done over the past few years. She has that "LA face" now: Hollow cheeks, plumped lips, tightened, wrinkle-free skin, and a small, near-invisible nose.

Naomi wonders what she would look like if she had the same amount of money as Harlow. She likes to think she wouldn't overdo the Botox or plastic surgery, but she knows herself well enough to guess that the pressure to keep up with everyone else would eventually get to her and she'd slowly morph into another clone. She runs her fingers across the deepening lines in her neck, imagining how amazing it would be to make them vanish with a simple procedure, no concern for costs. Naomi tsks, chiding herself for letting her mind drift. She never used to obsess over her imperfections and she wonders if she notices them more now because she's nearing thirty, or if it's just a side-effect of living in Los Angeles.

Back on task, Naomi studies the image of Harlow again, this time focusing on her expression. The events of the last few days make it look as if Harlow's emerald-green eyes are daring the camera to photograph more than her external persona. Like she wants the lens to reveal who she really is.

A killer? Naomi wonders.

She scrolls down the page, past a variety of merch and tour information, before landing on the retro-style film reel promoting her latest album, *Legacy*.

One thing that really stands out to Naomi is the juxtaposition between Harlow's first album and her last. How she went from girly and lighthearted to a much darker aesthetic over the years, now only wearing tones of deep emeralds, midnight blues, reds and blacks, and rarely smiling for photos. She even ditched her platinum-blonde locks for rich shades of copper and brown.

Curious, Naomi opens a new tab and searches for information about when Harlow changed her style, clicking on an article from *Avant* titled "Harlow Hayes Shocks Fans with Dark New Look" from August 2023. The article features various photos of a young Harlow next to promo images for her *Apotheosis* album. In the photos, Harlow looks away from the camera, not making eye contact.

Naomi scans other articles linked at the bottom of the piece, intrigued by one titled "The Evolution of Harlow Hayes: From Darling Debut to Grammy-Winning Style Icon."

A weird excitement courses through her as her mind races with theories and questions.

Why did Harlow change so much? What prompted the reinvention? Did her breakup with Colton Scott hurt her more than anyone realized? Enough to plot his murder? And the biggest question of all: Who is the person behind the persona?

AVANT

The Evolution of Harlow Hayes: From Darling Debut to Grammy-Winning Style Icon

BY CINDY ALEXANDER – JULY 1, 2024

Everyone in Hollywood knows the importance of reinventing yourself to stay relevant, but few nail it as perfectly as Harlow Hayes.

When the recent Grammy-winner first debuted at nineteen, she was another spray-tanned, skinny bottled-blonde dressed in sequins and ruffles. And as her career progressed into her mid-twenties, her fashion and beauty remained safe for the most part, leaving much to be desired from the doe-eyed doll. But after a year of mishaps and another year out of the spotlight, Hayes returned with a brand-new look.

In the late summer of 2023, Hayes shocked the nation when she swapped out her platinum-blonde pop princess persona for a darker aesthetic, complete with chocolate-brown locks, bold makeup looks, and a sultry, old-Hollywood-inspired wardrobe—all to match the enigmatic vibes of her long-awaited new album, *Apotheosis*.

In honor of the star's birthday this month and the one-year anniversary of *Apotheosis* in August, we compiled a collection of Harlow Hayes' most memorable looks, from debut to now. Check out the photo gallery.

Music Journal

HARLOW HAYES *APOTHEOSIS* REVIEW: DARK INDIE POP MAKES WAY FOR HARLOW'S FUTURE STAR

★ ★ ★ ★ ★

BY DANY BELLADONIS   *August 14, 2023*

The breakup with Colton Scott must have been worse than we imagined, because this album holds no prisoners. It kills them.

Following her breakup with longtime on-and-off-again partner Colton Scott at the end of 2021—before his quick engagement to Meghan Rhodes—fans were devastated but also hiding a twinge of excitement… because a breakup usually meant a legendary album was on the horizon. I don't think anyone expected it to be this dark or iconic, though.

The announcement of the album was as cryptic as the titles on the track list, with fans realizing she'd taken a leaf out of Taylor Swift's book and started leaving Easter eggs in the months leading up to its release. At first, she started by sharing seemingly random lyrics, photos, and videos with little to no context on all her social media channels. Like a clip from Baz Luhrmann's *Romeo & Juliet*, featuring the famous "Violent Ends" line. Then there was a clip from the 2004 film Crash, plus references to the Rolling Stones' "Shattered" and BTS's "Idol" and "Persona" tracks, all of which ended up being hints to song titles on her own upcoming album. But she didn't stop there, posting at specific times to hint at both the track order and length of the songs. For example, track three, which was posted on the third of the month at 4:39 a.m.

Since this was new behavior for Harlow, fans didn't know what to look out for. But we have a feeling they won't be making that mistake again.

Apotheosis has already been hailed by critics and fans alike as a songwriting masterpiece on par with the likes of Swift and Lana Del Rey. The success of the album proves Hayes' music can stand on its own, regardless of the tabloids.

Apotheosis is largely constructed around sounds of glitchy electronics mixed with soft cascades of piano, and fractured snippets of white noise. While her best yet, it's also her most experimental, signaling a strong departure from her first three classic pop albums. Most notably, she's transcended lyrically, swapping out usually shallow lyrics about love and "livin' the good life" for deeper, doleful (sometimes even sinister) themes.

More than one song evokes visceral emotions, like "Tortured Soul," "Crash," "Invasion," and the attention-grabbing lead single "Violent Ends." At the opposite end of the scale,

"Shattered," "Midnight," and "Chasing the Darkness" grow in orchestral breadth as Hayes' voice hovers over the tracks like a ghost in a breathy, ethereal register.

It's hard to imagine the mellow Colton Scott triggering such dark yet passionate lyrics, but, as Harlow sings in "Persona," can you ever truly know somebody?

Comments:

Mark Porter · 8.14.23

It's giving Ultraviolence by Lana and reputation by T. Swift vibes

Chris Viviano · 8.14.2023

She didn't come to fuck around did she

Dee Bifalco · 8.17.2023

Anyone else notice the hidden layers of images in the album art? I thought it was just black, but there seems to be artwork, some areas looks like trees, others skyscrapers?

> Sian Motley · 8.17.2023
>
> I spotted that too. I think I can also make out the ocean (callback to RW&B perhaps?) and some roses.
>
> Dee Bifalco · 8.17.2023
>
> Also, the bolded letters in the track list spell out a date – March 14th? Unless it's not a date and it's "Charm," a future song maybe?
>
> Sian Motley · 8.17.2023
>
> Could be when tour starts!
>
> Emma-Anne Dutrond · 9.25.2024
>
> Harlow was baiting us…guess it's her, not Colton, who we didn't know at all

Chapter 7

Naomi has to force herself off the couch to get ready for her "date." Not that she's worried about it; dating is like networking in a way. She just doesn't want to stop researching, already engrossed in the mystery of it all, more so than any story she's worked on—possibly ever.

It's only when she reminds herself that Leo could have crucial insider info that she gets up and prepares for the usual: A night of polite small talk and a series of leading questions to get to the information she's after.

But when she lays eyes on him, waiting patiently outside the entrance of Ribalta's Pizzeria, she finds herself pleasantly surprised—and uncharacteristically nervous.

Naomi expected Leo to be good-looking based on what Amelia said, but he's giving a new meaning to the phrase tall, dark, and handsome. His hair is cut short and neat, accentuating his strong jawline, and he's dressed in a pair of dark faded jeans and a black V-neck tee that looks like it's about to rip open if he flexes his muscles. She can't look away.

"Naomi?" he asks, tilting his head to the side as she approaches. His eyes are warm brown, like honey.

"That's me," Naomi waves. "Leo?"

"That's me," he says, returning her line as he leans in to greet her with a kiss on the cheek. "It's so nice to meet you. You look beautiful."

"Thanks." She blushes, unable to remember the last time someone told her that. Even if it was just a line, he managed to make it sound genuine.

You're here for work, she reminds herself, trying to ignore the butterflies in her stomach. *He's a source.*

Not that it's stopped her before…

"Well, shall we?" Leo gestures inside. "Can't disappoint Amelia for setting this up."

"We definitely can't. She's probably watching us now, actually," Naomi jokes, looking around.

"You're probably right. We'll have to keep an eye out for a couple in hats and sunglasses."

Naomi laughs and follows Leo inside.

"Name, please?" asks a hostess with a long blonde braid.

"Leo Valencia, table for two."

"Sure, right this way." The hostess grabs two menus and guides them to a table in the back of the restaurant under a softly lit, neon-red sign that showcases the restaurant's name. It's surrounded by couples and groups of friends laughing as they chew their food, some with cheese dripping from their mouths. She can tell by their reactions and the heavenly scent of fresh garlic, basil, and dough that it's as good as it looks.

"Amelia tells me you live in LA now, so I figured you could go for some real pizza." Leo pulls out her seat before taking his.

"You were one hundred percent correct," Naomi smiles. "It's probably the thing I miss most about New York."

"What's LA like then? You like it there?"

"It's alright. Aside from the terrible pizza. Can't complain about the weather, at least."

"If you don't mind me asking, why'd you move?"

Naomi tenses at the question, not wanting to get into the details. "Just needed a change of scenery, I guess. And the company I work for has a West Coast office, so it was an easy escape."

"An escape. I feel you. New York can be... a lot."

"Have you lived here your whole life?" Naomi asks.

He nods. "Mmhmm. I love traveling but still can't imagine myself anywhere but New York. It's home, you know. You from here originally?"

"Upstate a little bit, near Poughkeepsie. But I moved down here for college, so this was home for about nine years."

"Where do you work? Amelia said you're a reporter..."

"Sorry, is this an interrogation? Did I miss the memo?" Naomi jokes.

Leo smiles sheepishly, deep-set dimples now on full display. "Sorry, sorry, I ask a lot of questions when I'm nervous."

"Oh, so you're nervous?" Naomi retorts, smirking.

He bites his lip and shrugs. She holds his gaze.

"I work for C*Leb News..."

"Oh shit, I know that one." He eyes her suspiciously now, like most people do when they find out.

"It's fun, I like it."

They both look up as the waitress comes over to take their order.

"Water and a Merlot, please," Naomi says.

"Should we get a bottle? Dinner's on me if that's alright with you?"

Naomi likes how he asked. "Fine, but I'll get the next one."

Leo smiles before turning back to the waitress, his left dimple facing Naomi. "Can we actually do the 2015 Cabernet from Napa? And I'll have a water as well. Oh, and some garlic knots too, please."

"Uh oh, do we have a wine snob on our hands?" Naomi teases.

"Hey, in this crazy world, you need to learn to enjoy life's little pleasures. Like food and good wine…"

And sex, Naomi wants to add, but stops herself. She shifts in her chair, sitting up straight. "So Amelia tells me you're in the NYPD? How's that going?"

He tilts his head. "It has its good and bad moments. Not easy being a cop in New York, as you can imagine. Most people hate us…"

"Should've been a firefighter," Naomi jokes. Her face turns red as she thinks about Marcus, the fireman she was hooking up with in LA.

"I know, right," Leo snorts. "Anyway, I'm hoping I can be one of the good guys. Make a difference, especially in communities like the one I grew up in."

"Where did you grow up?"

"In the Bronx. My parents moved here from Ecuador, hoping to give me and my brother a better life. So we both try to do our best to make their sacrifice worth it. Make them proud."

Naomi's heart sinks at his answer, thinking how she doesn't have any parents to make proud. Sure, her dad is out there somewhere, but she wouldn't even recognize him if he was sitting next to her. And her mom is dead. Even though Naomi had a complicated relationship with her mother and resented her for things, she still loves and misses her. Like Faye used to annoyingly say, "Mom's like a wild horse among wildflowers. She can't be tamed." Seeing her through Faye's perspective helps Naomi remember the good times, though. And she knows her mom would've been proud of her, would've been asking her for all the updates on the Harlow case, no doubt. But Faye dying would've killed her if she hadn't died first. So it was no use wishing she was still around.

"And how about you, what's it like being an entertainment reporter?" Leo asks.

Naomi shakes her head before answering. A physical attempt to get rid of the depressing thoughts before refocusing on her date. "It's good. Sometimes depressing because, well, Hollywood can be pretty fucking toxic. But I'm working on something really interesting at the moment."

"Oh yeah?"

Naomi clears her throat, trying to ignore the guilt she feels knowing she only agreed to this date to get information from Leo. She's surprised how much she's enjoying herself, enjoying his company, but work is work and that's what she's ultimately in New York for. So she segues into it.

"I'm actually here to cover the Harlow Hayes case...

Amelia told me she thinks the victim is Colton Scott. Can you believe that?"

Leo shifts suspiciously in his seat.

"You know something, don't you?" Naomi leans forward, eyeing him. "What is it?"

He sighs, narrowing his eyes at her as he finishes chewing a garlic knot the waitress has just set down.

"I'll tell you on one condition…"

"Name it."

He leans back and smirks. His amber eyes gazing into hers. "You let me take you out on another date…"

Naomi raises her eyebrows, impressed by his boldness. "We've barely been here thirty minutes." She throws a hand out. "But, fine, it's a deal… IF your intel is interesting enough," she smirks, crossing her arms.

A warm excitement courses through her as she holds his gaze, unsure if it's from the rising sexual tension between them or the imminent prospect of a lead.

Leo holds his hand out across the table, the corners of his lips tugging in a smile. A jolt of electricity runs through Naomi as she shakes his hand. "Deal."

"So," he says, leaning forward. "You didn't hear this from me, okay? But Amelia might be on to something. We responded to a call at Colton's penthouse last week. I only know because one of the guys said, 'Mr. America needs the help of the NYPD,' or some shitty joke like that."

"So it really is Colton," Naomi whispers.

He shrugs. "I don't know for sure. But what I think you'll find most interesting is the other thing I overheard…"

Naomi cocks her head to the side.

"Well, when I was over at the courthouse on duty earlier,

I heard one of the DAs talking to his boss about Harlow's victims…"

Naomi frowns, looking down at the table and then back up at Leo, blinking as she catches on.

"Wait… did you say 'victims'?"

Social Media Post

C*Leb News ✓ @CLebNewsOfficial

RUMORED: Harlow Hayes being investigated for multiple murders, ex Colton Scott possibly among victims. Read more at: clebnews.com/did-harlow-murder-colton

22:03 · Sept 25, 2024 · **108.3K** Views
858 Reposts **3K** Likes

> **@MariahCM**: WHAT THE ACTUAL FUCK PLEASE GOD NO NOT COLTON
>
> **@ShivvyDivs**: Harlow Hayes is a serial killer, confirmed.
>
> **@WhiteRev9**: You guys should be ashamed of yourselves posting rumors like this, these are real people's lives!
>
> **@OnceUponASummerHH**: Harlow didn't write "caught in the spokes of the wheel, but to spend time with you, I'd spin for eternity" just so she could go kill him 🛞
>
> **@ApotheosisBitch5**: @OnceUponASummerHH that song is about her dog
>
> **@AFCNottsFan**: Anyone check on her other exes? 👀
>
> **@DavePetersonOfficial**: Don't worry guys, I'm still alive

Chapter 8

Huddled beneath an umbrella, Naomi waits near one of the Roman columns at the top of the towering courthouse's granite steps. The steady pitter-patter of rain and the drop in temperature are a stark reminder she's no longer in LA. Instead, she feels like an extra in a Batman film, waiting for the villain of Gotham to arrive.

Today's antihero, Harlow Hayes, is expected to pull up any minute for her arraignment. She'll either be granted or denied bail, and Naomi and the rest of the world will finally know for certain whose murder (or murders) she's being accused of.

Once Naomi left the restaurant last night, a bit later and tipsier than expected, she called Joel to tell him what she'd learned. Joel said one of his sources heard rumors about Colton as well, so he was happy for Naomi to run with the story. After posting it, she spent the rest of the night wondering who the other victim could be, constantly checking comments on social media, perusing the different theories piling up. Naomi thinks it's most likely to be someone Colton was close to or someone he was sleeping with. Maybe his ex, Meghan Rhodes? Or maybe it was just a friend who was there at the wrong place and time. Collateral damage. Or maybe Harlow went after another one of her exes. Had she moved on from writing songs about them to killing them?

Naomi laughs in disbelief. As if she's actually standing here, genuinely contemplating who else Harlow Hayes potentially murdered. She's still struggling to believe this is seriously happening. But the abundance of paparazzi, reporters, and cameramen gathered outside the courthouse tells her it's very serious.

Even the general public is out in force, some showing support for Harlow and others denouncing her, demanding the "demonic" pop star be locked up for life. Naomi watches in fascination as police hold back a group of protestors clashing with a swarm of fans.

"Both groups have been here since yesterday," C*Leb's cameraman, Chris, tells Naomi as he fixes his large camera on the tripod. He arrived at the courthouse early to get them a good spot near the door.

Naomi shakes her head, still taken aback by the level of passion these people have for a stranger.

"I hope you're wrong about Colton, by the way," Chris says, adjusting his camera. "That guy's one of my favorite actors."

"Guess we'll find out soon enough." Naomi shrugs, shivering, as she looks at Chris's exposed bald head, bent forward to check his equipment again. Even fully dressed in jeans, black Timberland boots, and an oversized rain jacket, his tattoos are visible, climbing up his neck to the side of his face.

"Do you really think there's more than one?"

Before Naomi can answer his question, two black SUVs pull up in front of the courthouse and chaos commences. Camera gear clicks into place as reporters and paparazzi buzz into action. Chris follows suit, hoisting his furry mic into position, as Naomi stumbles forward, trying to hold her ground on the front line. She instinctively shields Chris with the umbrella to make sure his lens doesn't get wet, sacrificing her hair so he can get a better shot.

Reporters call out and cameras flash as the district attorney arrives with his small army of lawyers and paralegals, but the excitement quickly dies down as everyone waits in anticipation for the real star of the show.

As Harlow Hayes steps out of her SUV, panicked whispers of "Over there" and "That's her" rapidly turn into shouts of "Harlow!" and "Did you do it?"

Naomi strains to get a look but is boxed out by pushy paparazzi. She balls her hands into fists, channeling her inner Faye. *She* wouldn't have let anyone get in the way of seeing her favorite celebrity. Naomi can almost hear her voice. *You didn't wait there for hours only to get pushed out. Do something about it.* So Naomi inhales and barrels forward, not caring if her heels impale anyone else's feet in the process, and is finally able to score a glance.

Harlow is guarded by an entourage, hovering over her with giant black umbrellas. Her face is covered with large black sunglasses, her hair tied in a low, dark ponytail down her back. She's dressed in effortless luxury, wearing a beige blazer, wide black trousers, and black pointed heels.

Naomi stares in awe, feeling as if time has slowed. A shiver shoots down her spine and the hairs on her arms stand on end. She's unsettled and doesn't know if it's because she's only feet away from *the* Harlow Hayes, or because she's in the presence of a murderer.

The moment passes in a stunning, ominous rush of glittering gold, crimson, and black, and before Naomi can catch her breath, Harlow and her crew are safely locked behind the courtroom doors. Unfortunately, the arraignment is private, with no press or public allowed in the courtroom, so Naomi has no choice but to wait.

Once the hysteria tapers off and the reporters disperse, Naomi pulls out her phone. She wants to see if she has enough time to grab coffee for her and Chris before the post-arraignment press conference, but a message from Leo distracts her.

Her chest tightens, wondering what he's going to say. She's confident he had a good time too. It was he who suggested they order another bottle of wine after dessert. *He wouldn't have bothered if he wasn't enjoying himself. Right?*

She feels suddenly anxious, surprised by how much she wants to be right. By how much she'd like to see him again, not just for information. She opens up the message, hoping he's asking for a second date. He's not; but Naomi doesn't care. Because what he has to say is far more interesting.

Naomi glances around, observing the other reporters' facial expressions and body language. To see if they've been tipped off too. But none look particularly excited by anything. She attempts to mask her excitement as she reads Leo's text, wanting to kiss him even more than she already did.

Don't publish anything until after the press conference is over to be safe (don't want anyone suspecting a leak) but thought this would give you a head start.

Her eyes widen and her heart pounds as she zooms into the screenshot of Harlow's arrest warrant. Amelia was right about Colton being the victim, and Leo was also right—Colton isn't the only one.

Harlow Hayes is accused of not one, but two counts of murder.

But none of Naomi's theories about the second victim came close to the truth. Not only does she have no idea who the other victim is, but according to the information in front of her, the woman died three years ago.

C*LEB NEWS

THE "HITS" OF HARLOW HAYES

Reports confirm singer is being investigated for the murder of ex-boyfriend Colton Scott and mystery woman Jade Dutton

By Naomi Barnes – *September 26, 2024*

After her arrest yesterday, details have finally emerged of Harlow Hayes' alleged crimes. Official reports now confirm that the singer-songwriter is suspected of two counts of homicide in the death of ex-boyfriend actor Colton Scott and a woman named Jade Dutton.

Following the arraignment, a representative for the prosecution confirmed Scott was found unresponsive at his home in New York City last week. His family has not commented on the matter as of yet, but members of the Scott family were seen leaving the courthouse.

No details on the connection between either Hayes and Dutton or Scott and Dutton have been revealed; however, it's important to note that Dutton was found dead in October 2021, nearly three years ago.

Harlow Hayes was arrested in Nashville on Tuesday before being moved to New York by authorities, where she was arraigned by a judge this afternoon in a private hearing, as part of a very speedy interstate judicial process. Hayes pleaded Not Guilty to the allegations and bail was set at one million dollars, under the condition Ms. Hayes surrenders her passport and remains under house arrest at her Manhattan residence.

Another hearing is expected to take place in the next one to two weeks, in which evidence against the singer will be presented to a judge before a preliminary hearing date is scheduled.

In a statement to the press, Hayes' attorney Rudy Lodge said, "Ms. Hayes has been completely cooperative with law enforcement and we look forward to clearing her name on this matter as soon as possible. My client asks for privacy at this time."

Comments:

@**KamrynHartSings**: No no no no I just saw @RealColtonScott at Paris Fashion Week in June. This can't be real!

@**PaulShearsOfficial**: @RealColtonScott I can't believe the rumors were true. I'm going to miss you so much, brother. Heaven has gained an angel. RIP man.

@**HaileyAlexanderActs**: #RIPColtonScott My heart goes out to his family. He was a lovely man. So grounded and just a beautiful soul.

@**HarryTurnerFootball**: Absolutely shocking news @RealColtonScott can't believe you're gone mate

@**EstesGhost**: Fuck Harlow Hayes! Colton was my heart and she broke it. She needs to pay.

@**ApotheosisBitch5**: maybe they deserved it 🏃‍♀️#StreamLegacy

@RWBloverHH: Innocent until proven guilty remember! #FreeHarlow Hazies, let's have a buying/streaming party to show her we're here for her #WeLoveYouHarlow #Stream-Legacy

@ShesBack26: HH was rumored to have been the jealous type, must have caught them together…

@LarryBarry5: @ShesBack26 C+H broke up YEARS ago. Find it hard to believe she'd all of a sudden go kill him.

Chapter 9

Within an hour, Naomi's story has garnered millions of likes and reposts, plus tens of thousands of comments. She hated having to wait to post her article until after the press conference, when all the other reporters would have the names of the victims too, but in hindsight it worked out well since she was able to draft the piece before anyone could beat her to it.

She browses the comments, spotting an outpouring of love for Colton, illustrated by broken hearts and crying emojis, alongside vile abuse and hatred for Harlow Hayes.

In an attempt to drown out the negative news, Harlow fans are trying to get #FreeHarlow to trend alongside videos of her that "prove she's an incredible person and not what they say." These feature acts of kindness, like Harlow granting wishes with the Make a Wish Foundation, donating large sums of money to animal shelters, or doing meet-and-greets with fans, comforting them as they cry tears of joy.

But "antis"—those with an agenda to destroy Harlow's reputation, according to Harlow stans—are working hard to contradict these posts, responding with negative anecdotes about Harlow's character, claiming she's rude and abrasive and has jealous tendencies, and even going as far as to allege she's a drug addict with serious mental health issues.

It's strangely thrilling for Naomi to know that her article has prompted this tidal wave of response. Normally, she publishes a story and moves on to the next, unless she finds any new details to report. As far as she's concerned, she's just reporting on the truth, sharing the facts. Any outcry or resulting reaction isn't usually of interest to her, she's just the messenger. But this sort of fallout is different to anything she's ever experienced before, and she can't get enough.

She continues to scroll through the comments, getting more and more wrapped up in the reactions and theories, constantly refreshing for more. She wonders what Faye would have posted, imagining her as one of the fans defending her idol against all the haters. Whereas, at this point at least, Naomi is neutral. Neither for nor against Harlow. Just intent to find out what really happened.

Naomi refreshes the screen, trying to see if anyone who knew Jade has joined the conversation. Aside from the fact that she lived in New York City too, Naomi couldn't find any meaningful connection between the young model and Harlow or Colton to include in the article, and didn't have time to do much more research since she wanted to get the story out before anyone else. She was hoping she'd be able to learn more about Jade through the comments, but no one seems to know anything—or seems to care. They're more fascinated by the fact that Harlow allegedly murdered "some random girl."

But Jade wasn't some random girl. She was a person. Naomi swallows down the lump that's formed in her throat, imagining how Jade's family must feel, their grief being yanked back to the surface after all these years. Like how researching this case has brought back her own complex feelings, the ones she's been running from for so long.

Naomi's phone lights up with a welcome distraction. An incoming call from Joel. She taps the green button and answers.

"Great work, article's blowin' up!" Joel says proudly. "Crazy about that random girl, though."

Naomi rolls her eyes as Joel echoes the internet's insensitive comments. "Yeah, really sad."

"Got any more info on her yet?"

"Not really." Naomi looks down. "Aside from her being a young model who lived in New York, that's it really. Pretty girl. Social media is assuming Colton must have had an affair with her and Harlow killed her in a jealous rage."

"What do you think?"

"I really don't know. Part of me thinks it's ridiculous and the other part of me knows people have murdered for less, so…" Naomi nibbles at a broken nail. "What's getting me though is the timing. Why wait three years to kill Colton if that was the case? It doesn't make any sense."

"And they haven't released any other details about cause of death or motive?"

"No, nothing. All we got was her arrest warrant and confirmation of the victims' identities. The probable cause warrant should fill in the details, but I don't think we'll get that until her next court date."

Joel lets out a sigh. "Well, see what you can find before then. Would be fuckin' amazing if we could get ahead of that. See if your new police friend can get you any insider info."

"I'll see what I can do," Naomi responds, excited about the prospect of seeing Leo again. "Going to spend the next couple hours doing some digging, start making a list of people to interview."

"Sounds good, let me know if you need anything." He pauses. "And keep up the great work, kid."

Naomi's hands flit across her keyboard as her brain tries to make sense of the mystery. She's finding it hard enough to wrap her head around Harlow killing Colton, let alone anything else. The pair hadn't dated in three years, so what could have possibly happened between them? Was it that they secretly got back together after Colton ended his engagement to Meghan Rhodes, things went sour, and Harlow killed him in a crime of passion? Or was it more calculated than that? And, most confounding of all, how the hell does Jade Dutton fit into this?

After trying and failing to find any meaningful information on Jade through Google, Naomi types in "Jade Dutton Reddit" in her search bar, hoping true-crime enthusiasts have managed to dig something up. The Reddit sleuths are impressively fast these days and while many share baseless speculation, theories Naomi knows to take with a huge mound of salt, sometimes it's a goldmine of information. Thankfully, today is one of those days.

> Harlow Hayes' victim Jade Dutton's original cause of death listed as overdose. Found this article about it. Says woman found dead in drug den in the Bronx in October 2021 was identified to be twenty-three-year-old Jade Dutton of Millbrook, NY. Police speculated death was drug-related, judging by fresh track marks in line with heroin use. https://nystimes.com/drugoverdosevictimidentified_jadedutton

Naomi shifts in her seat, unsettled by the details. She skims the article and then the comments, pausing on a rumor about Colton.

> u/bethaninvestigates: my sources tell me Colton showed signs of drug-related death too. His body was found in his NYC penthouse. Guess they're thinking she tried to stage their suicides? Still weird the deaths happened so many years apart though. She'll most likely be released soon. Case seems flimsy AF to me.
>
> u/milliecrimesolver: Or maybe they'll find even more victims #HarlowIsASerialKiller

Another overdose? Naomi cocks her head to the side, chewing on her lip. She bites off a piece of dead skin, wincing at the sting.

The rumors baffle Naomi even more. As depressing as it is, these kinds of deaths aren't uncommon. So the prosecution opening an entire murder investigation and actually arresting someone as famous and influential as Harlow Hayes for two suspicious overdose cases—including one from *three* years ago—is very odd.

Naomi knows she needs to get her hands on the probable cause affidavit to try and make sense of it all, so she texts Leo. Guilt gnaws at her as she sends the message, but she justifies it by telling herself she isn't just using him for information. She wants to see him again. Plus, she did promise him a second date.

I owe you. Dinner later? My treat this time!

He texts back a smiley emoji followed by a text. *No prob, happy to help. Dinner sounds great though... not that I'll let you pay. I don't get off until nine though. That too late?*

Not at all, Naomi replies, excited. *Can meet near you round 9:15? Just let me know where.*

Leo sends a thumbs-up. *You familiar with K-town? Great place called Maze 32.*

Naomi hadn't been to Maze 32 before, but had been to Koreatown plenty of times. It was one of her and Faye's favorite places to celebrate birthdays, from the energetic atmosphere, to the great food, to the bad karaoke. Faye loved K-pop and would drag Naomi to any place that had been visited by her favorite Korean idols.

See you there, Naomi texts back, followed by a smiley emoji. She exhales and dives back into Reddit.

The next post to catch her attention is one claiming that Jade Dutton had a stage name: "Jade Joan." Naomi recalls her Instagram handle, @JadeJoanDuttonnn, having surmised it was just Jade dropping her last name. But why? For what? Curious, Naomi goes back into Google and types in "Jade Joan," and is surprised as tons of YouTube videos fill the screen. She clicks the first one, titled "Acoustic Cover of Once Upon a Summer." In the clip, Jade comes into view. She looks to be in her early twenties. Long blonde hair, a small button nose with big eyes. She seems sweet. Innocent. "Hey guys, it's Jade Joan here. And in today's video, I'm going to play a cover of Harlow Hayes' 'Once Upon a Summer.'"

Jade strums the guitar and sings, her voice breathy and light. Naomi can't help but draw comparisons between Jade and Faye. Jade clearly had aspirations to be a singer too. As beautiful a voice as Jade has in this video, though, Faye's was better.

A dull ache fills Naomi's chest at the realization that it doesn't matter. Because neither Jade nor Faye are alive to compete. Neither of their dreams ended in glory and fame. They ended in a fiery blaze for Faye and a pool of her own vomit for Jade.

But Jade's story isn't over. In fact, something tells Naomi that Harlow's arrest is only the tip of the iceberg.

Chapter 10

Naomi's entertainment reporting is usually a far cry from investigative journalism. She gets a tip and then writes a story—no need for hours of painstaking research and inquiries. And while this case has been abnormal from the start, she figured it would be straightforward coverage once the victim was revealed. That she'd write a story on the victim and their death, cover what their relationship to Harlow had been, and then eventually write another story based on the evidence.

But it turns out it's much more complicated than that—especially since there are still so many pieces of the puzzle missing—so she starts making notes, listing everything she knows alongside any questions, old and new theories, plus any actions to take.

Harlow Hayes arrested for 2024 murder of Colton Scott + 2021 murder of Jade Dutton

Evidence:
- *none revealed*
- *most likely will reveal a connection between the two*

deaths—*investigation into Colton's death must have led them back to Jade?*

- *probable cause affidavit* should be made public next week during hearing

Cause of deaths:

- rumors both were drug-related—possible Harlow staged accidental overdoses (see Reddit article)
- need Colton & Jade's autopsy reports for confirmation

Motive:

- Jade was a model and aspiring musician, Colton an A-list actor, Harlow a world-famous pop star
    - Did H somehow feel threatened by J career-wise?
    - Did C have eyes for J?
    - Did H hurt J, and then C recently found out, so H killed him to cover it up?

To do:

- get probable cause affidavit for H's arrest—ask Leo
- get C + J's autopsy reports—ask Leo
- check J's social media and see who she was particularly close to at time of death (roommates, co-workers, etc)—see if they can give connection to H or C
- talk to officers involved in J's original case, why foul play was originally overlooked, where was she last seen (before her body was presumably dumped?)—ask Leo if he can find anything out?
- talk to officers involved in Colton's murder investigation— might be difficult, ask Leo if he can get any more info about the callout to C's penthouse that night
- attend C's funeral? Best opportunity to meet with family/

friends who might know more about the case against H—
find out date

· *text Jessie, see if her friend at Machinist can get her an*
  interview with anyone that worked with H, like Charlie Roy,
  head of Machinist Records, who "discovered" her

· *talk to any other associates of H, want to know what people*
  close to her think—do they think she's capable of murder?
  Do they know anything about her recent relationship with
  Colton?

· *text Amelia, see if there's any way she can get more info from*
  colleagues or get me in touch with Sam Brixton (H + C
  manager)

Naomi looks at the list and takes a deep breath before opening her phone to tackle the easier items. First, she googles "Colton Scott funeral" and quickly learns it's to be held this Sunday in his home state, Maine. The bottom of the article claims it's a private event for family and friends only, no press or media. Naomi crosses her arms, unsurprised. She'll have to come up with a plan to sneak in. At least she has a date and rough location; she can figure out the rest later.

She texts Leo next, not even bothering to beat around the bush.

Hey! Thanks so much again for helping me out earlier,
I can't even tell you how much I appreciate what you did.
I feel horrible asking so soon, but before I see you later,
is there any way you can help me with even one of these
highlighted bullet points? I'm a bit stuck again and really
could do with some more info. Obviously don't do anything

that will get you in trouble, but even if you're able to ask around and get some intel that would be SUPER helpful. I'll get you the finest wine you can find later, I promise!

She adds a smiley face before sending the message along with a photo of her bulleted list, things for him highlighted.

Next up is Jessie, Naomi's friend who works for a popular music magazine. They met while they were both waitressing part-time during college, and Jessie quickly became the go-to party friend, often helping Naomi with Faye on nights out. Faye had a habit of picking fights after drinking too much, or sometimes she'd pass out on the bathroom toilet, and when Jessie was there, she would always help Naomi get her home or play damage control with the bouncers.

Jessie! How the hell are you? I'm back in NY covering the Harlow story and really want to meet with someone from Machinist Records, ideally someone who has worked with her for a long time like Charlie Roy or a producer. Any way you can get me in touch with someone who knows someone? P.S. let's do drinks soon! Here until at least next week.

Naomi watches as the dots pulse, heart racing in excitement as Jessie's response comes through within seconds.

Ahh you're back! 1. Yes, let's! I'm away this weekend, but how about next Tuesday? 2. I think it's going to be impossible to get Charlie based on experience, but I could link you up with the producer of her first two albums, Bobby Park? He's super nice, you'll love him.

Naomi deflates a little at not getting the chance to talk to Charlie. But she knows it was a long shot anyway. She does a quick search of Bobby, clicking into a profile piece from *Music Journal*. She skims it, impressed by his credits and experience working with Harlow, and asks Jessie to set up a meeting.

Next, she texts Amelia to see if she can get her in with Sam. But, as expected, the answer is no. *Sorry hun, Tabby says Sam isn't speaking to any press since one of his biggest clients is in jail and his other is dead xx*

Dejected but not surprised, Naomi goes back to her list, crossing off the relevant items before reassessing. She sighs, knowing this isn't going to be easy. Getting first-hand information from family and friends of lesser-known celebrities for smaller scandals is hard enough. She can only imagine how difficult it will be to get confidants of A-listers like Colton and Harlow to talk about a murder investigation. They aren't going to just open up to Naomi Barnes from C*Leb News.

However, Jade's family and friends might.

Naomi tries to imagine how she'd feel in their shoes. If all of a sudden she discovered that Faye had potentially been murdered. The thought makes her queasy, instantly distressed. She wouldn't want to keep quiet; she'd do the opposite. She'd be so desperate for the truth that she'd talk to anyone who would listen in hopes it would result in someone coming forward with more information.

She pulls up Jade's Instagram account on her phone, her chest tightening with sadness as she views the photos. Jade looks so young, so happy. Oblivious of her fate. She selects Jade's "tagged in" photos, a quick way to see who Jade's closest acquaintances were so she can contact them, and selects the top post from @Emily_Dutton. It's a selection of photos, captioned: *Missing my @JadeJoanDuttonnn extra today. Happy birthday in heaven little sis xoxo.*

The queasiness Naomi felt moments ago returns in full force, her heart aching for Jade's sister, and also for herself. She googles Emily and sees that she's a social worker living in Millbrook, New York, only a two-hour drive north. She could potentially stop there on her way to Colton's funeral in Maine this weekend, if Emily is free. And happy to speak to her.

She takes a few deep breaths before sending a message.

Hi Emily, my name is Naomi and I work for C*Leb News. I'd love to buy you coffee sometime soon and ask a few questions about your sister Jade if possible. A lot of the media covering the case are focused on Colton, but I want to make sure Jade's story is heard too (I lost my sister a few years back as well for what it's worth).

She feels kind of low, using Faye as a tool to hook Emily, but if she has to deal with the shit that comes with losing a sister, she might as well use it to her advantage. She knows Faye would approve anyway. She was always encouraging Naomi to be more brazen to get what she wanted.

I don't understand what you feel bad about, she imagines her saying. *You're just telling the truth. Plus, you genuinely care. Stop being so noble.*

Naomi wonders if she should try reaching out to Jade's parents, but decides against it for now. She has a feeling she'll have better luck with Emily—sisters and friends usually know more than the parents do anyway.

Emily messages back almost instantly and Naomi fumbles as she opens the app, breathing a sigh of relief when she sees that Emily is happy to meet her. *Sure, I'm free Saturday evening if that works for you?*

That's great! Naomi responds. *How's 6 p.m. at the Millbrook Diner?* She figures this should give her plenty of time to talk to Emily and still make it to Maine before midnight.

After Emily agrees, Naomi wonders if there are any other stops worth making on her way up north, trying to avoid the obvious answer: Home.

Millbrook is less than a half hour from where she grew up. She thinks of her high school friends, but the only ones she still keeps in touch with have moved—Kim to Connecticut, Justine to Colorado, and Dee to Charleston. Their hometown isn't somewhere people stay if they can help it. Naomi thinks of Faye, her body rotting away in a graveyard there, and winces. If she felt up to it, she could visit her. Maybe with Aunt Mary, who still lives nearby.

The only remaining relative she has some sort of relationship with, Aunt Mary was Naomi's mom's only sibling, younger by five years. Naomi wasn't sure if it was the age gap or different interests, but for some reason or another, Lucy and Mary were never that close, not like Naomi and Faye. In fact, Naomi can count only a handful of times when they'd actually seen Aunt Mary growing up, usually at funerals or weddings. But she was always kind to the girls, especially after their mom died, helping them with the funeral arrangements and the wake. Always making sure they knew they were invited to Thanksgiving and Christmas dinners. But Naomi and Faye decided to start their own traditions instead, going on a different road trip every holiday, staying in grotty motels on the way and making some of her favorite memories. It always surprises her when other people aren't close with their siblings. It makes her feel both incredibly lucky and unlucky to have had that bond with her sister.

It's because you're a Capricorn and I'm a Pisces. That's why we get along so well. I'm the dreamer and you're the logical one—perfect pair. Naomi shakes her head, smirking at some of the absurd things Faye used to say.

As much as Naomi would like to skip the visit to her hometown, not wanting to face the onslaught of emotion and memories it would no doubt unearth, she decides to suck it up. Naomi would be mortified if Aunt Mary found out she was in town and chose not to stop by. Up until now, she's always rejected her polite invitations with the excuse of being too far. But with Millbrook only a half hour away, she doesn't have that excuse anymore.

Plus, Aunt Mary was nice enough to let Naomi store some of Faye's things at her house before she moved to LA. Naomi tried to donate or throw out as much of her sister's stuff as possible after she died, but there were still about five boxes worth of things she couldn't face getting rid of—old notebooks, photos, select clothes, and other keepsakes. Aunt Mary agreed to keep them in her basement so Naomi didn't have to lug them with her to California. The last time she saw Aunt Mary was when she dropped them off.

After taking a deep breath, Naomi presses the call button. Her heart pounds with increasing vigor at every ring.

"Well, look who it is!" Aunt Mary sounds cheery, making Naomi relax.

"Aunt Mary, how are you?"

"I'm doin' great, hun, doin' great." Her New York

accent is stronger than Naomi remembers. "Just puttin' some favors together for your cousin's gender reveal this weekend."

Naomi's face flushes as she remembers the invitation she ignored months back. "Oh yeah, you guys must be so excited…"

"We are! Shame you can't make it, we'd all love to see ya."

"Well, actually, I'm back in New York for work and might be able to stop by if that's okay?"

"Oh, fantastic! Of course that's okay. It's Saturday afternoon, one o'clock."

"Great, I'll be there." Naomi already regrets it, not sure she can withstand an entire afternoon of baby talk and questions about her plans for the future. But at least she'll have her meeting with Emily Dutton to look forward to.

"I'd offer a place to stay the night but I've already given the rooms to—"

"No, no, honestly, please don't worry," Naomi interrupts. "I'm actually heading up north to Maine after, to cover Colton Scott's funeral."

"Oh, that sounds depressing." Aunt Mary's tone shifts from mournful to angry. "That horrible singer. What she's done…" Naomi pictures her clutching at her chunky costume necklace as she shakes her head.

"Yeah, it's all very sad," Naomi replies, not wanting to get into the details.

"How you getting to Maine, hun?"

"Planning to just rent a car in Poughkeepsie."

"Okay, well don't forget it shuts around midday on Saturday. Closed on Sundays too."

Naomi quickly googles this and realizes Aunt Mary's right. "Oh crap, it does." She could rent a car from the city, but she doesn't want the stress of having to drive through Manhattan. "I'll just get a couple of Ubers I guess. It'll all be covered by my company, so…"

"Oh, I know!" Aunt Mary exclaims, startling Naomi. "How 'bout you borrow your Uncle Frankie's car? He's away on business—in Milwaukee for a conference, somethin' to do with trains and microchips, lawd knows—but it's just sittin' in the driveway."

"Oh no, it's fine, I'd feel—"

"Honey, please. It's the least I can do since I can't offer you a place to stay. And he has one of those third-party insurance plans, so as long as you have some sort of insurance for yourself, you're covered. I insist."

Naomi pauses. Having a car would be helpful. "Okay, that would be great, thanks so much."

"You gettin' the train into Poughkeepsie, I'm guessin'? Need me to send someone to pick you up?"

"No, that's alright," Naomi responds. "I'll get a taxi, it'll be easier." She adds an "I insist" before Aunt Mary can protest.

"Alright, hun. Well, I look forward to seein' ya!"

"You too, Aunt Mary. Bye!"

After hanging up, Naomi muses what her aunt would think if she was arrested for murder like Harlow Hayes. Would she tell reporters she didn't know her that well and distance herself? Or would she defend her regardless, and stand by her in court? She likes to think Aunt Mary would support her—so long as she believed she was innocent. Naomi thinks about her mom and how she'd react. She probably wouldn't do anything, disappear so no one could ask her questions or bother her about it. Faye, on the other hand, would defend her more fiercely than anyone.

"I'll always have your back," Naomi remembers her saying when they were stargazing on the hood of their old Honda Civic one night. It was just after she discovered that Faye was responsible for Naomi's cheating ex-boyfriend losing his full-ride scholarship to his dream school. Without telling Naomi, Faye anonymously sent "evidence" that Brad had been plagiarizing his papers to the assistant principal, which resulted in disciplinary action and in him ultimately losing his place at Michigan State.

"I appreciate you having my back, but you take things too far sometimes," Naomi replied, partly amused, partly reprimanding.

"Do I, though?" Faye questioned. "At least everyone knows he's a cheater now."

The question of loyalty makes Naomi wonder for the first time about Harlow's family in all of this. Realizing she hasn't seen any comment from them on her arrest, she quickly googles "Harlow Hayes family" to see what comes up.

Motherfuckers, she whispers, seeing the *Avant* exclusive.

CELEBRITY NEWS

"She Completely Cut Us Off, We Don't Even Know Who She Is Anymore," Says Harlow Hayes' Aunt

BY REBECCA PEEL – SEPTEMBER 26, 2024

With the recent allegations against pop star Harlow Hayes, we reached out to her family to get their thoughts on the matter. And to our surprise, they weren't defending her innocence, instead opening up about how she cruelly cut them out of her life years ago.

An only child, Harlow Hayes (born Harlow McHayton) hails from a small town in southeast Ohio. Her parents, James and Michelle McHayton, doted on her, even moving to New York when Harlow was sixteen so she could pursue her dreams.

"From such a young age she was so talented," says her Aunt Jocelyn. "We always knew she'd be a star. Her mother, my sister, gave up her life so Harlow could make it. And for years, they were so close. You've seen her acceptance speeches where Harlow would profusely thank them for her support… but then, out of nowhere, a few years back, she became distant. Stopped answering our calls, refusing to see us. And then she started releasing music with satanic references and the like. Just awful.

"I always told Michelle this would happen when she chose pop over country. Country stars don't go down those dark roads like stars do in Hollywood or New York. They're good Christian people.

"So I hate to say it, but when I saw the news that she'd been arrested, I wasn't that shocked. Just heartbroken at what had become of my niece."

Chapter 11

Interest piqued by the article, Naomi falls back down the Harlow Hayes rabbit hole, moving from tabloids and gossip columns to YouTube videos as she tries to better understand the mysterious pop star.

The various concert clips from Harlow's *Red, White, & Blue* tour remind Naomi how incredible a performer Harlow is. Naomi is captivated by her ability to command a stage, singing effortlessly through impressive choreography or playing her guitar—sometimes both.

Naomi's favorite moment is when Harlow comes on stage without any backup dancers or fancy sets. She just walks out with nothing but her guitar and a microphone. She doesn't rush the moment. Takes in the cheers and shouts from all of the fans in the arena. The camera pans away from Harlow to all the tear-stricken faces, before panning even further out to show an aerial view of a dark dome filled with thousands of twinkling lights. As Naomi watches from this angle, she can't help but think that in Harlow's world, she isn't the star. Her fans are—shining brightly for her.

In the clip, Harlow thanks them. Tells them what they mean to her. That they're what make her life worth living.

That they lift her up when she is down. She then asks them to shine their lights even brighter. "I see you," she says.

Goosebumps cover Naomi's skin, and she wonders once again if someone who seems so kindhearted and altruistic could really be a killer.

When the concert clip ends, a lyric video for "Melancholy," a song from Harlow's latest album, *Legacy*, starts automatically playing. Naomi closes her eyes as Harlow's whispery vocals open the track.

Do you miss me like I miss you? I hope you're not as melancholy and blue.

Her voice sends chills up Naomi's arms. If she had been asked yesterday to tell Harlow's voice apart from other talented pop singers like Sabrina Carpenter or Dove Cameron, she would've found the task impossible. But the more she listens, the more she can hear Harlow's unique tone shining through. It's breathy but rich, familiar yet distant. Her head voice is delicate and ethereal, while her lower register is powerful. In her earlier albums, Naomi can detect a slight country twang. Very subtle. But it's almost completely gone by album four. That album, *Apotheosis*, is clearly the turning point for her. She'd taken four years to release it, although the pandemic was smack in the middle of that timeline, so it wasn't as long as it seemed—everyone kind of lost two years then.

Harlow's voice understandably matured over those years. Now it's even richer, with some grit to it. Raw, in a way. She has stopped trying to belt out every note and sometimes even opts to whisper or speak the words instead, which gives the songs a sultry feel, with added layers of unsteadiness and intrigue when she builds to a belt. It's as if she decided to stop singing by the book and to perform from the heart instead. No surprise it's her most critically acclaimed work.

This growth is even more evident in Harlow's music videos. It's clear her first three albums were managed more closely by the label. The singles chosen for videos lacked substance but were catchy as hell. It was your typical pop music, with a bit of synth and bass alongside a catchy beat and corny choreography. She'd donned the classic pop star look, bejeweled and sparkling in the finest of fashions with eye-catching sets. And while Naomi enjoys watching those videos, she doesn't connect to them nearly as much as those from Harlow's last two albums, which some have called cinematic masterpieces. According to fans, Harlow's later music videos also contain Easter eggs—little clues that musical artists sometimes leave that act as callbacks to previous work or hints for something yet to come. Naomi remembers reading an article that mentioned something like this, but they were mainly hints Harlow left for future song titles and track lists.

Naomi wonders what other secrets Harlow could be hiding in her work—ones that fans didn't know to look out for before her arrest—and makes a note to look into them later.

Moving on, Naomi skims through the beginning of the *Harlow Hayes, America's Sweetheart* documentary, keen to hear the comments and opinions of Harlow and people close to her. But instead, it's filled with wishy-washy opinions of self-proclaimed "industry experts" who probably only met her once in their lives, if that.

Naomi laughs at the journalist who claims she would always be America's Sweetheart. *If only they had known what she'd be accused of in a few years' time.*

The host cites Hayes' handling of the "Jax Paulson incident" as her crowning moment, when "all of America fell in love with her." Paulson, a well-known but washed-up radio host, tweeted how Harlow was a talentless artist who didn't deserve to be nominated for the VMA for Artist of the Year, let alone win. Many people expected her to ignore the comment, like she usually did. But when she won the award, she said, "And for all the girls out there who keep being told they're not good enough, that they're not worthy. This one's for you. You are worthy. You are enough. Don't let anyone try and tear you down. Thank you!"

"And I thought that was really inspiring," the journalist says in the documentary. "It was a really classy thing to do. After that day, her fanbase kind of blew up."

Naomi bites her lip, remembering the incident. She also recalls how that radio host got fired a few years later, some scandal about call girls or something. She covered it for C*Leb.

Maybe Harlow didn't just forgive and forget, after all.

The thought switches on a lightbulb in Naomi's head. She opens an Excel spreadsheet, titling the tab "Evidence" and the first column "Harlow Doesn't Forgive & Forget."

While there isn't an obvious recent connection between Harlow and Jade, Naomi wonders if there's one from a very long time ago. Everyone, including she, seems to have looked for Harlow's connection to Jade and Colton around the time of their deaths, but if Harlow waited three years to get revenge against Jax Paulson over a media scandal, then what if she waited a lot longer to get revenge over an even bigger betrayal?

Interview Transcript from Late Night Talk Show

August 17, 2023

Interviewer: "Give it up for Harlow Hayes, everyone!" *applause*

Harlow Hayes: "Hi!" *waves to the crowd*

Interviewer: "Wow, Harlow Hayes. It's so great to have you. So great. First of all, you look fantastic. Absolutely fantastic." *gestures to Harlow, audience cheers* "Sounds like the audience is loving the new look too."

Harlow Hayes: "Thank you, thank you." *smiles* "It's so nice to be back. And yes. It was time for a change, so…"

Interviewer: "You know, I was thinking…"

Harlow Hayes: "What have you been thinking?"

Interviewer: "If you can look this great dyeing your hair black, do you think… I could pull off blonde?" *raises eyebrow* "With some frosted tips, perhaps?"

Harlow Hayes: *laughs* "It's giving NSYNC. Love it. I say go for it."

Interviewer: *turns to camera* "Early-2000s boy bands, watch out. I'm coming for you!" *looks at Harlow* "Hey, if I go through with this, I expect you to be there for moral support. I'll have my people call your people. You're going to hold my hand as they dye it blonde."

Harlow Hayes: "I'll be there, of course. You just tell me where and when."

Interviewer: "Hell yeah!" *turns to audience* "You heard it here folks, okay?" *turns back to Harlow* "Anyway, you know there's such a buzz all around the block tonight. Everyone's so excited you're here. The fans are dedicated, man." *audiences cheers, Harlow smiles, puts her hand to her heart* "I don't know if you know, but some have been camping out overnight. Mayhem. Chaos! But it's because they're DESPERATE to get a glimpse of you. Because you've been kind of MIA for, what... two years now?"

Harlow Hayes: "Um yeah, it's wild. So first of all, thank you all so much! I'm so, so incredibly grateful for all my fans and everyone who has stuck around while I've been... rediscovering myself. And yeah, I just needed some time. To figure out what artist I want to be rather than what I've already done."

Interviewer: "So tell me, what's this album about then? What does... Apotheosis... mean?"

Harlow Hayes: "Well, Apotheosis means the culmination of the highest point of something. The point at which a person transforms into a divine being, shall we say. So the songs kind of tell a story like that. And how you get to that place."

Interviewer: "How do you get to that place?"

Harlow Hayes: "By embracing the darkness." *smirks*

Interviewer: "Well, it looks like you've quite literally embraced the darkness. You are darkness."

Harlow Hayes: *purses her lips and shrugs* "Maybe I am."

Social Media Post

Apotheosis is my religion @ApotheosisBitch5

A thread of Harlow Hayes' most ominous lyrics…

♡ ◯ ▽   🔖

19:13 · Sept 26, 2024 · **43K** Views

58 Reposts **938** Likes

Apotheosis is my religion@ApotheosisBitch5

Echo:
Futile efforts and broken dreams / For a fleeting moment, it gleams
Deafening screams not what it seems

Apotheosis is my religion@ApotheosisBitch5:

Rose-Covered Grave:
I don't blame you for what I made you do
But for what you did to me / I'll haunt you
Until you're laid / Under a rose-covered grave

Apotheosis is my religion@ApotheosisBitch5:

Invasion:

The voices in my head whisper sinister things / Show me images I don't want to see
Unraveling slowly, spiraling fast / I don't know how long I can last before I snap

Apotheosis is my religion @ApotheosisBitch5:

Melancholy:

You laughed as you took your final breath / Your words hanging in the air

I'll never know what you were trying to say / Cursing as I walked away

Now I'm haunted, haunted by the memory of you

Apotheosis is my religion @ApotheosisBitch5:

Footsteps in the Snow:

Now I'm far beyond redemption / At an all-time low

So I follow the call of the devil's crow

To the grave beneath the bloody footsteps in the snow

Apotheosis is my religion @ApotheosisBitch5:

Violent Ends:

Silk town, godless town, naive girl about to drown

Now blood stains my hands since that night

If you guessed this wouldn't have a happy ending, you were right

---

Apotheosis is my religion @ApotheosisBitch5:

Idols:

Bleeding poison from a heartless shell

Have to sell your soul to survive this hell

Apotheosis is my religion@ApotheosisBitch5:

Cruel Delights:

I want to taste the blood, let it pour like rain

Baby I know I'm insane, but I'm craving you

Apotheosis is my religion@ApotheosisBitch5:

No Way Back:

It's a million arrows, piercing the skin / The fatal blow from the poison within

Digs its way in and won't let go / Embrace the pain and get on with the show

Chapter 12

A variety of potent scents waft through the crisp night air as Naomi makes her way down West 32nd Street, following her navigation toward the place in Koreatown Leo suggested. From garlic and chili sauce to car fumes and trash, she inhales a different smell with every stride. People shout, some in English, some in Korean, and cars cruise by, wheels spraying water on photo-taking tourists with their bubble tea as they pass.

She moves quickly through tunnels of scaffolding before continuing to push through the crowded sidewalks lined with various illuminated shop fronts and restaurants, flickering neon signs beckoning her in. The lingering scent of rain on the pavement mingles with the smell of barbequed meat, and her stomach rumbles.

She checks her watch, annoyed at herself for being late. She lost track of time earlier, as she often does now—sucked down the Harlow hole, as she's started to call it, unable to think of anything else. Her research has only fed her new obsession, though, and the more she's learned, the more engrossed and conflicted she's become.

While it's impossible to ignore the various mentions of

graves and blood and death, especially across Harlow's two most recent albums, there's still nothing else that points to her being a vicious murderer. No actual evidence that Naomi has seen that makes Harlow seem any more likely to kill than other musicians who write and sing about the same dark themes. But hopefully she can get some more insider information from Leo tonight.

She glances up and then back down to her Maps app, which tells her she's at the location, although she can't see a sign for Maze 32 anywhere. The distant echo of someone singing poor karaoke makes Naomi smile, remembering Faye's twenty-first birthday and how she turned into a drunk diva, refusing to share the mic.

She follows the sound, eyes darting to and from the abundance of Korean and English advertisements, and finally sees the yellow sign for the restaurant.

"Woah, careful!" Someone yanks Naomi back to the sidewalk just as she steps out into the road. A taxi speeds past, horn blaring.

Naomi looks up at Leo, heart racing. "Shit, thanks," she laughs nervously. "I must have spaced."

"You scared me. I thought I'd be skipping dinner for a trip to the hospital for a second." He tries to laugh it off, but she senses a hint of worry. He offers his arm to her. "I think you better take this, for safety reasons."

Her face flushes red, but she smirks as she loops her arm through his.

After safely making it across the street this time, Naomi and Leo walk into the bar, which looks more like a video game than a restaurant. The entire ceiling is lit by LED lights in the shape of a maze and the walls are lined with

KELLY AND KRISTINA MANCARUSO

green hanging plants. But better than the atmosphere is the smell of simmering sweet barbeque sizzling on hotplates as they pass smiling patrons on their way to the bar.

Leo pulls out a stool for Naomi and takes a seat next to her.

"So how's everything going?" he asks as they wait for the bartender, currently serving a group of early-twenty-year-olds in the corner.

She turns back to Leo. "Honestly, you've been such a help. I really owe you."

He nods. "Yeah, no problem. I'm kind of intrigued myself, not gonna lie." He puts his finger to his lips. "But shhh, don't tell anyone."

"You're a fan of Harlow Hayes?" She laughs.

"I didn't say that. Even though her songs are pretty catchy." Leo starts singing the chorus to "James Dean."

"Oh my god, I'm not going to karaoke with you, ever."

"What? I can sing!"

Naomi shakes her head in disagreement.

Leo smirks, eyes lingering on hers, before nodding at the bartender to make his way over. "I'll take a Terra." He looks over at Naomi, giving her a chance to order.

"Same," she says, before turning to Leo. "What, no fancy wine this time?"

"Gotta have beer with Korean fried chicken." He holds his hands out as if he had no choice and then turns back to the bartender to order the food. Naomi salivates at the thought of it.

"So how was work?" She hopes this prompts him to remember the text she sent earlier.

"Not too bad, thanks. You?"

"Interesting." She laughs, crossing her arms. "This case isn't straightforward, that's for sure."

It's hard to believe the arraignment only happened earlier today. With the way she's been uncharacteristically fixated on Harlow and her alleged crimes, Naomi feels like she's spent weeks rather than days looking into everything. "Oh, and once again, thank you SO much for…" She lets her words trail off, not wanting to say it out loud.

"No worries, it was about to be made public within the hour anyway, so thought I'd give you a sneaky head start."

"Well, it's much appreciated. You didn't happen to find out anything else, did you?"

Leo shakes his head as he takes a sip of his drink. "So I couldn't get you anything official—only the detectives have access to the actual evidence and other official documents…" He places his beer bottle on the bar. "But I did ask around. Word is they have some type of video."

"Video evidence?" Naomi gasps. "Do you know of what? Of who?" Naomi imagines footage of Harlow slaying Colton or Jade.

Leo shrugs apologetically. "No idea, sorry. But," he holds a finger in the air. "Here's where things get interesting… One of the other cops said he was working in the Bronx when Jade's body was found. He said they didn't make the connection until last week, after Colton Scott's death. Said it was a weird case at the time because while she clearly had needle track marks, there were also bruises around her neck…"

Naomi raises an eyebrow. "Bruises?"

"Yeah, like she was strangled—that's what he said, at least." Leo nods knowingly at Naomi, whose eyes are now

KELLY AND KRISTINA MANCARUSO

wide with horror. "The guy said he pushed for it to be investigated but that it never was."

"What? That's—" Naomi opens her mouth and closes it, fumbling over her words in disbelief. "Her family didn't push for a full investigation?"

"Apparently not. He said he was told to stop wasting time looking into it."

Naomi scoffs, shaking her head. If she was told Faye had strangulation bruises, she would never have let that go, pushed until she had answers and found out who hurt her and why.

But maybe they were never told, she thinks, feeling unsettled.

The thought is galvanizing and she's even more motivated now to get answers. Not just to satiate her own curiosity, but for Jade and her family too, who no one really seems to care about.

Naomi tries to fall asleep but can't, thinking of Leo and his bombshell that Jade could have been strangled—a fact that was clearly covered up.

Could sweet, fragile Harlow really have choked someone to death? Physically holding her hands around Jade's neck until she died? It's difficult to imagine; although, it fits with the "jealous rage" theory—still the most popular one among internet sleuths.

Naomi reaches for her phone, wanting to read some more of the fan conspiracies with this new information in mind. As she scrolls through the Harlow Hayes hashtags on social, she views posts ranging from plausible, to unlikely, to completely ridiculous, including one from a user convinced that "Harlow is a robot who malfunctioned and killed." There's another one that's also far-fetched, but Naomi can't help but be intrigued by the prospect that "Harlow is a serial killer."

After watching ten ridiculous videos on this theory, Naomi is about to write it off completely until she stumbles upon a user called @BobTheFlopppp. He has a boyish face that suggests he's in his late teens or early twenties. His curly, unkempt hair is crying out for a barber and his pale skin is praying for some sunshine. Appearance aside, @BobTheFlopppp makes a very convincing argument. The crux of his theory hangs on the fact that in between the death of Jade and Colton, another one of Harlow's enemies died under mysterious circumstances. A third murder, which, if proven, would indeed classify Harlow as a serial killer.

Video transcript from @BobTheFloppp

9.26.24 8:00 p.m. EDT

Hi guys, Bob the Flop here! How we all doing? We're all in our feels, aren't we? Obviously absolutely tragic about Colton bae and Jane, Jade whoever, but let's not leave out my fellow Hazies. We are going THROUGH it, okay.

Well, I don't mean to stir the pot or anything, but I think I might be onto something. Before I get into it, though, don't forget to click like and subscribe if you want more piping-hot tea and celeb goss!

Okay, so here we go:

In early 2022, executive producer Bill Lever was found dead in his apartment. It had been ruled a suicide. But the ruling was sus. Bill didn't leave a note. He didn't have a history of depression or mental illness. And according to his friends and family, death by suicide didn't make sense to any of them.

Upon further digging, I found out that a sexual assault allegation against Bill had been made by an unnamed artist and that it was settled out of court. About six months later, he hung himself. Allegedly.

I know. I know. I'm clowning. Like I'm putting my red nose on and am clowning so hard over here but I want you to take a look at this…

So this is an image of Harlow's second-album credits. And yes, that is Bill Lever's name circled in red under "One Heart."

Now look at the lyrics from "Midnight," a song from her fourth album, *Apotheosis*.

"I know who you are / I know what you did / Don't act surprised / You know I'm right / You deserve what you got for what you did at midnight."

Remember those words as you look at this photo, which was taken right around the time the allegation was made, in August 2021. I don't know about you, but to me, it looks like Harlow screaming at Bill Lever in a parking lot at night…

Don't hate me, please don't hate me. I'm a Hazie through and through. You know this… But… do we really think this is all a coincidence? That a third person, who clearly had some sort of beef with our girl, happened to suspiciously die in the last few years? In between the two murders she's now accused of?

For those of you who still need more convincing… look at these lyrics from "No Way Back" from her latest album, *Legacy*. She lit-er-ally mentions him by name:

"Hey Billy, help me understand / How did you live with yourself, when it all got out of hand?"

But according to "official reports," Billy didn't live with himself, though! Do you get it?

Listen, I'm not saying our Ho-ho went on some killing spree. But I will ask you a serious question.

What do you get the girl who has everything?

Revenge.

Chapter 13

The lobby of Machinist Records is a microcosm of the building itself, tall with granite walls, marble floors, and giant stone arches. But the first thing Naomi notices when she walks inside the legendary building is the familiar "MR," written in industrial font and enclosed in a saw-edged circle—the logo that appears on screen before every one of Harlow's music videos.

"I'm here to see Bobby Park," Naomi says to the receptionist after passing through security.

The woman gives a generic smile as she points to the right. "Down this hall, third door on your left."

Naomi knocks on the studio door three times before Bobby answers. He's taller than she imagined, and handsome, with large almond-shaped eyes, shiny black hair, and a flawless complexion. In fact, he looks more like he should be the lead singer of a boy band than the producer behind them.

"Naomi?" Bobby asks, reaching out his tattooed hand. He's wearing a pair of worn jeans and a baggy hoodie. "Great to meet you, I'm Bobby."

"Thanks so much for meeting with me, especially on such

short notice," Naomi says. Jessie confirmed the interview only last night.

"No prob, anything for Jess! Anyway, come on in. I was just finishing up a new track." Bobby gestures for Naomi to take a seat on the couch across from his swivel chair.

She admires all the equipment in the room, realizing that Harlow might have once sat on this exact couch, looking at this exact view.

Plotting her next murder, maybe?

On the other side of the glass, behind the equipment, is a room the size of Joel's apartment, its floor, ceiling, and walls covered in wood of varying thicknesses. But instead of furniture, it's filled with microphone stands, keyboards, a drum set, a piano, and a wall full of guitars.

"Pretty sweet, huh?" Bobby says. "Costs 500 an hour, this space." He raises a hand and slicks his hair back. "So Jessie told me you wanted to know more about Harlow?"

"If you wouldn't mind, I'd love to know anything you can tell me—what you think of her, the charges against her, what she was like to work with, anything."

He nods in understanding.

"Do you mind if I record this?" Naomi holds up her phone.

He hesitates. "Can it be off the record, though? I don't really want my name in any articles, Charlie doesn't like anyone blabbing to the press."

She nods, willing to compromise, and hits record. "So Harlow..."

He sighs. "I've been in the business for a long time. Longer than I care to admit. So, safe to say I've seen some crazy shit. But I'll be honest, I think this one takes the cake. I did not see this one coming."

While Naomi suspected as much, it was interesting to hear someone in the music industry, who knew Harlow personally and professionally, confirm that it took them by surprise as well.

"So you don't think she did it?"

"No," Bobby says. "I haven't actually worked with her in years—not since *Red, White, & Blue*. But the Harlow I knew didn't have it in her to do something like this. She had her issues, sure, but she wasn't capable of murder. No way."

Naomi bites her lip, surprised at his matter-of-fact tone. She was hoping her visit here would add weight to the serial killer theory, but now she's doubtful. Maybe she has been spending too much time online...

"But what about her lyrics, they're pretty dark, no?"

He waves his hand dismissively. "They aren't any darker than anyone else's. Plus, so many different people work together on creating those songs, it's hard to tell who the lyrics even come from most of the time."

"So she doesn't write her own songs?"

"No, no, she definitely does now. From what I've heard, she's killing it." His face reddens. "Sorry... poor choice of words, but yeah, I always thought she was a really talented songwriter actually. Especially with lyrics. But she was pushing for songs that were a bit too 'indie.' And the label had already acquired their 'singer-songwriter' artists like Kamryn Hart, and I knew Charlie didn't want to lose his golden pop star, if you know what I mean." Bobby drops his elbows to his knees, hands clasped in front of him. "Listen, at the end of the day, music is a business. More of a business than an art nowadays. So Harlow had to do what most other artists have to for their first few albums—until they get big enough to tell whoever they want to fuck off—and just do what the label wanted, and work with who they wanted her to work with."

"Like Bill Lever?" Naomi prods. Bobby shrugs, looking slightly confused at the mention of the late producer. "There's rumors…"

Bobby cocks his head. "Oh yeah?"

"That Harlow could also be behind Bill Lever's death."

Bobby cackles. "You can't be serious?"

Naomi shrugs, playing the fool.

"No." Bobby shakes his head. "No way."

"You worked with both of them, right? Did you ever notice anything strange between Harlow and Bill? It's weird they only worked on one song together, right?"

"Not at all. The label will mix up producers and collaborators for songs now and then, especially for hit singles like the lead track from *One Heart*." Bobby strokes his chin and looks up at the ceiling. "But strange between them? I don't think so. Not saying they were best friends or anything. Harlow could be flaky at times, anxious. And Bill wasn't the sort of person to have patience for that. He was all business. So I could see them clashing."

"She was always anxious?"

"Yeah, long as I knew her. But it was more than frustration over not being able to sing her stuff. It definitely was rooted in her personal life. There's lyrics she shared with me that have never made it into her songs. But they came from her heart and I think they were about Colton. Everyone thinks he's this can-do-no-wrong hero, but judging by her emotional state during the times they dated… he can't have been as great as everyone makes him out to be." He raises his hands in defense. "But hey, that's just my opinion."

Naomi cocks her head, debating how to classify this interesting bit of information. *Could Colton have been the bad guy?* she wonders. But then she remembers he was killed, which makes him the victim. Not Harlow.

She thinks of her next question carefully. "If, as you say, he wasn't as great as everyone believes, perhaps he provoked her, then? Pushed her to a point where she finally snapped?"

"Nah, I stand by what I said. The songs she wrote tended to be very sad. Not angry. That's why I was so shocked when I heard the news. If anything, I worried she'd try to harm herself. Not someone else. Harlow had a lot of heart but that's not necessarily a good thing in this business."

Naomi bites the inside of her cheek. Wanting to make sure she covers all bases, she unlocks her phone and finds the screenshot she saved of Bill and Harlow fighting in a parking garage.

"So does this change your mind at all? It looks like they were fighting?"

Bobby narrows his eyes, studying the photo. He slides his fingers over the screen to zoom in before handing it back to her.

"Um yeah… huh." He seems conflicted. "I really don't know. I never heard of any drama between them."

"Do you know if the allegations made against him were true? Sexual assault…"

Bobby rubs his hand over his chin. "I heard a rumor or two. It's the reason I wasn't too upset when I heard he'd passed, to put it bluntly."

Naomi is impressed by his candor on the matter. "I'm trying to figure out if there's a pattern. If she killed Bill, then…"

Bobby cups his hand to his face. "No. I really don't think she's a killer."

Realizing he can't give any more insight into the serial killer theory, Naomi changes tack. "So tell me more about working with her."

"Well, outside of her self-titled album, *One Heart*, and *Red, White, & Blue*, I worked with Mama Money's team on 'To the Nines' and also did some mixing on 'Endless Summers' in 2021—not that many people liked that one—but the last album I worked on with her was 2019. Last one that was released, at least…"

Naomi raises an eyebrow.

He looks sheepish, like he shouldn't have mentioned that. "Well, there was a scrapped album in between *Red, White, & Blue* and *Apotheosis* that we started, but with COVID and everything, it kept getting dragged out and then everyone would change their mind on the songs and the sound. Harlow really wasn't happy with it… she was getting real sick of the generic pop stuff at that point and wanted to break out, write her own stuff, as I said, but there was a lot of pushback from the label at that time."

"This was in 2021?" Naomi asks. "Around the same time 'Endless Summers' was released?"

"Yeah, it was ongoing but that not doing well only made matters worse. Harlow tried to argue that that was proof she should be able to take a new direction, but Charlie said it was her fault… and yeah, I don't know."

"Her fault how?"

KELLY AND KRISTINA MANCARUSO

"Uh, I just think Harlow wasn't into it. Her and Colton broke up around that time and it was a love song. She hated it but was kind of pushed to release it."

Naomi thinks of the timing of everything, and how Jade's death also occurred around then. "This is a long shot, but she never mentioned Jade Dutton to you back then? She was an aspiring musician." Naomi quickly pulls up a photo of Jade.

He's silent when he looks, but shrugs. "Nah, sorry, not ringing any bells. That the girl she's accused of murdering?"

Naomi nods. He looks genuinely sad about it. Naomi bites the inside of her lip as she thinks. "What about Colton? You mentioned Harlow wasn't in a good place whenever they were together. Do you think he was cheating? Possibly with Jade?"

"I mean, I wouldn't put it past him, but I genuinely don't know."

Naomi makes another note. "Last question. You say you haven't worked with Harlow in a few years. Not since *Red, White, & Blue*. Why did you stop working with her?"

Bobby runs his hands through his dark hair. "Good question. I wondered the same thing myself. But Charlie told me she wanted to go in another direction."

"And she never gave an explanation herself?"

"Nope, never heard from her again."

Naomi frowns, her intuition telling her there's more to it. She ends the interview, eager to get back home to mull over the new questions swirling around her head.

Did Colton push Harlow to her breaking point? If so, how? By cheating with Jade? And does any of this connect to Bill Lever? Bobby seems sure Harlow isn't a killer, but he hasn't worked with her in years, doesn't really know her anymore. Plus, would someone as sweet and innocent as he claims not even extend him the courtesy of firing him herself? Or at least giving him an explanation?

Naomi doesn't need all the answers to know something isn't adding up.

Chapter 14

Once home, Naomi heads straight for her laptop, not even taking a break to eat. She's too fixated on getting answers to bother with anything else. So she dives back into her research, choosing to focus first on the Bill Lever connection and the serial killer angle. Bobby seemed to think the idea was ludicrous, but Naomi isn't so sure. Two days ago, she thought the idea of Harlow murdering anyone was ludicrous, but she's since been accused of murdering *two* people—so why not three?

Naomi reads the comments on the video by the TikToker who presented the theory in the first place, fascinated once again by how polarizing the star is. So many people in the comments seem to loathe Harlow. And sure, if she is a murderer, maybe she deserves it, but as Naomi stumbles across the Harlow Hayes hate-train, sifting through tons of articles, videos, and social media posts full of disdain for the star, she can't help but feel it's all a bit unfair.

Harlow Hayes is a talentless industry plant
Harlow Hayes makes a mockery of the music industry
Don't let your children listen to Harlow Hayes
The devil in disguise: Harlow Hayes and the evil elite

Ten reasons why Harlow Hayes deserves none of her success

Harlow Hayes' worst looks

A thread on Harlow Hayes' cringiest lyrics

Why the world would be better off without Harlow Hayes

And those were the tame titles. Naomi can't believe how incredibly mean some people are. She can't fathom how someone could emotionally cope knowing people have so much contempt for them for just existing. How did Harlow deal with it all? Maybe she didn't and it's one of the reasons she snapped...

But then she recalls Bobby's words. *The songs she wrote tended to be very sad. Not angry. That's why I was so shocked when I heard the news. If anything, I worried she'd try to harm herself. Not someone else.*

One second, Naomi is sure Harlow is a cold-blooded killer. And the next, she's feeling sorry for her. Either way, Harlow is all she can think about, and it makes Naomi want to rip her hair out. It's maddening.

Feeling like her brain is about to short-circuit, she decides she needs to get out. Do something. Something that will help her get closer to the truth. As she looks around the apartment, she knows just the thing.

Naomi returns from her errand an hour later with red string, a giant pack of thumbtacks, five-packs of Post-it notes, painter's tape, and some ink for Joel's printer.

For the past week, thousands of thoughts and data points have been swirling around her mind, multiplying at an uncontrollable rate. And while she's been keeping track of them in Excel and Word, she needs a better way to organize them, a way in which she can lay her thoughts and theories out in front of her, alongside the facts.

First, she prints out photos of all the relevant people, along with any relevant articles, scanning her spreadsheets and lists for starred content to refer back to. Then she moves the couch out of the way and rolls up the rug, so she can lay everything out on the floor, but it's not working. The papers slip out of place every time she moves something. She needs a bigger space, a spot where she can step back and assess.

She stares up at the rectangular wall, where a huge canvas painting hangs. It's a modern piece, with streaks and splotches of different shades of red and black strewn across it. Naomi doesn't understand art. This looks like a crime scene to her. She has a much better use for the space. She'll just carefully tape up all her documents instead of thumb-tacking them. Joel will never even know. She carefully lifts the piece off the wall, holding her breath until she safely places it down in front of the TV.

She picks up Harlow's photo from her pile of papers and tapes it to the center of the wall, the familiar sense of unease bubbling through her as she meets the alleged killer's stare. Naomi continues taping various other photos and pieces of paper to the wall, connecting some by string and adding Post-its wherever necessary. She's in the zone, feeling lighter with each and every thought she transfers from her brain to the wall. She keeps writing, scribbling her thoughts as fast as possible, practically feeling the paper fly out of her fingertips. The thoughts pour out of her like a waterfall, her hand almost unable to keep pace.

She writes and tapes, writes and tapes, until finally her brain is empty. She collapses into the couch and stares at the wall. Instead of feeling exhausted, she's invigorated. Ready to finally start connecting some of the puzzle pieces. She feels a sense of pride as she steps back to assess her creation.

A photo of Colton hangs from the top-left corner of the wall, in line with a photo of Jade in the top-right—both victims dangling above Harlow's photo dead-center. Articles and Post-it notes, detailing everything from their respective dates of death, relation to Harlow (or lack thereof, in Jade's case), and other relevant information or theories surround each of their photos.

Both photos are connected to Harlow with a red string. String also connects Jade and Colton's photos, with a Post-it with a big question mark in the middle of it.

Another line connects Colton and Harlow, with a few Post-its summarizing their relationship history. Also surrounding Colton are notes with names, including his ex-fiancée Meghan Rhodes and those of his immediate family, plus his uncle, Senator Kenneth Scott—an uncle in politics always makes the murder board.

Similar Post-its also surround Harlow's photo, detailing people she has or had ties to: Ex-boyfriends, rumored flings, rumored enemies, and friends. It surprises Naomi at how little she's found about Harlow's current circle of friends. She used to be seen out all the time, but in the past few years she seems to have kept to herself. Naomi remembers her aunt claiming she completely cut her family out of her life. In 2021, she lost Colton, then cut ties with her family and her music team—Bobby included.

One person she is still connected to, however, is manager

Sam Brixton, whose photo hangs between Colton and Harlow, red string connecting the three of them. From what Naomi gathers so far, Colton introduced Harlow to Sam Brixton when they first started dating and he helped skyrocket her to fame.

To the bottom-left is a section for Machinist Records, and beneath it a list of people associated with Harlow through music, such as label head Charlie Roy, producer Bobby Park, and other producers, songwriters, dancers, and collaborators (like Mama Money) who worked with Harlow over the years. Adjacent to this section is a photo of Bill Lever, alongside a Post-it: "Another victim of H?"

The bottom-right corner is reserved for theories and "other," and includes a printout of the Twitter thread of Harlow's darkest lyrics, plus any potential relevant tabloids or other fan theories she's come across.

Naomi studies the wall, eyes darting back and forth between the various Post-its and photos. She purses her lips, wondering for one brief moment if it's a little over-the-top. She immediately shakes her head, though. There's nothing wrong with being thorough.

She refocuses her attention, looking for something— anything—to stand out, until she notices a connection between two of the notes.

VMAs, 12 Sept 2021: Harlow falls down stairs during performance

Jade Dutton: Last seen alive on 11 Sept 2021. Body found in Oct 2021. Death deemed overdose, but rumored to be asphyxiation (source: Leo)

The VMAs incident was the day after Jade was last seen alive.

Naomi fumbles for her phone and brings up a video of the fall, her breath catching as she sees it. She replays the video, studying the exact moment Harlow messes up. Right before the fall, her backup dancer tries a dance move that involves putting his hands around her neck.

Naomi imagines the bruises around Jade's throat.

It doesn't take Naomi long to find Trevor Gray, the dancer in the video—now famous in his own right as a star on Broadway.

She clicks through to his Instagram. His profile is a picture of him in the middle of a pirouette. His body, although tiny on the screen, is the epitome of human perfection, like he's been manufactured in a lab. Every lean, long muscle on full display. She taps the message button on his profile and slides straight into his DMs.

Hi Trevor! My name is Naomi Barnes. I'm doing a story for C*Leb and would like to ask you a few questions about Harlow Hayes, if you wouldn't mind sparing some time?

Naomi adds another string to the wall, connecting Jade to the VMAs Post-it. Her heart pounds with a weird excitement as she scrawls, *Was Harlow's mis-step a reaction to her having choked Jade Dutton to death the night before?* onto another note.

"Holy shit," she says after sticking it to the wall.

Social Media Post

C*Leb News ✓ @CLebNewsOfficial

Harlow Hayes takes a tumble at VMAs during "To the Nines" performance with Mama Money. Read about the best and worst moments of the night on C*Leb News here!

21:05 · Sept 13, 2021 · **56.3K** Views
401 Reposts **11K** Likes

> **@SpringDayRising**: So when Harlow told C*Leb News to expect the unexpected, did she know she was going to eff up the entire choreography mid-song?

> **@MaterialGworl3**: What a disaster. Heard she missed rehearsals that morning. Clearly cares more about partying than performing now…

> **@StipmoreHH**: She's been working so hard, hope she takes a break #weloveyouharlow

> **@baddiefonts**: She looked drunk or high to me.

> **@ClioNovelist**: I remember reading an article about how she was weird the entire night even in the crowd. Constantly touching her nose. Constantly looking at Colton, who seemed to be ignoring her.

> **@AbbeyRoadKnows**: @ClioNovelist he was probably embarrassed.

Interview Transcript from UK Radio Show

December 2021

Host: We have the brilliant Harlow Hayes with us today, everybody. Welcome to the show, Harlow!

Harlow: Hi! Thank you so much for having me.

Host: The pleasure is all ours. So how are you enjoying London?

Harlow: Oh, I'm loving it. It's always been one of my favorite cities, ever since I performed here for my very first world tour. The UK has some of the best crowds, for sure.

Host: You know, I have to agree with you on that one. Us Brits do know how to have a good time. At a concert or festival at least... Anyway, we can't wait to hear you perform in a bit in the Live Lounge, but first, I need to ask you a question. Only because my mate loves you, okay, and he begged me to ask.

Harlow: I'm scared now...

Host: Harlow Hayes... are you single? And if so, will you go on a date with my mate Jack?

Harlow: *laughs* I am single, yes, but I don't think I'll have much time for romance on this trip, unfortunately. Sorry, Jack.

Host: Ah, you hear that, Jack? Sorry mate. But fair enough, fair enough, thanks for humouring us, Harlow. Now

another cheeky question, apologies, but speaking of trips...
what happened at the VMAs?

Harlow: *sighs* Well, I found out that wearing new heels
and doing choreography on top of a flight of stairs isn't the
best idea...

Host: Tell me about it. I tried it last night, fell down not one,
but two flights.

Harlow: Well, at least it wasn't broadcast to millions of
people.

Host: Erm yes, I must say I am grateful for that. And you're
sure it didn't have anything to do with an ex-boyfriend? A
Mr. Colton Scott?

Harlow: *laughs awkwardly* So about my song...

Chapter 15

Naomi tries her best to avoid bumping into strangers as she speed-walks down Broadway. She's desperate to make it to the theater in time after the last-minute response from Trevor Gray, who has invited her to talk before his next show.

Her eyes dart between her phone and the colorful screens advertising the many different shows before she turns the corner on 45th Street. Adorned by its famous bright-yellow-and-black show logo, the theatre entrance is just like she remembers when she saw the show with Faye a few years back. It's weird, she thinks, how the world continued on as normal after her death, barely changing, while all the color was drained from Naomi's life.

Doing as Trevor instructed, Naomi bypasses the entrance and enters through the side of the building before sending a text. *Here*.

She stares at her phone, feeling a bit awkward as she waits for a response.

"Over here!" a friendly voice calls out seconds later.

Naomi looks up and sees Trevor waving at her, standing halfway out of his dressing room. He's shorter than she expected but he makes up for it in personality. He's wearing jeans, a hoodie, and a pair of red Air Jordans. Naomi passes racks of costumes and props as she makes her way over.

"You made it." He reaches out for a hug.

"Of course," Naomi replies, a smile tugging at her lips. "Thank you so much again for agreeing to speak to me."

His warm brown eyes and genuine smile make her feel at ease, like they've been friends for years.

"Sit, sit," Trevor says, gesturing to a rolling chair. Aside from the extravagant vanity with the Hollywood-style bulbs, the room isn't anything special. White walls, white curtains, and dark wooden furniture.

She turns her attention back to Trevor, who's beaming with pride. "So what's it like being the star for a change?"

He blushes, waving his hand dismissively. "Please, I'm not the star."

Naomi tilts her head, smirking. "You just won a Tony. I think it's safe to say you're one now."

He purses his lips and pretends to fling invisible long hair over his shoulder.

"Is it as glamorous as it seems?" Naomi asks.

"If you consider taking the subway here and eating a cup of noodles for dinner glamorous, then sure." His laugh is infectious. So loud and boisterous it makes her laugh.

"But being here, at one of Broadway's best theaters—I mean, I know you've performed at Madison Square Garden and other huge arenas—but this is pretty amazing."

Trevor sucks in his cheeks and looks away before grinning widely. "Okay, yeah, it's pretty fucking glamorous."

"I knew it." Naomi says, waving a finger at him. "So

what made you make the switch, anyway? From backup dancer for Harlow to theater?"

Trevor purses his lips. "Well, a few things. I come from a small town." He raises his eyebrows in emphasis. "Like, a really small town, with so few people that everybody knows everybody. And all I wanted to do was to explore the world." He uncrosses his arms, extending his right arm, palm up. "So as you know, I did that for a while but it got to be a lot. Mostly because I fell in love and it sucked leaving my boyfriend all the time." He leans back. "Anyway, Brandon had the idea for me to audition for Broadway and, well, here we are."

Naomi's about to comment on how sweet that is when Trevor adds, "But I'd be lying if I said Harlow had nothing to do with the decision." His smile fades, replaced by a set of pursed lips.

"Why?"

"Because she's a stone-cold bitch."

Naomi's eyes widen, surprised by the outburst. Bobby was so complimentary of Harlow, even sympathizing with her. But Trevor clearly feels differently.

"Wait. I thought you two were friends?" She thinks of the countless photos she's seen of the two of them on tour, laughing hysterically. Harlow even posted birthday tributes to Trevor, and he did the same for her. "What happened?"

He raises a brow. "Well, we used to be friends. Close friends. She'd confide in me about Colton or whatever was going on." He rolls his eyes at the mention of Colton's name. "Sorry, not to talk bad about the dead, but I wasn't a fan."

Naomi's surprised to hear Trevor has a similar opinion

to Bobby. "Can you elaborate on that for me? You're the second person today to say something like that, which surprises me since, before then, I hadn't really heard a bad thing about Colton."

He lets out a laugh, as if Colton's glowing reputation annoys him. "I mean, I can't pretend I knew the guy well but I just have a sense for people. And I had a bad one about him. Not only would he make Harlow cry and pick constant fights with her, but he just always seemed too smooth. Too polished. Fake."

"Do you know what they'd fight over?"

"Harlow never went into too much detail, but with how quickly he moved on to Meghan, I assume him cheating was one of many reasons."

Naomi makes a note, confirming her suspicion that Colton may have cheated on Harlow with Jade.

"But anyway, I was there for her. In fact, the last time I spoke to her was when she called me in tears after a fight with Colton. I calmed her down, told her she deserved better, and that I'd always be there for her. And she told me she'd always be there for me. Fucking heartbreaking." Trevor pauses, swallowing. "And then, out of nowhere, she stops replying to my texts, won't answer my calls. And then, boom! Charlie fires her entire dance team, citing bullshit 'budget' reasons. And the worst part is, Harlow completely ghosted me after that. Not even bothering to explain or apologize."

Just like Bobby, Naomi thinks. "When was this?"

"End of 2021."

Timing fits, Naomi thinks. "And you haven't spoken to her since?"

"No. The last time—" He stops, then shakes his head. "Well, the last time I *saw* her, about a year after I last *spoke* to her, she just completely blanked me. Walked right past me without saying a word…" He laughs in disbelief. "I was livid, as you can imagine, but also so shocked I didn't bother saying anything. I wasn't going to chase her down. If she didn't give a shit about me, I didn't give one about her… Ball was in her court and she stabbed it with a knife. She was finished with me, so I was finished with her. And that was that."

His eyes glaze over with tears as he looks down, face flushed. Naomi can see how much Harlow's hurt him.

"I'm sorry she treated you like that," she says, a new picture of Harlow forming in her head.

"It is what it is. Worst part was that I watched her hurt my other friends too. She should've at least had the balls to do it herself. Not send Charlie to do her dirty work."

After her interview with Bobby, when she learned of Harlow dumping her music crew, Naomi wondered if it was a coincidence. But now, after learning she also fired her dance crew and completely cut off one of her good friends, it's apparent it was purposeful.

"Do you think there was something major that happened around that time that perhaps affected her and was causing her to kind of cut everyone out?"

"Well, this all kind of happened around the time she went to rehab. End of 2021. After Colton's engagement. But honestly, she'd been acting off for a few months at that point. Kind of all over the place, distracted. Usually she never let her bullshit with Colton interfere with her work, but…"

Naomi thinks about the timing of it all again and the reason she wanted to speak to Trevor in the first place.

"So Colton got engaged to Meghan end of December 2021, and a few months before that was the VMAs…"

Trevor rolls his eyes knowingly. "Exactly. That was when it all started. That trainwreck of a performance. Trag-ed-y."

"Did you know that performance was the night after Jade Dutton was last seen alive?" Naomi says, a little more excitedly than she meant.

"Who's Jade—" Trevor starts, before the lightbulb goes on. He stares at Naomi with an expression of horror and curiosity.

Naomi nods. "There are rumors that Jade was killed by asphyxiation." She brings her hands to her throat to get the point across.

"Oh my god." Trevor stands up and starts pacing back and forth. He pauses, ready to speak, but nothing comes out. He paces again. "Are you telling me you think she freaked out during the dance move…" He stops and mouths "No" before continuing. "That she freaked out when I put my hands around her neck—like we'd rehearsed hundreds of times—because she'd just choked someone to death the night before?"

He stares at Naomi, eyes bugging. Naomi shrugs, implying that's exactly what she thinks. Especially after hearing Trevor's timeline of events.

By the time Naomi leaves the theater, the daylight has all but faded, replaced by the glow of the bright city lights. She does a three-sixty turn as she walks through Times Square, taking in the scene. Tourists smiling, taking photos. Groups of friends laughing. Couples holding hands. Vendors selling hot dogs, candied nuts, and light-up balloons for children. Street performers dressed up in costumes. Celebrities' faces plastered on huge digital billboards.

It's a beautiful sight. But when she listens closely, when she takes a deeper breath, the sounds and smells start to paint a different picture. She starts to notice the unpleasant undercurrents of her surroundings, hiding beneath the city's glamorous facade. Like the sirens behind the upbeat music. The stench of body odor masked by cheap perfume. Arguments drowned out by laughter.

Naomi imagines all the poor souls who come to New York to "make it big" but only manage to leave behind a legacy of broken dreams and disappointment, still palpable in the polluted city air.

Back at Joel's apartment, Naomi doesn't waste any time getting the details Trevor spilled about Harlow onto the wall. She writes two new headers on pink Post-it notes in black Sharpie, both branching from Harlow's image in the center. She moves a few pieces of paper from the "other" section to below the relevant headers, and quickly scrawls down new details, before adding them too.

Harlow doesn't forgive and forget

- *Jax Paulson: Radio host blasted her nomination as VMAs' Artist of the Year in 2015; fired in 2018*
- *Colton: Trevor seemed to hate him, Bobby also hinted H*

wasn't happy with him—both implied he gaslit, and possibly cheated on her

- *Possible Colton cheated with Jade?*
- *Bill Lever's "suicide" after sexual assault allegations—some think Harlow could've been involved, citing photo of them arguing, lyrics mentioning him*

Harlow's reinvention after Jade's death

- *Completely changed style (see Avant article from August 2023)*
- *Cut ties with family and friends*
- *Cut ties with dance crew and music team*
- *Darker lyrics, new sound (see Apotheosis album review)*
- *Possible scrapped album in 2019—could she have spilled more clues in these lost lyrics?*
- *Harlow implies she's embracing "the darkness" in interview, in response to question about the meaning of her Apotheosis album*
- *Starts leaving Easter eggs around Apotheosis (i.e., social media posts hinting to upcoming tracks—see Music Journal article dated August 2023—plus callbacks to past and future work in music videos for "Cruel Delights" and "Violent Ends")— are there others that fans haven't picked up on yet? Ones that hint to her darker secrets/personal life?*

Despite all her questions, Naomi feels like meeting with Trevor and Bobby allowed her to make good progress. It's clear that something major happened at the end of 2021, an event significant enough to make Harlow cut ties with family and friends and to prompt her to completely reinvent herself over the next year and a half. And, whether she committed murder or not, Naomi is convinced that event has *something* to do with Jade's death.

And now she has reason to believe that Colton wasn't a good boyfriend and that it's very possible he could have cheated on Harlow with Jade, there's motive.

Naomi hopes it's not as clear-cut as that, though. If she's learned anything from her research, it's that Harlow is far from a cliché. She might be a killer, but Naomi doesn't think "scorned woman" is her modus operandi.

Her eyes drift over the board, moving from the Easter eggs to photos, landing on Bill Lever's. Even though Bobby was unconvinced, she thinks about the possibility of Harlow having killed him as well. Lets herself consider the fact that Harlow could've killed three people, which would make her a serial killer. Then, Naomi thinks about how some of the most notorious serial killers left clues, almost wanting the police and public to figure out who they were, so they could get the "glory."

A chill prickles at the back of her neck as she stares at Harlow's photo, feeling like she's trying to tell her something. *Go on, figure it out.*

Other clues are out there, Naomi is sure of it. She just has to find them, and piece them all together.

Chart Topper Magazine

HARLOW HAYES ISN'T ALL BAD: HERE'S THE PROOF

By Meg Koestner
09/27/2024

Harlow Hayes' recent arrest has been dominating headlines, including our own. But with so many articles hinting at her guilt, we thought now was the perfect time for a reminder that Hayes is innocent until proven guilty. And if her track record of giving is any tell on whether or not she did it, then I don't think she did. But don't take my word for it. See for yourself by taking a look at some of Harlow Hayes' most generous moments below.

October 2018
Hayes donates to victims of Hurricane Michael

After the Category 5 hurricane devasted parts of the southeast, Hayes, who was scheduled to perform in the panhandle state that weekend, donated both her time and money to help out victims. Sources claim the star contributed $100,000 to the official victim fund.

December 2018–2019
Hayes grants twenty-five wishes for the Make a Wish Foundation

Harlow went above and beyond during this time, granting twenty-five wishes for the Make a Wish Foundation. She granted a child the Disney World trip of a lifetime, gave away special tickets to her concerts, did meet-and-greets, and even paid a substantial amount toward various medical bills.

March 2020–2021
Hayes helps out during the pandemic

From schools, to hospitals, to charities, Harlow's reported donations amid the coronavirus crisis totalled over $1 million. Recipients included the Red Cross, the First Responders Fund, the National Coalition Against Domestic Violence, as well as the Covid-19 relief fund in her home state of Ohio.

August 2022
Hayes supports Haven Animal Shelter with monthly donations

For the past three years, Hayes has been one of the most important donors to a New York City animal shelter, making monthly donations of $1,500. When asked for comment, CEO Anne Doyle said, "I've known Harlow for years, she's donated well over half a million dollars to our shelter so far. And she loves animals, loves them. And people who love animals don't kill for no reason. I want to go on the record and state my belief that anyone who loves animals is a good person. I repeat: Harlow Hayes is a good person."

March 2023–present
Hayes donates more than $200,000 to fans' GoFundMe pages

Over the past two years, Hayes has taken to various fans' GoFundMe pages to help them out, donating a total of more than $200,000 in sums ranging from $1,596 to one donation of $31,498. The lucky recipient of the latter was Jaycee Hill, who was raising money for her sister's cancer treatment. "She's our angel," Jaycee said in a thank-you post.

Chapter 16

Naomi stares out the window as the train rushes out of New York City the next morning. Her view rapidly shifts from towering glass skyscrapers and high-rise apartment blocks to brick buildings, chain-linked fences, and housing developments, some more unkempt than others. In less than an hour, all she sees are trees. Some still hold onto summer, green leaves hanging proud, while others have started to turn shades of orange, red, and yellow.

Sprawling estates and colonial-style mansions peek through the wooded area to her right as a wide expanse of the Hudson River reveals itself to her left. It still surprises her how stunning the landscape is, with its mountain-lined riverbanks painted in the early shades of fall. But even they do little to quell her mounting anxiety. She's almost home.

She rolls her sleeves, heat creeping up on her, as the mountains close in. *You're here now*, the wind seems to whisper. *No turning back.*

Naomi closes her MacBook once the train starts to slow toward its last stop, wishing she'd been more productive on the journey. She wanted to draft a new article about the

Harlow investigation, but instead spent most of the time typing and deleting, typing and deleting.

Was Harlow Hayes' Infamous VMAs Fall Tied to Death of Jade Dutton? Former Dancer Thinks So...

Did Harlow Hayes Strangle Jade Dutton to Death?

Usually, she's able to come up with a snappy headline, covering tons of information in a small number of words, but nothing is clicking today. It's all fog.

The train jolts to a halt as it reaches its final destination, Poughkeepsie, New York. The city is part of the Hudson River Valley region, midway between the core of the New York metropolitan area and the state capital of Albany. Founded in the seventeenth century by the Dutch, Poughkeepsie was a major hub during the Revolutionary War, and more recently became known for being voted as Forbes' "Eighteenth Most Miserable City to Live In," citing long commute times, bad weather, and crime as some of the reasons. Naomi has her own reasons, though.

She grabs her weekend bag and the gift for her cousin before shuffling down the aisle. A cool breeze hits her as she steps off the platform, greeting her with the smell of train fumes and chicken wings from the bar next door. She makes her way toward the taxi rank and hops into the first cab, directing the driver to her Aunt Mary's house about fifteen minutes away.

The view from the taxi presents a similar juxtaposition as the one from the train, but the small-town version. One second, they're whizzing past a brightly colored sign for an apple orchard, and the next they're passing a dilapidated house and abandoned barn. Then they pass the immaculately groomed grounds of Vassar College, followed by a grotty townhouse complex, like the one Naomi grew up in.

When she first moved to New York and told Joel and her other colleagues she was from upstate, their reactions usually included an "Aww, how nice" or "That must've been a great place to grow up," as if their first thought was of a quaint little town where everyone waltzed around in their Sunday best. Pumpkin patches and ice cream shops. Candy-apple-red covered bridges and fresh air. But the air around where Naomi was from wasn't fresh. It was full of cigarette smoke and the lingering scent of weed. And her painted front door was peeling and faded.

Naomi counts two more dilapidated houses as they drive, chest tightening with each sight, before a road lined with sprawling mansions on acres of land is closely followed by a decaying shopping mall, most shop fronts boarded up. Only the dollar store and nail salon are left.

A man takes a swig from a paper-bagged bottle, looking at two young girls walking past him in their crop tops and short shorts, despite the cool weather. The taller girl glances back at the man, while the other laughs, blissfully unaware of her surroundings. Naomi smirks, despite her concern; that was her and her sister once: Naomi, always on alert; Faye, living in a dreamworld.

Her phone vibrates in her hand, bringing her back to reality.

"Hey Joel," she says, worried he'll ask for a status update when her mind is so all over the place.

"Just wanted to check in and see how it's going—any updates?"

Her brain swirls with everything she's learned, realizing she hasn't updated him in a couple of days, hoping instead to simply present him with a hard-hitting article. She launches into everything, from the different theories circulating online to the eerie themes in Harlow's music and the alleged Easter eggs.

"Some are through social media, but others are in her music videos and her lyrics and even album artwork. Most hint at future songs, music videos, tour dates, that kind of thing, but I bet there are more that fans haven't even picked up on. Maybe even hints about her personal life, like how serial killers leave clues…"

"Hah," he laughs, before she can tell him about the latest developments following her meeting with Bobby and Trevor. "Reminds me of The Beatles all over again."

"The Beatles?" Naomi frowns, caught off-guard by his seemingly random connection.

"Yeah, not the serial killer part, but fan conspiracies surrounding album art and lyrics and other things. Back in the day, when I was a staff writer for a music mag, I did an article all about Easter eggs in music and learned some cool shit. Did you know the first musician to do it—that I know of, at least—was Bach?" Joel laughs.

"The composer?"

"Yep, he essentially wrote his name in musical notes. Since then, loads of artists have done similar things to what you're talking about. My niece, who's around your age, is always telling me about Taylor Swift Easter eggs, but in my era the fascination was all about The Beatles. You ever hear about the 'Paul is dead' theory, about how fans think

McCartney died and the other members slipped hints about it into their work?"

"What? No!" Naomi laughs, but her interested smile drops as she thinks of her mom, who loved The Beatles.

Lucy Barnes loved the band so much that she gave both Naomi and Faye middle names referencing her favorite songs: Jude for Naomi, Prudence for Faye. Naomi can almost hear her mother's raspy vocals as she pictures her on stage, ethereal bell sleeves flowing, hair fanned out, as she covered "Hey Jude" and "Dear Prudence," giving her girls—whichever one it was for—a wink as she sang. At Lucy's funeral, Faye returned the favor by singing a beautiful acoustic rendition of "Lucy in the Sky with Diamonds," changing the song's second-person pronouns to the collective first person. She looked at Naomi reassuringly the entire time, singing "picture us" and "we drift" and "our head in the clouds," as if to tell her they'd be fine. They still had each other.

"So is that your angle for the next piece, then? Harlow's 'killer' lyrics?" Joel asks, interrupting her thoughts.

Naomi shoves the memory aside and clears her throat. "Oh no, maybe a follow-up eventually, after I find a few more meaningful ones, but I actually have something much better…"

Naomi quickly gives Joel the rundown about everything she learned from Leo, Bobby, and Trevor, including the possibility Jade was strangled, and how she's meeting with Jade's sister later, before she tries to sneak into Colton's funeral tomorrow.

"Fuck me, look at you go," he says proudly. "Would be

great if we could include a comment from the sister in the article, that would be a real hit piece."

"For sure."

Naomi relaxes her shoulders, knowing this will buy her more time before she has to complete a draft. But an unusual feeling of guilt also niggles at her, imagining how awful it would be to find out in an internet tabloid that her sister might have been strangled to death before her body was dumped in a drug den. She thinks of all the celebrities and their families she's probably upset in the past, writing articles based on the usual rumors and whisper reports, never giving any thought to the heartbreak it could unleash. At least she'll be giving Emily Dutton a heads-up. She's teeming with questions for her, desperately curious to know more about Jade. But her questions will have to wait.

A bundle of pink and blue balloons attached to a mailbox bob in the wind, marking Naomi's destination. She inhales as the taxi accelerates up the familiar steep driveway of her aunt's house, wiping the sweat from her palms on her jeans.

Not finding anyone inside the front of the house, she makes her way toward the back deck, where she sees her cousin Katie and Katie's husband, Nick, greeting guests under a giant balloon arch. Katie is wearing a baby-blue fitted dress, which accentuates her massive baby bump. All the other guests are wearing either pink or blue too. Naomi looks down at her red flannel shirt and black leather jacket, cursing herself.

"Naomi!" Katie squeals as she walks up, gift in hand.

Naomi is thrown off-balance as she remembers the last

time she saw Katie, at Faye's funeral. Even though Katie is standing in front of her in a blue dress, cheery as ever, Naomi can't help but see her frowning in a black woolen coat.

"I was so excited when Mom told me you were coming!" Katie says, giving Naomi a half-hug and kiss on the cheek. "It's so nice to see you."

"You too!" Naomi says, trying to muster as much enthusiasm as possible.

They'd always gotten along, but were never that close, not like some cousins were. Naomi chalks it up to Katie being a couple years older, but part of her wonders if it's because she had a more stable upbringing, spending her childhood playing soccer instead of coloring on the wet floor of a bar while her mom rehearsed. Plus, Naomi and Faye had each other. They didn't need anyone else.

"When are you going to join the mommy club and move back here?" Katie sways, grinning from ear to ear as she cradles her bump. "We miss you!"

Naomi laughs awkwardly and shrugs. She wants to tell Katie not to hold her breath, to explain how she no longer pictures herself playing happy families. How her dreams of having children have now morphed into nightmares, her mind constantly wondering how anyone can cope emotionally with worrying about all the bad things that could happen to them. She figures these are details Katie would prefer to be spared, though, so she avoids the question.

After a quick chat about life in LA, Naomi moves aside so the newly arrived guests can greet Katie, while Naomi moves onto Nick.

"Thanks so much for coming," he says, arms outstretched for a hug. Nick was a year ahead of Naomi in school and lived in their neighborhood, so she hung out with him more than Katie when they were younger.

"Of course, it's really nice to see everyone," she says, pulling away. Her gaze lands on the faded scar on his forehead, more visible now than ever thanks to his receding hairline.

"Still have the scar, I see."

Nick's face flushes as his hand moves across it. "Have your sister to thank for that." He laughs.

She smirks, remembering the night Faye chucked a piece of splintering firewood at his head. Unbeknown to Naomi, freshman Faye had been hooking up with Nick, a senior at the time. When he broke it off with her—either because he got what he wanted or because he was about to turn eighteen and realized it wasn't a good look to be dating a minor—she didn't take it well. He needed eight stitches.

Naomi hears her aunt before she sees her, talking loudly about "pa-tay-ta salad." She uses it as an excuse to break away from Nick and turns to find her.

"Ah, there she is," Aunt Mary exclaims, engulfing her in a hug. "So happy you made it! Been too long…"

Naomi's heart aches at the words as she squeezes her aunt, breathing in her pungent flowery perfume. It takes her back to Faye's funeral, where Aunt Mary must've been wearing the same exact scent. Feeling her eyes get teary, Naomi clenches her jaw, looking around for something else to focus her attention on as she pulls away.

"Great job with the decor," Naomi says, eyeing the white tent and dozens of pink and blue balloons.

Aunt Mary swats a fly away with her hand, covered in rings and bracelets like some pirate merchant, before answering, "Why, thanks hun."

Being here now, seeing her aunt after so long, makes her feel even more guilty for distancing herself. They exchange messages around the holidays, but Naomi doesn't put in much effort. Sometimes, if she remembers Aunt Mary's birthday, she thinks of calling. But the thought of having to have conversations, even just answering a simple "How are you?", makes her feel sick with anxiety, so she never phones. It's wrong of her, especially after how much Aunt Mary helped with both her mom's and Faye's funerals, but Naomi simply hasn't been able to face it. All she has wanted to do is distract herself from her old life.

"My god, you look so thin," Aunt Mary says, looking Naomi up and down. "Come on, let's get you some food, fatten you up."

Relenting to her aunt's command, Naomi follows her to the gazebo, where bowls are filled with the usual selection of cold salads, next to a stack of burgers and hot dogs.

She picks at a plate of macaroni salad as she mingles with some of the guests, a few extended family members she saw occasionally as a kid, and unfamiliar others. Her conversations mostly consist of awkward greetings and intrusive questions. "Why'd you move to LA?" "What happened to Matt?" "Do you want to get married?" "Don't wait forever, your biological clock is ticking." "A family is so much more fulfilling than a career." And on and on.

She loiters next to her Aunt Mary and her friends, preferring to nod along as they chat at her rather than having to endure more painful small talk.

"I just had the weirdest dream last night," Lori, Nick's mom, says to the group. "I saw my grandmother—I was very close with her—and she told me everything would be okay with the baby and not to worry."

"Well, it was very foggy last night," Laura says. Naomi frowns, eyes darting from brown-bob Laura to blonde-bob Lori, who also furrows her brow.

"You know… what they say about fog and spirits?" Laura waves her fork in the air, looking befuddled, as if she merely asked what five plus five was.

She chomps down on a cube of watermelon. "When it's foggy out, or misty…" She holds a finger in the air, still chewing. "…spirits are able to more easily enter through the human realm and communicate with us."

Naomi shovels in a forkload of macaroni salad so she doesn't have to speak, eyeing the group. It's not that she doesn't believe in any sort of supernatural phenomena. In high school she worked at a creepy bed-and-breakfast, where multiple parents reported their children talking to a tree. The same tree. Naomi later learned that a man was reportedly hanged there during the Revolutionary War.

"I've never heard of that, but it makes sense," Lori replies, as Aunt Mary, Kath, and Donna nod in fascination.

Naomi sneezes and all the women turn their attention to her. She curses the Hudson Valley air.

"God bless you!" Kath says, placing her hand on Naomi's back.

"Thanks," Naomi replies. "Allergies." Her allergies have been acting up since she stepped foot in Poughkeepsie, almost like she is allergic to the place itself.

Laura lets out a laugh. "Allergies. More like government intervention!"

Naomi's eyebrows shoot up, taken aback.

"It's got nothin' to do with the pollen, honey, believe me." Laura waves her fork around again. "The government orchestrates it all, dumps the chemicals round here as a test twice a year."

"Don't want us feeling well enough to fight back," Lori chimes in, taking Naomi by surprise. But then she remembers all the other conspiracy theories she's seen Lori's kids, including Nick, post about on Facebook and decides to just nod along.

She tunes out, gaze drifting behind her to the woods where Nick's young nieces are playing. She smiles, remembering how magical the woods felt when she was a kid. She recalls the time when she and Faye, nine and seven, found an intricately carved miniature door at the base of a tree, painted yellow. The fairy door, they called it. It soon became their spot, a sort of safe haven. It was where they'd go if their mom was having one of her "days," when she was too hungover to do anything, or when she was having a spat with her latest boyfriend. Then, as they got older, it became the party place for them and their friends. They'd play beer pong with Hennessy and Peach Schnapps and drink by the fire pit they dug out.

Naomi pulls her jacket tight around her as a cold wind moves in, thinking about how life changes you. As a child, the woods represent magic. As a teen, excitement. As an adult, danger. She pictures the ramshackle house, hidden by trees. The one Faye was found in, not too far from here.

Naomi moves her shoulders around and adjusts her neck from side to side, feeling squeamish.

She's catapulted from her thoughts back to the party when Nick makes an announcement for everyone to gather around the big box near the side of the house. She breathes a sigh of relief, knowing the party is about to be over and she can make her way to Millbrook. She considers visiting her sister's gravesite first, but the mere thought of it puts her on edge. She just wants to get out of the area. Something about being home feels wrong. A constant tightening in her chest, shortness of breath. A feeling that will worsen tenfold if she goes to the cemetery. No, she'll visit when she has answers about Harlow, like she originally planned.

"Five!" Guests begin counting down excitedly, eager to see what color balloons will be unleashed from the box in front of Katie and Nick.

"Four!" Naomi imagines pink balloons flying toward the sky. Her sister's face flashes in her mind, snapshots of her as a little girl through to adulthood.

"Three!" Naomi pictures Jade Dutton, another sister lost.

"Two!" She envisions blue balloons and thinks of Colton Scott.

"One!" Everyone cheers as blue balloons fly out of the box. But Naomi stays silent, stuck in a daze, with Harlow Hayes' smirking face imprinted in her mind.

Chapter 17

Naomi pulls up to the Millbrook Diner in Uncle Frankie's white sedan, twenty minutes before she and Emily Dutton have agreed to meet. The diner is an old-fashioned structure, adorned with stainless-steel siding and an LED neon sign above the entrance. It's in the center of town, with rows of vintage lampposts and perfectly trimmed trees lining the street, their leaves a mix of green, yellow, and orange, giving it a charming aesthetic akin to the setting of a Hallmark movie. But seeing as she's there to discuss the murder of one of the town's former residents, Naomi isn't charmed, only able to focus on the gray clouds rolling in.

Once seated in a corner booth, her server, Logan, grins widely as he hands her the menu. He looks like he's popped out of a children's book. Long and lanky, with a wide, friendly smile. A bell rings and they both turn their attention to the entrance, where the hostess is pointing Emily in their direction.

Emily's resemblance to Jade is as prominent in person as it is on her profile. She looks similar to her photos, but on Instagram she's usually more done-up. This morning, she's dressed casually in a pair of white sneakers and a gray sweatsuit that hides her figure. Her short brown hair is pulled tight into a low bun, slicked back with what looks like a bottle of hairspray, with a full face of heavily contoured makeup that doesn't seem to match her attire.

Naomi stands as Emily comes over. Logan gives Emily a menu and excuses himself.

"Thank you so much for agreeing to meet with me." Naomi extends her hand to Emily, who shakes it before taking a seat.

"Yeah, no problem. You were actually the only journalist to reach out, so…"

"Really?" Naomi asks, taken aback.

Emily nods. "Yeah, everyone else seems to care more about getting clicks than the truth. They're all focused on Colton and Harlow, no one really seems that interested in Jade."

"Typical." Naomi grunts in annoyance and shakes her head, before looking Emily in the eye. "Well, I care very much about what happened to Jade."

Logan interrupts to take their order. A black coffee and pastry for Naomi; a Reuben and Diet Coke for Emily.

Once Logan walks away, Emily leans back and studies Naomi. "Well, I guess you know what it's like. To lose a sister."

Naomi swallows the lump in her throat, biting her lip to distract from the stinging in her eyes. "Yeah, I do, unfortunately." She stares at the window as she answers, imagining Faye walking toward her, smiling as her blonde hair blows in the breeze. A car drives past and her ghost disappears. "And while I've made peace with her death, there are still so many unanswered questions, closure I'll never get. But I'm hoping I can get it for Jade."

Emily's shoulders loosen. She bites her lip, nodding in understanding.

"Do you mind if I take some notes?" Naomi asks, pulling out her notebook and pen.

Emily shrugs. "Sure."

"So first of all, I'm so sorry for what happened to your sister. And I know it must be really hard to talk about, but can you walk me through everything? What happened..." Naomi opens and closes her mouth, struggling to find the right words without coming across as insensitive. "Were you surprised when you learned they were reopening the investigation into her death after all these years?"

Emily laughs, crossing her arms. "Uh yeah, just a little. Wouldn't you be?" Naomi's face flushes, slightly embarrassed at the obvious question. Emily softens. "But I always thought something was off anyway. No one listened to me before, though, said I was just in denial." She rolls her teary eyes.

"What do you mean by 'something was off'?" Naomi asks.

"Like, it just didn't seem right that my sister would die like that, you know?"

Naomi holds her question as Logan walks over with their drinks.

"'Like that', as in... overdose?"

Emily swirls her straw, staring intently at her drink. "Jade wasn't into drugs—not the kind in her system when they found her. I mean, she liked to party, sometimes she would take molly or smoke a little weed, but heroin?" She scoffs. "No."

Naomi chooses her next words carefully. "Moving to a big city, though... trying to make it in the modeling and music world... two of the most brutal industries... that can cause a lot of stress on anyone and that stuff would have been everywhere. You don't think she maybe started hanging out with the wrong people? Or that it all became too much for her? It isn't uncommon for aspiring actors, models, musicians to turn to drugs." She feels her cheeks redden.

Emily is shaking her head before Naomi can even finish. "No, believe me. I literally visited her like two weeks before she died. And there was no way she died of 'laced heroin.'" She puts air quotes around the last two words. "She was on a health cleanse, for Christ's sake. She was so conscious of everything she put into her body." Emily takes a sip of her soda and laughs. "Well, not everything, I guess."

Naomi raises an eyebrow.

Once she swallows, Emily dabs the corner of her mouth, a nostalgic grin on her face. "Let's just say, if Jade had any vice... it wasn't drugs. But she... I guess you can say she was promiscuous."

Naomi smirks. "Oh?"

Emily nods as she takes another sip of her drink.

Naomi bites her lip, thinking. "Do you think it's possible Jade slept with Colton? And Harlow..."

"Killed her in a jealous rage?" Emily interjects. "It's honestly so ridiculous." She throws her hands in the air and laughs. "Like, as if Harlow Hayes killed my sister? And then what, staged an overdose to cover it up?" She exhales shakily and dabs her eye with the side of her napkin. "But yeah, maybe Jade finally picked the wrong guy. I guess it's the best explanation we have…"

Naomi nods, agreeing that the theory Harlow snapped after Colton cheated with Jade is the most plausible. And if Jade was as "adventurous" in the bedroom as Emily said, maybe they made a sex tape.

Video evidence, she thinks, recalling Leo's tip on what the prosecution had against her.

"Have the police shared any of the evidence with you and your family yet? Video evidence, maybe? Or something else they have against Harlow that ties her to Jade's death? Because this is the thing that's stumping me. How they managed to connect it after all these years. Especially since we know the DNA tests haven't even come back yet…"

"Don't even get me started on the police," Emily says angrily. "They've just ruined our lives all over again, without even giving us any real details. Our lawyer is pressing them, but all they're telling us is they have 'substantial evidence' against her and we have to wait until the probable cause affidavit is read out at the next hearing."

It shocks Naomi that even Jade's family doesn't know. "Did they mention anything about the connection between Harlow and Jade, or Jade and Colton? Do you know if they ever even met for certain?"

Emily shakes her head. "Nope, nothing. The only concrete connection I'm aware of at all is Sam Brixton. I think he's Harlow's and Colton's manager? The last party Jade went to, the night before she went missing—the night before she died, I guess, based on the autopsy's findings—was at Sam's mansion in the Hamptons…"

Naomi freezes, alarm bells going off. "The night before the VMAs... fuck."

"What?" Emily sits up in her seat, looking concerned.

Naomi fidgets with her fork before explaining the VMAs connection and how she thinks Harlow falling during that performance the night after the party was a reaction to something that upset her.

"I have a friend in the police, and he mentioned that when Jade's body was found, there might have been bruising around her neck..."

Naomi can tell from Emily's expression, changing between horror, anger, and despair, that this is news to her.

"Can you recall any mention of that on the autopsy?"

"Of bruising? Like she was..." She runs her hand over her throat and then shakes her head, sniffling. "No, not that I remember. And I never saw her body. Closed-casket funeral too, so..." Naomi's heart thumps, remembering Faye's closed-casket funeral.

Naomi nods, wondering why this would have been left off the autopsy report if the detective Leo spoke to was so sure about it. *They told them to stop looking into it.*

A pit forms in Naomi's stomach as the words "major cover-up" flash across her mind in bright-red letters.

"Is there any way you can send me a copy of Jade's autopsy? I won't publish it or anything, I just want to verify a few things."

Emily hesitates before agreeing. "Yeah, sure. I know it was sent to my email, so I'll forward it to you."

"Thanks."

They both smile at Logan as he sets down their food.

"Are you going to write about the... strangling... thing?"

Emily asks once Logan leaves, before taking a bite of her sandwich. Naomi's relieved she brought this up.

"Is that okay with you?" She prays Emily doesn't say no, because she's going to have to run the article either way. "I won't include any of our conversation here if you don't want me to, but you can have a comment included if you want. Or not."

Emily shrugs as she takes another bite, looking at the window as she chews. "Write what you want. Maybe it'll actually prompt the police to start giving us more information, put some pressure on them."

"Hopefully."

"You can include what I said about her not being into drugs. How I always thought something was off."

"Amazing, thank you," Naomi responds.

"But nothing about the sex stuff, okay? She'd haunt me forever." She laughs. "Not that I'd hate that." She smiles, tears filling her eyes again.

"I know what you mean," Naomi says, understanding full well.

"If you don't mind me asking," Emily says, "what happened to your sister?"

Naomi swallows and takes a sip of her water before answering. "Well, it's kind of similar to your story, sadly. Her name was Faye, she was an aspiring musician too, like Jade. Died about six months after, in March 2022. Her body was found not far from our hometown, in Poughkeepsie. Cause of death was officially listed as drug overdose and/or smoke inhalation. There was a fire, but she also had a lot of drugs in her system, also 'laced heroin', aka fentanyl, hence why she didn't escape…"

"Shit," Emily says, rubbing her hands up and down her arms. "Wonder if you'll get a phone call next saying she's another victim of Harlow."

Naomi laughs awkwardly at the ridiculous thought. But the burn at the back of her throat, the creeping chill on her neck, and the sudden sound of her heartbeat thrashing in her ears makes the notion impossible to ignore.

Chapter 18

Given the right circumstances, human skin can melt. It can fuse together with synthetic fabric to the point where skin and pleather are no longer distinguishable. Naomi never knew this could happen until it happened to her sister.

Naomi stares at the thick drops of rain falling on her windshield, unsure how much time has passed. The engine is running, but she's still in the parking lot of the diner. Physically, at least. Mentally, she's in the past. Back two and half years. Back to the worst day of her life.

She was on her way to work, coffee in hand as she strode down the city street, when her phone rang.

"Naomi Barnes? This is Officer Delgado with the New York State Police Department. Is your sister Faye Barnes?"

Her heart sank in apprehension, assuming Faye had been arrested for something. Drunk driving, maybe. "Yes. Is everything okay?"

"I'm afraid not." What he said next shattered her world forever.

Everything after that was a blur. People bumping into her as she stood, frozen in place. Hot coffee burning her hand as the Starbucks cup tumbled to the ground. The taste of copper in her mouth. The ringing in her ears.

She rushed to Grand Central and got on the next train to Poughkeepsie. When she arrived, she got a taxi straight to the scene of the crime—a neglected property set back from the road, obscured by trees, not far from where she grew up. The police wouldn't let her past the yellow tape toward the remnants of the once-boarded-up house, said they were still gathering evidence, mumbling something about a "known hotspot for junkies."

She forced them to take her to the morgue to see Faye's body. She couldn't look at the horrifying corpse for more than a few seconds. Half of her melted, the other half charred bone and flesh.

The grief hit Naomi when they handed her the bag of Faye's belongings. Her ID, phone, and silver "N" bracelet were mostly melted and all that was left of her favorite shirt was a sooty scrap.

After an investigation, police concluded that she overdosed on a fentanyl-heroin combo and passed out on a pleather sofa with a lit cigarette in her hand. The highly flammable sofa caught fire, sending the rest of the abandoned house she was in up in flames.

Naomi closes her eyes, placing a hand over her mouth, nauseous at the memory. She tries to focus on the sound of the rain outside. *Drip. Drip. Drip.*

She can't stop replaying the conversation with Emily in her head. Noting the similarities between their sisters and their deaths. Two beautiful aspiring musicians apparently overdose from "laced heroin" within six months of each other. Bodies found within a hundred-mile radius. And as far as both Naomi and Emily know, neither of their sisters had ever even done heroin before. But unlike Emily, who is adamant Jade never did any kind of drugs, Naomi can't say the same about Faye.

Faye had fallen in with the wrong crowd before. Nothing as serious as heroin, that Naomi is aware of, but she did have a habit for turning to drugs and alcohol when things got tough. It first started to get bad after Naomi moved away for college. Even though she visited home whenever she got the chance, almost every weekend, Faye struggled. Her grades dropped and she started experimenting with drugs other than weed. At her junior prom, Faye had to get taken away in an ambulance with alcohol poisoning. Apparently, she hadn't eaten anything all day except for her antidepressant and then downed a bottle of tequila before the dance. They also found traces of MDMA in her system.

Like their mother, Faye had high highs and low lows, with her ups and downs continuing into her twenties. When she was up, she was constantly on the go, constantly trying to better herself and make things happen. Always singing, writing, gigging, exercising, studying, working harder than anyone Naomi had ever met. But then, she'd burn out or rejection would strike. Sometimes she'd stay in bed for days, not wanting to be bothered. Or she'd disappear, not letting Naomi know where she was or what she was doing, like in the months leading up to her death. There was even an instance, about a year before that, when Faye's boyfriend at the time called Naomi in a panic, telling her Faye was at the hospital because she "mixed" and "took too much" and "wouldn't wake up." Thankfully, she was okay. That time, at least.

"Why the fuck would you do that?" a distraught Naomi asked Faye in her hospital bed. "You think doing shit like that is going to get you anywhere aside from six feet in the ground? Like Mom?"

"You wouldn't understand," Faye replied. "It was just so... loud. I just wanted it to be quiet."

It's why when the police called Naomi, passing on the world-shattering news that her sister was dead, it wasn't unimaginable to think she overindulged or slipped up. Naomi knew better than anyone that Faye didn't know her limits. Or was prone to ignore them when she was in a bad place.

She thinks back to the days after Faye's death. How she was so overcome with despair and anger—but anger at her sister over anyone else. Wondering how she could be so reckless. Naomi had been so shattered, she tried to force herself through the stages of grief to the acceptance stage. Her sister was dead. She saw her corpse. And the police said they "didn't think" there was anything suspicious, so she left it. No sort of investigation would have brought her back. But now, Naomi is starting to think it was cowardice and fear that made her accept her sister's cause of death so easily. Because the more she thinks about it in light of what she knows now, the more something feels off.

Tears sting her eyes and a wave of guilt washes over her as she thinks of Faye dying all alone in that wretched place. Where did she get the drugs? Who was she with? Did she inject herself, knowing it would kill her? Or was it an accident? The police said that it was a known hotspot for drug users to convene, saying that she probably showed up, paid to get high, and then passed out. If she overdosed before the house set on fire, they probably left her, not wanting to get themselves into trouble. Naomi feels angry, wanting to know who was responsible. Why had she not pushed harder before? She can't remember why she didn't ask more questions, didn't put more pressure on the police to find out.

She pulls out of the diner, her mind warring with itself as she thinks about the multitude of kids from her high school that overdosed, a few of them from Faye's friendship group. She even saw a Facebook post a couple weeks ago about another guy they went to school with who died. It wasn't abnormal, especially not for their hometown. But no matter how hard she tries, she can't shake the terrwible feeling that it's all a lie.

Maybe Faye did fall in with the wrong crowd, but not the one Naomi originally thought.

From: Emily Dutton <emily.dutton@gmail.com>
Subject: Follow-up
Date: Sept 28, 2024 09:24:44 PM EDT
To: Naomi J. Barnes <naomi.barnes@clebnews.com>

Hi Naomi,

It was really nice to meet you earlier. As promised, see Jade's autopsy report attached. Please don't share/publish this, but I hope it helps in some way. I've also attached a photo of her – one I know she loved – so if you could try to use that in your article instead of the one most outlets are using, that would be much appreciated.

Also, after meeting you, I looked up your sister and was surprised to see that we share a mutual

Facebook friend — Jade. I checked Instagram too and they both followed each other. Not sure if this is important or why I'm even bothering to tell you, but thought it was interesting that they knew each other and thought you'd want to know.

Anyway, thanks again for dinner (and for caring) and good luck with everything.

Best wishes,

Emily

Chapter 19

Halfway through the arduous three-hour drive to her hotel in Maine, fighting off one painful memory after another, Naomi stops for gas and more coffee. And to read the email from Emily. She removes the lid from the Starbucks cup to let some of the steam escape and breathes in the soothing earthy scent. Her heart flutters as she takes a long sip—protesting at the intake of more caffeine. She can't remember if it's her fifth or sixth cup of the day. Maybe seventh. The liquid burns her throat on the way down, but it's a welcome feeling.

She exhales as she opens her email, trying to ignore her racing heart. *Think like a journalist*, she tells herself. *Be professional, not emotional.*

But Emily's email doesn't help calm her. Her hand trembles as she reads the second paragraph, and she winces in pain as coffee scorches her hand.

"Fuck!" She drops the cup into the holder, cursing again as it spills over the plastic console. She'll have to clean the car before dropping it back off at Aunt Mary's. She forces herself to breathe.

Jade and Faye knew each other?

How had she not made the connection before? She supposes it's because she was logged into C*Leb's social accounts at the time. Usually, that was more beneficial when researching a case, more likely to show her connections between celebrities. Her personal accounts are almost dormant and useless. She lets out a frustrated laugh, knowing she might have seen this sooner if she had been logged into her accounts instead. But would she have even thought anything of it? They were Facebook friends, which didn't mean anything. Of course they probably ran in the same circles...

But what if Faye knew something about Jade's death, so they killed her too...

She runs her hands over her face, hating that she can't control her thoughts. Feeling herself spiraling and in need of a distraction, she closes the email and calls Joel.

Once he picks up, she quickly lets him know she got an exclusive with Emily Dutton and that she plans to have the piece about Jade potentially being strangled—and that being connected to Harlow's VMAs fall—ready to publish on Monday. Joel is pleased, but can tell something is up.

"You alright?" he asks.

The simple question nearly causes Naomi to burst into tears, which scares her. Matt used to joke she had a heart made of ice because he'd never seen her cry. Not until Faye died.

"Yeah, I'm okay, thanks." She wavers on whether to share her thoughts about Faye but decides against it. "Just exhausted."

He doesn't buy it.

"Naomi," he starts. "What's the matter?"

She tells him about Faye, and how she thinks her death could possibly be connected to the Harlow case. "I know it sounds stupid, but there are so many similarities to Jade, and I just found out they were Facebook friends too and I don't know…"

Still on the verge of tears, she tilts her chin up and opens her eyes wide while pressing her tongue hard against the roof of her mouth.

You're being ridiculous, she chides herself. *Harlow Hayes didn't kill your fucking sister. That's crazy.*

"Oh sweetheart," Joel says. It's the first time she's ever heard a genuine softness in his voice. "Listen, it's not stupid. I don't know how many times I have to tell ya you're one of my best reporters, it's why I snapped you up straight outta college, okay?"

Naomi laughs, wiping the snot running from her nose with the back of her hand.

"And it's completely understandable for you to make those connections. For this to undoubtedly bring your grief to the forefront. If I had known that covering Harlow would have taken this turn, I woulda never sent you, never put you through this." He sighs.

Naomi's throat stings as she fights back tears. *Jesus Christ, pull it together*. She bites at her cuticles, wincing at the pain as she tears off another piece of skin.

"But try and think objectively for a second," he continues. "Is it really so strange that Jade knew your sister? Two young, beautiful aspiring musicians living in New York. They could have easily met at a party and linked up on social media. It makes perfect sense for them to know each other, run in the same circles. While it's a huge-ass city, the gigging circuit ain't that different to the reporting circuit. How many times do you run into the same reporters, photographers, paparazzi from other outlets? I bet you're Facebook friends with some of them."

A small weight lifts off Naomi's chest. He's right—she is. She exhales the breath she's been holding, feeling another small weight fall away.

"And I know us reporters from New York pretend like this stuff we cover doesn't bother us. So I'm going to tell you something my California-born-and-bred ex-wife told me when I first met her. It's okay to feel things. Feeling things doesn't make you weak. It makes you human. And humans write better stories."

It's the cheesiest thing she's ever heard him say, but it makes her feel miles better in the moment. "Thanks, Joel, you big sop," she jokes, sniffling.

"I don't like to remember most things my ex-wives have said to me, but I always try to remember that one. Because in all seriousness, Nay, AI is comin' for us writers so the only way we don't lose our jobs to these computers is by using being human to our advantage."

She laughs again, thinking of one of the outlandish theories she saw online about Harlow being an AI who got out of control. "Right, I'll keep that in mind."

"But anyway, try and stay focused. Colton's funeral is tomorrow, right?"

She confirms, thankful for the change in subject.

"How are you planning on—"

"The less you know, the better, probably," she says before he can finish his question.

Joel doesn't necessarily encourage breaking rules, but he

isn't against it if one of his reporters thinks it worthwhile. "Just don't do anything illegal…"

"Well, make sure you're on standby tomorrow afternoon in case I need you to bail me out."

"Hey, you get arrested, you're on your own, kid."

"Yeah, whatever," she replies before hanging up and pulling out onto the interstate.

She knows Joel will be there for her if she needs him, something she didn't realize was so important to her until now. The fact somehow comforts and disquiets her at the same time.

Two hours later, Naomi arrives at her hotel in Haverhill, Massachusetts, about an hour south of Colton's hometown in Maine. It's late and she knows she should get some sleep before tomorrow's event. But, once again, her anxiety keeps her up.

She decides against re-opening Emily's email, vowing not to view the autopsy report again until after Colton's funeral; she'll need to be focused for that and obsessing over connections between Faye and Jade's death isn't going to help. So instead she tries to be productive, spending time practicing her cover story for tomorrow and scanning photos of people attending, trying to memorize the different faces she can expect to see. She wants to be prepared and know who to avoid. Not that anyone should recognize her, but some people, like Colton's and Harlow's manager Sam Brixton, might be able to poke holes in Naomi's cover story of previously working on Colton's PR team. So as much as she wants to talk to him, especially now she knows Jade was last seen at his pre-VMAs party, the funeral probably won't be the best place. She jots down certain questions and notes for herself before checking her outfit one last time, feeling somewhat confident in her plan.

Naomi turns the light out again, desperate for her brain to shut off and stop tormenting her for a few hours, but her heart and mind are still racing, made worse by the copious amounts of caffeine flowing through her system. All she can picture is Harlow Hayes attacking her sister. Strangling her like Jade and then pumping her full of drugs before lighting the house on fire.

Groaning in frustration at knowing how sleep-deprived she's going to feel tomorrow, she rolls over and grabs her phone, intending to put on a sleep story from the Calm app, but instead she instinctively opens Twitter one more time.

None of the posts contain anything new, just more of the same hate-filled posts lacking actual substance or evidence. Nothing like @BobTheFloppp's first video, which actually contained facts and brought new information to light. She goes to @BobTheFloppp's profile, but he hasn't posted any updates since his original video. In fact, she can't find the video at all. She feels unsettled, wondering if he was forced to take it down. Threatened.

Naomi realizes she didn't do much digging into the Bill Lever case aside from asking Bobby a few questions. She hasn't even looked into Harlow's whereabouts the night of Bill's death. Her heart races as a new wave of adrenaline shoots through her.

Bill Lever was found deceased in his home in Los Angeles the morning of February 1, 2022, so Naomi searches for "Harlow Hayes February 1, 2022."

She breathes a sigh of both relief and disappointment when she sees a post from user @MilaLovesHH from the date in question. It's a photo of Harlow in the window of an Italian restaurant, sitting across from another thin blonde woman. According to Mila, Harlow was spotted out for dinner with Colton's sister-in-law Casey Scott, on the night of Bill Lever's death. In Maine. On the other side of the country from where Bill Lever died.

Naomi frowns, confused by a different photo of Harlow in the post below, also dated February 1, 2022. This one is from @CrazieHazie414HH: *Harlow grabbing a green juice on Rodeo Drive this AM. BRB actually dying.*

Naomi looks back up at the previous post, rereading it. She realizes the fan must have meant that Harlow was out the night before, judging by the nighttime shot. Of course, Naomi thinks. *The one day I need to know where she was, it can't be simple.* Spotted in Los Angeles the morning of, but on the other side of the country the night before. So did she kill Bill Lever and then go get a green juice? Was that her pick-me-up after a kill?

She zooms in on the photo of Harlow and Casey Scott, interested that Harlow was still hanging out with Casey after her final breakup with Colton. That means they must have been close. That Casey felt some sort of loyalty to Harlow, and not just to the Scott family.

Naomi shuts her eyes, finally able to relax now that she has a specific person to target at the funeral tomorrow.

DAILY NEWS

COLTON SCOTT: LAVISH MEMORIAL SERVICES TO TAKE PLACE TODAY FOR THE BELOVED ACTOR

By Felice James, Showbiz Editor
09:35 Sunday, 29 September 2024

Actor Colton Scott will be laid to rest today in Port Wendigo, Maine. The coastal community, usually a playground for the rich and influential, will take a pause from golfing on pristine greens and sailing along its shores to mourn the death of one of its own.

The late star, who tragically passed away last week, will be buried in a small ceremony attended by close family and friends. A larger, invite-only memorial reception will then be held at the local Country Club. It's rumored that Scott's *Mr. America* co-stars will be in attendance, among other Hollywood titans and political magnates.

The investigation into Colton's death is still ongoing, although a statement from the family noted that his body was no longer needed for analysis: "On Sunday, we will bury our beloved son, brother, nephew, and grandson. We're thankful to the NYPD and the coroner's office for completing all autopsies and examinations in a swift manner so we can lay him to rest sooner rather than later. Please note that this is a private memorial service, only to be attended by invited family and friends. We ask the public and the media to please respect our privacy during this difficult time."

While we anxiously await news on the investigation, our hearts go out to Colton Scott, his family, friends, and all of his fans who continue to share tributes for their beloved actor. Musician Nikki Rix recently released a tribute song for his longtime friend Colton along with a music video in his memory. In the video for "Cielo," Colton Scott makes a final appearance via CGI imaging, before disappearing into the clouds. An angel called to heaven, indeed.

Chapter 20

Naomi glances at the choppy waves of the deep-blue Atlantic as she drives north toward Port Wendigo. A red-and-white-striped lighthouse comes into view as she turns the corner, surrounded by rocky shores.

She imagines Harlow driving along this same route with Colton, the first inspiration for "Once Upon a Summer" stirring in her mind. Instead of gray and cold late September, it would've been a sapphire and golden July, tranquil water sparkling under the high sun and boats filling the bay. Naomi pictures their beginning like a polaroid-perfect romance. Old money, new money, young, beautiful, famous, and in love. Skinny-dipping under starry skies. Sunbathing on the rocks. Lobster dinners. Sailing into the sunset... Little did the lovers know they were heading into a deadly storm.

Or maybe Harlow did know, but didn't care, Naomi muses. It's clear their relationship was more complicated than it appeared.

Goosebumps prickle Naomi's arm as she takes another bend. Across the inlet, perched atop a tall cliffside, a large Georgian-style mansion peeks through a row of pine trees. Harlow's vacation home.

According to an article Naomi read in Architectural Digest, Harlow purchased the property when she and Colton were still dating but continued to spend her downtime there well after their final split. Maybe she loved the location. Or maybe she wanted Colton to have a constant reminder of her, even in his hometown.

Naomi casts her gaze to the cliff below the mansion and, seeing how the waves crash violently against the rocks, her picture-perfect visions of Harlow and Colton become spliced with scenes more fitting of a horror film than a romance. Colton's laughter is replaced by a scream. Harlow's kind eyes, usually clear and bright, are bloodshot, devoid of emotion.

The thought unnerves Naomi as she pictures her sister in Colton's place, and she wishes she could forget everything she learned yesterday. Just for now. She's already on edge as it is, knowing she's sneaking into the wake, and obsessing over Faye's death—wondering if she was actually murdered, like Jade—isn't something she can handle now. She can't spiral, not today.

Naomi exhales loudly, telling herself to focus on the scenic drive in front of her instead. The rocky coastline soon turns into rolling hills of green grass, lined with trees in rich tones of red and orange, and the nervous pit in her stomach flares as she drives up the freshly paved road toward her destination.

She switches from Spotify to radio, feeling it's in poor taste to pull into the post-funeral gathering playing songs from the alleged murderer.

Naomi looks down at her white shirt and black tie, the uniform of the country club's servers, before fixing her side braid. Since press is strictly prohibited and invitations will be checked at the door, her plan is to covertly enter the memorial service as if she's one of the staff, before changing into guest attire and posing as a former colleague of Colton's.

She breathes deeply as she passes through the wrought-iron gates, ready to find out if this is either an incredibly clever or foolish plan.

The security guard eyes her suspiciously as she rolls her window down, a clipboard in his hand. She's about to speak, but then he quickly waves her through, after spotting a few black limousines pulling up behind her. A rush of relief and adrenaline courses through her as she realizes she's made it past the first obstacle.

A spectacular white dome comes into view as Naomi reaches the top of the emerald hill. The multistory structure is lined with windows on the first floor and a wraparound porch on the second. Guests are already standing outside on the balcony area, smoking and conversing.

Naomi parks her car and surveys the entrance. She notices numerous servers, wearing the same outfit she's currently wearing, coming in and out of the door to the left. To the right, elegantly dressed guests, all clad in expensive black attire, are making their way through the glass bifold doors. It doesn't look like any security is checking guests' identification or stopping anyone trying to walk into the main entrance. Aside from the men at the second gate, the only security are those looking out onto the golf course and surrounding property.

Naomi smirks, realizing they're probably trying to make sure no press or paparazzi sneak through the wooded area.

"And I drove right through the checkpoint," she whispers to herself.

She inhales, absorbing the boost of confidence, and takes off her black tie. Underneath her white shirt, she's wearing a satin-black camisole tucked into black trousers. She chucks the shirt and tie into the footwell of the passenger seat and pulls on a black blazer before swapping out her flats for stilettos and grabbing her clutch bag.

Brown leaves crunch beneath her feet as she steps out of the car. She shouldn't be surprised by the cool breeze that greets her—it is Maine, after all—but still she shivers as she marches forward.

The mood inside the country club isn't as somber as Naomi expects. She was worried that going to a funeral would put her off her game, that it would bring back floods of painful memories. But this lavish event is a far cry from the low-key gathering she held for her mom and Faye.

Aside from the black attire, it feels more like a wedding reception with the impressive tables of food, loud chatter, and laughter.

Naomi scans the crowd for Casey Scott, taking in the sea of famous and influential cliques. A group of politicians, including Colton's uncle Kenneth Scott, are gathered around a high-top table to her left, while a group of bank CEOs and hedge fund managers are huddled by the bar to her right. She can almost smell the money coming off them, that group alone worth the GDP of a small country. Then there are the lone wolves, using the wake as a networking event.

Naomi pushes through the crowd, stopping when she

notices the impressive ensemble in front of her, including most of the *Mr. America* cast alongside a few supermodels and musicians. It's strange to think Harlow isn't here. Of course it makes sense, but still. It's also odd that Colton's ex-fiancée, Meghan Rhodes, doesn't seem to be among the guests. But one face in particular stands out—because it's impossible to miss.

In the center of the room, a giant oil painting of Colton stares back at her. She recognizes him by his boyish grin and lush eyelashes. But the warmth of his appearance is gone—as if his ghost has taken possession of the photo and is waiting to haunt everyone here.

Everyone thinks he's this can-do-no-wrong hero, but he can't be as great as everyone makes him out to be.

Not to talk bad about the dead, but I didn't like him.

A shiver crawls up Naomi's spine as she recalls both Bobby and Trevor's comments. Until now she'd chalked them up to him potentially being a cheater, a playboy who'd toy with Harlow's emotions. But staring at his painting now, hypnotized by his dark-brown eyes and thick lashes, she can't help but wonder if his heroic persona was hiding more than that. If, like Harlow, the world thought they knew him, but really had no idea.

What was your secret, Colton? she thinks. *Did we not know the real you either?*

Naomi almost doesn't recognize Casey Scott with her new bob haircut, but the former model is one of the tallest women in the room. She's wearing a loose-fitted black dress and a deep-red lip, reminding Naomi of Daisy Buchanan. Casey says something to the bartender and then looks down at her phone. Her husband, James, Colton's brother, is next to her, casually leaning on the bar as he quietly speaks to another man, his face turned away from Naomi.

She decides to take her chance.

"Excuse me," Naomi says exasperatedly as she approaches the bar. Once Casey turns, Naomi reaches past her and grabs a napkin from the tray.

"Sorry." Naomi grimaces. She points to her top, which she pretends has just been soiled by something. She dabs at the dry fabric with a napkin.

"Well, at least it's black," Casey says. "I can't even see anything."

A metaphorical lock clicks in Naomi's mind, and she is relieved Casey didn't just smirk and turn away.

Naomi sighs, throwing the napkin down at the bar. "It's only from Target anyway. Don't tell anyone, though."

Casey smiles, and Naomi knows her self-deprecating comment worked. Naomi has a strategy planned for various people she might encounter today, and her strategy for Casey is to appear down-to-earth and utterly average. She read that Casey's parents were both public school teachers, so figures she'll respond better to someone who doesn't seem pretentious or materialistic. And she's right.

"I'm Faye," Naomi says, mentally cursing herself the second her sister's name comes out of her mouth. She was planning on using Amelia's name for a cover, but Faye slipped out instead. Just when she thought she was keeping it together...

Forcing herself to quickly recover from the mistake,

Naomi stretches out her hand to Casey. "I used to work on Colton's PR team."

Casey shakes her hand and smiles. "He's my—was my—brother-in-law. I'm Casey." She thanks the bartender as he hands her a dirty martini.

"Nice to meet you. And so sorry for your loss. You must have been really close with him…"

Casey stirs her martini with an olive stick before taking a sip. "He was like a little brother to me. Always causing problems for James and the family, as I'm sure you know…"

Naomi tries not to look confused. *What does she mean?* From her experience working in the industry, knowing how hard publicists work to sweep things under the rug, she guesses that maybe Colton's PR team had to work harder than she imagined. Maybe Bobby was right. Maybe Colton wasn't so perfect. Maybe it only seemed that way because they *made* it seem so.

"Don't I know it." Naomi laughs awkwardly, signaling the bartender. She quickly orders herself a glass of Pinot.

"I still can't believe Harlow did this. It doesn't seem right."

She studies Casey's response, noting a sadness sweep over her face.

"Were you close with her?" Naomi presses.

"We were, yeah." Casey stares into her martini, lips pursed in a sour yet distant expression.

"Do you think…" Naomi grimaces as she lets the words hang in the air. She's on tenterhooks as she waits for Casey's response. After all, Casey was close to Harlow just before Faye died.

Casey chews on the olives and shrugs. "If you asked me three years ago, I would have said never in a million years. But I guess I don't know her at all anymore."

Naomi swallows hard, feeling a small weight fall off her shoulders. "So you don't think she was just…" She waves her hands in the air. "Going around killing people?" She lowers her voice to a whisper. "Young aspiring musicians. Like that other woman, Jade?"

Casey side-eyes Naomi. "No. I mean she had her jealous moments. Who doesn't? But as angry and sad as I am about everything and the possibility she could've done this to Colton, and of course that poor girl, who definitely is Colton's type, I don't know. A part of me just doesn't believe it at all. I desperately hope it isn't true at least, as much as I'd like closure for James' family." She gestures toward her husband, who is still deep in conversation at the bar.

"When was the last time you saw her?" Naomi presses, racking her brain for how to ask the question she's really interested in—was she with Harlow the night Bill Lever died?

Casey sips her martini and then cocks her head to the side, blowing air through her cheeks. "Pshh, I honestly can't remember."

Naomi leans in. "Sorry, I only ask because there's a rumor going around that Harlow killed someone else in January of 2022—Bill Lever, I think?" She waves her hand dismissively, as if it's ridiculous. "But I don't know, seems crazy. Right?"

"Bill Lever?" Casey lets out a laugh. "No. I remember when that happened. Don't get me wrong, she didn't like the guy—total sleazebag, but I remember texting her about it when the news broke. Because we'd been together for my birthday the night before. She was with me in Maine until at least midnight." She stares down at the floor, frowning again. "Can't believe that was almost three years ago now."

Naomi tries to do the math in her head. No way Harlow made it to California in time to kill Bill Lever then. And that photo in LA was taken of her closer to lunchtime, so she probably had gone straight to Rodeo Drive after her flight.

Casey's eyes glance at something behind Naomi and she smiles.

"Sam, hi." A sad smile crosses her face as she reaches out her arms.

The man comes over, and Naomi gets a whiff of his musky cologne as he squeezes past to greet her.

Naomi flounders, realizing who it is. Colton and Harlow's manager, Sam Brixton.

She inhales through her nose, trying to calm herself as he turns around, his wavy brown hair bouncing as he moves, unlike his tailored suit, which fits perfectly to his body. Naomi watches his pearly-white smile fade into a scowl.

She looks around, wondering what could have irked him. Until she realizes it's her.

"How'd she get in here?" he asks, his small dark eyes now boring into hers. "It's astounding how low the media is willing to stoop these days."

Fuck, she thinks. *How the hell did he know?* Naomi's eyes dart toward the possible exits, worried she's about to be thrown out by security.

"Sam," Casey interjects, trying to calm him down. The

room has quieted and people are starting to stare. "This is Faye, she used to work with Colton's PR team."

Sam's face drops for a second, looking from Casey and then to Naomi, perplexed. "No, Casey," he says, exasperated. "She's a reporter. From fucking C*Leb News."

Before they can call security, Naomi slips into the crowd and makes a dash for the parking lot.

Chapter 21

Naomi glances at her rearview for the third time in thirty seconds, wondering why the same Toyota Corolla has been tailing her since Maine.

She wonders if the Scotts have sent their henchmen after her, imagining them bullying her off the road before they smash her phone and laptop to pieces to ensure she didn't record anything. Or maybe it's an undercover police officer about to pull her over and arrest her, if you can even do that for crashing a funeral. *But surely undercover police officers and henchmen drive something fancier than a Toyota*, she thinks. If it was a black SUV, she'd be really nervous.

Naomi inhales, willing herself to relax before pressing on the accelerator. She's done things like this plenty of times in her career. Snuck into places, pretended to be someone else to get intel. But she's never once felt this anxious about it, even the times she's been found out.

How the hell did Sam Brixton know who I was? Before I even said anything?

She's baffled. She's only ever talked to the administrative staff at Machinist and his agency, never met or seen him in person. Has he memorized what every single journalist covering the case looks like? Seems an odd thing for someone of his importance to worry about. Then again, her article on Harlow did just go viral a few days ago, so perhaps he recognized her from her headshot. She realizes then her mistake, cursing herself for being careless.

Thinking of Sam, Naomi recalls her conversation with Emily last night and how she mentioned Jade attended a pre-VMAs party at his house before she disappeared and subsequently died. Naomi knows these sorts of parties are far from intimate affairs, especially those that take place at fancy mansions before big industry events. There would have been hundreds of people coming in and out all night, but it's a connection between Jade and Colton and Harlow that can't be ignored.

Harlow must've been there too, Naomi thinks, betting it's one of the links prosecutors found as well. She wishes she could confirm with Sam but knows she's blown any chance of that now.

Did something happen at the party that upset Harlow? Did Jade do something in particular that set her off?

Naomi imagines Jade and Colton kissing in a secluded space at the modern estate, no idea that Harlow, seething with rage, was watching. Still, why would Harlow kill Jade then, but wait years to enact revenge on Colton? No, it doesn't make sense.

Naomi thinks back to the serial killer theory and shudders as goosebumps prickle her arms. *Was Jade her first victim, then Bill Lever, and then, before Colton... Faye?*

The thought of her sister being entangled in all this is haunting. *What's the pattern, though? Was Harlow picking off beautiful, aspiring musicians she felt threatened by? And then Colton and Bill Lever were just for fun?*

Stomach twisting in knots, Naomi tries to rein in her thoughts. She's missing too many pieces to draw proper conclusions. Even if the events surrounding her sister's death seem suspicious in retrospect, Naomi has no evidence or reason to suggest Faye could've been murdered by Harlow.

You're getting too absorbed in the case, she warns herself. *Don't blur lines between Jade and Faye, they're completely separate.*

But are they? a voice questions, before immediately being contradicted by another.

Don't ask questions you don't want answers to.

Naomi breathes a sigh of relief as she pulls up to her aunt's house in Poughkeepsie, the Toyota no longer in sight. But the relief soon shifts to discomfort after she kills the engine, the once-welcoming atmosphere now unnerving. Devoid of daylight and the buzz of partygoers, fog hovers over the ground, obscuring the front entryway path save for a single lamppost that flickers in the dark.

Naomi takes a minute to open the car door, recalling Aunt Mary's friend's words from the party about fog and spirits. *"When it's foggy out... spirits are able to more easily enter."* She surveys the hilltop property in the woods, wondering if Faye's spirit is trying to break through to tell her something, or if something more sinister lies in wait... if someone had followed her here and is now lurking in the shadows. She tells herself to stop being ridiculous, before huffing out an exhale and pushing the car door open. Her heart races as she grabs her bag from the back seat and speed-walks to the front door.

Naomi digs the nails of her shaky index fingers into the cuticles of her thumbs, constantly glancing around as she waits for Aunt Mary to answer. Naomi should've called beforehand to give her an estimated time of arrival, but she'd been too distracted on the way back.

"Hey hun," Aunt Mary says, opening the door. The smell of tomatoes and garlic mingles with her perfume as she leans in for a kiss. "How was your trip?"

"Good, thanks." Naomi scrapes the bottom of her black heels on the welcome mat, kicking them off after her aunt ushers her inside. "Definitely made better by having a car, so thanks again." She holds up the keys and hands them over.

"Oh, anytime," Aunt Mary says, taking the keys and placing them on the sideboard. "Want some ziti? I saved you some. Wasn't sure when you'd be getting back."

"I'm okay—thank you, though! I have to get going soon if I want to get the next train."

"Need a ride? I've only had one glass of wine so far..."

"No, I'll get an Uber, honestly, you relax. Been such a busy weekend for you!"

Naomi senses the relief in her aunt's expression.

"Okay, hun, as long as you're sure."

"There is one thing I was hoping to do, though, before I head back to the city." Naomi chews on her lip. Aunt Mary, who has returned to drying dishes, cocks her head to the side.

"Do you still have Faye's things here? Those boxes I left you…" Naomi picks at the scab on her thumb.

Aunt Mary studies Naomi, clearly concerned. "Course I do. Everything okay?"

Naomi swallows the burn in her throat. "Oh yeah, all fine." She waves her hand dismissively to mask her lie. "There's a couple things I've been meaning to grab for ages, didn't remember until I was back here. Just some sentimental stuff."

Naomi really wants to see if she can find any useful information or tenuous connection to Harlow or Colton— clues as to how she could fit into all of this—in Faye's old notebooks and paperwork. It's a long shot, but she needs to at least check.

Aunt Mary frowns, placing her recently lotioned, wrinkled hand on Naomi's. "Follow me." She guides her to the basement door. "It's all down there to the left. Sure you don't want me to heat up some ziti for you?"

"I'm sure!" Naomi smiles for half a second before journeying down into the musty basement.

A bare lightbulb hums over her head as she stares at the four cardboard boxes piled up on the cement floor. All that's left of her sister. She checks her watch and gives herself twenty minutes to sift through the things before she has to order an Uber to the train station. She's too edgy tonight to take a train after 10 p.m.

Naomi peeks into the two boxes on top and shakes her head. She doesn't know why she bothered keeping any of

Faye's clothes and makes a mental note to sort through those another time. She lifts them and places them to the side, crouching down to analyze the contents of the other two boxes on the floor, seemingly filled with notebooks and photos. She coughs, dust filling the air, as she removes a stack of polaroids from the top.

She sifts through them quickly, trying not to get too emotional at the memories. Some from their road trips, making silly faces on the drive. Some on the beach, cliff-jumping and playing volleyball. Some from karaoke nights and others from Faye pretending to pose like she's on the cover of Vogue.

Naomi bites down hard on the inside of her cheek as she places the photos to the side, deciding to take them with her, before opening one of the notebooks.

Her chest tightens as her fingertips slowly graze the velvety cover of Faye's black leather journal. She bites down harder on her cheek, tears stinging her eyes as she remembers her sister's obsession with writing in this threadbare notebook. She took the tattered thing with her everywhere, constantly writing down her ideas, transferring them from her phone to her book.

"Why don't you just keep your notes in your phone?" Naomi asked once.

Expecting some sassy response said with a hand on her hip, Faye surprised Naomi with a poetic answer. "Because I like seeing the words written imperfectly perfect on an organic piece of paper. It makes my lyrics feel more special, like writing them down is an art form in itself."

Naomi wipes a tear away as she opens the book, seeing her sister's handwriting on the front page.

~ ideas for future number one hits ~
Faye P. Barnes
2015

Naomi swallows hard as she flips through the pages, eyes casting over teenage Faye's musings, ranging from rhyming prose and notes about melodies through to random lists of words she'd like to use.

Seeing how talented a songwriter she was even at sixteen makes it all the more tragic. She was so smart. Seemed so close. What the hell happened?

Naomi recalls the last few months of Faye's life, how she struggled to find her feet when Naomi said she was going to move in with Matt in the summer of 2021. Naomi even fronted three months of rent to give Faye more time to find a roommate or a new place, and almost offered to move back in at one point following one of Faye's mini-breakdowns.

But toward the end of the year, things seemed like they were turning around for her, despite her mood swings. She moved into a new studio apartment in Union Square, started getting her hair and nails done and buying designer clothes. To Naomi's shock, when she eventually asked Faye how she was affording her new lifestyle, she said she had sold a song to a record label.

"What the hell, that's huge!" Naomi said. "Why didn't you tell me!?"

"Didn't wanna jinx it," Faye replied, cheeks red. "I hoped you wouldn't notice and I could just surprise you when it came out. It may not even get made, they just bought the rights. But hopefully I can keep writing some more good ones and one of them will hit or I can bag a longer-term contract and get paid yearly advances."

Naomi tried to get more details from her, on both the song and who she had sold it to, but Faye stayed uncharacteristically secretive. It worried Naomi at first, when she started disappearing for days and weeks on end after that, especially considering only a year before Naomi had received a call telling her Faye was in the hospital. But Faye was no longer with that guy and had promised Naomi she was doing much more exciting things, that she was doing well.

"I've been off working with some songwriters and producers," Faye told Naomi when they eventually caught up one day for dinner. "Good things are happening, I promise!"

Naomi struggled to read her, though. She seemed happy and, judging by the restaurant she had picked and the hefty tip she left, she also seemed to be doing well financially. But she also seemed on edge. Looked tired and stressed. Her collar bones and hip bones were more prominent than ever before, jutting out from her cashmere sweater dress.

"And they're paying you for that? Have you sold more songs?" Naomi always thought songwriters got most of their money off royalties or major contracts. She still couldn't work out how Faye was affording her new lifestyle.

But once again, Faye was evasive, just nodding and then changing the subject. Naomi chalked it up to Faye just being desperate for things to work out that time, something Naomi also deeply wanted for her, so she let it go, figuring she could press her for more details some other time. She had no idea her window for questions would close so soon.

A sinking feeling takes root in Naomi's stomach. Knowing what she knows now, she's surer than ever that she was right about Faye's story not adding up. That she wasn't telling the whole truth. That the money wasn't just coming from songwriting. Naomi wonders what Faye could have gotten involved with. Drug dealing? OnlyFans? Escorting or some other kind of sex work?

There were endless possibilities, from good to bad to fatal. Because, as smart and witty as Faye was, she could also be reckless and impulsive, often letting her ambitions and desires get in the way of rational thinking, making her put her trust in the wrong people. She was the sort of kid who would have most certainly followed a stranger into a van if he told her he had candy, with tunnel vision for her prize. "I'll worry about the consequences later," she'd say.

Naomi imagines her investigation revealing answers she doesn't want. But she needs the truth. She puts the songbook on top of the photos, deciding to take it with her so she can pore over it later.

Seeing as she only has ten minutes before she needs to leave, Naomi throws the photos and songbook into a nearby empty IKEA bag before sifting through the remaining contents, hoping to find any bank statements or contracts that could point to where the money came from.

She adds a stack of paperwork, a few more notebooks, and a yellow envelope to the bag before heading upstairs to order an Uber.

★

On the train back to the city, after picking at a container of cold baked ziti her aunt insisted she take, Naomi pulls out the yellow envelope.

Her stomach churns, marinara sauce and bile rising in her throat as she reads the letters on the top of the stack of papers.

Dutchess County Medical Examiner's Office

AUTOPSY REPORT
Name of the deceased: Faye Prudence Barnes
Birth Date: March 14, 1998 **Death Date:** March 3, 2022

Following Faye's death, police ordered an autopsy to ascertain the official cause of death and make sure there wasn't anything suspicious. And while neither the police nor the medical examiner were able to provide answers for everything, nothing was deemed suspicious enough to warrant opening an investigation.

But Jade Dutton's family was told the same thing.

Heart thumping, Naomi pulls Emily's email up on her phone and opens the attachment. She's unsure what she's looking for as she compares Faye and Jade's autopsy reports. Jade's autopsy doesn't mention bruising around her neck, so if Faye's death was also a cover-up, it's not like her report would reveal anything.

Naomi sighs, wondering if these are just meaningless pieces of paper full of lies. But as she scans the cause of death section, something catches her eye. She glances to and from both reports, over and over again, sure she hasn't misread the small details.

According to the documents, Faye and Jade died by poisoning from almost exactly the same amount of fentanyl.

Naomi glances over her shoulder, feeling the same uneasiness she felt in the car. Could someone still be following her, watching what she's doing? She angles herself toward the window as she rereads Faye's report, taking in every gruesome word.

She covers her mouth, gasping when she sees something even more alarming than the matching drug dosage. How could she have possibly missed this before? Did she ever even look at the autopsy report? She thought she did but maybe she didn't. Everything was such a blur, never thinking to question what the police told her. *Cause of death: Smoke inhalation and/or drug overdose.* But they never mentioned the minor detail that Naomi is staring at now.

SKULL: Possible fracture on the right parietal bone. Difficult to determine severity due to third-degree burns.

From: Naomi J. Barnes <naomi.barnes@clebnews.com>
Subject: Question
Date: Sept 29, 2024 09:58:09 PM EDT
To: Glen M. Hill <glen.hill@yahoo.com>

Hi Glen,

Hope you're well! I'm investigating a case and
have a couple questions I need your expertise
on. I have two young women who died of apparent
overdoses, months apart. Autopsies list nearly
identical dosage of fentanyl in their system. Is
it common for unrelated overdoses to match like
this?

Also, one of the reports notes a possible skull
fracture. Wondering why something like this
wouldn't be deemed suspicious? (For reference,
this woman was found deceased of an apparent
overdose after a house fire.)

Thanks,

Naomi

From: Glen M. Hill <glen.hill@yahoo.com>
Subject: Re: Question
Date: Sept 29, 2024 10:33:57 PM EDT
To: Naomi J. Barnes <naomi.barnes@clebnews.com>

Naomi,

Nice to hear from you.

Re: the skull fracture, I often see injuries
like this with drug overdoses or house fires from
people passing out/falling over. Sometimes an old
injury. Most likely it was looked into and I would
trust the coroner's decision to not highlight
that.

Now in regard to the drug levels, I would say that is uncommon, especially if the deaths took place months apart. Only time you see similar matches in levels of fentanyl/heroin is when drugs come from same source.

Hope that helps,

Glen

Chapter 22

Naomi barely remembers getting back to Joel's apartment. She's supposed to have an article ready for tomorrow, but she spent what should have been her writing time obsessing over her sister's death. She still can't believe what she found in the autopsies, possible proof that Faye was murdered by the same person as Jade.

And that person was most likely Harlow Hayes.

She expected to feel relieved being back in the city, away from home. But her feelings are only amplified now. A shiver runs up her spine as she thinks of the Toyota tailing her earlier. And the feeling of someone watching her on the train. What if someone followed her back to the apartment too? She double-checks the lock and heads over to her investigation board on Joel's wall.

Before this weekend, she felt like she was nearing the precipice of the mountain, so close to the truth. But now the wind has been knocked out of her and she realizes she's at the base of an even bigger, hellishly daunting climb.

A mix of trepidation, anger, and confusion stirs inside her as she shakily writes her sister's name on a Post-it note and sticks it on the wall, along with a photo and a few questions.

Where did her money come from in late 2021?
Was she sleeping with C?
How did she know J?
Any evidence of her and H crossing paths?
Overlooked head injury?

She runs string from Faye to Harlow, Colton, and Jade. Then, on a sheet of A4, she scrawls Casey Scott's name in large letters, and notes below anything interesting from their conversation. Like how Colton gave his PR team headaches and how the Harlow she knew all those years ago wouldn't have murdered anyone. Naomi also flags Casey's comment about Harlow being jealous and Jade being Colton's type.

Her eyes flit to Sam Brixton's photo as she places Casey Scott on the wall near Colton. She traces a line from Sam to Jade, and then writes on a piece of painter's tape alongside it.

Last seen at SB party before 2021 VMAs—Harlow there too? Saw something that upset her?

Naomi backs away and scans the huge web of photos, papers, and connecting strings, trying to see if she's missing any other connections. Her eyes flit between Faye, Jade, and Bill Lever, who all died between September 2021 and March 2022. She then narrows her eyes at their potential killer, Harlow, who coincidentally went through a major reinvention throughout the next year, not only in her image and music but in her personal life, cutting out family and friends.

Wanting to analyze these changes more closely, Naomi grabs the roll of red string from her desk and cuts a seven-foot piece, taping it in the blank section to the left-hand side of the wall. She writes three new headers.

Before Jade's death
September 2021–March 2022
After Faye's death

She takes her time reordering the wall, moving all her research that references the time before Jade's death in 2021 to the "Before" side, everything to do with the 2021 VMAs, Jade, Bill Lever, Casey Scott, and Faye to the middle section, and anything that happened after March 2022 to the "After" side.

As she assumed, the first two sections are filled with the most information—tons of lyrics, video references, and Harlow interview clips all relating to hits from her first three albums and her one flop, "Endless Summers." There are also relevant quotes from Naomi's interviews with Trevor and Bobby, plus tabloids referring to the singer's relationship with Colton.

The most interesting details on the sparse "After" side are lyric snippets from Harlow's two recent albums, interview clips, Trevor's claim that Harlow gave him the cold shoulder, and the Avant article from Harlow's Aunt Jocelyn. Surprisingly, there's little from her new music team and nothing else from her family.

Naomi plucks a note she left for herself from the wall, a reminder to analyze potential Easter eggs in Harlow's music, and crumples it in her hand. She eyes the Amazon package sitting on the kitchen island and opens it, unwrapping Harlow's latest two albums, *Apotheosis* and *Legacy*, which she ordered earlier in the week. They're both gorgeous, glossy vinyl versions, accompanied by stunning lyric posters.

Upon her first few reads of the accompanying lyrics, she recognizes a pattern of references to revenge. She writes down some of the most notable lyrics and posts them on the right side of the wall.

Underestimated me from the start / And now you have to watch it all fall apart / I'll slash a lasting legacy across your heart / Watch me rise / While I watch you crash.

There's no such thing as happy endings in a world so violent and cruel / You rolled the dice / I finished the game / But who's the fool?

She also adds lyrics from "No Way Back" and "Midnight," which the TikToker theorized was about Bill Lever, as well as a line from "Cruel Delights."

Hey Billy, help me understand / How did you live with yourself, when it all got out of hand?

I know who you are / I know what you did / Don't act surprised / You know I'm right / You deserve what you got for what you did at midnight

Is it wrong. Or is it right. To get high off these cruel delights.

Another pattern Naomi recognizes is the constant reference to death, but while *Apotheosis* seems to reference death in a vengeful way, Harlow's latest album is much sadder, almost remorseful. Like the lyrics from "Garden of Bones."

A garden of bones, watered with tears. Blood-soaked soil, saturated with fear. No one knows I laid her here. Alongside a part of me buried for years.

Naomi's stomach twists at the words. She initially ignored the hundreds of internet sleuths who theorized this was some sort of lyrical confession, sure it was just a metaphor. But now she thinks otherwise. Her throat burns, wondering if the lyrics are about her sister. Picturing Harlow laying her on a filthy sofa and then lighting a match.

Naomi scans the *Apotheosis* and *Legacy* lyric posters again, looking for more mentions of death and blood specifically, but nothing else stands out.

She goes to her Twitter bookmarks to find the posts that conveniently compiled Harlow's darkest lyrics to check she hasn't missed anything and adds a few more to her wall. She does a quick search for #HarlowHayes and Easter eggs and finds a thread noting mostly trivial stuff, like hints that led to eventual song names and music video release dates, or small references to past albums. All the Easter eggs seem to be in her two latest albums, though. Strange. Naomi writes a new Post-it—"Easter eggs start with *Apotheosis*"—and adds it to the "After" section.

As Naomi stares from the left to the right side of the

board, there is a glaring fact she can't ignore. That at the end of 2021, after Jade died, Harlow changed forever.

She reasons that this type of change in behavior can't be a coincidence. People don't just wake up one day and change everything about themselves. Style, sure. Artists change their style all the time. But personality? Lyrics? How they interact with fans? Not to mention cutting out family and friends.

Such a big reinvention must be the result of some type of trauma. Something major. Like killing someone for the first time. And maybe Harlow's "apotheosis" was transforming from an innocent woman into a lethal one—into a serial killer. Many serial killers see themselves as gods...

Naomi's mind swirls with questions. *Were Harlow's lyrics truly about murder? Did Harlow, like so many other killers before her, leave clues in the hope she'll get caught? Did she have someone change Jade's autopsy to hide the bruises on her neck? Did she have help covering it up? Is she responsible for her sister's head injury? Is she really so evil that she pumped these women full of drugs and then, in Faye's case, let her burn?*

It's possible.

Naomi spends the night tossing and turning, thinking of all the ways she could get justice for Faye. In the past, justice wasn't an option because there wasn't anyone to blame. But now everything has changed.

The second Naomi notices the bright light beaming through the window, she knows something is wrong. The sun doesn't rise until close to seven, and her alarm was supposed to wake her at six so she could draft and post the article she promised Joel.

Heart pumping, she reaches for her phone.

9:47 a.m. *Shit.*

If Joel is in California, he might not ask about it for another couple hours, she reasons with herself.

But when she glances at her screen again, she sees he's already texted her. It's not about her article, though. It's a link to a different one.

"No," she whispers, scanning the news release. "No, no, no! Fuck!"

AVANT

All Charges Against Harlow Hayes Dropped

The star's lawyer confirms the case has been thrown out due to insufficient evidence

BY NICHOLAS CLARK – SEPTEMBER 30, 2024

Safe to say it's been a doozy of a week for Harlow Hayes…

After being arrested in Nashville ten days ago on suspicion of murder, then being extradited to New York to face a judge for not one, but two counts of murder, the question on everyone's lips has been: Is America's pop princess Harlow Hayes a killer? Looks like we have our answer. And it's great news for all the Hazies out there…

According to Rudy Lodge, Hayes' attorney, the prosecution failed to provide the DNA evidence that the judge requested at Hayes' initial arraignment. Instead, lab results confirmed the samples being tested were not a match in either of the alleged murders.

"We are thrilled that the judge has decided to drop all charges against Harlow after DNA evidence proved that Ms. Hayes had no involvement in these crimes," Lodge told reporters outside the courthouse. "DNA does not lie, and my client has staunchly denied all allegations made against her from day one. The fact she was arrested and charged for these crimes so prematurely was a true injustice, so we're happy the City of New York has finally come to its senses."

Hayes was suspected of being involved in the recent death of actor Colton Scott and the 2021 death of aspiring model Jade Dutton. No further details have been released about either of the alleged crimes, and authorities have declined to comment on whether they will continue to look into foul play. The "Violent Ends" singer has been on house arrest at her Manhattan residence, but is expected to be cleared of all charges. She's rumored to have already fled the state to her beachfront property in Maine.

Harlow

Finally, I'm free. Not that my release means I'm innocent.

You'd probably argue I'm not free at all, though, never have been. That this level of fame is a prison in itself. Everyone watching my every move, wishing for my downfall. Unable to leave my glass cell without being chased down. Except instead of prison guards, it's paparazzi with zoom lenses, reporters with too much ambition, and deranged losers with absurd vendettas.

But it's all about perspective. And I'm grateful that I can now see that these aren't problems. No, I've had those. And I've dealt with them. These are simply proof that the dream I'm living is real, and if "celebrity" is a punishment, I'll take it. Live out my glamorous sentence behind gold bars and velvet curtains willingly, begging them to throw away the key.

I know better than anyone that you can't have the good without the bad. I fought too hard, gave up too much to be ungrateful now. I remember what it was like to withstand the rejections in the beginning. To be cast aside. My arrest was just a little blip on my journey. There's no such thing as bad press, right?

I giggle at the absurdity of it all—at everything that's happened, what I've done. The delirious laughter ceases in my throat and my smug smile drops as I stare off into the distance.

"But did you do it?" I imagine you asking.

You'll hate me when you learn the truth.

PART II

CRUEL DELIGHTS

If time heals all wounds, darling, we're the exception.
We'll sip bloodstained champagne as our lesson.
— Harlow Hayes, from the album *Apotheosis*

Harlow

Six Months Before the Murder

I'd learned long ago how deceptive appearances could be. How, up close, plush velvet curtains were thin and patchy, gold trophies that gleamed from the stage were tarnished and rusted. And sometimes, the most revered idol—the smiling hero atop the highest pedestal—was actually a monster once the cameras stopped rolling.

The thought reminded me to smile, to remember where I was. *Don't let them see*, I imagined my mother saying. *You can be upset later, when no one is watching.* So I pushed my shoulders back, lifted my chin, and tried to pretend that I was happy. But behind my closed-mouth grin, my teeth were gritted, jaw clenched tight.

I looked ahead, assessing the other stars already posing for photographers. I could tell some felt like me, by the way their smiles didn't meet their eyes. How, in between poses, they hunched their shoulders, masks slipping as they let out shaky breaths.

I winced as my middle fingernail jabbed into my thumb's stinging nailbed. I shook my hand out to relieve the pain and then studied the bloody cuticle I'd started picking at in the limo. A tiny pool of blood formed between my polish and skin, its bright-red hue matching the carpet beneath my feet. My first instinct was to suck it off, but my mother's judgy voice stopped me once again. *Get your filthy fingers out of your mouth, for Christ's sake. Act like a lady.*

If only she knew what I was doing last night with Colton. I faltered at the reminder, suddenly wanting to vomit.

"You okay?" my makeup artist Courtney asked, steadying me.

"Fine," I nodded, forcing the onslaught of memories away.

Was it really over for us this time? Before anyone even knew we were back together? Was this the final, final break?

My heart ached as I realized that it had to be.

I inhaled deeply and closed my eyes, forcing myself to focus on the present once more. I had to get through an entire red carpet and needed to get my shit together before I embarrassed myself.

Three things I can hear: An obnoxious laugh to my left. Muffled chatter to my right. Cameras clicking ahead.

I exhaled and opened my eyes.

Three things I can see: Emerald ring on my right ring finger. The red carpet beneath my diamante Louboutins. Courtney's makeup brush coming toward my face.

The coping mechanism, in tandem with Courtney's powder application, stopped the racing thoughts. But I still yearned for something to relax me, more than the Xanax and two shots of whiskey I'd downed in the limo. Something to numb my mind completely.

My eyes darted around the venue, landing on various acquaintances I could get everything from weed to cocaine from. But I had to perform in a couple of hours and couldn't risk anything else in my system. I'd just have to suffer through and deal with my heart later.

It was a shame I'd come to loathe these events so much. I used to love them—everyone clamoring to talk to me, desperate for sound bites or photographs. But the glamorous novelty wore off over time, and the process became more painful than enjoyable. Starving myself. Stressing about puffy eyes. Having to be "on" the entire night. Plastering a fake smile across my face as I answered the same question fifteen times in a row. It was exhausting. But, like my God-fearing Aunt Jackie would say, there's no peace for the wicked.

Sweat pooled around the nape of my neck, making me instantly regret wearing my hair down and not slicked back in a bun like my stylist suggested. Panic crept through me as I imagined my slinky satin dress, which I could feel clinging to my back, covered in wet patches.

Silk gown, godless town.

I quickly typed the words into my notes app so I wouldn't forget them. It was how I kept track of any spur-of-the-moment lyric ideas when I didn't have my songwriting book with me.

Fake smiles… something… drown?

I finished adding the incomplete musing as my publicist Rebecca guided me down the carpet. A camera flashed as I turned the corner, followed by another and then another. I flinched at the bright lights, forcing myself to breathe before handing my phone to Rebecca and stepping into the firing line.

"Harlow, over here!" photographers shouted from all directions. I inhaled as I posed, changing my stance every two seconds. I pushed my hair behind my shoulder and straightened, sticking my neck out at different angles as I shifted from pouty lips to a varying range of smiles with ease. I was thankful for the distraction, being forced to focus on tightening my body, sticking out the right parts just enough while I held my breath.

Rebecca stepped in front of the cameras with her hand held up before gesturing for me to move down the carpet. I exhaled a sigh of relief. But the feeling was fleeting.

"Kamryn, Kamryn!" the photographers shouted as I exited, their cameras pointed toward the young pop star behind me. It was a sobering reminder of what I used to be. An innocent eighteen-year-old with the world at my feet, excitement in my eyes, and a genuine love for the attention and glamor of it all. I wondered if Kamryn would one day become as jaded as me, see these events for what they really were—a circus. And we were just animals, trapped. Our only purpose to entertain, no matter our mental state.

I followed Rebecca over to one of the shouting faces, Leyton Russo of STAR, who was waving excitedly in her pink jumpsuit behind the gilded rope. If she weren't media, I'd be tempted to think she was a sweet lady. But everyone had an angle in this business. Everyone.

"Slayyyy!" Leyton screeched as I walked over.

I air-kissed Leyton and winked at the camera.

"How are you, girl?" Leyton said, waving her hand in circles. "You look insane. IN-sane."

"Thank you, thank you!" I beamed with my first and last genuine smile of the night.

Being complimented was the best part of the red carpet. Regardless of whether or not they were sincere, it was nice to hear something kind in the moment, especially since later, once photos from the event circulated online, it'd be difficult to find many niceties among the hateful comments. Some would call me too fat, others too thin. Some would say I had had too much work done, others that I was looking old and haggard. It was impossible to win.

"So first, I gotta ask…" Leyton said, bringing me back from my thoughts. "Who are you wearing?"

"Gucci," I responded, holding my arms out so the STAR camera could capture the dress.

"Well, the navy is stunning on you. Simply stun-ning." Leyton snapped her fingers in the air as she replied. "Now, tell me, are you excited for your performance? I know I am."

"Of course, can't wait!" I added a fake squeal to help mask the lie.

"What can we expect? Anything you can tell us?"

"Ummm…" But before I could answer, Rebecca pressed a hand on my shoulder and pulled me away.

"Expect the unexpected!" I winked at Leyton before disappearing into the crowd.

Expect the unexpected? I rolled my eyes at the lame response. Even after all my success, all the awards, I was still another cliché.

Rebecca motioned me toward a familiar middle-aged man with frosted tips. Despite his hair, which was stuck in the 2000s, Conor from *Avant* was one of the best-dressed men in the room, donning a suit from Tom Ford's recent collection.

I told him the same thing I had told Leyton at STAR but with a few extra details. In the middle of explaining once again how the idea for my latest song came about, Conor pressed a finger to his earpiece, his expression changing from focused to mischievous. I followed the cheers, my heart flying into my throat when I saw the reason: Colton Scott.

I tried to swallow my mounting anxiety, praying my three layers of makeup hid the red flush in my cheeks. I knew eyes—and cameras—would be on me, studying every twitch of my face for a reaction. A faltered smile. A split-second, downcast glance. Something, anything they could use as proof of my feelings for him.

I wanted to laugh. No one could comprehend how I felt about him. The overwhelming, almost unbearable sensation I felt in his presence. Sometimes joyful, often painful. Always uncontrollable. For nearly all of my adult life, he'd been both my greatest source of happiness and my greatest source of pain. My safe haven and poison all at once.

But not anymore. This was the end. I wouldn't be dragged back in, wouldn't lose control again.

I allowed myself one final look as he posed for the cameras. His eyes met mine for a fraction of a second before he glanced away, as if I was no one to him. I dug my nails into my palms, trying to pierce skin with my sharp acrylics while his mouth turned up into his famous crooked smile.

It was a weird feeling, to want to escape into someone's arms and also murder them at the same time.

Chapter 23

No. No. No. *This can't be happening*. Naomi's phone drops to the floor. She lifts her hands to her head and squeezes.

When? How? For the police to have arrested Harlow in the first place for not one but two murders, they must have had strong enough evidence to convince a judge to sign off on the warrant. So how the hell does the case just get dropped in less than a week?

Naomi rereads the article, scouring the page for further details of what prompted them to drop the case or if they have another lead. But there's nothing else. All it says is the DNA wasn't a match, and the judge felt that was grounds for dismissal.

Naomi clenches her hands into fists as anger bubbles inside her. How could they let her go, this potentially deranged murderer, without even having another lead? How could they just rip justice away from the families like that? From Emily. From Naomi.

She scoffs, shaking her head. She knows exactly what got her released. Money. Power. Influence. People like Harlow always get away with everything.

"Fuck!" she yells out in frustration, hot tears stinging her eyes.

Her hands tremble as she bends down to get her phone. She exits out of the article and calls Leo, desperate for answers.

He answers on the first ring. "Hey."

"Harlow," Naomi cries. "She's been released. All charges dropped."

"Well, yeah. Must be innocent."

He sounds wildly confused by her intense reaction. "Sorry, I feel like I've missed something. You find some evidence I don't know about?"

She pinches the bridge of her nose, imagining how crazy she must seem to him, not knowing everything she does. She became so absorbed by the case over the weekend, she forgot not everyone else's life revolves around it too.

She thinks of the autopsy reports. Of the same level of fentanyl in both Jade and Faye's systems.

"Well, I found some stuff out. Some pretty crazy… I don't know… this weekend…" She huffs, unable to form a coherent sentence.

"Everything alright?" he asks.

No, everything fucking isn't alright, she wants to scream. *My sister was probably murdered and her killer has just walked free.*

But Leo doesn't even know Naomi ever had a sister, as far as she's aware. "Everything's fine." She bites her lip. "But I could do with a big favor."

"Okay…" He waits for her to explain.

"Could you try to find out who the detectives

are—were—on the Harlow case? I need to speak to them. Or, if you can talk to them first, just try to get any info you can."

He sighs reluctantly, but she presses on. "I know it's really annoying and I'm sorry to ask. But I need to know what they know—what evidence they had, if they think she really did it, or if they have any other leads…"

"Uhh…"

"Please? It's… I just need to know. I promise I'll explain later. Or whenever you're free. Are you free later?" She knows she sounds frantic, can hear the frenzy in her voice, but hopes it will convince him to do what she is asking and not ask any questions.

"I can meet you around four? Just let me know where."

"Thank you! I'll text you the address."

After convincing him one last time she is indeed fine, Naomi hangs up, slightly embarrassed she called him so hastily. He must think she's a mad woman. But she doesn't care. She needs answers.

She stares at her wall, filled with photos, news clippings, lyrics, Post-it notes, and thread. She should start taking it all down. Case closed, right? But it's not even close to over for her. Her investigation has only just begun. Not that Joel knows that.

Joel: Did you see the news? Guess you can come back to LA now…

Naomi: It's bullshit. Going to stay and keep looking into some stuff.

Joel: Okay. Feel free to write a wrap-up piece, but remember… be objective.

Joel: Anyway, big scandal happening with cast of Bravo show, about to meet a source. Talk later.
Naomi: Good luck!

The rest of the day seemingly disappears as Naomi arranges and rearranges her investigation wall, only feeling more frustrated than she did in the morning. She's caught off-guard when her phone vibrates, a text from Leo coming through alerting her he's outside.

"Thanks so much for coming," she says once she opens the door. "I'm sorry to be a pain."

"Hey, no worries." He smiles and hands her a six-pack of Budweiser. "You sounded like you might need a drink, though."

His smile fades as he studies her. "Shit, your lip's bleeding…"

Naomi's hand flies to her face, suddenly aware of the copper tinge of blood in her mouth. She vaguely remembers picking at the peeling skin earlier. She looks up at him, about to explain, but he's not looking at her anymore. He's staring straight ahead at the wall, eyes wide, jaw slack.

"Woah…"

Her face flushes, realizing how it must look. Like she's lost her mind. The papers, photos, and string take up the entire wall now, stretching from the breakfast bar to the living room windows.

Naomi pulls out two bottles of beer from the pack. She twists the caps off both, not flinching as the sharp corners bite into her flesh, and then hands one to Leo.

He takes a swig, shaking his head as he stares at the wall. His gaze moves to her, his eyes wary. "You sure everything's okay?"

"Yes, I just… I have a lot to catch you up on," she says. "But first, did you find anything out?"

"DNA wasn't a match," Leo shrugs. "Apparently, they were comparing DNA found under Jade's fingernails to Harlow's. Had reason to believe it would be hers, based on the evidence found at Colton's place…"

"The video evidence? Any more details on that?"

"Yeah, some sort of sex tape. From 2021."

Naomi nods, her suspicions confirmed. She turns away from Leo to look back at her wall, eyes shifting from Jade's blue-eyed, innocent gaze to Harlow's mysterious smirk.

"So they didn't find Harlow's DNA on Jade, but what about on Colton?"

"Apparently, Harlow claimed they started seeing each other again, so any DNA found on him or at his property had a simple explanation. She said he must've taken the drugs after she left. They tested the packets and she never touched them."

"Right," Naomi scoffs. She guides him into the living room, gesturing for him to sit on the couch. "I just don't understand how they can just drop it all based on DNA under Jade's nails not matching if they have all this other evidence."

"Well, DNA is DNA. It doesn't lie. Must be someone else."

"So they have another lead? Another match?" Naomi plops down on the couch, cross-legged.

"Don't think so, no."

Naomi huffs, blood rushing to her face.

"Honestly, the detective I talked to seems as baffled as you do. Said the prosecution was convinced she did it. In Colton's case, they even had a video of her arriving at his penthouse that night. Text messages that gave her motive…"

Naomi grabs her notebook and pen from the side table and quickly jots down what Leo said.

Text messages proving motive?

He rubs his chin. "Well, I didn't get the specifics, but sounds like he was holding something over her."

Blackmail?

As Naomi writes, she recalls her previous suspicions about Colton. But if he was the one holding blackmail over Harlow, then *she* was the one with the secret.

"So with those links plus the video evidence, they were shocked when the DNA came back as not a match. They were sure it would be. So now, everything else can be explained away—they have no concrete proof that shows she injected them with the drugs. Her lawyer is obviously saying he simply overdosed after she rejected him, and the Jade murder charge was already flimsy to begin with, and certainly falls apart when the Colton charge does."

Naomi chomps on the inside of her cheek as she yanks off a cuticle. She presses down on it to stem the blood.

She watches Leo's Adam's apple bob in his exposed throat as he takes a swig of beer. She imagines Harlow leaping on

Colton, putting her hands around his neck and strangling him like she did to Jade.

"But what if there are other victims out there?" she asks.

Leo furrows his brow, darting his gaze to her. "What makes you say that?"

Naomi nods toward the investigation wall and finally tells him about her sister.

Chapter 24

As Naomi finishes her explanation of everything that happened to her sister and how she thinks Faye's death may be connected to the case, she pauses to gauge Leo's reaction. But she's unsure what he's feeling, his blank, wide-eyed stare making it clear he's still processing.

He opens his mouth to speak but nothing comes out. Naomi feels the urge to fill the silence but holds her tongue for a moment, wanting to give him a chance to react. He rubs a hand over his jaw, looking from her to the wall.

"Listen…" The concern in his eyes is more pronounced now.

Shit, she thinks, knowing that she's lost him. She changes her mind and interjects before he can say anything. "There's more." She holds a hand up, launching into all of her discoveries, including all the "coincidences" and connections. He still doesn't seem convinced, so she pulls out her smoking gun: The matching drug levels cited in the autopsy reports.

"You can't tell me this is all a coincidence. That these two aspiring musicians, both living in New York where Colton and Harlow were, died from the same exact levels of fentanyl in their system, within months of each other. Not to mention they both had other suspicious injuries..." Naomi huffs. "I mean, come on. You of all people should believe how weird this is given what you told me about Jade's neck bruises and how they told your co-worker to stop looking into it."

Leo looks at her with warm, sympathetic eyes. "Okay, the dosage level is weird. But why cover up Jade's neck bruises but not Faye's head injury? As bad as it sounds, head injuries on an autopsy are more common than you think. Especially with that level of drugs in your system. Or maybe she did try to get up during the fire but passed out. It's easy to slip and fall."

Naomi throws her hands up in frustration. "But she was on the couch, basically glued to it. You don't fracture your skull falling on a fucking sofa!" Floods of hot tears run down her face.

"It could be an injury from earlier that day or week, even," he rebukes. "I promise you, if they believed it warranted further investigation they would have told you," Leo says, echoing Glen's prior email.

Naomi thinks of the countless celebrity deaths she's covered over the years. Some of them trivial, unimportant dirtbags, yet still somehow more important than her sister to the public. "No, they wouldn't have because no one gave a shit about her," she mutters. "And they were all probably in on it, I don't know."

He opens his mouth to argue, but decides against it.

"Believe me," Naomi says, forcing herself to calm down. "I know it sounds fucking crazy, but..."

Leo puts his beer down and reaches out for Naomi's

hands. He leans down so he's eye-level with her. "Listen, I don't think it's crazy. I'm so sorry about your sister and that you had to go through that. But I've seen family members do this. Spiral over the death of their loved one. On a mission to have someone or something to blame."

"I'm not—"

"No, I know," he continues. "I'm not saying that's what you're doing and I'm not even saying I think you're wrong." He exhales. "But even if you're right, it will be almost impossible to prove."

Naomi wavers. She knows deep down Leo has a point. But she isn't ready to accept it.

"Why don't you just take a breather? I think you need to get out of this apartment, so how about you let me take you out to eat? I can text Tom too, see if he and Amelia are free to join?"

She crosses her arms, eyes darting from him to the wall.

"The wall will be here when you get back." He raises an eyebrow. "And then you can reassess with a clear head..."

Naomi blinks away a tear. "Okay."

Not far from Joel's apartment, Feliz's is a swanky Mexican restaurant with floor-to-ceiling shelves of tequila. Naomi feels better the second she enters the lively atmosphere, looking forward to a strong margarita. After taking seats at the bar, she and Leo scan the colorful happy hour menu as they snack on still-warm salted tortilla chips.

"Hiii!" a voice rings out, accompanied by the rapid click-clack of heels against the wooden floor.

Naomi covers her mouth, still chewing as she turns. She

easily spots Amelia, her furry burgundy coat contrasting with her platinum-blonde hair. A smiling Tom trails behind her like a golden retriever.

Leo greets his brother and future sister-in-law before leaning over a bright-pink chair to signal the bartender. Naomi is glad he forced her out of the apartment. She needed this. The salty-sweet margaritas and prospect of conversations about things other than the case are calming.

"Check us out, on a double date." Amelia waggles her eyebrows at Naomi as she searches for her straw with her tongue. She has a cheeky grin plastered across her face.

Naomi rolls her eyes, suppressing a smile as she finishes off another margarita. She glances over at Leo, who catches her eye and winks. The more she drinks, the more she wants to rip his clothes off. She imagines him lifting her up onto the table, running his hand through her hair as he kisses her neck. She's grateful her hormones are helping distract her.

"He's just been helping me get some info about the Harlow case, that's all, don't get too excited," Naomi says, trying to convince herself as much as Amelia.

"Oh, how's that going, by the way—I saw she's been released?"

Naomi sighs, mad at herself for bringing up Harlow when she promised Leo that she'd take a break. She even convinced herself that she wanted one too. But now, given the chance to talk about it, she can't resist. So she orders another margarita and explains what she's learned since she last saw Amelia, from the bruising on Jade's neck and Trevor's details on the VMAs to getting kicked out of Colton's funeral.

"Yo, did you just say you got kicked out of Colton Scott's funeral?" Tom chimes in.

Leo stares at her blankly. She left that part out earlier.

Continuing to ignore Leo's suggestion to not think about Harlow Hayes, Naomi—now four margaritas deep—explains to Amelia and Tom how she doesn't believe she should have been released. How there are too many coincidences. How she changed too much following Jade's death. Not to mention the fact she believes there could be more victims.

Tom, who was silent for most of Naomi's rant, responds wide-eyed. "Wow, you really are invested in this." Amelia nudges him, giving him a warning look, before turning to Naomi.

"So who do you think did it, then, now that Harlow's been released?"

"No, that's what I'm saying… it's her! She shouldn't have been released."

Amelia raises an eyebrow, scrunching her face in disagreement. But Naomi doubles down. "You don't understand. Emily's sister was adamant Jade didn't take any drugs. And she was last seen at the manager's house of Harlow-freaking-Hayes. She was there. One of the last people to see her. And Jade was clearly Colton's type. And if she was his type, so was Faye… and before you say anything, listen to this…" Naomi sees Leo cringe out of the corner of her eye, alerting her to how crazy she sounds. She knows she should rein it in or change the subject. But impulse takes control and she presses on.

"I compared Jade and Faye's autopsy reports and their 'overdose' levels"—Naomi makes air quotes—"are the exact same on both." She flails her arms. "I mean, can it be more obvious? Harlow Hayes killed Jade Dutton and then she killed my sister. And covered both up to look like overdoses."

Amelia narrows her eyes. But Tom is the one to speak first. "Wait. You think Harlow Hayes, the pop star, killed your sister?" he scoffs, looking to Amelia for confirmation.

Amelia greets him with a stern look before she turns back to Naomi, a sad smile on her face. "I mean, anything is possible, hun." She's using her extra-chirpy PR voice to soften the blow. "But don't you think maybe it's a bit far-fetched? And even if it is true, it's going to be impossible to prove now. There's nothing else you can do. Maybe... just let it go."

Naomi's jaw tightens in frustration. How can they expect her to just let it go? She looks from Amelia to Leo, taking in their concerned expressions. Then she looks at Tom, eyeing her like some deranged animal. She can't take it a second longer and stands.

"I have to pee." She grabs her bag and walks away, on the verge of tears.

Are they right? Is it too far-fetched? Am I just trying to find someone or something to blame for Faye's death?

Instead of going to the bathroom, Naomi heads outside to clear her head. The cold breeze and misting rain are welcome on her flushed face. She feels so misunderstood. She thinks of Tom and Amelia. The look of concern and confusion plastered across their faces, like Naomi has lost it.

Annoyed, she opens Twitter and types in #HarlowHayesIsGuilty, desperate to find others who share her viewpoint, even if it's for different reasons than hers. She could show him these posts to back herself up.

> **@LovelyLauraaaX0**: #HarlowHayesIsGuilty idgaf what the fucking corrupt justice system says, she deserves the death penalty

> **@JesusStan009**: Not surprised Harlow Hayes case was dropped, she's one of them, only trying to sell sex and evil #HarlowHayesIsGuilty #illuminati

> **@MrAmerica08916**: It's always the good ones that get hurt in the end. Nice Christian boy like Colton Scott taken from the world by an atheist whore #HarlowHayesIsGuilty

> **@HHevangelist**: #HarlowHayesIsGuilty is trending even though the case has been dropped! Leave her the fuck alone and get a life

> **@ColtonStrongxx**: She basically confesses to murder in her lyrics this is bullshit #HarlowHayesIsGuilty #Praying-ForTheScotts

She scrolls through the posts, including commentary from all sides—from stans using the hashtags to defend Harlow to antis hating on her. Both of these groups give Naomi pause, as she finds it once again fascinating how one group of people would probably murder Harlow if they got the chance, and the others would forgive her for being a murderer with no questions asked.

Naomi keeps scrolling until she finds what she's looking for, a critical, somewhat objective opinion sprinkled among the rants.

> **@ThatHazieLawyerLady**: As a Harlow fan, I'm so relieved she's been released. But as an attorney, I'm skeptical. People want to believe Harlow is a daft pop singer, but they'd be

wrong to misjudge her. If you study her career, she's actually an incredibly clever woman. And to withstand the pressures of the music industry and maintain her level of success— that takes more than just talent. It takes someone with thick skin. Someone willing to do whatever it takes. I have a lot of questions and I'm sure you do too. So comment with your Qs below and I'll try to break down whether #HarlowHayesIs-Guilty or #HarlowHayesIsInnocent

Until now, Naomi has purely been an observer, analyzing and dissecting everything she sees online. She's never liked or reposted anything, only lurked, reading from afar for the sake of research and work. But tonight, she finds herself feeling the need to be a part of the conversations. To talk to other people who actually understand.

And the best thing about the internet is that she can remain completely anonymous.

Chapter 25

Naomi wakes up to a strange snore. She cringes as she turns to her side and sees Leo's shirtless body sticking out from under the covers. Then she realizes she's naked as well. *Goddammit.*

The memories come back to her in a haze. Leo coming outside to console her, asking if she wanted him to walk her home. Naomi begging him to stay. Naomi kissing him. Him pushing her away, saying he didn't want it to happen like this. She was drunk. Him finally caving. Her groaning as his tongue slipped inside her mouth. Him pulling back, asking if she was sure. Naomi saying "I want you" as she rubbed her hands over his groin. Him groaning as she unzipped his pants and kneeled down, taking him in. Him pulling her up to share another kiss as he undressed her and lifted her up as he slid inside. Them moving as one all the way into the bedroom.

She feels turned on all over again, wanting to rip off the sheets and mount him. But the urge disappears when she recalls the rest of last night, the hangover anxiety kicking in.

You think Harlow Hayes, the pop star, killed your sister?

Her heart rate spikes, face flushing red as Tom's mocking words come back to her, shifting her embarrassment to anger. As if the notion is so wild to believe, even though Harlow was arrested just last week for murder. Tom tried to make Naomi feel like she's crazy, make everyone think she's gone insane. But she isn't crazy. She's on to something, she knows it.

"Hey," Leo says, rolling over, breaking her out of her spiral. "What time is it?"

Naomi checks the time and clears her throat. "Eight."

"Shit, I should get going."

"You sure? I can order some breakfast if you want…" Her face reddens, and she worries his brother got in his head. Does he really need to leave or does he just want to get away from her—this insane reporter?

"I would love that, but I gotta be at the precinct by nine." He runs his hands over his face and through his hair, somehow managing to make himself look even sexier. He rolls over and kisses her on the cheek and her head spins for a moment. "Last night was incredible," he says. "We should do it again."

"I'd like that." She blushes, heart pounding. Maybe she hasn't scared him away. He said he believed her at one point yesterday. Didn't he?

"Mind if I use your shower?" he asks.

Naomi hands him a towel and heads to the kitchen. She puts on a pot of coffee and pops three Advil. After his shower, Leo walks down the corridor, looking sexy in the same jeans and T-shirt as the night before.

Naomi holds up the pot of coffee. "Want a cup?"

"Nah, I really need to head out, but I'll call you later?"

Not knowing whether to kiss on the lips or cheek, they end up in an awkward half-kiss goodbye.

Naomi closes the door behind him, letting out a loud sigh. She sinks into the couch and opens her Twitter account to where she left off the night before. She leans forward, excited to see new posts from @ThatHazieLaywerLady.

> **@ThatHazieLaywerLady**: My main issue here is that they wouldn't have arrested Harlow if there wasn't real, concrete evidence for BOTH murders. Something clearly led authorities to believe she was guilty.

"Exactly!" Naomi says out loud, feeling somewhat vindicated.

> **@ColtonStrongxx**: They need to release the evidence against her to the public. NOW! This is so unfair.
>
> **@ThatHazieLaywerLady**: @ColtonStrongxx unfortunately, they don't and they won't. The case has been dropped and sadly we'll never know why.
>
> **@UndercoverJayne**: @ThatHazieLaywerLady: DNA not being a match doesn't prove she's innocent. She could have been careful, could have planted someone else's or could have been let off on a technicality. Just think of OJ and the glove...
>
> **@ThatHazieLaywerLady**: @UndercoverJayne Yup – so much room for error in these cases.

Naomi would never dare to interact with accounts like this from her normal account, but now that she has an anonymous one, she can finally join in.

> **@JusticeForFaye31498**: @ThatHazieLawyerLady So in your honest professional opinion, you think she could have killed both of them?
>
> **@ThatHazieLawyerLady**: @JusticeForFaye31498 not enough evidence to prove it clearly, but yes I think she's involved.
>
> **@JusticeForFaye31498**: @ThatHazieLawyerLady Do you think it's possible she's killed other people too (i.e. Bill Lever)? There's also rumors of other aspiring musicians dying under similar circumstances to Jade…
>
> **@ThatHazieLawyerLady**: @JusticeForFaye31498: Is there? Idk about these, but usually when there's smoke, there's fire…

Naomi wants to take a screenshot of the thread and send it to Tom with a note saying, "See, I'm not fucking crazy."

She digs her nails into the palms of her hands, thinking more about his reaction. *The nerve to think I'm crazy*, she silently scoffs. *It's ridiculous. I'm not a stan or an anti, going on here with all sorts of wild claims like Harlow is in the Illuminati or some shit. And I don't think she's guilty for no reason. I'm genuinely going off facts and only believing credible sources, like this lawyer.*

She can't sit back and keep quiet any longer, thinking of all the Toms out there, unaware and misinformed. It's her job to educate them. To spread the truth, let people know what's happening.

They need to know, she thinks as she powers up her laptop. She drafts her article, almost unable to type fast enough as the words pour onto the page.

When the article is finished Naomi exhales, feeling better.

She wonders if all she needed to do was to get her thoughts out on paper. Then she recalls Amelia's words. "There's nothing else you can do."

"But there is," she says, hitting *Publish*.

C*LEB NEWS

LET OFF ON A TECHNICALITY? "WHERE THERE'S SMOKE, THERE'S FIRE," SAYS SOURCE CLOSE TO HARLOW HAYES CASE

Sex tapes, blackmail, MORE bodies—the pop star may have had charges dropped, but that doesn't mean she's innocent. In fact, insiders think there may be other victims out there.

By Naomi Barnes – *October 1, 2024*

Harlow Hayes is officially a free woman. But that doesn't mean she's not guilty of her alleged crimes. In fact, the truth might be more heinous than we think.

After being arrested on suspicion of murder for the deaths of beloved actor Colton Scott and aspiring musician Jade Dutton (2021) exactly one week ago, charges against pop star Harlow Hayes have officially been dropped. But with enough evidence to arrest her in the first place and the absence of any other leads, it's troubling, to say the least. Especially with mounds of new information coming to light from sources close to the case.

One such piece of information is the fact that Dutton's cause of death may not have been a drug overdose. It's instead rumored to have been asphyxiation, according to officers at the 2021 crime scene who noted bruising on Dutton's neck—a fact that was conveniently left off the autopsy report in a clear attempt to cover up a crime.

Dutton's case was reopened after evidence found in Colton Scott's apartment pointed to Hayes being involved in not just Scott's death but Dutton's as well. Among this evidence are damning text messages from Hayes to Scott as well as a sex tape(!), most likely starring Scott and Dutton. Believing a possible struggle ensued between the two women (perhaps Dutton clawed at Hayes as the pop star held her hands around her throat), police compared Hayes' DNA to fragments found underneath Dutton's fingernails. However, the DNA wasn't a match.

This small detail somehow prompted the judge to ignore all the other damning evidence (including the fact that the pop star's DNA was present in Scott's Manhattan penthouse) and throw out the case.

"Detectives are baffled," a source close to the investigation said. "They still think she did it. They had a video of her arriving at Colton's penthouse that night, a sex tape, and text messages that gave motive." When asked what the text messages said, the source all but confirmed blackmail. "Sounds like he was holding something over her."

Could Scott have found out Hayes killed Dutton, so Hayes silenced him too, once and for all? And was the sex tape of Scott and Dutton what set Hayes off on Dutton three years ago?

Many, including the victim's sister Emily, believe it's possible. When asked about her sister's death, Emily Dutton confirmed, "She didn't do drugs, so I knew something was off."

Others say the truth is even more sinister, going as far as to link other suspicious deaths to Hayes, including that of music producer Bill Lever (found dead in his home in early 2022) as well as another aspiring musician with links to Dutton.

"People want to believe Harlow is a daft pop singer, but they'd be wrong to misjudge her," said a lawyer with insider knowledge. "If you study her career, she's actually an incredibly clever woman. And to withstand the pressures of the music industry and maintain her level of success—that takes more than just talent. It takes someone with thick skin. Someone willing to do whatever it takes."

Hayes isn't the first celebrity to have a taste for blood, though. Even today, over a quarter century later, rumors still swirl that O.J. killed his ex-wife. He had motive, a proven record of jealous tendencies, and even wrote a book detailing how he "would" commit a crime. All eerily similar signs to the case of Harlow Hayes. Only instead of writing a book, Harlow is practically confessing through her lyrics. All you need to do is simply look up some of the songs on *Apotheosis* or *Legacy* to see the alarming connection—some say an outright confession—to murder. Just take this lyric from "Violent Ends":

Now blood stains my hands since that night. If you guessed this wouldn't have a happy ending, you were right.

We shouldn't let those with power, influence, and money get away with their crimes. We deserve the truth and for all evidence to be released. They wouldn't have arrested Harlow if there wasn't real, concrete proof. Something clearly led authorities to believe she was guilty—including the previous unreported strangulation marks found around Dutton's neck—and I only hope our system corrects this egregious denial of justice and decides to reopen the case.

Comments:

@**HarlowsHarlot94**: Go to hell. This is complete libel against Harlow and Colton and you should be sued. Fuck, even O.J. should be suing you for this fake news article!

@**SianGilbz**: Jade Dutton was strangled!? Why isn't anyone else taking this more seriously?

@**HHevangelist**: @SianGilbz Because she's clearly making shit up. No proof of that or any of her other claims whatsoever—hence why the judge dropped the charges!

@**StrawberryFields4eva**: This batshit reporter was probably the one who framed her in the first place…

@**CruelSophieXoXo**: Hundreds of my moots are following this delusional, clout-chasing publication, suggest you unfollow before I block.

@**ApotheosisBitch5**: Apotheosis was her first album post PANDEMIC, of course there will be mentions and allegories to death. We don't know what she went through! So why don't you just shut the fuck up, Naomi Bullshit Barnes!

@**TorturedSoulHH**: Naomi Barnes hope someone kills you, you dumb fucking cunt

@**HHevangelist**: Someone should teach this dumb bitch a lesson!

@**TorturedSoulHH**: @HHevangelist found out where she lives in LA…

@MirrozNSm0ke: Finally a reporter brave enough to speak the truth without hiding from the repercussions of the evil elite!!!!

@HarryTurnerFan: @MirrozNSm0ke @SianGilbz happy someone else is taking this seriously. Too many fans with no lives in the comments ignoring these horrifying facts!

@RoseAndValerie9: I don't disagree Harlow should be locked up, but how fucking dare you slander Colton like this, claiming he was blackmailing her – appalling and heartless, his poor family #victimblaming

@OceanBlvdsTunnel: This makes no sense, Meghan Rhodes is still alive. If Harlow was such a crazy murderer, why not kill the woman Colton actually got engaged to?

@LiviaStoneHH: @OceanBlvdsTunnel exactly! Naomi Barnes lost all integrity. Comparing to O.J.!? Are you effing kidding me? Just another journalist willing to say anything for clicks. Pathetic.

Harlow

Four Months Before the Murder

I inhaled, letting the smoke fill my lungs as I watched the waves crash against the jagged cliffs below. I knew the THC was kicking in because I started thinking of the waves as a metaphor for my life, on the cusp of crashing into a million little pieces. The perfect mindset for songwriting.

I cry for a life that's shattered, like the shards of glass on the floor
You've tainted anything that mattered, now I fear what's in store

I scribbled the lyrics down in an old composition notebook I found in the kitchen drawer. I usually wrote in my phone, but I wanted to disconnect for a couple hours.

Because no one can hear me, I'm a powerless ghost
Devoured by darkness, got too close

As I let the lyrics flow onto the page, I started to forget my anxiety; when my brain was piecing words together, it provided a distraction from the heavy weight pulling my heart into my stomach. I cocked my head to the side as I reread the lyrics, sighing.

There were a few with potential. The rest were garbage. But I knew that to improve them, I had to keep going. Tell myself no one would hear them anyway. This was just for me. So I strummed the chords of my guitar—A minor to C to G minor—and sang softly.

"If you were a different shade… of red. And I wasn't… held captive by the thoughts in my head…"

My throat stung as I repeated the last two lines.

"Maybe it would have worked. Maybe it would have lasted. But we're… we're…"

I paused, trying to think of two toxic substances that shouldn't be combined. But "we're like ammonia and bleach" didn't have the poetic ring I was looking for.

"But your… darkness is overpowering. Slowly devouring."

I nodded, writing it down.

"And my heart breaks…" I continued. "To watch this love souring."

God, you're pathetic. Rolling my eyes, I scratched out the last line. *Useless. Basic. Talentless.* I could hear the cruel comments in my head.

"Three things you can hear. Three things you can see." I whispered the command to myself as I threw my pen down, trying to stop the downward spiral in its tracks.

Waves crashing. Seagulls squawking. Wind whipping…

A ship on the horizon. Grass beneath my feet. The beach beyond the cliffs below.

I instantly felt better by remembering where I was. At my beach house in Maine, away from the chaos of the city. No paparazzi or crowds. Just me and my guitar.

And the Scott family, ten minutes up the coast…

I groaned, annoyed at my own brain for the reminder. I had bought the home when Colton and I were at our happiest. Like with him, it was love at first sight when I saw the Georgian-style mansion. Its understated extravagance, arched hallways, and intricate carved-wood walls made me feel like I'd been whisked away into another time.

Starry nights, champagne on ice. Bodies as one, souls intertwined. Once upon a summer.

I silently sang the lyrics to my bestselling song as I reminisced on the summer that had inspired it. Before it all went wrong. I remembered the first time Colton had brought me to his parents' lavish estate in Maine to meet his family. How nervous I was, terrified they wouldn't like me, especially after I'd mentioned it to my own status-seeking mother.

What are you going to wear? You should really plan all of your outfits ahead of time. Do you know who his grandfather is? Don't mess this up!

I sucked in another hit of weed, embarrassed at all the energy I'd spent worrying back then. When, now, it didn't matter one bit. Sure, they were nice to my face, but I would have never fit into his family long-term. The only one I got along with was Casey, Colton's brother's wife. We still stayed in touch, but the rest of them could go fuck themselves as far as I cared. Especially his mother.

Denise Scott liked to pretend she was a modern-day Jacqueline Kennedy. She carried herself with the right amount of grace and elegance, balanced by a slight coldness. Or maybe that was just how she was to me. I could tell from the moment we met that Denise hoped I was just a phase her golden boy would grow out of.

If Denise Scott only fucking knew what her son was really like. What he liked to do behind closed doors.

I pulled my woolen coat tight, shivering as the cold breeze whipped around me.

I tapped the screen of my phone once I got inside. I'd left it on the kitchen counter on purpose, to ensure uninterrupted songwriting time, and now I'd have to deal with the consequences. Face the fact that both my personal life and professional life were hanging on by a thread, despite how successful and happy I appeared to the rest of the world.

"You were supposed to be in hair and makeup an hour ago. Where the hell are you?" the first text from Sam read.

"This isn't cute anymore. You can't keep showing up late. I'm happy to give you time if you need it, but this isn't the way to go about it. Charlie is starting to lose patience and frankly so am I…"

I let out a loud exhale before responding. *"Just reschedule, I'll head back tonight, okay. Relax."* I added a "sorry" for good measure. Not that I meant it.

I flung the phone back on the marble counter and walked over to the couch, grabbing a cushion to squeeze tight. Going back to New York was the last thing I wanted to do, to keep singing a song I hated. I wanted to stay holed up here as long as I could. Until I could shake this feeling. Of guilt. Shame. Sadness. Eating away at me like parasites.

Trying to stay in control, but I'm slipping away
I'm spiraling down, wondering what to say
Not that it matters, no one need listen
All that's worth saying are the secrets I'm keeping

I curled up in a ball and cried hot tears as the lyrics came, not bothering to write them down.

Present Day

If I had to share one lesson learned from this tumultuous year, it's this: You have to look out for yourself and take control, no matter the cost. Because the price of sitting back and crying, of playing the victim, is far too high. It's a dog-eat-dog world out there, and you have to fight to survive.

So even though part of me knows I deserve to rot in a jail cell for life, the other part tells me everyone gets what they deserve in the end. And that I did what I had to do. I shouldn't be punished for that. And if put in the same situation, I'd do it again.

The truth is, I only have one regret. And it's not what you think.

Chapter 26

Right after Naomi posts the article, she feels lighter, like a weight has been lifted. But as the day goes by and the article is shared by tens, then hundreds, then thousands of social media users, she starts to panic, wondering if she should've run it by Joel first. She knows why she didn't, though—because he would have stopped her, forced her to completely reframe it.

Would have also called out the possible legal ramifications of it, a voice says in the back of her mind. But she ignores it. People need to know the truth. A potential serial killer is back on the streets.

Her anxiety spikes as her phone buzzes, assuming it'll be more of the same death and rape threats she's been receiving from Harlow stans since she posted the article. She knew the fans would go on the defensive, but she didn't expect the reaction to be *this* bad.

She cringes at the continued vibrating, realizing it's a call. Expecting it to be Joel, she's surprised to see Leo's name on the screen when she finally looks. Her heart sinks, knowing she probably shouldn't have quoted him in the article, even anonymously.

She huffs out a short breath before picking up, bracing herself. "Hey," she says, too cheerfully. Her whole body is tense.

"What the hell is with this article?"

She closes her eyes and deflates.

"Those conversations were supposed to be confidential. Me helping you out on the down-low. But now I see my words verbatim all over the internet…"

Naomi opens her mouth to defuse the situation, but Leo talks before she can. "My boss is pissed, knows someone's been talking to the press, wonder how long it'll take for them to figure out it was me." He mumbles something she can't quite make out.

"Listen, Leo, I'm really sorry… I mean technically you never said it was confidential, so…" She knows she shouldn't have added the last bit, but couldn't help herself.

He laughs, annoyed. "Right, yeah, sure. Well, don't bother asking me for any more favors. I see what this was now. You got what you wanted. I'm done." He hangs up.

She rubs her hand over her eyes, slamming her phone on the countertop with the other. "Fuck."

She's tempted to hurl the phone across the room when it vibrates again, but refrains when she sees it's her friend Jessie.

Still up for going out tonight? I can get us VIP at the Standard! 9 p.m. if you're in. She's added a smirking emoji followed by toasting champagne glasses.

Naomi completely forgot about her plans with Jessie and the thought of socializing makes her head hurt. But she could do with a distraction. And a drink. Many drinks. *I'll see you there*, she replies.

*

Rising tall against the Hudson River, the Standard, High Line is a New York City staple with every luxurious amenity imaginable. Rooms with floor-to-ceiling windows, sweeping views of Manhattan and the Hudson, a legendary rooftop club, rotating art installations, a German beer garden, and a steakhouse. The perfect place for Naomi to try and take a break again, hopefully a successful one this time.

Not that Joel would be happy about her going MIA after unleashing that bomb of an article into the world. He already tried calling her twice, once just before she left the house and again before she got on the subway. She can tell by his "Call me. Now." follow-up text that he isn't pleased. She's not ready for the fallout, though, so she decides she'll enjoy her night and face him tomorrow.

Naomi stares at the white textured walls of the hotel as she waits in the lobby, imagining herself being transported to an alternate reality, a world where no one is angry with her or wants to kill her. One where her sister is alive.

"Hi!" a voice calls out behind her.

Naomi swings around to face Jessie. She's grinning from ear to ear, her hazel eyes sparkling against the colored LED lights. She is wearing a black mini dress with Doc Martens and a black beanie that half-covers her long caramel-colored hair, an outfit Naomi could never pull off. She leans in for a hug and they hold each other for a moment. It's been almost a year since they last hung out.

"It's so nice to see you," Jessie says, squeezing her again. "How's it been being back?"

Naomi sighs. "It's been... a lot."

"I bet." Jessie shoves Naomi playfully.

Naomi shakes her head. "Harlow Hayes has been the bane of my existence for the past week."

"Betcha never thought you'd say that," Jessie laughs.

"No, I did not. How about you, how's everything?"

"Yeah, all good thanks, just busy. Currently working with my boss to put together the list for the Songwriters Hall of Fame's next induction." She smirks mischievously. "I could probably sneak you a name or two next week if you need a story."

"That would be amazing, thanks," Naomi says instinctively, although she's not nearly as excited as she normally would be about a future tip; she's too swept up in Harlow Hayes and the suspected murder of her sister.

The elevator dings and people pile out as the doors open. Jessie gestures for Naomi to follow her.

"Look familiar?" Jessie gleams as she darts her gaze around the silver walls.

Naomi frowns, racking her brain for why an elevator would be familiar, and then it hits her. This is where the infamous fight between Solange Knowles and Jay-Z took place. Naomi was only a senior in high school when it happened ten years ago, but it's something every entertainment reporter knows about.

"Is this the actual elevator?"

"Mmhmm." Jessie smirks. "There should be some celebs hanging around tonight too. I heard Nikki Rix is in town, usually shows up when DJ Sea is playing. We'll start on the rooftop but then head inside for his set."

Naomi nods. If she could get some gossip tonight or

witness anything like a Solange–Jay-Z-level scandal, Joel would hopefully forgive her for ignoring him.

The elevator opens and Naomi is immediately greeted by a smoky neon-lit club with views of the city skyline, sparkling in the distance like starlight. Jessie guides her through the dance floor, where disco lights reflect off the swaying, sweating bodies. Once across, Jessie pulls up a red rope and guides them to a velvet couch in the corner. A promoter, smelling of cigarettes and shaving cream, is popping champagne for a group of models, their twig arms swaying in the air as they celebrate.

Jessie introduces Naomi to Izzy, the promoter. She's happy when he doesn't reach out his greasy hand and instead hands them a glass.

"To a fucking good night!" Izzy shouts, holding up the bottle.

Naomi clinks her glass against the others' and downs half the contents.

"Want one?" Jessie smirks as she dangles a dime bag containing small white pills in front of Naomi. She hasn't taken molly in years, not since her early twenties.

"Why not?" Naomi says, holding her hand out. What's one more bad decision?

The two of them let the pills dissolve on their tongues before knocking back another glass of champagne.

"This one's for all the bad bitches out there!" The DJ yells into the microphone. Everyone cheers, but Naomi's smile drops when the trap remix of Harlow Hayes' "Violent Ends" blares through the speakers.

She tilts her head back, annoyed by the DJ's song choice for reminding her of everything just when she finally started to forget about it all.

"Yassss, Harlow!" one of the models calls out. "Finally free!"

Naomi rolls her eyes as the crowd erupts in cheers and laughter. She turns to follow Jessie on her way to the dance floor, but freezes when she hears one of the women bring up her article.

"Did you see that article from C*Leb earlier?"

Another woman, this one with thick eyebrows that look like they've been glued into place, laughs. "Hell yeah. It was just the wild conspiracy I needed to start my day. I think the writer's got it all wrong though."

Naomi bites her lip, not in the mood to hear her defend Harlow.

"I was there that night, at the pre-VMAs party—the night before that girl... well, we know what happened to her now, but I think it was the last place she was seen alive."

Naomi's heart races with excitement and she moves closer. The corners of the model's lips curve into a smirk.

"I saw Jade, Harlow, and Colton together. Walking up the stairs. He had one hand wrapped around Harlow's shoulders and the other placed right above Jade's ass."

Naomi's mouth falls open at the comment. She now has an eyewitness putting the three of them together, the night before Jade disappeared.

"Hi, sorry to intrude, but I couldn't help but overhear what you were saying." Naomi's worried the woman will be annoyed she was eavesdropping, but thankfully, she's eager to share her theory.

"Yeah, basically just saying that I don't think Harlow's the villain in this story. I think we'll all find out Colton Scott is—was."

Naomi thinks about how Colton was allegedly blackmailing Harlow and wonders if her intuition about Colton not being completely innocent in all this was right. That maybe he's done worse things than toy with Harlow's heart and emotions, as mentioned by Bobby and Trevor. That maybe he was an accomplice. Or worse.

"Do you think the blackmail the writer mentioned had to do with that night then? That Harlow and Jade got in a fight and Harlow killed her? Or do you think Colton played more of a role?"

The model shakes her head before Naomi can finish, taking another swig of champagne before leaning in closer as the music and crowd get louder, nearly screaming in Naomi's ear. "One of my friends slept with Colton. Said he was creepy as fuck. Like, vile. She told all of us to stay away from him."

Naomi frowns, unsure of how to process the information. "Vile how?"

"I don't know. She wouldn't tell us. She just said stay away."

"So you think he's the one that killed Jade?" Naomi asks. "And then what? Killed himself?" Naomi thinks of Harlow's DNA found in Colton's apartment, knowing she must somehow be involved. But she wonders if the police checked Jade for his DNA. Probably not. She also wonders if this night, right before the VMAs, was when the sex tape was made. But that would mean Colton kept it, despite Jade's fate. Alarm bells sound in her mind like sirens.

Naomi is about to ask more questions, but then Izzy arrives with a tray of shots. The model squeals, disappearing into the crowd, holding a couple of glasses in the air. Naomi's head spins, and she can't tell if it's from the pill–champagne combo or from this crucial new piece of information.

This changes everything, she thinks. It's too much for her intoxicated brain to process properly right now, so she quickly writes down the exchange in her Notes app and takes two shots before meeting back up with Jessie on the dance floor.

Within a couple of hours, Naomi has completely lost count of how many drinks she's had. Everything is a blur, just like she wanted.

Her head spins as if she's on a merry-go-round. She wobbles, reaching out for the wall. Once she regains her balance, she closes her eyes and inhales, not realizing someone is vaping right next to her. She retches after ingesting the plume of smoke, but thankfully nothing comes up. Exhaling, she forces herself to stand up straight. But her knees buckle at a memory of Faye.

Naomi had just gotten dumped by her college boyfriend, the one before Matt. Faye had encouraged her to get blackout drunk, promising she'd stay sober and look out for her. But Faye ended up getting wasted too, and Naomi somehow remained just coherent enough to hail a cab to take them home. She looks around for Jessie but can't seem to find her through the fuchsia and lavender haze.

You can do this, she tells herself. *You're fine. Just get downstairs and hail a cab.*

She stumbles forward, gripping onto various strangers for support as she tries to make it to the exit. But she struggles to see, everything blurring together like a neon-colored, long-exposure photograph.

The music seems to disappear, replaced by silence and the sound of a heart beating faintly in the background. She shakes her head, wishing she never took the pill. A scream bursts through the silence and she freezes. *Where is it coming from?* She whips her head around, the movement making her dizzy, and she stumbles again, tensing at the sound of a wailing woman. Then she hears the crackling of a fire, followed by laughter, deep and drawn-out, like in slow motion. She shakes her head and everything is normal again. And the laughter returns. But this time, it sounds just like Faye.

Naomi stumbles again, calling out for her sister. Warm liquid spills down her cheeks as a pair of arms wrap around her shoulders. "Faye?"

"Naomi… it's Jessie. Are you okay?"

It's three in the morning by the time Naomi sobers up enough for Jessie to trust she'll be alright sleeping alone. Still, Jessie shares a cab with her, waving her off into Joel's brownstone. Once inside, Naomi hobbles barefoot up the stairs, desperate to get into bed. But when she goes to unlock the door to the apartment, it's already open.

Chapter 27

Naomi slowly pushes the door inward, peering inside as it creaks open. She takes one step, then another, listening for any signs that someone is there.

As she moves, she thinks of the Toyota trailing her back from Maine, then the death threats from fans.

> **@TianaJadeHH**: i hope you fucking die like Colton & Jade you stupid bitch
>
> **@DarkDemise**: who's coming to the C*Leb office with me to k-word this clout-chaser?
>
> **@JennaT56**: wouldn't it be so sad if Naomi Barnes suddenly ceased to exist?

She swallows hard, wondering if they have really come for her so soon, brazen enough to make good on their threats. She counts to three and dashes to the kitchen, letting her heels and purse clatter to the floor. Worried the noise will have startled the intruder—if there is one—she grabs a knife from the drawer and holds it out in front of her, eyes wild, ready to fight.

The sound of blood pumping in her ears drowns out any

noise, so she forces herself to focus on her breathing so she can hear. Sweat trickles down her clammy forehead as she tentatively moves through the apartment, knuckles white from clutching the knife.

Another threat flashes through her mind like static. *One day you'll get what's coming to you, you ugly cunt.*

Could one of them have doxed her, released her address online, or figured out where she was staying? She kicks in the bedroom door. Nothing.

Could they be lying in wait right now, planning to attack once she falls asleep? She pulls open the closet door. Nothing.

With only one place left to check, Naomi lunges into the bathroom, throwing the shower curtain to the side. She lets out the breath she'd been holding and relaxes slightly. She knows she's been a bit wrapped up in the case and all over the place lately so she convinces herself that she just must have forgotten to lock the door.

After doing one more sweep of the apartment, Naomi barricades the bedroom door with a chest of drawers. Even with the light on and the knife on the bedside table, she can't sleep, unable to get her heart and thoughts to stop racing.

Naomi recalls what the model said at the club, convinced now that Colton is even more of a villain than she originally thought.

Like @ThatHazieLawyerLady said, *Where there's smoke, there's fire…*

AVANT

Hollywood Heartthrob Colton Scott is Unrecognizable as He Preps for *Mojave* Shoot in New Mexico

The actor is set to lead Clint Caruso's latest action film alongside MMA fighter Riley Joseph and newcomer Lindsey Mitchell

BY HALLE SKIDMER – MARCH 12, 2017

A boost of serotonin for fans of Colton Scott who live in Albuquerque this week, as the actor temporarily moves to town to film scenes from the new Clint Caruso flick Mojave, which will see Scott's character Eddie Silver fight his way through the desert after a deal gone wrong with a ruthless gang leader.

While much of the movie will be filmed in the actual *Mojave* in southern California, New Mexico's largest city also plays a big part.

Avid fans have been quick to catch on, spotting the actor around the city, but the dramatic change in his appearance has eluded many. Out for a casual drink in town sporting a blue tank and red baseball cap, Scott was spotted with matted, shoulder-length locks and unruly facial hair—not the usual, clean-cut look we're used to seeing for the *Fact of the Matter* star. But while the guise may seem strange for fans, it sounds consistent for the role of a man who finds himself left for dead in one of the unkindest terrains in the United States.

This is Scott's second time being directed by Clint Caruso following the success of *Doomsday* in 2015. MMA fighter Riley Joseph and newcomer Lindsey Mitchell will also star in the film.

NEWS ALERT

21-Year-Old New Mexico Woman Missing: Penelope Lopez Last Seen Leaving her Albuquerque Home

Date: March 28, 2017

Posted by: Kristen Carerra

A loving daughter, friend, and sister, Penelope Lopez has been missing for four days.

Penelope's roommate, Julia Getner, was the last person to see the University of New Mexico student on March 24, 2017. Getner says she exchanged a brief greeting with her roommate, who said she was "going out for drinks," before she went inside to change for her night shift at the local diner.

Diana Lopez, Penelope's sister, confirmed Getner's claim, stating that her sister had texted her that night before she went out. It was the last she heard from her.

"She wouldn't tell me who she was meeting, but she seemed excited. I told her to be careful and text me when she was home, but she never did. I pray she didn't arrange to meet up with some psycho she met on Tinder."

After making several attempts to contact Penelope, Diana contacted the Albuquerque police, who are currently looking into the matter.

Penelope is 5'7", of slim build, with tan skin, brown eyes, and long blonde hair. If you have any information regarding Penelope's whereabouts or her disappearance, please contact the Albuquerque Police Department at (505) 555-2677 or the New Mexico Department of Public Safety Missing Person Hotline at (800) 555-3463.

Social Media Post

RavenRumours   Subscribe…

Not naming names since I haven't seen any evidence, but a popular A-lister, most famous for his action roles, allegedly took things too far in the bedroom with an aspiring (unknown) singer. Promised to help her with her career, but instead she claims he r*ped her. When she threatened to go to the police, his team of lawyers shut her up. Guy comes from money, family members in politics, so they were able to 'make it go away'. For now at least. Source also says it's not the first time something like this has happened either.

10,986 likes

RavenRumours *Aspiring starlets beware: this A-list actor isn't the hero, he's the predator… *screenshot from email above**

Comments:

@notasitseemz: Gotta be Brandon Haim. Mom's an ambassador, dad's attorney general. 'Dynamite' franchise puts him in A-list… Plus, he's always seemed like a creep.

@AndrewBatemanOfficial: BH has women falling at his feet, why would he do that? Smells like bullshit to me. Another slut who couldn't handle being rejected so she's trying to paint the town red *yawn*

@mianancy271: @charamykate maybe Patrick Merlino?

@charamykate: @mianancy271 my first thought too, but

wouldn't call him A-list. What about Colton Scott? Uncle is governor of Maine 👀

@LDRsJimmy: @charamykate lol nah man's way too vanilla for that. Probably Brandon H judging by the comments here

Harlow

Three Months Before the Murder

Yawning, I scrolled through Instagram as I waited for the interview to begin. I should've been excited to be in Paris, but it was five in the morning and I was jetlagged as hell. Not that I could remember the last time I had a decent night's sleep.

From my feed I could see Sam was celebrating his wife's birthday in LA, Kamryn Hart was recording a new music video, and Colton... well, I didn't follow him anymore. The thought made me feel weak and powerful at the same time. Weak that I still thought of him, but powerful that I'd managed to stay away for so long. I hadn't seen or spoken to him in months and felt like I was finally moving on. Not that I forgot about what happened. No, that's what truly kept me up at night, even after all this time. I had good and bad days, but I really felt like I finally had a handle on things. In the past two weeks, I hadn't missed one work function, recording session, or event. Charlie was still annoyed at me, I knew that, but Sam seemed pleased. He could tell I was trying. And I was. I was going to fix it. I was good now.

But just when I felt I had it under control, a news story brought me back down. These algorithms were annoyingly good, keeping track on things they knew I was the most interested in, even though I didn't want to be.

I fumbled in my bag and popped two pills into my mouth. One Xanax to help me relax and one Adderall for focus and energy, drowned with champagne to help me forget. I'd mastered my prescription cocktail years ago and knew what worked well together and what didn't. For example, a beta-blocker like propranolol or sedative like Xanax worked great to calm my nerves, but would make me drowsy. When combined with an amphetamine like Adderall, however, the drowsiness was counteracted and I could sing and dance for hours on end. This was my usual cocktail for days like today, finding it worked much better than cocaine or ecstasy—which I saved only for parties or festivals I was attending for fun.

I wasn't an addict, but I probably should have tried to rein it in. Now wasn't the time, though.

"Ready?" the host asked, crossing one long leg over the other. She had short, curly, blonde hair and wore a bright-blue pantsuit that clashed against the green screen behind us.

I nodded, ready to get it over with, and held out my bag for Rebecca to take.

Once Rebecca was out of shot, the woman nodded at the cameraman, who counted down from three to one with his fingers.

After filming for the interview wrapped, I went straight back to my hotel, popped a few more pills, and slept for hours. It seemed the only time I could sleep was in the daytime; something about the nights unsettled me too much to switch off. My heart pounded as I woke from my nap, anxious that I fucked the interview up, worried Sam and Charlie would be able to tell I was on something. It didn't help that everything I'd taken in the morning had worn off by now.

You have to get your shit together, I chided myself as I reached for more pills. *You're so close.*

I walked out of my suite's bedroom and opened the balcony doors, inhaling the Parisian air. It had a sweetness to it I couldn't quite put my finger on. Bread? Flowers? Perfume? The scent mingled with the bitter stench of fuel being released into the air from the taxis and mopeds buzzing through the street below. From my balcony, I could see the twinkling lights of the Eiffel Tower in the distance, reminding me of the first time I'd seen them. With Colton. I was only twenty at the time; a naive child in the blissful newlywed phase of our tumultuous relationship. Completely oblivious to the darkness ahead of us.

A car horn blared, ruining the solace I'd been searching for. The high-pitched sound brought me back to the present, fixating my mind on the commotion of the city, amplifying everything from sirens wailing to engines revving to people shouting and laughing. I returned inside, instantly relaxing when I shut the doors and muffled the noise.

I'd just started drawing a bath in the elegant clawfoot tub when there was a knock at the door. I groaned, expecting it to be Rebecca with a soul-sucking request like filming an Instagram endorsement for some brand desperate to appeal to a younger audience. I tried to think of my excuses to get out of it, surprised when the knocking continued, louder and more urgent this time.

Boom. Boom. Boom. My heartbeat echoed the banging on the door as I apprehensively walked toward it.

Maybe it's not Rebecca, I thought, disconcerted. *Maybe it's the police...*

Fear flooded my body as I stared through the peephole and saw it wasn't either of them.

It was worse.

Even through the thick wooden door, I could feel the magnetic pull between us, feel the hum of electricity in the air. That connection used to be filled with love and longing, but now it sparked with something rotten.

"Har, let me in," Colton said. "We need to talk."

Present Day

I'd been so close to getting away with it. *So very close*. But then he tried to ruin it all, tried to back me into a corner. And I couldn't have that. He gave me no choice.

Thankfully, he mistook my cunning for compliance, not realizing I was sharpening my claws behind my back, waiting for the perfect moment to strike.

Chapter 28

Naomi wakes to the sound of a plate whirring against the countertop, followed by the shuffle of utensils. She bolts out of bed and throws on a robe, heart hammering as she stares at the chest of drawers barricading the door. Deciding to face her foe head on rather than stay put, she shifts the furniture as quietly as possible, giving herself just enough room to squeeze out the door. She hears the fridge open and close as she tiptoes down the hall, knife in hand.

She takes a step forward, holding the knife out, and turns the corner.

"Jesus Christ!" she yells when she sees him. "What the hell, Joel? I thought someone broke in." She drops the knife onto the counter and wipes the sweat from her brow. "Was it you who left the door open last night?"

He stares from her to the knife and shakes his head. "Did I? Well, it is my place, remember. And seeing as you wouldn't answer any of my phone calls…" His white teeth contrast with his tanned skin and pink polo shirt as he smiles sarcastically.

"I'm sorry—" she starts, but he doesn't let her talk.

"So I thought I'd stop by, see how it's going, see how you're doing." He gestures to the wall spanning from the living room to the kitchen and Naomi cringes. "And at least I've been able to confirm you've lost your fucking mind."

Naomi doesn't say anything. Her head is pounding and she needs lots of coffee and water for this.

He pinches his fingers together in front of his face. "I'm not going to lie. I was pissed when I first saw the article, knowing I'd have to spend hours I don't have talkin' to legal. Which I did, by the way, after a furious Sam-fucking-Brixton called me after you somehow managed to libel two of his most famous clients—one posthumously." The color of his face grows closer to the bright shade of his shirt's pinky-red as he presses on. "And then, to add to my embarrassment, I learn he personally kicked you out of Colton's funeral—another thing you conveniently failed to mention to me. He said he was going to let that slide—he gets it, overambitious reporter doing her job, admires your initiative as much as he questions your ethics… But then you go rogue, publishing that brazen bullshit suggesting not only that Colton was blackmailing Harlow but that she's potentially a fucking serial killer?"

Hearing him call her work bullshit is like a knife to the heart. But she tries not to take it personally. He's mad, she understands. So she doesn't say anything, just crosses her arms and looks down as he admonishes her. She glances up, seeing his eyes dart to the board and back to her. His face softens.

"I know this case has taken an unexpected turn and that it's reminded you so much of your sister. But we've been over this—"

"We haven't, though!" Naomi throws her hands in the air. "You have no idea everything I've found out since we last spoke."

Joel runs a hand down his face before holding it out in question. "Please enlighten me then."

"Both Faye and Jade—both young, beautiful aspiring musicians, neither of whom had drug problems—die of drug overdoses six months apart."

"Yeah…" Joel says, noting this is something he already knows. She told him this after her meeting with Emily.

"And then, I not only learn they knew each other, but after comparing their autopsy reports, they both died with the same exact levels of fentanyl in their systems." She rattles through the facts quickly so he can't interrupt. "And I checked with a medical examiner who said that's not normal and he would bet the product probably came from or was administered by the same source."

Joel purses his lips as he considers this.

"And on top of that, we obviously know police sources have claimed Jade had bruising on her neck years ago, but then in my sister's autopsy, I learn she had a head injury. A possible skull fracture, Joel!"

He runs a hand over his face. "Don't you hear yourself? You're literally contradicting your own argument. You told me yourself Jade's bruises were missing from the autopsy. Which makes sense because her death was actually suspicious. But if Faye's head injury was reported then they left it because there was clearly nothing to hide."

Naomi deflates, now having heard this same argument from not one but three level-headed people. Glen, Leo, and now Joel. Was she really reaching so much? Trying to force the evidence to fit her narrative?

He sighs, crossing his arms. "And even if Faye's death was suspicious, why are you writing libelous articles about Harlow Hayes after she's been cleared? Shouldn't you be onto the next lead?"

She wants to defend the article, stand her ground, but she's not as sure as she was before. After learning more about Colton last night, she thinks it's more complicated now. Which reminds her.

"Well, now that you mention it," she says, ready to change the subject away from the article, "I do have a new lead. Some new information that could turn out to be something big."

He eyes her skeptically.

"This girl at the club last night said she saw Colton, Harlow, and Jade together that night and she thinks Colton is actually the one who killed—"

"Woah, no, no, no, let me stop you right there…"

"But I even found some more stuff last night about a girl who went missing when he was filming in New Mexico in 2017!"

"Naomi!" Joel shouts, startling her. "No. We're not the fucking New York Times. We're C*Leb News. Me and you taking on the fucking Scott family? Are you crazy? Oh god, I have a headache." He pinches the bridge of his nose again. "One second you're sure it's this, the next it's that… No, we are absolutely not messing with the Scott family. Not after they just buried their precious golden boy. Don't even think about it."

She opens her mouth to argue but instead throws her hands in the air and paces the room. "Fine, should I just write something about Harlow's latest makeup look? Fashion choices?"

"No, what you're going to do is take a break. You're not going to write anything until you've taken a step back and can look at things objectively again. If you want to talk to the police about reopening the investigation into your sister's death, then by all means, let me know if you need any help. But if not, I'll have Angie book you a flight back to LA—it'll have to be in a few days when we can get rid of the Harlow army camped outside the office, but in the meantime, you cannot go rogue on this. And you absolutely cannot write one more piece about Harlow Hayes, and definitely fucking not a whiff of anything bad about Colton Scott, based on something one drunk girl said in a club."

Naomi grunts in frustration. But she doesn't have a leg to stand on. Doesn't have any tangible, foolproof evidence. Yet.

After Joel finally leaves, Naomi gets back to work; she's come too far to give up now. She opens the Notes app to double-check what the model said about Colton before writing it on a Post-it and sticking it to the wall.

"Vile/stay away" Potential 3some with C, H + J gone wrong? H got jealous or something else?

Naomi's eyes dance across the photos of the beautiful people, three of whom are dead. She recalls Emily telling her about Jade's promiscuity and sexual appetite. She reflects on her own sister's bad taste in men. Two naive young women. One powerful man...

She originally presumed Harlow was jealous, but was she? Or was she somehow involved? Did she and Colton get off on something sadistic together?

Naomi ponders this, shaking her head in frustration. She needs to learn more about Colton. Speak to someone who knew him to see if the rumors are true. Her eyes land on the small picture of actress Meghan Rhodes, Colton's ex-fiancée.

Why weren't you at the funeral, Meghan? What do you know?

AVANT

Colton Scott Talks Heartbreak After Failed Engagement to Meghan Rhodes

The Hollywood hero opens up about love, loss, and self-doubt, calling the breakup with his former co-star "challenging all around"

BY SIAN GILBERT – MARCH 5, 2024

After ending his engagement to actress Meghan Rhodes in January, Colton Scott opened up for the first time about how he's coping with their split.

"Breaking up is never easy. It's hard. Not only on an emotional level—realizing you'll no longer be with the person who was the center of your world for so long—but also on a self-doubt level. I really thought she was the one. So yeah, it's just challenging all around, ya know? But I'm finally starting to feel like myself again and am looking forward to everything that the big man upstairs has in store for me."

When asked what's helped him overcome the heartbreak, Scott revealed his main source of comfort has been his nephews.

"They're at that perfect age where they actually think I'm

cool," he laughs. "They came to visit me on set last week and yeah, it was an incredibly 'proud uncle' moment for me."

Scott is currently filming the sequel to *Mr. America*, *Mr. America: Retaliation*. Luckily for him, Rhodes' character was killed off in the first installment so they don't have to worry about working together.

Scott and Rhodes met in 2019 on the set of *A Highland Love*. In the romantic dramedy, Rhodes played a librarian who had never experienced love outside of books, while Scott played a Scottish Highlander who thought romance novels were inauthentic and unrealistic.

Despite an undeniable on-set chemistry, nothing was rumored to have happened between the two since Colton was dating pop star Harlow Hayes at the time. Throughout the years, they continued their "friendship" until they eventually fell in love and lived a whirlwind romance in real life, with Colton proposing to Meghan in late 2021 soon after they began filming for *Mr. America*. The pair's engagement lasted for just over two years.

Meghan is currently filming *I'm Sure She's Fine*, an HBO adaptation of the hit psychological thriller novel by the same name about a paranoid mother who goes missing and a daughter, played by Meghan, who doesn't care—until, that is, she believes her mother may have had a reason to be paranoid after all.

When asked for a comment, Meghan declined.

Direct Message

Meghan Rhodes ✓

@meghan_rhodes_official
15M followers · 405 posts
View Profile

9:06 a.m.

Meghan,
I'm a reporter for C*Leb News
and need five minutes of your time.
I'm onto him.
Please call me at 845-555-5908 when you see this.

Chapter 29

Naomi wastes no time, reaching out to Meghan across all her social media, sending the same direct message to her Instagram, Twitter, and TikTok, even though she knows they'll most likely never be read. She leaves messages and emails for her PR contact and manager, but knows it could take them days, if not weeks, to get back to her. With all the other reporters trying to get a comment on Colton, coupled with promotions for her new HBO show, Naomi will be lucky if she gets any response at all.

She grunts in frustration, knowing she needs to think of some other way to get Meghan's attention. She goes back to her Instagram account and scrolls through countless photos of the blonde bombshell. There's a recent cover for Vogue, sexy lingerie shoots, red-carpet snaps, and artsy vacation photos. She clicks onto one of Meghan floating in an infinity pool somewhere exotic, looking off into the distance.

Saint Lucia, you've been incredible. Until next time, the caption reads, followed by a camera emoji and a tag for @AnnieRhodesPhotography.

Naomi clicks on the tag, curious if Annie Rhodes is Meghan's sister. And she's right. She smiles, imagining an alternate reality where Faye is alive and famous and Naomi is the proud sister behind the scenes. Then she thinks about Emily Dutton, someone who suffered a similar fate, and how she was happy to help Naomi. Could it work with Meghan's sister too? It's worth a shot.

Hi Annie, my name is Naomi Barnes, she begins her message. Usually she notes her job title next to lend credibility, but she thinks in this case it might just cause Annie to scroll past. Instead, she uses a similar tactic to when she messaged Emily—the personal angle.

I think Colton Scott may have played a part in the death of my sister years ago. I was wondering if there's any way you could get me in touch with your sister so I could ask her a few questions? I can be reached at 845-555-5908. It's very important. Thank you!

With nothing to do but wait, Naomi decides to go for a walk. When she left the apartment, it was a cool but sunny Wednesday morning; now, it's pouring rain.

Every step she takes squishes against the cement, soaking her socks. But she doesn't care.

Naomi is surprised when she looks up to see the famous arches and spidery wires of the Brooklyn Bridge. It's barely visible, though, caught in between a mist of gray clouds encircling the structure. It makes the landmark look gothic, like the bridge is a gateway to a giant medieval cathedral in the sky. Up until a minute ago, she felt lost. But now she knows exactly where she is, and is surprised to be an hour's walk from Joel's apartment. She should turn around, but she doesn't want to. She wants to keep going.

Amid all the gray mist, buildings, and clothing, an artist's colorful stall sticks out like a picture that doesn't belong. She's usually in such a rush to get somewhere or do something that she never takes the time to stop and admire. But this time she does, drawn to the vibrant paintings like a moth to a flickering flame.

"See anything you like?" the artist asks, sliding out from under his tattered tent. Naomi imagines it must have been white when he first bought it, but has since become so dirty that it almost looks yellow. She feels a twinge of guilt and sadness. Yet another starving artist failing to make their dream come true, unlike the subjects of his multicolored portraits—icons like Marilyn Monroe, Michael Jackson, and Heath Ledger. Naomi lets out a sarcastic huff, realizing that even though his subjects "made it," they all met tragic, early ends.

"Just looking," she says, out of habit. The man nods, deflated. She can tell from his baggy clothes and thin frame that he could use the money. "I mean, these are all beautiful," she corrects. "I'm just trying to figure out which one I'm going to buy."

His eyes brighten. "Thank you."

Naomi continues to study the paintings, her eyes glossing over other celebrities' faces who also met premature ends. Aaliyah, Kobe Bryant, Paul Walker, Selena Quintanilla, and… Naomi pauses. "Is that Paul McCartney? Isn't he alive?"

The man looks up at her, a strange look in his eyes. "Paul is dead," he replies, matter-of-fact.

Naomi opens her mouth to argue but stops herself. Maybe something happened to him and she was the one out of the loop? But then she remembers Joel mentioning the theory that some fans believed he was dead, so she pulls out her phone and googles "Paul McCartney death."

At the top of the search results is an excerpt from the "Paul is dead" Wikipedia page.

"Paul is dead" is an urban legend and conspiracy theory alleging that English pop musician Paul McCartney of the Beatles died in 1966 and was secretly replaced by a look-alike.

Naomi smirks, amused by the crazy conspiracy. It fascinates her how anyone could believe something so outlandish.

Either way, she's drawn to the piece and the nostalgia of home, reminding her of her mom and the Beatles records she had on display. Usually she avoids sentimental things like that—anything that might make her feel something— but today, she wants to feel. She asks the artist how much and hands him a fifty, letting him keep the change.

With her new piece of art tucked under her arm, she wipes the raindrops off her phone and puts it back in her pocket, staying a moment to look over the edge of the bridge, at the dark water thrashing in the wind below. She hasn't walked the bridge in years, the last time with her sister.

Naomi remembers waking up to a door slamming at four in the morning that day. Worried, she got up to check on Faye, who had seemingly arrived home in a huff. But Faye refused to open her bedroom door, said she was tired and just wanted to go to sleep. So Naomi let her. That afternoon, Naomi walked in on Faye in the bathroom, studying her naked frame in the mirror, fingers tracing blue bruising on her ribs and wrists.

"What the fuck happened?" Naomi asked, horrified.

Faye slammed the door on her, angry at the invasion of privacy.

"Did someone hurt you?" Naomi pressed, heart pounding.

"No," Faye snapped. Silence hung in the air, almost as thick as the door between them, until she spoke again.

"I fell down the stupid stairs at the party last night." Faye's nasal tone hinted she'd been crying. "And before you start, yes, I was drinking. Yes, I know I need to be more careful. And no, I don't need a lecture from you, I'm literally fine."

Even though her intuition told her Faye was lying, Naomi dropped it. She knew her sister well enough to know she wouldn't get the truth out of her in that moment.

A couple hours later, she convinced Faye to go for a walk with her. They walked all the way to the Brooklyn Bridge, not speaking a word until they stopped at a viewpoint halfway across.

"If something happened, you can tell me. You know that, right?"

Faye linked her arm around Naomi's and pressed her head on her shoulder. "I know," she whispered.

Inhaling, Naomi closes her heavy eyes, tears ready to spill over at the memory she'd forgotten about until now. With everything she's learned recently, and with all the new questions swirling in her mind about what Faye could've been involved in before her death, about how she died, Naomi is recollecting the events in a whole new light. An even more disturbing one.

She presses her hand into her shoulder, imagining her sister's head there once more. She wishes she had never let it go, kept pressing Faye to tell her what really happened. Naomi knew deep down she didn't just fall down the stairs. Maybe if she had tried harder to get Faye to open up, she'd still be alive.

Naomi recalls the blind item she found last night, the one accusing an A-list actor of rape. She closes her eyes, the thought making her nauseous.

What if Colton hurt Faye? she thinks. *Maybe she met him at a party...*

Naomi huffs, watching her breath turn to angry smoke in the cold air. If Colton wasn't already dead, she'd kill him herself.

But was it even him? she questions. *Will I ever know?*

A passing truck rattles the wooden slats beneath her feet as she stares at the city skyline in the distance, the same view she and Faye gazed at. The only difference is that today it's shrouded in mist. A gust of wind blows, as if it's Faye's ghost, egging Naomi on to solve the mystery. She once again thinks back to what Aunt Mary's friend said. *"When it's foggy out, or misty, spirits are able to more easily enter through the human realm and communicate with us."*

She knows it's a stupid, childish notion, but she's desperate for it to be true.

What happened, Faye? Give me a sign.

And that's when her phone pings.

Chapter 30

Naomi shakes the rain off her umbrella once she steps under the glass shelter of the Bowery Hotel. She rubs her hands, slick with sweat and rain, on her beige trench coat before fixing her hair. A man in a bowler hat and red waistcoat greets her as he holds open the doors to the famed East Village property.

The moment she steps inside the warm lobby, she's transported to what feels like another century, the rich decor of velvet, leather, and wood drawing her in. She scans the room, filled with plush sofas atop patterned rugs, searching for Meghan Rhodes. That's who she assumes is waiting for her, at least.

1 p.m. Bowery Hotel lounge.

Her heart races, thinking back to the anonymous text message from a number she didn't recognize, wondering if she was wrong about who contacted her. *Maybe it's a trap*, a voice warns. She imagines a crazed fan hiding behind one of the velvet curtains.

The lobby is dimly lit, so she squints, eyes drawn to the fireplace across the room. A crown of blonde hair peeks out from the back of one of the large brown leather chairs, which almost seem red in the firelight.

Naomi traipses across the patterned rug, chest tightening with nerves. She's both relieved and even more nervous once she spots her, gazing into the flames, cupping a mug of steaming liquid. The light dances in Meghan's gray eyes as she looks up.

"Meghan?" Naomi says, voice low. She grows lightheaded as she takes the actress in, almost glowing, with a golden aura surrounding her. Naomi stumbles over her tongue for a brief moment but manages to pull herself together. "I'm Naomi, nice to meet you."

Meghan gives her a half-smile in return, and for a second Naomi is worried it's all a coincidence and Meghan never contacted her at all. But then she shifts in her seat and shakes Naomi's outstretched hand.

"Please, sit," she says, gesturing to the chair across from her.

Naomi takes a deep breath. She's been up close with plenty of celebrities before but she's never sat down intimately – not like this. Normally she would be over the moon to have landed a fireside chat with someone like Meghan Rhodes, but she hasn't come here for gossip. She came for answers.

"Thanks so much for meeting me." Naomi takes her jacket off and places it on the floor on top of her purse and umbrella. Her eyes flit across the room from the intricately carved stone fireplace to the vintage lamps on the dark wood-beamed ceilings. It's cozy but in an old, haunted mansion kind of way. "This is a beautiful hotel."

Meghan nods, smiling. "I love it. Used to come here all the time to read scripts when I was just starting out."

She's soft-spoken, with a warm and welcoming air, not at all what Naomi expected. In her red-carpet interviews she often seems aloof and cold. But tonight, she looks at home. Minus the distant, sad look in her eyes. "I usually don't do this, you know."

"I know," Naomi says. It's widely known that Meghan is very private and barely speaks to the press about work, let alone anything about her private life. "This isn't for an article. It's personal. Everything is off the record unless you tell me otherwise."

"I'm afraid it will have to be, I'm under a strict NDA. The only reason I agreed to this was because my sister told me it was personal. And she hated Colton, so the fact that you thought he wasn't the good guy made her forward it to me. It's my last night in New York for promotions before I go back to LA, so…" She turns her gaze back to the fire.

"An NDA from who? Colton?" Naomi interjects, astonished. She doesn't know why she's surprised. She's always just assumed Meghan was private, not silenced.

Meghan turns back to Naomi. "From his family and army of lawyers. Yes. Anyway, you know I looked you up before we met and I was surprised to see your latest article didn't really match your message."

Naomi sighs. She can't believe she went rogue like that and vows to never publish another article in the heat of the moment, promising to always send it to at least one other reader for fresh eyes.

"Yeah, well I'm starting to think I was a bit hasty with that, which is why I wanted to talk to you. See if I missed something. I got into all this because I was investigating the case against Harlow Hayes and while I originally thought she was to blame, I now have reason to believe that Colton isn't as innocent as everyone thought he was, and that he may have been involved in the death of two young women—maybe three." She thinks of the missing girl in New Mexico from 2017, when he was filming *Mojave*, of the model, and of the blind item. And she thinks of Faye, bruised and broken. She coughs, trying to clear the sting in her throat. "One of whom is my sister."

Meghan exhales and places her tea on the wooden coffee table. She runs her hands through her hair and props her elbows on her knees, clasping them together. She's wearing a thick black cable-knit sweater on top of a calf-length satin skirt, an inch of her skin peeking out above her black leather boots.

She gives Naomi a sad smile. "I'm truly sorry about your sister. I would freeze hell over if I thought someone hurt mine. Unfortunately, I don't know anything about anyone's death. Not even his…"

Naomi nods, about to ask a question, but then Meghan continues.

"But… and this is completely off the record, okay? You can't tell anyone you've spoken to me. As I said, it's a strict NDA." She eyes Naomi, waiting for confirmation.

"Of course," Naomi says, sitting up. "You have my word."

Appeased, Meghan speaks. "I have to say I wouldn't be completely surprised if your theory is true." She pauses and glances around the room as she lowers her voice. "Colton wasn't the true gentleman—hero—everyone wants to believe."

Naomi's heart starts pounding. She leans forward, waiting for Meghan to continue.

"So in the beginning everything was so great. Then after about a year and a half, he started to get a little controlling, didn't like me doing sex scenes with other men, hence why I moved into more PG roles for a time."

Naomi thinks of her film list, not having noticed the shift before from raunchy romcoms to children's movies and cheesy action films.

"Things became rocky, and we temporarily broke up for the first time last year, when I insisted I wanted to sign on to *I'm Sure She's Fine*. I think I have, like, one sex scene, so he got over it." She clears her throat. "Anyway, earlier this year… and I've never told anyone except my sister about this before," she says, eyes darting around the room once again. "But I found messages." Her voice is no more than a whisper now, but her eyes are wide and telling.

"What kind of messages?" Naomi asks.

Meghan shakes her head, a look of disgust on her face.

"Disgusting, perverted messages. To multiple women." She blushes. "We had a great sex life, especially in the beginning. Couldn't keep our hands off each other. And I enjoy it a little rough. Hair-pulling, all that. But, apparently, that wasn't enough for him. And when I turned down his more… hardcore… requests, he searched for it elsewhere…"

Meghan's hands tremble as she clasps her mug of tea, bringing it to her red lips.

"Would you mind sharing what sort of requests? And you're sure they couldn't have been taken out of context? Just kinky stuff?"

Meghan scoffs. "Call me a prude, but saying things like you want to slice little pieces of flesh off someone to cook and eat, or that you want to slit someone's throat just enough so they bleed but don't die so you can fuck them while they teeter on the line of life and death is more than 'just kinky.'"

Naomi's eyes widen, sure she misheard her. But then she recalls the words from the model at the club. *My friend slept with him, said he was vile. To stay away.* She swallows her growing nausea, thinking of the blind item and Jade's bruising, Faye's injury.

"Like rape fantasies..."

Meghan nods, face paling.

Naomi can't imagine how anyone could be into something so depraved, let alone put it in writing, but she knows how fucked-up people can be. It tends to be the ones you least expect too. Cold and calculating behind the scenes, meticulously careful until they get cocky, confident they'll never get caught, and finally they make a mistake. Goosebumps prickle her arms as she thinks of all the horrible people still out there, getting away with whatever they want.

She breathes out a shaky exhale, forcing herself not to think of what her sister possibly went through.

"Do you know if he was into choking specifically?" she asks.

Meghan tenses and then nods.

Naomi's heart rate spikes at the confirmation. "And how did you find the DMs? Were you looking through his phone because you had suspicions or did someone tip you off?"

Meghan purses her lips, then sighs. "I rarely did things

like that. I prefer an ignorance-is-bliss approach. Don't go looking for things you don't want to find. But he'd been acting… off. And my intuition just told me to look."

Naomi opens her mouth to speak but Meghan continues. "Oh, and there is one thing I forgot to mention. Before all this—we're talking 2022—literally just months after we got engaged, I got a message. Something like 'He's not the perfect man you think he is. He's a monster.' But I'd received so many messages over social, especially from so many Harlow fans who hated me, so I just ignored it. After that point I almost never checked my socials, handed them off to my PR team. But yeah, when I found the DMs later, I remembered that message. Assumed it was one of the women he… you know."

"When in 2022?"

"January… February maybe?"

Naomi bites the inside of her lip, nodding as nausea roils through the pit in her stomach. Less than five months after Jade. Only one month before Faye.

"Do you have the username?"

"It was just 'user' something followed by random numbers. I checked afterward because I wanted to go back and ask questions but they never responded. Account deleted."

"So you say you found these messages on his phone. Did you confront him?"

"I did. I threw his phone at him, one of the messages open on the screen. Asked him what the fuck they were." She laughs angrily as she turns away from Naomi. "I was desperate for them not to be true. He begged me to stay, told me they were from when I was filming away for months and he was weak… and, goddamn him, I wanted to believe it so badly. I tried to work through it. But I just couldn't get those messages out of my head. His words. Like he was Jekyll and Hyde, you know? And I couldn't continue sleeping next to a monster. So the next day, when he left for work, I called my dad, packed my bags, and got the hell out of there. Went back to Indiana for a bit."

"How did he take it?"

"Not well. I think he tried to call me fifty times. Showed up to my parents' house. My dad had to threaten him with a gun to get off the property. And the anger in Colton's eyes. He was so angry, I almost left with him then and there, worried he'd rain hell and highwater on my parents." Meghan tucks a lock of golden hair behind her ear as her eyes fill with tears.

"But I stood my ground. Told him if he didn't leave me be I'd send screenshots of the messages to every news outlet in the country. And I think it spooked him."

"Do you still have the screenshots?" Naomi asks.

"No," Meghan says. "I actually never even took any. Stupid, I know. But he didn't know I was lying."

"And is that when you got slapped with the NDA?"

Meghan nods. "The terms were that he wouldn't speak negatively about me but that I couldn't speak about him at all. I knew it was unfair but I didn't care. Just wanted to put it all behind me. So I signed it, wanting to be done. He was due to start filming the sequel to *Mr. America* so thankfully he was distracted. Contractually obligated to be elsewhere."

Naomi is about to ask if she dropped out of the project because of Colton, but then she remembers Meghan's character gets killed off in the first film by the villain, who follows her back to her apartment from a hotel bar. Suddenly, Naomi is more aware of a man dressed in black who's been lingering at the end of the room, staring at his phone. *Has he been listening?* She shivers, despite the heat emanating from the fire nearby.

Meghan moves her head, which blocks the man from her peripheral vision, and Naomi is brought back to the present.

"So when you guys got engaged, he seemed fine. Normal? Because if I have the timeline accurate... you got engaged right in between the two murders."

She shifts uncomfortably, eyes downcast. "I was so smitten with him. Like, head-over-heels, blind love. Now we know how blind, I guess... but yeah, the only problems or fights we had during that time had to do with Harlow."

Naomi notices the change in her tone from wistful to irritated as the conversation shifts to Harlow. "What was your experience with her?"

"Well, when we first got engaged... she was... she showed up a few times. They'd get into these heated arguments." Meghan waves her hand. "I don't hold it against her, though. She was young." Meghan's gray eyes stare back at Naomi. "I really thought she had grown up a little, but not so sure now."

"So even knowing now what you know about Colton, you still think she could be..." Naomi searches for the right question. "Do you ever think she'd go so far as to kill him?"

"I would like to think not," Meghan shrugs. "But if I had her fire or temper... maybe I would've killed him after finding those DMs. Instead, I just succumbed to my own cowardice and scurried away." Her eyes glisten as she looks to the side.

The admission slightly annoys Naomi, who can't help but judge Meghan for letting Colton continue to roam free for so long. But then she corrects herself. Meghan isn't to blame. Colton is.

"I mean, it took me two years to notice his dark side, so maybe she didn't know," Meghan continues. "But honestly, I don't see how she couldn't have. The way they broke up and then would get back together. It was so toxic." Meghan throws her hands in the air. "I mean, she was with him for, like, six years? I honestly don't see how she couldn't have known."

Naomi feels warm again, her blood starting to boil as she thinks about Harlow. Despite Colton turning out to be a villain in all this, she's still not convinced Harlow is completely innocent, her intuition still telling her she either knew what he was doing or was involved herself.

Meghan sighs deeply. "Once again, I'm so sorry about your sister. Truly. And I'll never forgive myself for not saying anything."

"Maybe you can help me make things right one day," Naomi says, imagining writing an exposé on Colton Scott.

Megan laughs, unamused. "If I can give you any sort of advice, it's to never, ever mess with the Scott family. Please trust me on that." She looks Naomi dead in the eye when she says this, making sure she's hearing her. "Plus, Colton is dead. Can't hurt anyone else now. If you want answers…"

Naomi finishes her sentence. "There's only one person left to talk to."

It's strange how time quickens or slows depending on the situation. Like when Naomi is on the verge of cracking a story, time flies and there's never enough of it. Whereas now, as she waits for the F Train back to Greenwich Village in a dark, dank subway tunnel, time has stalled. Each minute taking an eternity to pass.

The station is nothing special. An underground mosaic and cement tunnel like every other that smells like trash and piss. Naomi spots a boarded-up hole in the wall and walks toward it. She tugs on a note pinned to the boards. "Newsstand closed due to Covid-19." Naomi shakes her head, imagining the sign being taped up four and half years ago, when everything shut down. It still shocks her how many businesses never recovered.

She walks toward the platform, standing away from the edge. A man walks in front of her and her heart starts to race. *Is that the guy from the hotel?*

She swallows, feeling sweat prickle on her forehead. She thinks of the other times this week when she's felt like she's being followed. Watched. She thinks of what Meghan said about fearing the Scott family. What if they knew they were meeting? What if they were listening?

"Come on, come on," Naomi whispers at the distant whir of a train down the tunnel, urging it to arrive. She grips the bottle of pepper spray in her purse, letting go once the train screeches to a halt in front of her.

She feels safer onboard, surrounded by people. She thinks about everything she learned from Meghan and what that means for the murders. Her stomach churns, thinking of her sister and Jade suffering something abhorrent at the hands of Colton Scott. She laughs in disgust when her eyes land on something scribbled in permanent marker on the door.

"RIP Colton Scott, forever our hero."

She wants to vomit. Wants to yell from the rooftops what a sick fuck he is.

But she wouldn't be hasty again, not like last time. If she wants to save what's left of her journalistic credibility, she'll need to do things properly. Get evidence, real proof, before she publishes anything. Which leads her straight back to the woman at the center of it all—the only one with answers.

Harlow Hayes.

Harlow

One Month Before the Murder

I crossed and uncrossed my legs, thumping them against the couch as I waited in the colorful seating area surrounded by patchwork cushions and blankets. Inhaling the warm, woody incense burning nearby, I admired the familiar surrealist art on the wall. Every time I sat here, I saw something different. Today, the paint strokes showed me a woman, but with two faces, one smiling, one screaming. I looked away, feeling uneasy.

It had been two months since Colton showed up at my hotel room in Paris, furious. He'd come to confront me, claiming I had some sort of vendetta against him.

I recoiled as I remembered the fight that had ensued. Him stalking toward me, clamping a hand around my mouth when I'd said something he hadn't liked.

"Remember, if I go down, so do you."

I remembered struggling beneath his grip, lashing out before he eventually let me go, satisfied with himself. I remembered his disgusting smirk. Me throwing a bottle of champagne against the wall, glass shattering around him. Him throwing my bottle of pills at me, calling me crazy. Him leaving, delivering his final threat.

"Don't do anything fucking stupid, Har. I'll know if you do."

I jumped as the door to my left opened and Dr. Grayson called my name, pulling me out of the traumatic memory. Sunlight spilled in through the window behind her, framing her in a golden aura like a saint.

"How have you been?" she said as I entered her office. She motioned for me to take a seat on the cream sofa.

I sat with my palms under my legs, trying to wipe off the sweat. "I've been okay, thanks. You?"

"I'm well, thank you." Dr. Grayson took a seat in her swivel chair across from me. Dressed in her classic style of a beige-toned neutral sweater and matching slacks, she wore her gray-blonde hair as she usually did, in a neat, low bun.

"Can you elaborate on 'okay' for me?" she asked. "What does that mean for you?"

"Um... well, you know, the usual ups and downs," I replied. "But I've been good this week in terms of the pills—managed to not take any again."

After my fight with Colton, I'd been so distraught that I ended up downing an entire bottle. I'd thrown them up almost immediately after, panicking at what I'd done. But it'd shocked me into realizing that I really did need help. That I couldn't continue on this path of self-destruction. I knew if I truly wanted to sever any sort of connection with Colton, any sort of control he had over me, I had to first sort myself out. And Dr. Grayson had been there for me every step of the way, helping me see that Colton was just as toxic as the pills.

Dr. Grayson eyed her notes and then looked up at me,

smiling. "That marks two months, Harlow. That's a huge achievement, you should be very proud of yourself."

My face flushed at the look of pride on her face. My mother had always been so tough on me growing up, always pointing out my flaws, barely celebrating my wins, that I rarely ever was proud of myself. Pride was reserved for winning awards or performing perfectly. Not for abstaining from drugs, something that isn't even a challenge for most people. But most people had no idea of the power an addiction could hold over you. How your body begged you for the thing you were trying so hard to avoid, reliant on the poison more than air, more than water. How your mind was a warzone, the logical voice drowned out by the cruel whispers wielding intrusive thoughts and painful memories as weapons to cast you down.

"And how's everything else going?" Dr. Grayson asked. "I know you mentioned last time that there was something that had upset you with work?"

I pressed my lips together, stiffening at the reminder. "Yeah, there's been some disagreement over some of the tracks that should feature on the next album," I said, ignoring the thing that had upset me the most. "I'm meeting with Sam next week to talk about everything, hopefully iron things out."

It was funny how life worked, how when you felt like you got control back in one area, it slipped in another. Sam and Charlie, my label head, had become increasingly overbearing and controlling of my work recently, even more so than in the past. I understood to an extent—I'd lost focus—but soon everything would be back to normal.

"That's good. Remember what I told you, about standing up for yourself? If there's a song you really love, fight for it."

I nodded. "There is a song I feel really connected to, actually. It's about being caught between a rock and a hard place, not knowing if what's best for you is actually the right thing to do. How every option feels wrong, so you just stay silent. Do nothing."

Dr. Grayson studied me, nodding in understanding. "It's so great that you have a creative outlet to explore those topics. Do you mind if I ask what inspired that song? Is it something you'd like to discuss, talk through with me too?"

"Um…" I looked down at my nails, surprised by how far my acrylics had grown out, wondering what to say as I thought about the inspiration for the song.

Tick, tick, tick. The clock was nearly as loud as my thumping heart.

"Well," I mused, ignoring her question. "I guess it would be useful to get your opinion…"

"Of course."

I cleared my throat. "If you knew someone was… bad, let's say… but you knew no one would believe you because you didn't necessarily have evidence, what would you do?"

"Is this about Colton?" she asked. Dr. Grayson had already made clear her dislike for Colton during previous sessions, highlighting his track record of manipulative, coercive behavior based on how I described our relationship over the years, things I had never flagged before.

"Don't do anything fucking stupid, Har. I'll know if you do."

"I'd rather not say," I replied, feeling unsettled by his

threat. *What if she's working for them?* I quickly shook the ridiculous thought off, couldn't let myself spiral like that.

"Well," Dr. Grayson sighed. "If I thought this person was a danger to other people, I would tell someone. Even if it's not enough to have someone arrested right away, maybe exposing that person could result in 'trial by media,' which could then lead to a criminal investigation, once the professionals have a chance to look into it. We've seen that before, like with the MeToo movement and Weinstein. So yes, depending on what it is, of course, I'd speak up. Tell them my story, if I experienced or saw anything first-hand."

My mind raced through all the potential consequences of talking. Colton's wrath, or, worse, his family's. And where that would lead. Ruined career and reputation. *They'll come for you*, I thought, unsure if I was more scared of the Scotts or the public's reaction for bringing down the nation's golden boy. Not to mention potential jail time…

"But what if by talking… you incriminate yourself?"

Dr. Grayson frowned, studying me. I swallowed hard, not wanting to imagine what she'd think of me if she knew the truth.

"Well, I'm a big believer in the phrase 'The truth will set you free.'" She shrugged. "So take from that what you will."

I tossed and turned in bed that night, thinking about what Dr. Grayson had said.

"The truth will set you free."

Was she right? Was coming clean the only way to truly regain control—over myself and my career? My life? But I couldn't bear the thought of that. Of the consequences. Not until I explored every other avenue first—see if there was any way to take Colton down without implicating myself.

"If I go down, so do you."

Unable to sleep, I got up and poured myself a scotch. The bottle, which I'd only bought two days ago, was nearly half gone. I told Dr. Grayson I'd given up pills, which was the truth. I just left out that I'd replaced them with more alcohol.

I stumbled from the kitchen to the window, wincing in pain as my hip bone collided with the edge of the table, sure to leave a bruise. Looking out across the city skyline from my beautiful glass cage, I thought back to that night in Paris. To the blind item Colton had showed me, the catalyst for him flying halfway across the world to confront me.

In the anonymous social media post, the user had accused an A-list actor of rape and, as expected, people had jumped into the comments trying to guess the culprit. The majority of people seemed to be accusing another actor, but a couple also mentioned that Colton fit the description too due to his "Old Money" status. For some reason, he'd been convinced that I was the reason for this, accusing me of "spreading lies." At the time, I hadn't understood why he'd been so angry about online gossip; there was so much shit out there about every celebrity, true or not. I chalked it up to it being the first time he had read something negative about himself, but even now, months later, my intuition told me that the reason for his intense reaction had been because he was scared someone was onto him.

The thought sent chills up my arms, making me wonder if perhaps there were other things like that out there, more anonymous tips from over the years that could be linked to him.

It was as good a starting point as any—my only lead—so I created a fake email address and anonymously emailed the contact listed on the blind item poster's Instagram profile, offering money in exchange for tips. I didn't explain who I was looking into, though, worried they'd take the info and bring it to the Scotts for an even bigger payout, so I simply asked for any other tips the user had received that were similar to that one—accusations made about famous, beloved actors.

There had to be more out there, it was just a matter of finding things that his family hadn't already wiped from the face of the earth. I downed the rest of the scotch, caressing my throat as the liquid burned on its way down. It was like fuel to a fire, igniting my determination to destroy Colton Scott.

Chapter 31

Trying to plan her next move, Naomi stares at the wall, still organized in sections of "Before," "After," and "During." She wonders if she should take it all down and start again, this time with Colton at the center, but decides to first write out all her new theories and questions on a piece of paper.

Theory 1: Colton is a sick bastard, but not the murderer. Harlow is a potential serial killer, murders Jade (potentially Faye and Bill as well) and then kills Colton when he finds out and blackmails her.

*Theory 2: Colton (accidentally?) chokes Jade to death during sex. Harlow is an accomplice, helps him cover it up. She's traumatized, hence the fall at the VMAs and potential rehab stint later that year. *This doesn't explain Faye, Colton, or the alleged blackmail*

Evidence:

- *Sex tape (of Colton and Jade?)—is this what triggered Harlow?*
- *Model from club said she saw C+H+J walking up the stairs together, looking cozy, at the pre-VMAs party—sex tape*

potentially made this night
- *Harlow's DNA found in Colton's apartment—she claims they were seeing each other again*
- *Text messages between Harlow and Colton show motive; C was blackmailing H—this makes most sense with Theory 1*
*Side note: Could the blackmail have also implicated Colton somehow, which is why the case got shut down? Because his family didn't want this leaking?

*NEW THEORY: Colton and Harlow were in on the killings together!?

Naomi drops the pen, wondering if she's getting too caught up in crazy conspiracies. A million questions swirl in her mind.

Who drugged Jade and dumped her body? Colton? People who worked for his family? Who would have killed Colton years later, aside from Harlow? Could it really just have been suicide? How does Faye's death fit in? And Bill Lever's?

Groaning in frustration, she turns on her heels toward the fridge and twists open a beer. She takes a giant swig, pacing back and forth as she thinks, her intuition telling her she's missing something major. Something that would change everything.

She instinctively opens her TikTok and types "Harlow Hayes theories" into the search bar, hoping she'll see something new from a vigilant fan and have a lightbulb moment. She skips through the videos claiming Harlow is a robot or devil-worshipper and pauses on a video titled "Harlow Hayes Is An Imposter," making her briefly remember her encounter with the artist earlier today. He was so confident the real Paul McCartney died and was replaced by someone else.

The video from user @BorrillsWeerdWorld" opens with a disclaimer, saying that their videos are theories meant for entertainment value and not meant to harm any person or company. Naomi watches as the user comes on screen, their face shakily hovering over an image of Harlow. They start by recapping the title of the video, that they believe Harlow isn't Harlow—not always, at least—and that Harlow either has a body double or "she isn't Harlow Hayes at all."

Naomi sighs, tempted to scroll. But she decides to keep listening, unable to ignore her curiosity, intrigued to know how this person came to such a wild conclusion.

The user launches into a brief bio of Harlow's past, explaining how she got started and rose to fame quickly—so quickly, in their opinion, that she didn't know how to handle it. They did some digging of their own and found out from multiple sources that Harlow wasn't happy.

"She had a toxic on-and-off relationship with Colton Scott and was known for being depressed and unsatisfied with the fame." A B-roll of Harlow crying and looking sad during performances plays in the background while the user explains. "In December 2021, Harlow canceled a few appearances and then came back better than ever in the new year. But also, with some noticeable differences. And no, I'm not talking about her style evolution for *Apotheosis*, I'm talking earlier than that…"

A photo of Harlow appears on screen with the year "2022" at the top. In the image, which appears to be a paparazzi photo, Harlow is looking down, smirking as she walks. An unsettling feeling washes over Naomi, knowing that by this time Harlow could have made her first kill.

"As you can see, this photo is high-res and unedited, probably taken with a really great zoom lens. We can see the sweat on her face here, a bit of puffiness. But what we can also see, if we look closely…"

The user moves, so only their eyes and forehead are visible on screen, as well as their finger, which is circling Harlow's nose.

"… is a prosthetic nose."

Naomi rolls her eyes, annoyed at how desperate people are for views that they make up anything.

"Look closer," the user says, as if they know what Naomi is thinking. The entire screen is now a close-up of Harlow's nose. "See the lines?"

Naomi sits up straight when she notices. She doesn't think it's obvious enough to be positive, but the more she looks at the line slightly curling up beneath Harlow's powder, the more she wonders if it is in fact some kind of prosthetic. But still, Harlow could've just been insecure. This was before she got most of her fillers and other procedures done.

"Like I mentioned in my Avril Lavigne video last week, I think it's possible the label hired a body double to fill in for Harlow when she was struggling, and that at some point Harlow died and they took over completely." The user raises a brow and then in an attempt to remain neutral offers a counter-argument. "On the other hand, the label can make just as much money on an artist's death as they could a replacement, but just humor me for now, okay?"

The image on the screen changes and a side-by-side photo comparison appears, showing an old image of Harlow with a much more recent one from a red-carpet event. The old photo is a sweet shot of innocence, while the new one radiates a darkness Naomi can't quite put her finger on.

The user talks as red circles appear over Harlow's nose and arm, while arrows point to her skin, hair, and teeth. "So these two photos are about seven years apart. On the left we have Harlow circa 2017, after the release of *One Heart*, and on the right is Harlow this past summer in Paris. Before you get annoyed at me, yes, I know people's faces change as they age, that hair color and skin tones can be changed with dye and fake tan, and that makeup can make a huge difference, but it certainly doesn't explain all of... this."

The unnerving feeling in Naomi's stomach grows as she more closely studies the photos. She doesn't want to rule out photo editing, age, or plastic surgery, but the video creator is right; the two Harlows in the photos don't look like the same person. Similar? Yes. But one hundred percent? No.

"Now, let's go from looking to listening..." The user plays a video of Harlow singing in early 2021, followed by one of her singing in 2024. In the first video, her pitch is high, while in the second, it's much lower. The user explains how differences in sound systems can change an artist's sound, but not by that much. Naomi agrees, although she acknowledges that the same artist can often sound completely different when singing in a different genre, so she finds this argument less convincing.

Next, they explain how in recent years, Harlow started signing her autographs in a new way, signaling a change in handwriting, before moving onto some other strange things.

"Here's something really bizarre: One of the names in the credits of Harlow's latest album is Addia S. Howler...

who *doesn't* exist. Could it be a top-secret pseudonym? Or maybe an anagram of Harlow's imposter?"

Even though the photos have made her question herself, Naomi still feels like this whole thing is ridiculous, albeit entertaining. But @BorrillsWeerdWorld reels her in with their final point, when they mention how Harlow guest-starred on a podcast about the Beatles where she said her biggest influence for her latest album was Paul McCartney.

"'Paul is dead' theory, anyone?" they say. "Could Harlow's body double have taken this as inspiration... and then taken things too far? Let me know your thoughts in the comments!"

Naomi eyes the photo she purchased from the street artist earlier. A pit forms in her stomach, expanding with every racing thought.

Harlow

Three Weeks Before the Murder

"There's my girl." Sam stood as I approached the private booth at the back of his favorite restaurant in the West Village.

"Sorry I'm late," I said, giving him a hug. I cringed, knowing the phrase was becoming my new greeting.

"No worries, everything okay?"

I tensed at the question, feeling him studying me. "Yeah, all good. Did you like the recording I sent?" I asked eagerly, leg thumping against the table. "I was actually working on the song before I came here, it's why I was running late." It was a lie, but I wanted Sam to think I was focused on my music and nothing else. "Do you know if Charlie has listened yet?"

I nervously shook my leg up and down as I waited for his reply.

He took a swig of his beer, nodding, but not looking at me. "Right now, he's thinking it might be a little sad for this album, for the direction he's thinking, so maybe it's one we save for the next one. Beautiful song though, I loved it!"

I pressed my lips into a thin smile and nodded. *"If there's a song you really love, fight for it.*" I recalled Dr. Grayson's words, but I wasn't in the mood to fight for it. Not today.

I jumped when the waitress appeared to take our order. I wanted a real drink, but needed Sam to think I was completely clean, that I had everything under control, so I just ordered a water.

"You sure you're okay?" Sam asked again, shattering my hope that I was putting on a good front. "You seem on edge…"

He was right, I was on edge. After reaching out a week ago, I'd finally received a reply from @RavenRumours yesterday, the blind item account. They'd warned me to take everything with a grain of salt; they had no sort of vetting system and just had to go off their hunch whether they thought these stories were true or lies fabricated for attention, as horrible as that sounded.

It was why I was late, because I was trying to compare the anonymous tips with my own knowledge, to see if I could connect any to Colton. Most I didn't think were related to him, but several stood out. Some because I knew he was in the location at the time and the pieces fit—like one about a missing woman in New Mexico—and others just because my gut told me. I knew "my gut feeling" couldn't serve as evidence in court, but it was enough for now.

"What is it?" Sam said, concerned.

My mind warred with my heart over whether to tell him. I'd been so desperate to tell someone what I'd been doing, but didn't trust anyone enough. I could trust Sam, though, right? Even if he was also Colton's manager, I'd known him since I was twenty; he had always looked out for me like an older brother. Searching his warm brown eyes, I remembered the time I showed up to his house, a puddle of tears drenched in the rain, after Colton had told me he wanted to take a break the first time. Sam and his wife had ushered me inside, plying me with tea until I fell asleep on their couch.

I can trust him, I told myself. *It's Sam.*

"I've... come into some information..." I clutched my necklace as I glanced around the empty room, fingering the grooves of the chunky crucifix. "I think... Colton might be a really bad guy."

I could feel my cheeks turn beet-red once the words came out, surprised when Sam's face dropped into a mask of sympathy. He took my hand.

"Harlow, I know the two of you have a long, long history. And breakups are really hard. I have a lot of love for you both."

"No, Sam. Just listen to me, please. It started that night," I whispered. "After the party at your house, before the VMAs..."

Sam rushed to swallow his drink and then started laughing uncomfortably. "Hey, hey, hey, I know you two got in an argument that night, no need—"

"No, that's not it, though, you don't know why—"

"Yes, I do, Harlow, and I think we should leave it." He stared at me sternly and my heart felt like it shattered into a million pieces, realizing he already knew.

My mind battled between helplessness and anger as I tried to find the words. "Okay, well then you know why we need to go to the police!"

He slammed his beer on the table, face growing red as he

turned to me. "With what evidence?" he snapped. "You're going to say... what?"

A fresh wave of embarrassment washed over me as I realized what a fool I'd been. On so many levels. I started to sob.

"Listen, I am trying to help you here," Sam said, softening. "We both know that you can't just make accusations about a member of the Scott family and expect it to be sorted. No, you need cold, hard proof. And a damn good legal team."

I wanted to argue, say I had information on other instances, but I knew what I had wasn't strong enough. I laughed, thinking how five minutes ago I thought my "gut instinct" was worth anything.

"It's just so frustrating," I said, letting out a groan. "To watch him out there... thriving... everyone loving him." I wiped my nose with my sleeve.

"Hey, hey, look at me."

I reluctantly met his gaze.

"It was a long time ago, okay? He's grown up a lot since then. I promise. It's affected him too, believe me."

I rolled my eyes.

"And whatever else you think you might have on him," Sam continued, "if you don't think it's strong enough to bring to the police, then maybe it's nothing. Okay? So promise me you'll keep this between us? For your own safety."

I bit the inside of my lip, thinking maybe I was wrong. But deep down, I knew I wasn't. I just needed more evidence.

"Fine," I replied, deciding it was best to appease Sam for

now, hoping I could use it to my advantage. "As long as you pull the plug on that other thing."

Sam pursed his lips, nodding. "I'll see what I can do."

Present Day

All my life people have underestimated me. Thought they were better than me. Tried to control me. So once I earned my place, understood the power I had, I wasn't going to let it go. I was finally going to use it. It felt so good—almost euphoric—to take back control. Be the one holding the power. But then it was almost taken from me. Because I was careless.

Stay away. Stay out of it. The words still echo in my mind.

But I didn't listen. I let my guard down and then it was too late. If I wanted to keep my secrets safe, I needed to act. I figured I was already going to hell, had already sold my soul, so it made my decision easy.

You probably sensed it, but I've always had a darkness in me. I just hadn't fully embraced it.

Chapter 32

According to the theorists, Paul McCartney died in a car accident in 1966 and the band—and allegedly British intelligence services—replaced him with an imposter. The first article on the conspiracy was published in an Iowa university's student newspaper in September of 1969, but public interest peaked the following month when a caller told a Detroit radio host to put on the Beatles' *White Album* and to spin the intro from "Revolution 9" backward. When the host played it, he confirmed that he heard the words "Turn me on, dead man." After that, the rumor quickly spread across the nation, prompting other radio hosts to discuss the theory on air as fans searched for even more clues in the band's music, especially in the newly released *Abbey Road*.

And now, fifty-five years later, there are detailed articles, subreddits, social media threads, videos, and even entire websites dedicated to the topic.

Naomi knows about Beatlemania—who doesn't—but she's still shocked to see how deep the theory goes. As she continues to read about it, she discovers that some fans believe the album cover for *Abbey Road* is symbolic of a funeral procession, with John as the preacher in white, Ringo as the undertaker in black, Imposter Paul as the barefoot corpse, and George as the gravedigger in denim. Fans point out that Paul is holding a cigarette in his right hand, even though the "real Paul" was a lefty, and they also reference the license plate of the Volkswagen in the background as a sign, saying "28 IF" is how old Paul would have been *if* he were alive.

Diving deeper, Naomi learns that it's not just *Abbey Road* that holds clues, but *Sgt. Pepper's Lonely Hearts Club Band* as well. Naomi studies an image of the cover shot, which features the four members of the Beatles in colorful band outfits. Behind the quartet is a crowd, made up of various cut-outs and images of celebrities and other notable faces, like Marilyn Monroe and Edgar Allan Poe. Red flowers in front of the group spell out *BEATLES*. According to some fans, though, the cover includes a treasure trove of clues from the band, hinting that Paul is in fact dead. A fansite's blog post breaks it down, claiming that the black color of Paul's instrument represents death, while the wood represents a coffin. Then, there is the fact that Paul is facing straight, while the others are angled toward him, almost like they're propping him up—like a corpse. Finally, there are the flowers: Red hyacinths aka the mythological flower for death, which are reminiscent of a memorial, inferring that the entire album cover could be symbolizing a burial ceremony... Paul's burial specifically, since the yellow hyacinths next to the red ones spell out the letter "P" when turned sideways.

Naomi laughs in astonishment. She knows it's ridiculous to even consider whether it's true or not, but the incredibly specific details make the theory hard to dismiss. She also knows the more she digs online, the crazier and deeper the conspiracy will get, so instead she decides to call someone who she trusts. Someone level-headed and logical.

"Naomi?" Joel answers. "Everything alright?"

"All good," she says, her face flushing as she thinks of their conversation earlier this morning. She pitches her voice higher than usual, feigning innocence. "I just wanted to quickly ask you about something if that's okay? It's nothing to do with... you know..." She doesn't dare speak Harlow's name to him.

"Okay..." She can hear the trepidation in his voice.

"So I've been doing what you said, taking a break and trying to forget about the case..." She clears her throat, hoping he can't tell she's lying. "And in my quest to distract myself I've stumbled across something really interesting. Something you actually mentioned to me before, to do with the Beatles..."

"Oh yeah?" He sounds intrigued.

"Yeah, you briefly mentioned the 'Paul is dead' theory a few days ago, and then today I met a street artist who truly subscribed to the conspiracy. That then prompted me to research it a bit more, which then made me think an article on it could be of interest to our readers. I already did some research but wanted to see if you think I'm missing anything and if it sounds like a good piece."

Her heart thumps wildly in her chest as she waits for him to respond, hoping he doesn't see through her half-truths.

"Hmmm, that could work as a feature piece... what do you want to know?"

After exhaling a sigh of relief, Naomi explains everything she's learned and pauses for Joel's reaction.

"I'm impressed," he says. "You got most of it."

"What am I missing?"

"Okay, well at the end of 'I Am the Walrus,' you can hear 'O, untimely death!' from a broadcast of King Lear."

"Interesting..." Naomi's eyes widen, intrigued, as she quickly jots it down.

"If you think that's good," Joel continues, "you'll have a great time with this one... So it sounds like you're aware of most of the clues from the front of the iconic *Abbey Road* album cover. But did you also know that if you hold a butter knife to the back cover, you can see a reflection of a human skull?"

Naomi's head spins as a memory comes to her. One of her mom doing something with a butter knife and an album in the kitchen.

"Oh, and you can't forget about 'Strawberry Fields Forever,' where at the end of it John Lennon mumbles 'I buried Paul.'"

"Seriously?" Naomi laughs. "I can't believe I never heard all this before."

"Well, it's just a conspiracy theory, obviously. He's not actually dead..."

"Right, of course," Naomi says, not one-hundred-percent certain anymore. "But say he was, are there any theories about the imposter? Like who they are—were?"

"Oh yeah, apparently some guy named Willy—no, Billy—something. Billy Shears, I think, although a lot of fans think Ringo is Billy, but I won't get into that."

Naomi freezes, sure that name means something to her.

She furrows her brow, racking her brain. Joel continues to ramble, mentioning a look-alike contest and something about "A Day in the Life" and "With A Little Help From My Friends."

She's barely listening, though, her brain instead recalling Harlow's lyrics. "Oh my god," she says when it hits her.

"Crazy, right?" Joel replies, thinking she's responding to him. "Anyway, I've gotta run, but let me know if you have any other questions while you write."

She thanks him before hanging up, feeling like she's in a daze. Fueled by adrenaline, Naomi immediately reaches for her Harlow albums. She studies the onyx black cover of *Apotheosis*, embossed with layers of images that she previously overlooked, before pulling out the lyric booklet inside. And there it is, right in front of her, under "No Way Back":

Hey Billy, help me understand. How did you live with yourself, when it all got out of hand?

Was Harlow actually singing about Billy Shears, Paul McCartney's rumored replacement, and not Bill Lever? As Naomi grapples with whether it's just a coincidence or a bombshell discovery, her eyes land on the glossy *Legacy* vinyl cover, sitting upside-down on the floor next to *Apotheosis*.

In the artwork, Harlow is wearing a red jacket, the bright color in contrast with the dried-up, empty field in the background. But as Naomi looks closer, she sees that Harlow isn't in just any field.

She's standing in a dead *strawberry* field.

Harlow

The Day of the Murder

I ran a finger across my broken nail, jagged and sharp, imagining what it would feel like to scratch Colton with it and watch him bleed. It was what he deserved, I was sure of it now.

I shook my head, sickened at how I almost let Sam trick me into thinking Colton wasn't a bad person. In truth, we were all bad people, but Colton was the bottom of the barrel.

I looked around my Manhattan apartment as I read over the newest additions to my digital folder, worried someone was spying on me through the glass windows with some military-grade camera, watching what I was doing.

"Don't do anything stupid, Har. I'll know if you do."

I shifted in my seat, making sure no camera could see my screen, filled with my own witness testimony plus new intel from @RavenRumours. I'd asked them to look further into a few select tips and, without even asking for more money, they did. I had been careful not to make it obvious from their end who I was investigating, just to be safe.

I don't know who you're trying to take down, but I hope you get the bastard, their message read, alongside crime scene photos, hospital records, and other documents—things that, when combined with my own knowledge, painted a horrifying picture.

But infuriatingly, even though I could put the pieces together, even though I had proof that Colton was in the area around the time a couple women that fit his type went missing or died in drug-related deaths, I knew it still wouldn't be enough to take him down. There wasn't much that would be admissible in court. He covered his tracks well and if I tried to expose him using only the random files, no matter how horrific they were, he'd get out of it. And then he'd bury me instead.

Sam's voice resounded in my mind. *"You can't just make accusations about a member of the Scott family … No, you need cold, hard proof. And a damn good legal team."*

Creeeeak. I froze at the noise behind me, whipping my head around. *It's just the pipes*, I told myself, looking back at the screen. At the blinking cursor next to where I just signed my name.

The only thing that would mean something to a jury, to the police, would be my testimony. But coming clean about what happened would mean I'd go down too, like Colton had warned. Sam would have also been at risk, but it wasn't like he had kept his word to me about the one thing I had asked, so why should I have kept mine?

It still won't be enough, a voice cautioned, making me want to throw my laptop across the room. I smacked my forehead, groaning in frustration as I weighed my other options.

You could find a way to live with the guilt, just let it go.
But I'd tried that, hadn't I?

You could kill him… And then expose him posthumously… he wouldn't be around to say you had anything to do with it…

I balked at the idea, not even taking it seriously. It was wrong. And messy.

But wouldn't it be a relief? To have him out of the picture forever? To know he could never hurt anyone else?

I swatted the voice away.

Craning my neck, I darted my eyes across the room, once again making sure I was alone, before ejecting the USB. I wished I could slot it into my skin to keep it safe; for all I knew, the Scotts were already onto me and would send their people in to extract the files when I wasn't home, tearing every single one of my properties apart until they found them. I picked up my phone, wanting to check the live feed of the new security cameras I had installed outside of my door and throughout the rest of the house, but got distracted by a notification waiting for me.

What the fuck… My heart hammered with every second I watched, switching between rage, devastation, and a sense of powerlessness.

But you're not powerless, I thought, blood boiling. I *could* do something. I could take back control. *You can put an end to this. Right now.*

I grabbed my keys and slammed the door behind me, ready to do what I should've done long before.

I tried to calm myself as I drove through the city streets, trying to focus. *Three things you can hear. Three things you can see.* But all I could see was red.

Chapter 33

Naomi searches "Harlow Hayes and the Beatles" to see if Harlow ever made any references about them specifically or the Paul theory over the years, aside from paying homage on her album cover and the possible lyrics about Billy Shears.

A slew of results load, showing everything from videos of Harlow covering their songs to fan edits to news articles. The first headline, dated from last year, reads, "Harlow Hayes Rescues Two Pups and Names Them after Beatles Members."

Lennon and Ringo, Naomi shakes her head. It had been in front of her face the entire time. She just didn't know what she was looking for.

The next reference she finds is from an "unofficial Beatles podcast" that Harlow appeared on, where she mentioned her love for Paul McCartney and how he was a major influence on her latest album, *Legacy*.

The podcast only has ten episodes, so Naomi puts it on double speed and listens for anything else that might be important, but there isn't much else. However, one of the episodes prior to the one where Harlow guest-starred goes into depth on the "Paul is dead" theory. So while Harlow never mentions the theory herself, she made an indirect reference by simply being on the show and by saying he influenced her latest album.

Naomi plays back the line, analyzing exactly what Harlow says and how she says it, and realizes she's referring to being influenced by the way the Beatles left Easter eggs about Paul in their albums.

She stares at the back cover of *Legacy* again, where Harlow's standing with the red jacket, looking down, in the dead strawberry field. Chills run down Naomi's arms when she remembers that Faye is potentially another victim in all this.

Could Harlow looking down symbolize her looking at a grave? Could the red jacket symbolize blood?

Both Joel and the podcast host said fans found hidden messages on the front and back covers of the Beatles albums by holding a mirror up to them. An idea dawns on Naomi. She runs into her bathroom and grabs a mini eye shadow palette that has a mirror on the top. She holds it to the back cover of *Legacy* and sees a hyacinth flower appear in the top-left corner of the cover, where the sun rays are parting through the clouds.

She checks the lyric poster to see if the flower exists elsewhere and pauses on "Garden of Bones," the album's fifth track. Next to the title is a yellow hyacinth flower, like that used on the cover of the Beatles' *Sgt. Pepper's* album—the yellow hyacinth believed by theorists to form a P to mourn Paul. Her heart is racing. This cannot be a coincidence.

She analyzes the glossy paper, looking for something out of the ordinary. She checks for odd spacing in the lyrics.

Nothing.

She checks for unusual capitalized letters.

Nothing.

But then she notices a familiar name in the songwriting credits—Addia S. Howler. *They don't exist*, she recalls the TikToker claiming in their video. *Maybe it's an anagram, who knows.*

Naomi grabs a piece of paper and scrawls down the letters in a circle, mixing them up—a strategy Amelia taught her when they went to a quiz night. She first tries to form names, mixing letters in various combinations. It doesn't take her long to find it. *Harlow.*

Naomi frowns, not expecting that to be it. But she shrugs and crosses the letters out, seeing she's left with I-S-E-A-D-D.

A wave of mixed emotions, horror and satisfaction, crashes over her as she cracks it. Addia S. Howler isn't an anagram for another name. It's an anagram for a statement. The confirmation she's been looking for.

Harlow. Is. Dead.

Naomi's hands, her legs—everything is trembling. She gets up and starts pacing, taking deep breaths as if there isn't enough oxygen in the room. Is this some twisted homage to Paul and the Beatles? A joke? A coincidence?

She can't believe she's even open to the idea that this could be real. It's absurd. She only kept watching the imposter video in the first place because she found the idea entertaining. She never imagined it would lead her to these clues, which would actually make her take the theory seriously. That Harlow Hayes is dead, replaced by an imposter.

Naomi walks back to her board and fixates on the note that reads, "DNA wasn't a match." She says the words out loud to herself, repeating them in the form of a question. She recalls what Leo said when he told her that DNA doesn't lie.

DNA is DNA. It doesn't lie.

Maybe the DNA wasn't a match for Harlow Hayes because the Harlow they got the DNA sample from *wasn't* actually Harlow—the one that was with Colton and Jade that night, at least.

No, absolutely no way, she chides herself again. *Don't be ridiculous. You're a reporter for a major outlet. Not an online armchair conspiracy theorist.*

But is it really that implausible? a voice questions.

Naomi has walked around LA before. Seen how similar so many of the "aspiring actresses" look. Hasn't she herself said that Harlow now has an "LA face"?

Then there are all the competition shows, where so many unknown singers showcase vocals better than best-selling artists. Naomi recalls various times where she pretended she was a coach on *The Voice*, closing her eyes before a contestant started singing, only to be positive they were the original artist pranking the panel. But no, they just sounded nearly identical to the star. In fact, judges of these shows often complain how difficult it is to find contestants who sound unique.

Is it really so wild to think someone who looks like Harlow could sound like her as well? Naomi wonders.

There are countless fans out there spending every waking minute trying to look like her and sing like her. Is it really so far-fetched to think that someone achieved it? Not a robot or a clone, but an imposter...

Heart racing, Naomi's eyes dart from one clue to another as it all falls into place. It's as if each piece of relevant evidence is lighting up in her head, like she's John Nash in *A Beautiful Mind*.

She's on the cusp of a huge breakthrough; she can feel it.

Chapter 34

Naomi lets out a long exhale, shaking as she tries to keep focus. Pieces of information, pictures, lyrics, videos—so many things—race through her mind as she grapples with her new theory.

She swallows, trying to ignore the burn at the back of her throat, and studies the section of the wall that denotes when Harlow seemed to change in style, personality, and behavior. It all happened after Jade died. On the left-hand side, or before Jade's death, Harlow is described as being depressed but nice, while on the right, or after Jade's death, Harlow is described as being cold-hearted and rude.

Naomi bites her lips as she frantically scans the wall again, noting the other changes, like the complete reinvention of Harlow's image in 2022. She thinks of all the other pop stars that majorly reinvented themselves at one point—everyone from Taylor Swift, with her groundbreaking *reputation* comeback, to Miley Cyrus' shock transformation from Hannah Montana to her "Wrecking Ball" phase. Even Christina Aguilera did it in the early 2000s. And then, of course, Naomi's favorite, the transformation of Lizzy Grant into the iconic Lana Del Rey. So Harlow reinventing her image doesn't prove someone else took over. But... dying her hair and changing her image would be a genius way to cover up the fact that she isn't the real Harlow. It would certainly explain the change in sound too. The imposter would have a different voice, different lyrics, and a different musical style—albeit similar enough for it to be believable.

Naomi slams the enter key on her laptop, impatiently waiting for it to wake up. Once she opens Chrome, she searches for celebrity body doubles. She scans through all of the results, learning it's not as uncommon as one would think.

It turns out management companies use body doubles often, kind of like how actors use stunt doubles, to fill in for certain things like promos and meet-and-greets. Naomi even learns that Miley Cyrus briefly used a body double for a small part on her "Best of Both Worlds" tour. After a fan recorded Miley sneaking through a trap door while someone else dressed as her Hannah Montana alter ego continued to perform, management had to come forward and admit the truth. Of course, Miley was playing two characters, so the situation was understandable. But the most notorious pop star body double-related theory out there is about Avril Lavigne, who tons of true crime enthusiasts believe died and has been covertly replaced by her body double, Melissa.

When Harlow reinvented herself for the launch of *Apotheosis*, the album was all about revenge and other dark themes, and while *Legacy* was similar, it also had other themes running through it. Rebirth, immortality, and remorse. Naomi scans the various excerpts of lyrics stuck to the wall and on the table next to her, landing on "Garden of Bones."

A garden of bones, watered by tears. Blood-soaked soil, saturated with fear. No one knows I laid her here. Alongside a part of me buried here for years.

Naomi exhales a shaky breath as the words take on a brand-new meaning.

In the "Garden of Bones" music video, Harlow is pictured burying herself. And while Naomi used to think it was all metaphoric, now she wonders if it was Imposter Harlow reenacting burying the real Harlow. Then there's the music video for "Cruel Delights" where Harlow is wearing an orange jumpsuit and dancing behind a cage. Was she hinting she should be in jail for what she did?

Naomi removes the header above the red string and replaces it with "Imposter Replaces/Kills Harlow!" and "Addia S. Howler Anagram for HARLOW IS DEAD." Then she takes a step back, stopping to think about the implications of it all.

She thinks of the Avril conspiracy theory, how management was rumored to be behind it. She tenses as an uneasiness washes over her. Sam Brixton recognizing her at the funeral. Then the Toyota following her. The man on the subway. Joel mentioning how angry Sam was and to back off…

Did Sam want to make sure no one found out about Harlow's replacement? And he knew if any reporter would go digging, it would be Naomi, since her sister was a victim in all of this?

Nausea ripples through her as she considers how big a cover-up this could be. She can't stop digging, though, not when everything is finally starting to fall into place.

Not when she's finally figured out that Harlow Hayes was replaced by an imposter at some point after her third album.

This can't be real.

This can't be real.

This is crazy.

But what if...

Naomi freezes, a thought occurring to her.

Could this be the blackmail Colton was holding over Harlow—fake Harlow? That he knew she was an imposter?

Naomi never thought it made sense for Harlow to kill him so long after he killed Jade. It was one of the major holes in her latest theory that Harlow witnessed Colton kill Jade and felt guilty about covering it up. But with this theory, killing Colton when she did makes all the sense in the world. He was going to reveal her secret and she couldn't have that happen.

Bingo, she thinks, adrenaline gushing through her like electricity. *Got ya, bitch.*

Naomi inhales and picks up the album, to search for any more clues as to her identity. She thinks of all the Easter eggs in Harlow's music, realizing they were all from the imposter since she took over during *Apotheosis*. Maybe she left more clues, ones Naomi didn't even know to search for. She'd have to study everything from a completely new angle now...

She looks over the back cover again, the one of Harlow's imposter in the strawberry field. She hits herself on the head, guffawing, as she realizes something else she didn't see before. She feels giddy, delirious.

She recalls the block lettering on the back cover of the Beatles' *Abbey Road* album cover and how fans realized that by organizing the blocks, a message was formed: "Be at Le Abbey RO." According to fans, the RO is part of the message as they refer to the eighteenth and fifteenth letters in the alphabet. And if you add them together, you get thirty-three. Since C is the third letter in the alphabet, the message would be "CC." CeCe is a nickname for Cecilia. And so, fans believe the message says Paul was buried at St. Cecilia's Abbey, a monastery in Ryde, Isle of Wight.

Naomi puts the block letters together and frowns at the message they form, "H7W2QR." She cocks her head to the side, wondering if it's even a message at all. But then she wonders if it's like the RO in the *Abbey Road* secret message. She writes down the corresponding number to each letter of the alphabet and tries multiplying, adding, dividing, and even subtracting.

But nothing makes sense.

She wonders if this is even an Easter egg at all and if she's lost the plot completely. So she discards it and goes back to the song where she found the anagram for "Harlow is dead" and searches to see if she missed anything. And there she notices two out-of-place letters—N and Y—capitalized in the songwriting credits in a phrase under the name Denis Saint. She looks up "Denis Saint songwriter" and, like Addia S. Howler, the name doesn't seem to exist. At all.

Blood pulses in her ears. *Another anagram? But for what?*

She tries to decode the name but again, none of the combinations make sense. She stares at capital N and Y, and the state comes to mind. Her heart drops the second her brain pieces together the location: St. Denis Church in New York.

Naomi blinks rapidly as she types the address into Google Maps, a horrible sinking feeling setting in.

"This can't be happening," she mutters, the hairs on her arms standing to attention.

But as she clicks into the directions, she lets out a gasp, realizing it really is. Because on the bottom of the Google sidebar is a pin location with the matching code "H7W2+QR."

She sits back in her chair, not believing where the trail of clues leads.

To her sister's gravesite.

Chapter 35

After navigating the tail end of rush-hour traffic, it's pitch black by the time Naomi makes it to the graveyard. She decided to rent a car instead of taking the train and then a taxi, thinking she wanted to be alone while she did this, but as she stares out at the cemetery, shrouded in darkness on an eerie October night, she wishes she had the comfort of a cab driver nearby.

Well, you're here now, she thinks, forcing herself out of the car.

A heavy mist greets Naomi as she steps outside, dim rays from the blood-orange moon bellowing down on her. Her stomach roils with dread, still disbelieving that a Harlow Hayes Easter egg led her here.

This was not how she intended to visit her sister's grave for the first time. She should've been walking in the sunshine, carrying a beautiful bouquet of wildflowers, not clinging to a can of pepper spray as crows squawk in the distance. She was supposed to come here *after* she uncovered the truth about Harlow. She never imagined that her search would lead her here before then. That her sister would somehow be a part of this mess. Whether her sister was a victim of

Colton, real Harlow, or fake Harlow, she still doesn't know. But if she continues analyzing Harlow's music and albums, will she find even more victims? Like a sick, depraved scavenger hunt?

This is fucking crazy, she thinks, continuing forward.

She stops, whirling around at the sound of rustling in the trees. Warning bells blare in her head, and the hairs on her arms stand on high alert, telling her to leave. But she can't. She won't. She needs to see this through. She needs to get justice for Faye.

She picks up her pace, dead leaves swirling around her as she rushes forward, before her feet cement to the ground, as if she too is made of stone. Except, unlike the graves and statues, she has a heart that can't stop beating. It's racing a mile a minute as the memories of burying her sister here flash across her mind. Her kneeling at the closed wooden casket. Her whispering goodbye. Her following the procession to the burial site. The lowering of the casket six feet under. And throwing a rose over the grave.

A chill shoots through her as the lyrics to one of Harlow's imposter's songs come to mind. *Until you're laid under a rose-covered grave.*

She shakes her head, trying to shift the memories that cut her like a thousand knives. *Fucking psychopath*, Naomi thinks, growing ever more desperate to ruin this person. But this isn't the time to fantasize about her revenge. That comes next. Now, it's time to find out once and for all who did this to her sister.

Naomi's breath is shallow and shaky as she scans the cemetery with her flashlight, creeping past tombstones until she finds her sister's grave, marked by a statue of an angel, perched gracefully atop a square stone.

It's smaller than she remembers, grass now covering the hole where her casket was lowered. "A 'Garden of Bones,'" Naomi whispers under her breath, recalling the lyrics to the bridge.

A fortress is only as strong as what it's made of. An angel frozen in time. Her haven a kingdom of delicate glass. Shattered and rebuilt into stone made of lime.

Naomi pauses, wondering then if the song is referencing her sister's grave. The last hidden clue led her here, so nothing is out of the realm of possibility now.

She knows she should feel afraid, alone in a cemetery in the dead of night. But now she feels invincible, like she's on the brink of a discovery that will change everything. She moves her flashlight around the site, looking for something, anything that will lead to another clue. And then she spots it. A plaque, laid to the right of the gravestone.

Even though Naomi hasn't visited the site since her sister's funeral, she knows this wasn't there before. She picked the gravestone herself. And this wasn't part of it.

She steps closer, crouching down as she shines her light over it. She squints, trying to make out the writing. *Is it Latin? Or another anagram?* But something tells her it's neither of those.

She reaches into her purse for her compact eyeshadow and holds up the mirror, her breath catching in her throat as her mind processes what the inverted text says.

"Here lies Harlow Hayes."

Harlow

The Murder

Lightning flashed in the distance as I pulled up at the oceanfront property, warning me of a storm on the horizon, urging me to turn back. But I ignored the sign, and instead followed the eerie tune of the guitar to the garden. The sound of blood whooshing in my ears mixed with the foreboding chords to create an off-kilter backing track as I approached. *Whoosh. Strum. Whoosh. Ding. Whoosh. Strum.* It grew louder with every step, hitting its peak as I pushed through the wooden gate.

"It's over," I shouted once I saw her, sitting in *my* rose garden.

The second-rate stand-in Sam hired when I was in rehab two and a half months ago stared at me in confusion, oblivious to my rage.

As I stalked closer, I couldn't believe that I even let this happen in the first place. I should've shut it down the second I found out. I tried, telling Sam I didn't need a stand-in, but he claimed she was only there to help out for a little while. That it was a way for me to focus on my wellbeing while she did the tedious things I didn't want to do anyway. The things I was already not showing up for, like photo ops, radio appearances, or even recording the shitty songs Charlie wanted me to sing instead of my own.

"It's just temporary, to help you and the rest of us out for a little while. Think of it like a stunt double."

So I'd put my faith in Sam. Trusted when he said I was irreplaceable, that he'd pull the plug on it "soon." And I'd been so absorbed in my mission to take Colton down that I hadn't noticed the other predator, trying to creep from the shadows into the spotlight.

My spotlight.

She'd slowly been doing more and more to try and impress Sam and Charlie. Like going from lip-syncing to singing live at shows, and answering interview questions on the fly rather than following a script. And finally, the last straw, recording and performing her own song that was a complete departure from my own tone and style.

When I saw the video, I was just as mad at Sam as I was at her—for allowing *her* to sing *her* songs as *me*, when I couldn't even release *my* music—but I knew it was a waste of time to go to him. I'd already given him three whole weeks to sort it out. Three fucking weeks. And not only had he done nothing, he'd let it get worse.

I'd been allowing people to walk all over me for far too long, from my parents, Sam, Charlie, Colton, the media... But no more.

She stared at me in confusion when I told her she needed to leave. It annoyed me, the blank look on her face after she finally placed her guitar down.

"You need to go," I said again, tempted to shove her into the fountain. "This..." I flailed my hands around. "Is over!"

A cloud covered the setting sun, casting a dark shadow across the usually whimsical space.

"But why? What did I do?" she stammered.

I scoffed, tears now filling my stinging eyes. "You know exactly what you did—are doing. You can't just *be* somebody else. Take over someone else's life because you couldn't make your own, weren't good enough. This is *my* life. *I* built it. Me! It's *mine*!" Thunder rumbled in the distance as I croaked the final word.

A cool breeze blew wisps of hair in front of her face, moments ago a picture of hurt and innocence, now hostile and hardened, fitting in with the stone statues surrounding us.

"You can't fire me, Harlow," she said, crossing her arms. "It's up to Sam and Charlie."

I balled my hands into fists, furious both at her words and the implication of them. That I had no control. That I was powerless.

"I don't need anyone's permission to get rid of you," I spat. "You're nobody! Just a shittier version of me."

She narrowed her eyes at me, shaking her head. I could see the tears in her eyes, though, like I'd hit a sore spot. "You know, I was always such a fan of yours. But I guess this is exactly why they say never meet your idols... And actually," she said, squaring her shoulders, standing her ground. "I think you know that I'm the *better* version of you, and that's what scares you so much."

The words pierced through me as I shook in anger and frustration. Part of me knew she was right. I'd grown so used to hateful comments, especially on my appearance, that when she started doing things and getting positive comments like "Harlow looks better than ever!", it stung.

But how dare she, of all people. I was so, so sick of people disrespecting me and my space. *Don't take your anger out on her*, the logical side of my brain urged, desperately trying to rein me in as my fight-or-flight responses battled each other. But the way she stood there, like a distorted mirror image of me, taunting me through the glass—I couldn't bear it.

I screamed as I reached out, trying to shove her.

But she reacted quickly and grabbed my arms before falling back. It felt like time froze in that moment as we battled for control, eyes locked, arms shaking. Fear replaced my anger when I saw the hostile, volatile expression behind her glare. It was different from the vacant expression in Colton that night, but like him, like me, she didn't have herself under control, that was clear. But it was too late once I realized; she'd already snapped.

A splitting pain cracked through my head as my skull crashed into the hard stone behind me. My ears rang out with muffled silence as I stumbled to the floor. I pressed my hand to my head, immediately pulling back when I felt the sting of the gash.

"Oh my god, oh my god, oh my god." I could hear the words repeating over and over, like an echo. "I didn't mean to. Didn't mean to... Mean to..."

Yes, you did, I wanted to say as I stared at my blood-covered hand. But I couldn't speak, couldn't move.

Am I dying? Is this really how I'm going to go out? I thought, as the pain in my head intensified.

It was poetic, in a way, that this is how it would end. I

was always my own worst enemy. I wanted to laugh at the irony of it all.

No. This isn't real. I'm having a nightmare. My thoughts continued to race. *If I die, will anyone even know? Will they just replace me with this imposter? Surely not. Sam wouldn't. Would he?* But then I realized I didn't care anymore. I was sick of fighting. I'd lost.

You want to be me so badly? Go for it. Enjoy.

I couldn't tell if I said the words out loud or to myself. The throbbing in my head was starting to numb and I could feel myself losing consciousness. As I drifted, I imagined her dealing with the consequences of everything I'd put into play. Dealing with the Scott family. Potentially going to prison herself.

Adrenaline shot through me when the horrifying realization hit. *No, no, no.* I hadn't actually put anything into motion yet. I had some "evidence," but no one knew. I hadn't even set a backup plan with @RavenRumours to leak everything if something happened to me.

If I died, Colton's secrets—and any sort of justice—would die with me.

I used my final bout of energy to yank my necklace off and throw it at her feet. *Take this. You'll need it.*

And then everything went black.

I didn't know how long I'd been out when I briefly regained consciousness. I just remembered feeling cold. So cold.

"Shhh. It's all going to be okay. This is going to help you."

Those were the last words I heard before the needle went into my arm and flames engulfed me.

Chapter 36

Naomi's heart hammers in her chest, pounding louder with each passing moment in terror, shock, and bewilderment. She remembers the "Harlow is dead" anagram.

Harlow is dead.

Here lies Harlow Hayes.

No, she thinks. *That can't be right. This is just a sick joke.*

Because if Harlow Hayes is buried here, in Faye's grave, then where the hell is Faye?

Harlow

Present Day

The seagulls circle like vultures above the choppy sea. Everything is gray—the water, the birds, the foreboding clouds.

Crack! A door slams, making me jump. I look out the windows on the other side of the room, the ones overlooking the sprawling gated gardens out front, and see the gate has come unlocked, wind thrashing it against the frame.

A wisp of fog creeps through the gate like a ghost and I shudder. I debate leaving this place, hiding out in Nashville or Los Angeles instead, but this house has a hold on me. A part of my soul. A part of *her*. Even though she's no longer here. Her body, at least.

I shudder, remembering that night. The thunder rumbling in the distance. Her face in front of mine. And then her arms. Aiming for me.

Her expression changed from sour to pleading. The ground started to move beneath me. The sound of blood whooshed in my ears.

You take things too far! So impulsive. So reckless. I imagine you reprimanding me.

But I promise I didn't mean to hurt her.

Chapter 37

Pieces of the puzzle shift, rearranging themselves to form a new picture. The whole picture. And finally, Naomi sees it.

She falls to her knees, unable to keep them from buckling at the shock. The ground is cold and damp, the wetness seeping through her jeans. It isn't the first time she's ignored the signs. The clues that have been in front of her all along.

Like the time Faye cried to her over the phone, upset at yet another rejection, telling her that even though she was talented, she wasn't unique enough to sign as an artist. She was too much like Harlow Hayes.

Naomi remembers telling her sister to not give up. To try something different. Sing different songs. She remembers her sister agreeing. And then things seemed to completely turn around for her. Faye seemed brighter, had a new lease of life. She was finally making money—claimed she sold a song. But then she became uncharacteristically secretive and private, stopped posting on social. And now Naomi knows why. She purses her lips, annoyed at herself for not seeing through her sister's lies sooner.

Naomi doesn't know what to do, so she just takes a

photo of the plaque, clutches her phone—flashlight on—and dashes toward the car. She puts it in drive, heading back to the city as her thoughts spiral, recalling all the things in front of her face all this time, like lyrics she overlooked before.

"The yellow door," Naomi whispers, thinking of the song from *Legacy*: "If You Ever Get Lonely (Yellow Door)."

The line instantly brings back a memory. Of the marigold fairy door in the woods behind their house. Their spot. *Their* safe haven.

Naomi hadn't connected the lyrics until now because she hadn't been focused on Harlow's love songs. She'd been focused on her songs about death and violence. Not ones like this. So she continues to drive, letting all the clues align with her memories. Letting her thoughts go round and round on a carousel of disbelief and desperation.

She remembers the unsettling feeling she got when she saw Harlow at the courthouse that first time. The shivers that crept over her when she listened to her recent albums. And the uneasiness she got when she studied recent photos of "Harlow." Then there's the trail of clues inspired by the Beatles. The band their mother loved. Music that was so inextricably bound to their childhood...

No, you're crazy, she thinks. *You're crazy. You're crazy. You're crazy. You were wrong about Harlow murdering Faye, you're wrong about this too. You have to be. It's impossible.*

But she wasn't completely wrong about Faye being involved, was she? Naomi just never imagined it was on this scale. That her sister would be harboring a secret as explosive as this. Keeping *this* from her. Her chest tightens as her throat stings with anguish.

How could she not have noticed all these years? Regardless of all the plastic surgery, makeup, and weight loss, surely she would've seen it in her face? Heard it in her voice? She supposes it's because Harlow had always reminded her of Faye, even when she was alive. She just assumed Harlow made her uneasy because she missed Faye—because you don't just assume your dead sister is impersonating one of the world's most famous pop stars.

Naomi scoffs, slamming her hand down on the wheel, crying out.

Everything is a lie. A fucking lie.

She swerves the wheel, realizing she drifted into the other lane. Anyone watching probably thinks she's drunk driving. She might as well be; she feels drunk. Head spinning, stomach churning.

She pulls over, the nausea and overwhelming anxiety too much to bear, and flings the door open just in time, spewing her dinner over the black asphalt.

The action helps clear her mind. And as she sits back in her seat, forcing herself to breathe, she starts to accept the possibility that Faye never overdosed in a drug den that went up in flames. That she isn't buried in that grave; she's alive.

And that it's possible that *she* is the imposter. *She* is Harlow Hayes.

Chapter 38

It can't be true. It can't be true. The phrase repeats over and over again in Naomi's mind, the rational part of her brain pleading her to think logically. To consider that maybe Leo was right. Maybe coming home just dredged all her unconfronted grief to the surface, and this is all a psychological coping mechanism. She doesn't want to believe her sister is really dead, so she's made up a story. All this is just her mind playing tricks on her, and Joel is right, she needs to take a break. Because what Naomi is concluding is beyond preposterous.

Naomi illegally parks in front of Joel's apartment, not giving a thought to getting a ticket. She has bigger concerns. Hands trembling, she searches for videos of Harlow post-*Apotheosis*, desperate to see if she recognizes Faye this time. Because if it's true, she still can't comprehend how she didn't see it before.

The first clip that surfaces is a live performance of "Echo." Harlow is looking to the side, her long raven hair obscuring her face. She's wearing a black leather jacket with large hoop earrings. And her eyeliner is overdone, with a long wingtip. Naomi clicks into the video and presses play, needing a closer look. She watches as the camera moves, revealing Harlow's face.

She hits pause, studying the famous features. She bites her lip, frowning. It really doesn't look like her sister. At least, not like how Naomi remembers her. Her sister had a rounder face, a thicker nose, and long blonde hair like Harlow used to have. Her heart sinks, wondering if she really is mistaken.

But she could've gotten plastic surgery, Naomi thinks. *Look at how different some celebrities look now versus before they were famous... they're unrecognizable.*

She grunts in frustration as she gets out of the car, her mind at war with her heart as she races up to the apartment. She immediately opens another video as she falls onto the couch, this one an interview clip. In it, Harlow is sitting in front of a microphone in a radio station. She's wearing a burgundy blouse with dark copper hair. The host thanks her for joining the show and she smiles, thanking them in return. Naomi watches intently, waiting for a sign, any sign, of it being her sister. Five minutes in and Naomi still doesn't recognize her. That is, until the host makes her laugh.

Naomi shakes her head and drags the marker back across the red line. The blood drains from her face as she hears it once more. She rewinds it again. And again. And again. And again. She closes her eyes, picturing her sister behind the laugh. But when she opens them, it still doesn't look like the face she remembers.

Naomi scrolls down, sifting through the rest of the suggested videos, her heart stopping when she sees the Beatles cover that came up during her search earlier.

Harlow Hayes – Lucy in the Sky with Diamonds cover.

She hadn't thought anything of it then, but seeing it

now, assuming that Harlow is actually Faye, it takes on a completely different meaning. *Harlow Hayes – "Lucy in the Sky with Diamonds" cover.*

Naomi is trembling by the time the song starts to play, instantly taken back to the day of her mom's funeral. When Faye gazed at Naomi, eyes shining as she sang the first words, changing "picture yourself" to "picture us."

Tears run down Naomi's face as Harlow stares at her through the screen, the exact same way Faye did that day. Naomi lets out a sob, covering her mouth with her hand as she listens to the opening... with the same exact lyric change.

She shakes her head, tears soaking her hand as her brain refuses to accept it.

Harlow could've copied it, must've seen Faye perform it somewhere.

Naomi wipes her face with her sleeves and forces herself to breathe. She jumps up from the couch and rummages through the photos in the plastic bins she brought back from Aunt Mary's basement. She finds a photo of Faye, posing seriously for the camera. Naomi remembers that photo. Faye wanted to pretend she was a pop star getting a photoshoot done, so Naomi played photographer as Faye posed away— this one making it into the pile of Faye's favorites.

Naomi pulls it out of the plastic casing and searches for the fan video that opened her mind to the imposter theory in the first place. She finds it and skips through all of the explanation, pausing on the part she's looking for—two photos of Harlow with a red line splitting the image down the middle. Naomi waits until red circles and arrows start to appear over both noses, arms, hair, teeth, and freckles before pausing the screen again.

Like before, she's convinced the two Harlows in these photos are not the same person. She just never imagined the one on the right could be Faye. Because why would her mind ever go there? It's fucking ludicrous.

Despite every logical part of her brain telling her she's lost her mind, Naomi holds up her photo of Faye, comparing it to the photo on the right of the screen. While the nose and cheeks are definitely different, there is no denying that it's her sister's smile and eyes.

Naomi huffs out a few breaths, feeling lightheaded. Her eyes land on the *Apotheosis* album cover on the floor below her wall of "evidence."

She forces herself off the couch and picks it up, studying the back track list, looking at the bolded letters and numbers that a fan pointed out.

A date: March 14. Faye's birthday.

Naomi looks up, scanning the papers on the wall for other numbers. A shaky gasp escapes her as she spots the sums noted in the article about Harlow's GoFundMe donations: $1,596 and $31,498. She thought they were random numbers at the time, but they weren't at all. They were fucking birthdays.

Their birthdays. January 5, 1996 was Naomi's and March 14, 1998 was Faye's.

"What the fuck," Naomi screams, dropping down to the floor, feeling like she might hyperventilate.

She picks up the *Apotheosis* cover again, this time looking at the front. She holds it up to the light, which illuminates the different layers in the album artwork from skyscrapers and ocean and roses. But it's the trees that stand out to her, and the small, barely noticeable faded yellow door at the bottom of one of the trunks.

Heart pounding, Naomi thinks of the lyrics to the yellow door song and wonders what other clues from Faye she missed.

She frantically opens the lyric posters of *Apotheosis* and *Legacy*, eyes darting across the text.

Happiness is long drives with you by my side
Now those are gone forever, alone I ride

I'm sorry for my words but yours cut like a knife
When you were ready to abandon me, walk right out of my life

An imposter with good fortune, a pretty face that turned the key
I don't even recognize the real me

I do, Naomi thinks, a mixture of fury and desperation overwhelming her. She forces herself to breathe as she continues to scan the lyrics, her stomach twisting in knots as phrases jump off the page, slicing at her heart like jagged little razors.

Splintering wood, started a fight
Eight stitches on a cruel September night

To the reckless girl I used to be
I promise, I'll leave you a worthy legacy

Scribbles on my shoes, Tears on my face
A bond that can never be replaced

We'd sing it's us against the world
But you couldn't fix me, you tried

You meant the world to me, now I'm dead to you
What was I thinking, what did I do?

Now I'm dead to you. Naomi aggressively pushes the tears off her cheek as she rereads the lyrics to "If You Ever Get Lonely (Yellow Door)."

Home is where the heart is
Unfortunately it's true
When you get lonely, think of the yellow door
Think of us two
Memories of us will fade, like the peeling
paint on the tree
I'll tell myself it was everything I wanted
How it was meant to be
Yet I'll whisper on the wind, please forgive me.

Forgive me. Forgive me. Naomi can hear Faye whispering the words to her and she wants to cry in relief and scream in anger at the same time.

She flips to the back of the vinyl cover to the track list, to see if she can find anything else. And she finally sees it, spelled out right in front of her all along.

No Way Back
Footsteps in the Snow
One Step Ahead
Rose-Covered Grave
Garden of Bones
If You Ever Get Lonely (Yellow Door)
Violent Ends Part II
Endless Loop
Melancholy
Echo

"N, Forgive Me."

Chapter 39

Naomi closes her eyes, feeling nauseous as her world spins violently around her. She imagines Tom and Amelia, even Leo and Joel, questioning her sanity. *So now you think your sister ISN'T dead? And that she is impersonating Harlow Hayes?*

She lets out a hard, incredulous laugh. Because yes, that's exactly what she thinks.

The proof is right in front of her, staring her in the face. Messages to Naomi, from Faye. In Harlow Hayes' music.

Is it really proof, though? Could the lyrics have been stolen instead? That would be a much more logical explanation.

Her heart starts to race as she doubts herself. She begins pacing again, unsure of what to do. She's tempted to go back to the cemetery, start digging up the grave, demand DNA tests.

She pictures herself covered in dirt as she digs with her bare hands, chunks of grass and soil mixed with blood packed beneath her splitting fingernails. She imagines wedging open the casket with a shovel to find a pile of decomposed bones. Then what? Go to the police station and tell them she just dug up her sister's grave because she's convinced her sister isn't her sister but is actually Harlow Hayes?

They'd probably drag her away to an insane asylum. Or if they did somehow take her seriously, and if she is right, then they'd arrest her sister. Again.

Her stomach lurches at the thought. That her sister might actually be alive. That she might be a killer. Not Jade's, but possibly Colton's. And Harlow's.

Naomi knows all about the drastic things people do to get to the top. What craving fame and fortune do to people. Could Faye have really been so desperate, so delusional, that she killed Harlow? If it were anyone else, Naomi would be convinced that Harlow's imposter is the killer.

No, she thinks. *Not Faye.*

She let you believe she died in a horrific way, a cruel voice whispers. *Is it really so unbelievable that she killed Harlow too? Would it really be so shocking?*

She cries out in frustration, sick of wondering. Of second-guessing everything. Not knowing. She can't sit around asking herself "What if?" any longer. She can't keep questioning her sanity. She needs to know the truth. Now.

She scrolls through social media, trying to find clues to where "Harlow Hayes" could be. She checks Instagram, seeing if @HarlowHayesOfficial has posted anything recently. And there it is, a video of her two dogs, Lennon and Ringo, running on the beach. Naomi replays the story, noting the cliffs in the background.

She recognizes those cliffs. "Harlow" is at her beach house in Maine. And soon, Naomi will be too.

★

The Beatles' "Hey Jude" plays through the radio after Naomi turns the key in the rental car's ignition. She instinctively reaches to change the channel, but stops herself as the second verse begins. Goosebumps prickle her arms as the words set in. It's like her mother is singing to her through McCartney's voice, urging Naomi to "go and get her."

She peels out onto the road, not caring about the other car she sideswipes as the now ominous-sounding chorus of "na-na-na-nas" propels her toward the heart-wrenching, unfathomable truth.

PART III

VIOLENT ENDS

Oh, please believe me, this was not my intention.
A violent end for an honest confession.
— Harlow Hayes, from the album *Legacy*

Harlow

Present Day

Sam paces around my two-story living room, looking uncomfortable in his tight blue suit. He holds a glass of Macallan in one hand and gestures wildly with his other. He's complaining about what I did, but I'm not paying attention. My mind elsewhere, thinking of them. Thinking of you.

"Are you even listening?" he says, snapping me out of my thoughts.

I sigh, balancing my head in my hand as I sit on the sofa, trying to calm Ringo, who's eyeing Sam warily. Sam's beady eyes meet mine, and he gives me the warning, patronizing look I've come to despise. Like he's reminding me that he knows "my deep, dark secrets," so I should... what? Be nicer? More amenable? Afraid?

No.

I smirk, amused by his arrogance. How he thinks he has a hold over me, that I should be genuinely concerned about him turning me in. But his greed makes him predictable. And he already showed his hand the first time, three years ago.

"It was an accident... I'll take care of it... No one will

ever have to know… You're her… And she's you… Do you understand?"

I understood.

But what he didn't understand is that his actions showed me that he's a man who can see the bigger picture. And in time, he'll see that I did what needed to be done. That it was better for me, for him, for everyone. He should be thanking me, really.

The vein that's been pulsing out of his five-finger forehead finally recedes, but just as he chills out, his phone rings. He looks away from me, mumbling things like "I see" and "uh huh" before telling whoever is on the other line that he'll be right there. I relax into the sofa, glad he'll be leaving. I can't stand any more post-arrest crisis PR talk tonight.

"Everything okay?" I ask, studying my gold-flaked manicure.

He lets out a big sigh. "Security flagged someone outside."

Heat pools in my chest as the security notification comes through on my own phone and Lennon starts barking, causing Ringo to get up and do the same.

"Nothing for you to worry about, though," he says, grabbing his keys and heading for the door. "We'll finish this discussion in the morning, alright?"

"Sounds good."

I pretend like I'm unbothered by the prospect of a crazed Colton "fan" at the gates, but fear ripples through me. I see what they say about me. The detailed descriptions some write. How they'd hurt me. Torture me. Kill me.

They're finally coming for you, a voice whispers. Her voice, the one that's haunted me, ever since that day. It makes me wonder if the person at the gates isn't a Colton fan. But one of hers. Someone I should be even more afraid of.

They know what you did. All of it.

Chapter 40

After a four-hour drive, Naomi pulls up to the black iron gate guarding the entrance to Harlow's Georgian revival mansion. She hesitates before putting the car in park.

Am I really here? Am I really doing this?

She thinks of all her sleepless nights. Of her inability to truly move on with her life since Faye died. If there is even a shred of hope her sister isn't dead, that she's alive, Naomi can't ignore it. Even if she's proven wrong, even if she really has lost her mind, at least this nightmare of wondering will be over and she can get the help she needs. She exhales and finally steps out of the car.

A camera watches her as she moves toward the intercom. She clears her throat before pressing a finger down on the cold silver button.

"Faye?" Naomi's voice shakes as she speaks. "It's me."

She isn't sure what she'll do if Faye responds. Whether she'll buckle in relief and astonishment, cry her eyes out as she wraps her arms around her. Or if she'll scream and shout in a flurry of rage—livid that Faye forced Naomi to grieve her death, only for her to secretly live out her dreams.

She waits for the gate to open, imagining its metal

screeching against the pavement to beckon her in. But no one answers. She laughs. Feeling like all of this is suddenly hysterical. That she is hysterical.

The delirious feeling grows as she walks around the side of the house, wondering if she should scale the fence. A light flicks on in the distance, illuminating one of the windows at the back of the house. Naomi follows the gravel path around the edge of the property toward it, stumbling to her hands and knees when a shadow moves past the window.

It's her, she thinks, scrambling to her feet.

Naomi dusts the small stones and dirt off her jeans before using the back of her hand to push her hair off her face. The air is cold, but her head is slick with sweat.

"Faye!" Naomi shouts to the shadowed figure, despite being so far away.

Nothing happens.

She's about to call out again, this time trying Harlow's name, but Naomi's cry is muffled by a hand wrapping around her mouth.

Harlow

Wood creaks below my feet as I climb the stairs, Lennon and Ringo barking wildly behind me. I'm not sure if I'm looking for a better vantage point or a place to hide. I turn on the light once in my bedroom and quickly close the blinds. As I turn, a voice cries out in the distance and I freeze, paralyzed where I stand.

Chapter 41

Naomi tries to scream, digging her nails into the stranger's hand as she's dragged away.

"Stop resisting!" a deep, gruff voice demands as she flails beneath him. Her terror shifts to understanding as she realizes what's happened.

She's frustrated for being so close and annoyed at being manhandled, but she's also embarrassed. Of course Harlow would have security watching the property. She imagines how crazy she must look from their point of view. Naomi stops fighting, breathing in a sweaty metallic scent as the guard releases his hand from her mouth. He tightens his grip on her arm as she regains her balance.

"This is private property, ma'am," he says. "You're going to have to come with me while we wait for the authorities."

She imagines the headlines. *Crazed Woman Claiming Harlow Hayes is Her Sister Arrested for Trespassing at Singer's Holiday Home.*

Panicking, she tries to explain herself. "I'm… I'm a friend of Harlow's. She's expecting me, just please ask her to come down."

Jesus Christ, do you hear yourself? she thinks. But she's

here now, has to try. Do whatever it takes to get in front of "Harlow." See if she really is her sister.

The guard raises a mocking eyebrow, shaking his head as he continues to pull her toward the front gate. Returning from this angle, she can now see the small outhouse tucked into the treeline, a black Range Rover parked outside.

As they cross the driveway, the gates open. Naomi freezes, heart racing with excitement before pounding in alarm. The suited figure storming toward her isn't her sister.

It's Sam Brixton.

And she is completely fucked.

Sam stares at Naomi with pure disdain as their eyes meet. "Take her over here," he orders the guard, pointing to the wooden building nestled into a fortress of evergreens.

Once inside, he gestures for her to take a seat on a plastic chair in the middle of the small, brightly lit room. The air is musty and she coughs.

"You can leave us, Jack," he says to the guard.

"Arite, let me know if you need me." Jack closes the door behind him.

Sam sighs as he takes a seat across from Naomi. He clasps his hands in front of him as he assesses her with his beady black eyes, shaking his head.

"Wow." He leans back, letting out a hearty laugh. "Didn't I already talk to you about this? We thought you were some rabid fan or psycho stalker... I mean, maybe you are, you clearly aren't all there, are you?"

She rolls her eyes at the insult but a part of her worries it's true.

"Wanna explain what the fuck you're doing here?" He cocks his head to the side, his usual cheesy on-camera smile pulled into a thin line as he waits for an answer.

She chews on the inside of her cheek as she considers her reply, studying him carefully. She doesn't trust him, nor does she know how involved he was with the murders. But as one of the only people still working with Harlow after all these years, she has to surmise he knows the truth. About Harlow and Faye, at the very least.

If Harlow is Faye, a voice corrects her.

Her eyes are heavy from lack of sleep. She's tired. So tired of it all. She doesn't care if she's crazy. She just wants the truth. So she decides to risk it and tell him her theory. She didn't come all this way to back down now. She came here for answers and she's sure as hell not going to get them by hiding what she knows.

"I came to see my sister." Her voice breaks on the last word.

"Your... sister?" His cold expression turns confused and she wonders if he's a good actor or if he genuinely doesn't know. She notices him shift in his seat.

"Cut the bullshit," Naomi spits, hoping she sounds more confident than she feels. She knows what she's saying seems delusional. Insane. But she needs to come across as unwavering if she's going to make him crack. "I know she's not Harlow. I know she's Faye."

He laughs, shaking his head, which only angers her. "Wait, wait... a couple days ago, you were slandering Harlow, my client, in your 'article'—if you can even call it that—claiming she should never have been released and she was some serial killer..." His expression turns angry again. "Now you think she's your... sister?"

Her face flushes red, embarrassed, heart pounding as the thought crosses her mind once again that maybe she's wrong. But then she thinks of everything she's discovered since writing that article. All the clues, first pointing to Harlow being an imposter—the reinvention of her persona, the drastic change in her appearance and style, her haunting new sound and lyrics, photos placing her in Maine and LA at the same time, the Beatles references, all the hints... Addia S. Howler... Harlow is dead. Then she thinks of her sister's grave and the hidden inscription: *Here lies Harlow Hayes*. All the signs that were right in front of Naomi's face this entire time. The hidden messages for Naomi in the lyrics, like her sister was screaming *"It's me!"* from her gilded cage.

"I originally thought Faye was a victim, yes, but now I know the truth," she says, standing her ground. "I know the real Harlow is dead."

She holds his icy gaze as she says it. He laughs again, a deep chuckle. But forced. "Oh that's good. That's really good. And uh, what else do you think you know?"

"I know everything," she says. She swallows hard, throat stinging as if there's a rope around it. As if she's not about to hang herself on what anyone else would think is a wild conspiracy.

"Please humor me." He smiles, but it doesn't match his intensity.

Naomi takes a breath, ignoring the voice in her head telling her to shut her mouth. But she can't control herself, her impulses taking over. She says everything she's been thinking, piecing together over the last couple weeks, slotting the final pieces of her deranged theory into place on the drive to Maine.

"I think Jade died while she was with Colton and Harlow the night of the VMAs party at your house. I think Colton is a sick fuck and he strangled her to death during sex, potentially in front of Harlow." As she says it, the realization finally hits her. If her theory is true, then Sam must have been involved. "And I think you helped them cover it all up…"

His face doesn't give anything away, but he looks like he's holding his breath.

"Couldn't have your superstars in jail," Naomi continues. "But Harlow couldn't handle the guilt, which is when you started to worry about her and the future. Your future. Because when the guilt eventually got too much for her, she became unreliable. Unpredictable. And you couldn't have that. Especially after the mishap at the VMAs, then the failure of 'Endless Summers.' So smart, one-step-ahead Sam started looking for body doubles to fill in for her here or there. At first, just for promos and small appearances so Harlow could rest and reset. But then you hit the jackpot. You met Faye."

Naomi's throat stings as she says her name. "Not only did Faye look and sound like Harlow, she had the potential to be even better than her. Plus, you thought she'd be easier to control…"

She pauses to study Sam's face, watching his Adam's apple bob in his throat. And then it dawns on her.

Maybe Faye wasn't the killer. Maybe it was Sam. She thinks then of the matching fentanyl levels on the two autopsy reports. *Sam was the only one who could have helped cover up both murders...*

She shudders as his black eyes stare back at her. There's no point in holding back anymore. She needs to see this through.

"You killed her, didn't you? *You* killed Harlow."

"You have no fucking idea what you're taking about, Jesus Christ," Sam spits out, face flushed. "You need to see someone about these delusions, you really do. First, you sneak into Colton's funeral and upset his family. Next, you slander and defame both him and Harlow in your article, even after the justice system declared she was innocent—luckily for you, I've known Joel for a long time, so I refrained from pressing charges. And now? Now you show up to her home after a psychotic break, thinking she's your sister. And then you accuse me, the person who has been nice enough to not press charges *twice*, of these insane conspiracies? I mean..." He throws his hands in the air, shaking his head as he laughs angrily.

Naomi crosses her arms in a huff, realizing if she's right, he'll never confess. It was foolish of her to think he would tell her anything. Panic starts to set in as she realizes what she's done. That she's admitted to everything she knows. He'd probably do anything to stop her from seeing Faye, if it is her. From maybe seeing anyone ever again. Her breath quickens, chest tightens. She tries to calm herself, but the thought of possibly being so close to seeing her sister again and not being able to get to her is unbearable.

Her throat is on fire, voice unsteady as she makes one last desperate attempt. "I just want to see Harlow, okay?" She doesn't want to beg, but she doesn't know what else to do.

"Please, let me talk to her. I won't say anything to anyone, I swear. I just want to talk with her."

Sam's smile has been completely wiped away. And he isn't laughing anymore. He takes his phone out and sends a text before looking back at her. She senses a flicker of doubt. But it only lasts for a second. His face hardens.

"Naomi." He rubs his hand over his face. "I'm so sorry to hear about your sister. I know you want to believe she's alive. But she's dead. And this isn't healthy. You need to move on. You need to get help. Do you understand?"

Naomi fully understands that she needs help. Whether she's right about her sister being Harlow or not, she's going to need therapy after all this. But she'll never be able to move on unless she sees for herself. Not until she talks to "Harlow Hayes."

Sam won't let that happen, though, she's sure of it now. She needs to convince him to release her so she can go home and come up with a new plan of attack.

"I'm sorry," she says, changing tack. "I guess I just don't want it to be true. Was desperate for her to still be alive." Tears fill her eyes as she speaks.

Sam sighs, crossing his arms as he leans back in his chair and studies her.

"I'm so sorry," she says. "I've just gotten so carried away. What I said before is ridiculous, you're right. I have no proof of anything." She throws her hands in the air in a false display of surrender. "I promise I'll never write another word about Harlow or Colton. And I'm so sorry for accusing you. I…"

"Just wanted someone to blame?" Sam cuts in. "At least you see that now. I'm really not the bad guy here. I told you, I'm trying to help you. But you can only help yourself. Truly."

She swallows, trying to steady her breath as her plan starts to work. He hands her a tissue and she dabs her eyes. "I'm so sorry," she says again, standing up. "I'll get out of your hair and you'll never hear from or see me again, I promise."

He stands up quickly and blocks the door, and she wonders if he won't let her leave. Ever. Her pulse thrashes in her ears, the seconds feeling like hours.

Maybe I am right. And maybe I just made the biggest mistake of my life by telling him.

She takes a step forward toward the small gap in the doorway where only his arm is in the way. Her torso brushes against his forearm, and she presses forward, trying to get him to budge. But his grip remains steady. She looks up at him, blinking her lashes in quick succession. Like prey begging to be released from its captor.

His eyes narrow, and she imagines his heartbeat quickening. A hunter ready to pounce.

"Sam. Please, just let me go home. I promise I won't say anything," Naomi says again, as she moves her hand to the doorknob. She wonders what else she has to do. Drop to her knees and beg? No, she won't give him the satisfaction. So she presses forward with all her weight, turning the knob and pushing at the same time.

She expects to meet more resistance but instead she barrels forward, surprised as he just lets her walk out the door.

Harlow

I sit in my walk-in closet, scrolling through videos on my phone in an attempt to distract myself from what's happened. I scoff, annoyed by my own hypocrisy. A half hour ago I was downstairs with Sam, claiming to be fierce and unafraid, but now I'm hiding like a coward, while he rallies my security team.

Just look at the damn footage, I think, forcing myself to click the notification. *It'll just be an overeager fan or paparazzi. Nothing that bad.*

My heart hammers in my chest as I press play and the grainy figure comes into view. Goosebumps cover my arms, one inch at a time. I gasp, hand flying to my mouth as I register who it is. My phone slips through my fingers and crashes onto the hardwood floor. I try to breathe, but it's as if someone has punched me in the gut. Because it's not some crazed fan or stalker at the gates.

It's you.

I stand as still as a statue as I process the moment. A moment I've always dreamed about. And dreaded.

Did you find the clues I left in my songs? I left so many. It started as a coping mechanism, an outlet for the overwhelming emotions of missing you. But then somewhere along the way, I hoped maybe they'd lead you to me. I was inspired by the Beatles, of course. You remember, right? All the stories Mom told us?

I hope you being here doesn't mean you were agonizing over me all these years, though, missing me like I missed you. When Faye "died" and I became Harlow, you were happy, had your life together. That had been my only solace, that you had Matt—your own life, unchained from me. Your reckless little sister.

God, I've dreamed of this day for so long. To hug you again. Tell you everything—the good and the bad. Tell you I'm sorry. How I missed you every single day. How you'd been my muse.

But the problem with that is then you'd know what I really am: A killer.

For so long, I tried to think of ways to tell you. To let you know I was alive. But I swore to Sam I wouldn't tell a soul. He said the only way this could work is if everyone thought Faye Barnes was dead instead of Harlow Hayes. It was either that or prison.

But as I replay the video and hear you utter my real name for the first time in years, I know it can't wait.

Chapter 42

Naomi locks the doors the second she's back in her rental car, hand shaking wildly as she attempts to put the key in the ignition.

"Breathe," she tells herself. The engine roars to life and she puts her seatbelt on, allowing herself one final look at the house before reversing. A misty fog has settled on the property, and she imagines her sister striding through it. But Faye is nowhere to be seen.

Naomi has half a mind to make a break for it, bang on the front door, but she knows tonight is a lost cause. She needs to retreat. Clear her head and try again once she has a better plan, especially now that she knows Sam will be watching her.

Rain starts to fall as she pulls onto the main road, heading toward the interstate.

As she speeds down the highway, she tries to formulate a plan. But she's defeated. If she was right, then why would he let her go?

She flicks her windshield wipers on full power as the rain

turns to a heavy downpour, squinting as a pair of bright high-beams blind her in the rearview mirror.

"Fuckin' asshole," she mutters, trying to stay focused.

But the car continues to distract her, getting closer with every passing moment, until it's tailgating her. She's tempted to brake-check the driver, wondering who it could be. An idiot teenager? A drunk driver? She continues to drive, both hands tightly gripped to the wheel.

Or is it him?

Naomi accelerates at the thought, desperate to put more space between them. She's going far too fast for the inclement weather as she approaches a bend, panicking as she presses the brakes. But the car continues at pace. She hits the brakes harder, but once again the car doesn't slow. She's overwhelmed with fear as the car hydroplanes, realizing that if she dies, she might never learn the truth.

But there's nothing she can do now except brace for impact as her car spins off the road, straight into the trees.

Harlow

I grab my jacket and keys and head outside, ready to find you. But Sam's car is gone. Your car is gone. The hairs on my arms stand on high alert as a new panic sets in and my gut tells me that something is terribly wrong.

I click back into the camera footage, fast-forwarding until I see you leaving, and then peel out in the same direction, praying I'm not too late.

As I race down the road, my stomach twists into knots, thinking of Sam. *He wouldn't. Would he?*

But he was so adamant about no one ever knowing, especially you...

A wave of guilt washes over me as I realize what I put you through. At least I got to live with the hope that we'd reunite one day. But I took any shred of hope away from you.

I'm so sorry, Naomi.

I slow down, seeing headlights up in front of me as I reach the bend in the road. I squint, trying to make out the cars in the unrelenting rain. A black Mercedes. Sam's car.

My heart pounds as I pull in behind it and turn my high-beams on to see what's going on. And that's when my worst nightmare becomes a reality. When I see a white Jeep wrapped around a tree.

Ringing is all I hear as the nausea consumes me. I can't breathe, gasping for air as I take in the scene. I will myself to focus. Convince myself that panicking isn't going to solve anything. And somehow, I manage to calm down just enough to call for help, while I still have the chance.

I fumble with my phone, shaking as I draft a text to Jen, my assistant. "SOS. Send private ambulance. No police!"

I hit send, knowing I don't have much time. I take short, quick breaths as I share the pin location. I want to wait, to see if she received it. But there isn't time because Sam is almost at my door. I slide my phone into my pocket and open the door to the smell of damp earth and rubber. All I hear is the sound of rain and crunching rocks. Sam steps closer now, an umbrella shielding him from the downpour.

"What are you doing? You shouldn't be here." He sounds stressed. Panicked.

I get out of the car, flinching as raindrops pummel my face. "What happened?" I yell.

"I don't know, just saw this car hydroplane off the road."

I try to run toward you, but he grabs my arm. "You should go home, Harlow." He says the name harshly, a warning. A reminder.

"That's my sister," I yell, meeting his gaze.

"Your sister?" he frowns. "Funny, I don't remember Harlow Hayes having a sister…" His tone is icy, challenging.

Rage battles with my panic and desperation. The mud squelches beneath my feet, and I imagine him beneath me. My foot on his neck, pushing him into the mud to get to you. The urge to crush him, to hear every bone in his slimy neck crunch under my toes, grows stronger with every word that comes out of his mouth.

I shake Sam off. I'll deal with him later. Right now, I need to help you. But when I take a step around him, dead leaves crunching beneath my feet, he blocks me.

"This," he says, gesturing to your car, "is just an accident. Do you understand?"

It was an accident. I'll take care of it. Do you understand? His words from three years ago echo in my ears again.

"We had a deal, goddammit!" He grabs me tighter this time as I try to move away from him, fingers bruising my arm. "You know what you signed up for. Don't act all sad now, when for the past three years you let her think you were dead."

I look over at your mangled car, picturing your body lying limp and lifeless, surrounded in a pool of your own blood, before staring back at him, eyes wild with worry.

"And don't look at me like I'm the bad guy here!" he yells. "I'm the one who made your wildest dreams come true, remember?"

Sam's eyes flicker from your car back to me. He swallows as if he's battling with what he really wants to say. I inhale, getting ready for a fight. The silence between us is deafening but then the sound of sirens cuts through the void.

Sam grunts and turns on his heels toward his car, having the decision made for him. I buckle in relief, thankful Jen received my message.

"If she ever breathes a whiff of this to anyone…" Sam yells out his car window.

"She won't." I hold his gaze before he disappears into the night.

I run toward the ambulance as it gets closer, guiding them to the site. Once they park, it's as if everything slows. I watch helplessly as they carry a stretcher and large red medical bag out of the back and then bound toward you. I want to do something, anything, but I'm frozen.

My world silently shatters as they hoist your bloodied and broken body from the car, wondering if your death is my punishment.

Chapter 43

The sound of beeping and smell of antiseptic greet Naomi as she wakes. She swallows, but her mouth feels like sandpaper. She tries to push herself up, but the aching in her torso thwarts her attempt. It's like she hasn't moved in days.

Her mind pings with questions. What happened? Where is she? And then she remembers. The rain. The slick road. The car speeding up behind her. Hitting the turn too fast. Hydroplaning off the road and crashing into the trees.

She doesn't remember anything after that, but she remembers everything before. Arriving at Harlow Hayes' mansion in Maine. Calling out for Faye. Security hauling her away. Sam Brixton.

Her stomach sinks, remembering their exchange. He was lying, she's sure of it now.

Panic sets in and her rapidly increasing heart rate sets off the monitors. She needs to get out of here. Find her sister. She forces her eyes open, seeing nothing but a blinding white light. And then she hears a familiar, soft voice.

"Naomi?"

Her heart feels like it's stopped and she waits for the monitor to flatline. But it doesn't. It continues to beep. She turns to see Harlow Hayes, the white light surrounding her like a halo.

Naomi studies her warm, worried smile, searching her eyes for the truth. Without the heavy makeup her persona usually flaunts on screen, she can finally see it. Then the sheer magnitude of it all hits her. Overwhelming conflicting emotions of betrayal and relief, happiness and anger.

"Faye..." she says shakily, hands trembling with rage, eyes brimming with tears. "What... the... fuck..."

Faye cradles her face in her hands as she starts crying. Naomi doesn't know how to respond. Her brain is in overdrive, trying to process that this is really happening. That this isn't a dream or a hallucination. Faye's alive. Here with her. She was right. She tries to prop herself up, but the pain stops her.

"Ah," she groans, realizing she must've broken a few ribs in the crash.

"Naomi?" A woman dressed in dark-blue scrubs and lime-green Crocs runs into the room. "Welcome back. Just hang tight for a second there and we'll check you out." The woman crouches by her bedside, fiddling with the IV cables, before examining the clipboard.

"My name is Janet. I'm your nurse. I'm just going to press this button to prop you up a bit, okay?"

Naomi tenses as the bed moves and her bones ache. She doesn't want to look away from her sister, worried she's a hologram that will dissipate if she does. She presses her eyelids shut and then opens them, looking at Faye, still there. She breathes a sigh of relief.

Janet leans over and places a stethoscope on Naomi's chest. "Can you take a deep breath for me, please?"

Naomi abides, scanning her surroundings as she inhales and exhales, noting how the room looks like a cross between a hotel suite and a hospital. But the giant flatscreen and fancy gold and marble furnishings on the kitchenette throw her off.

"Where am I?" she asks, voice full of gravel.

Janet places the stethoscope down after making some notes and grabs a cup of water. "Here, drink this, you must be thirsty." She holds the cup to Naomi's cracked lips before answering. "You're at St. John's, a private hospital."

"In Maine?" Naomi finishes the water.

"Yes. You were taken here just after your accident a few days ago."

"A few days?" Naomi responds, shocked. Her heart hammers, wondering how she's going to pay for this private treatment.

"Yes, but that's nothing after an accident like yours. You were very lucky. Plus, your surgery went well and your leg should be fine in a few months."

Surgery? Months!? She lifts her neck, finally seeing the huge cast encasing her entire right leg.

"Fuck," she whispers, closing her eyes as she lets her head fall back into the pillow.

"Did I break anything else?"

Janet quickly consults the clipboard. "Two ribs and a fractured wrist."

The beeping on Naomi's heart monitor increases as her pulse quickens.

"It's going to be a tough road to full recovery, but you're

in great hands and Harlow's already let us know her plans for your outpatient care."

Naomi glances at her sister, who Janet of course thinks is pop star Harlow Hayes. Because she is, apparently.

"Now, I'm just going to ask you a few questions, okay?" Janet grabs her clipboard again. "Some are just formalities, things I need to verify. First, can you tell me your name and date of birth?"

"Naomi Barnes. January 5, 1996."

"Great. And on a scale of one to ten, what level of pain do you feel? Ten being like someone's cut off your leg."

"Um, a five, maybe," Naomi says, impatient to be done with these questions and talk to her sister. Something she thought she'd never be able to do again.

"Good, the pain meds must be doing their job then. Now, can you move your fingers?"

Naomi does as she's told and moves her fingers on both hands, even though they feel stiff.

"Now your toes."

She wiggles them and Janet nods, taking notes. When she looks up from her clipboard, she smiles. "You're going to be just fine. I'll go let the doctor know you're awake and she'll come check in on you in a bit. For now, I'll leave you two to catch up. Harlow, if your friend needs anything at all, just let us know, okay?"

Friend. The word is like salt in Naomi's wounds. Things would never be the same, would they?

Once Janet closes the door, Faye turns to Naomi. She looks so different. So much more like Harlow. But also so beautiful. Radiant. Like a goddess. A true star. Everything about her looks new. Her lips, her nose, the shape of her face and body. Her hair is long and thick, brown with copper lowlights mixed into what she's sure are expensive extensions. So different from the blonde shoulder-length cut she used to sport.

Faye grabs her hand, and for a moment everything is right with the world. It's all that matters. But then Naomi realizes that if this really, truly is her sister, she let Naomi believe she was dead for years. Let her think she suffered a violent, tragic end and it took Naomi almost dying to uncover the truth. Her younger sister has a hell of a lot of explaining to do.

Naomi scrutinizes Faye. *How could you?* she thinks. As if the words are painted on her face, Faye casts her eyes away from her stare, cheeks flushing red as she swallows.

"Naomi, I…" Tears fall from her reddened eyes again as she stumbles over what to say. She picks at her nails as she looks from Naomi to the floor and back again.

Naomi inhales, trying to organize all of the questions swirling around her mind like a tornado. "How could you? Why didn't you tell me?"

"I did, in a way," Faye says defensively. "All my clues that led you here."

Naomi scoffs. "So what, did you get arrested on purpose in the hopes I'd look into it? It's not like I've been obsessing over Harlow Hayes these past few years, dissecting her music. If anything, I avoided anything and everything to do with her—with you." She pinches the bridge of her nose with her only unbroken fingers, head aching, before throwing her hand out as she addresses her sister. "If anything, the clues nearly convinced me she—you, whoever—was a narcissistic serial killer. That was more plausible. One just doesn't assume their dead sister is Harlow-fucking-Hayes all of a sudden!"

Face flushing red, Faye crosses her arms and rolls her eyes, jutting her bottom lip out in a pout. A face Naomi is all too familiar with.

Naomi's throat burns as she grows hot with anger. "You let me think you overdosed and burned to death in a freaking drug den! Do you not see how fucked-up that is?"

"Shhh!" Faye says, eyes wide as she looks at the door.

Naomi gives her a challenging look. As if Faye has the gall to shush *her* after what she's done.

"I know it's fucked-up, believe me, I know!" Faye says in a harsh whisper, eyes brimming with more tears. "I never meant... things just got so out of hand so fast and then... it spiraled out of control... then it was too late and I didn't know how to... didn't know where to start."

"Hmm, I don't know, maybe try the beginning?" Naomi snaps.

Faye's face is as red as a beet. "This is why I never tried, I knew you'd get angry!"

"Of course I'm fucking angry, holy shit, what is wrong—"

"A lot is fucking wrong with me, okay, is that what you want to hear!?"

They bicker back and forth just like they used to. As if the past three years never happened. Naomi knows her sister, though—knows she needs to tread carefully, no matter how angry she is. If she doesn't, Faye will retreat, close in on herself. So she softens her tone.

"Please," Naomi sighs, reaching out for Faye's tense hand. She relaxes. "Just try to explain."

Chapter 44

Faye looks around the room, making sure no one is close enough to hear before she speaks. "So you probably remember how I'd been really struggling. Getting rejection after rejection. Depressed that maybe it was never going to happen for me…"

Naomi nods.

"Well, soon after, I got a call from Sam Brixton asking to meet."

"Sam contacted you?" There he was again, the common denominator in all this. *He's involved, no question, but how much?*

Faye nods. "Yeah, he'd watched one of my covers of Harlow online and said he wanted to talk. But the catch was I had to keep things confidential, so I did. I didn't want to get my hopes up again or jinx anything. So I met him and he offered me an opportunity I couldn't really refuse."

She looks down, picking at her cuticles. The same bad habit as Naomi.

"He was looking for someone to stand in for Harlow because apparently she had started to become 'increasingly difficult to work with,' and they needed someone to keep up appearances while she 'took a wellness break' at the end of 2021." Faye puts air quotes around the last phrase.

Naomi recalls the timeframe, when Harlow was rumored to be in rehab. A few months after the VMAs. After Jade's death.

"They didn't know how long she'd be gone for," Faye continues. "Nor did they truly know what the full extent of my role would be, probably just radio interviews and recordings, plus some music video work or appearances where they could get away with using a stand-in. Our figures and features were already pretty similar, we were the same height, same skin tone. All I'd need was a few good prosthetics, maybe a wig, good makeup…"

Naomi remembers the TikTok about Harlow being an imposter, how the user had noticed Harlow's—Faye's—prosthetics. And people calling him crazy in the comments.

"At first, when I realized he was offering me the chance to be Harlow's double, I thought I was being pranked, like I was on some reality show. But then I realized it was the opportunity of a lifetime. That maybe if I impressed him with this job, he'd want to sign me as an artist. So I said yes."

Naomi sighs at her sister's naivety.

"Obviously I couldn't tell you the truth," Faye says, noticing Naomi's judgmental expression. "I couldn't tell anyone. I had to sign an NDA and everything. I wasn't sure how long it was going to go on for or how—if—it would even work, but they said they'd make it worth my while. I'd get an insane new wardrobe, incredible stylist, makeup artist, personal trainer, personal chef… they'd cover all expenses and pay me a salary on top of it."

Naomi nods, now understanding where all the money was coming from those months before Faye's "death." And the real reason for her secrecy.

"Anyway," Faye continues. "I just kind of thought, 'Fuck it, this might be the only chance I get to make it.' It didn't take long for me to get up to speed. I already knew all her songs. All her choreography. I sounded like her, could move like her. I mean, you know I idolized her. How her music refocused me in high school, helped me get away from all the bad stuff." She waves her hand dismissively.

"I know," Naomi says, sighing.

"It's why I get so emotional when fans say that to me now. Because I was like them. And no one else really gets it. Most people just think it's silly pop music, but it's not."

"Well, especially not anymore," Naomi says, heart soaring as pride momentarily overtakes anger and suspicion. "You won a Grammy, didn't you?"

"Four, actually." Faye smirks. "But with the highs come the lows." Her smile fades as she looks out the window.

"I'd been so excited to meet Harlow when she finally came back. I wanted to impress her with my singing and choreography, show her everything I'd been working on, how well I could impersonate her. But Sam failed to mention that she had no idea about me. Not one fucking clue. And, well, let's just say she's the inspiration for my lyric, 'Don't meet your idols.'"

Faye's tone turns from wistful to harsh. Naomi eyes her cautiously.

"Harlow was either showing up late or not at all. It was so frustrating, her taking it all for granted. But I tried my best to be pleasant around her. To please her. But no matter how hard I tried, she wanted nothing to do with me. She loathed me." Faye lets out a huff, not bothering to hide her frustration. "So I chose to see her bad attitude as an opportunity. I stopped trying to please her and instead focused on looking out for myself. I wanted to show Sam that I was the better version of her. I could sing better. Dance better. And I could even perform better. But most importantly, I was reliable. And when Harlow didn't show up for an important pre-Grammy performance for the Recording Academy, and I was able to stand in last minute, I think Sam started to finally realize I was more valuable to him than she was."

A pit forms in the center of Naomi's stomach, worried where her sister's story is going. If she didn't know any better, she'd think this was all a story Faye had fabricated. A pretend, make-believe world where her dreams came true.

"The next few weeks were amazing, while we prepared to record the next album. Not only were they letting me do a lot of the demos, but Sam was keen to hear more of my songs, wanting to see if there were any that we could use. He and Charlie loved one of them so much they even encouraged me to do a TikTok and unofficially release it."

"Without running it by Harlow?" Naomi asks.

Faye shrugs. "I almost asked, but then decided not to. They'd kind of given up on her. Even though she was back, she seemed further away than ever, all over the place—which, now that I know why, I feel horrible about…"

Naomi furrows her brow, wondering what she means, but lets her continue.

"But at the time, I had no reason to feel bad. It was my chance. My plan was finally working and if the world loved my song, especially after Harlow's last single flopped, then Charlie and Sam couldn't send me away. If she no longer needed a double, surely they'd sign me, as *me*."

Naomi bites the inside of her lip, considering her sister, wondering if that's what she truly believes or if it's just what she is telling herself to make herself feel better.

"And, of course, everyone loved the song. Everyone except Harlow." Faye pauses, as if lost in a distant, unpleasant memory.

"I was working on some songs at the beach house in Maine—she allowed me to stay there when she was elsewhere. I'd just released the video for 'Idols' on TikTok and was really happy with it. I mean, even Harlow's harshest critics were giving it rave reviews. So when my security app alerted me someone was there, I thought maybe it was Sam coming to congratulate me." Faye lets out a laugh. "But it wasn't him. It was Harlow and she was seriously pissed off."

Faye's face turns red as she bites a piece of her cuticle off, clearly annoyed at the memory. It reminds Naomi of the countless times she came home after school complaining about a teacher or peer who dared question her about something.

"Harlow storms across the garden, shouting 'It's over!'" Faye says the phrase in a mocking tone. "I played dumb for a second, but deep down I knew. I knew it would only be a matter of time before she flipped on me. Not only had I released a song I wrote under her name, with lyrics taking a hit at her, but I killed it. And she was finally realizing I was better than her. More loved than her."

Naomi raises her eyebrows as she side-eyes Faye. She's

always been confident and fiery, but this is a level Naomi hasn't seen before. It unsettles her.

Faye ignores Naomi's questioning glare. "She started screaming, 'You're done. This is done. I don't need you or want you around, pretending you're me. It's my career. Mine!'" Faye throws her hands in the air as she imitates Harlow again. "Naturally, I started to panic, worrying if this could really be the end for me. If she got her act together, if this was her wake-up call, then maybe Sam wouldn't need me anymore. And I wasn't ready for that to happen. I needed more time."

The pit in Naomi's stomach continues to expand with dread.

"I tried to reason with her. But she wasn't having it. Said 'I don't need anyone's permission to get rid of you' and things like that." Faye huffs out another breath, shaking her head. Then she meets Naomi's gaze, eyes brimming with tears.

"You have to understand," she says, a pleading look in her eyes. "This cold treatment had been going on for months. I was so done. So sick of her taking everything for granted. Taking me for granted when I'd saved her from countless embarrassments. If anyone deserved to be there, it was me. So I told her I wasn't going anywhere." Faye swallows hard.

"And then she really lost it. I'd never seen her that angry before. She just came at me and... I don't know, it all happened so fast... I pushed her, trying to defend myself. I didn't even know I shoved her that hard, but she hit her head..." Faye's voice cracks as tears fill her eyes. She runs her hands through her hair and exhales.

Naomi squeezes her eyes shut, the sound of her heart

pounding in her ears. She feels like she might be sick as she imagines the events unfolding. Harlow ranting at Faye, barreling toward her, ready to attack. Faye shoving her to the ground. But then she imagines another scenario. One where Faye isn't defending herself. She sees red as Harlow's words cut her, scare her, so she goes on the attack first.

Naomi knows how volatile Faye can be, remembers their mother chiding Faye as a child. "Faye, you don't hit people! Faye, you don't bite people!" Faye's reasoning was always somewhat justified; it was never random. But where others would hurl insults, she'd throw a punch. Or a block of firewood. Couldn't help herself. Naomi thought Faye had learned to control herself over the years, but maybe she was wrong. And maybe Naomi was right about Harlow being an unhinged killer, except that "Harlow" is actually her sister. The notion is hard to swallow, but also impossible to ignore.

"You have to believe me," Faye pleads, now talking rapidly. "I didn't want her to die. I told her to hang on. That I was going to call for help. So I called Sam. I tried to explain everything that happened. That it was an accident. That I didn't mean to hurt her. I hoped that maybe she only had a concussion, but when Sam got there, he told me she was gone."

"Wait, you called Sam!?" Naomi says, baffled. "Not an ambulance?"

Faye stares at her, exasperated, and throws her hands out. "I was scared if I called an ambulance, they'd call the police... and..."

"And help a dying woman?" Naomi looks at Faye incredulously.

"Is that what you would've rather me do?" Faye says, pleading eyes narrowing. "Call an ambulance and then get hauled away to jail? Be the 'psycho' who killed Harlow Hayes?"

"Yeah, you know what, Faye? Maybe! Because then I wouldn't have had to go through almost three fucking years of hell, thinking you were dead!" Naomi's heart monitor starts to beep as she raises her voice.

"I know it was shitty of me, okay? I'm sorry." Faye's eyes fill with tears as she begs Naomi to understand. "But I had no choice. Sam said that he'd take care of it, that no one would ever have to know, but only if I became Harlow and left the old me behind."

A ringing silence fills the room.

"Prison or pop star," Faye says, red-faced. "What would you choose?"

Chapter 45

"But I still don't understand why you didn't tell me," Naomi says. "I would've kept your secret if I had to. Even a month later. Or a year... I would've listened. Like I am now."

Faye throws her hands in the air. "You were happy. You had a life. A good one. I was just constantly holding you back. I thought you would be fine..."

Naomi bites the inside of her cheek, tears stinging her eyes. "Well, I wasn't."

Faye looks down, not wanting to meet her eye. "I'm sorry," she whispers. "But you can't be mad at me for following my dreams."

Naomi opens her mouth to argue with her questionable reasoning. But Faye doesn't see things logically. She's all emotion. No use getting in the way of what she wants to do or think. For now, Naomi decides to be happy she has her sister back.

"So what happened next, then?" she asks. "Once Harlow was... dealt with."

The words feel sour on her tongue. She doesn't bother asking Faye for details on the cover-up, having a good idea what happened. If Faye could pass for Harlow, Harlow could pass for Faye, so Sam took Harlow's dead body to New York, put Faye's clothes on her, and surrounded her with Faye's personal effects. Naomi feels sick at the thought of Sam's gloved hands undressing Harlow, then dosing her up with drugs so the police and coroner would assume that was the cause of death, and then lighting the building on fire so it would be hard to truly tell. So that *Naomi* couldn't tell.

She wonders how much Faye knew about the cover-up, but doesn't ask, not wanting to know. Faye skips over this part too, instead launching into the explanation of how she truly transformed into one of the world's most famous pop stars without anyone knowing.

"Assuming her identity was the easiest part. She didn't even keep things in a safe, so her passport, IDs, wallets, etcetera were all so easy to get a hold of. I had access to everything—cars, private jets, bank accounts, and so on. When you're that famous, the less checks you have to go through anyway. The most awkward part was cutting out colleagues and friends. Thankfully, I learned from Sam that she'd already cut out a lot of her family after a big fallout over money a year prior, so it was a select few I had to ghost while Sam hired me new teams to work with. It wasn't that hard, I obviously had no emotional connection to them. I got a new phone, new number, and then if they tried Harlow's social media or even tried to talk to me in person, I just ignored them. I didn't enjoy that part, people calling me a bitch, but I had no other option, really."

Naomi thinks of Trevor, picturing him walking up to Faye and her just blanking him. She was surprised Faye was able to do it, just ignore someone like that. She had her shortcomings, but she was always friendly and kind. Naomi gulps, feeling unsettled at this new image of her sister.

"But then there were the fans, especially the diehard ones, who we knew would be the hardest to convince. Sam and I both thought it'd be best if 'Harlow' lay low for a while. Take a hiatus. This would give me time to regroup, and also some time to undergo a few procedures to make sure I looked as much like her as possible and didn't have to bother with the prosthetics anymore. He got me the best surgeons and stylists. They got me veneers, a nose job, buccal fat removal, lip injections, hair and eyelash extensions... By the end of it all, even I barely recognized myself. I wasn't Faye Barnes anymore. Or just Harlow's body double. I was the one and only, world-famous Harlow Hayes."

Naomi imagines Faye enjoying her "hiatus," being pampered while she suffered. It stings even more knowing what she was doing during that time, choosing not to contact her, to let her know she was okay. Naomi searches Faye's Harlow-fied face, making sure it really is her sister in there. The familiar determined look in her navy-rimmed blue eyes—devoid of the green contacts she must usually don as Harlow—confirms it.

Naomi shifts in her hospital bed uncomfortably, thinking of how one woman was just replaced with another, like that. And how her sister still doesn't seem to grasp that she just slotted into someone else's life. *Maybe it's the trauma,* she reasons. *Her mind's way of forcing her to not face the horror of it all.*

The thought brings Naomi back to what led her here in

the first place. The arrest of Harlow for the murders of Jade and Colton.

"If you didn't start working as Harlow's double until November 2021, then you don't know what happened to Jade, I'm guessing, but what about Colton?"

Faye sheepishly bites her lip and shifts her gaze to the floor. "I know what happened to both of them, actually."

Naomi's heart sinks, praying Faye isn't about to tell her she played a part in Jade's death as well.

"I didn't have anything to do with Jade," Faye says quickly. "But…" She looks around the room before lowering her voice to a whisper. "I gave Colton what he deserved."

Chapter 46

Rather than shrinking in on herself like she did when explaining what happened to Harlow, Faye holds her head up high as she details for a stunned Naomi what happened between her and Colton. How she'd had a crush on him ever since he started dating Harlow, saving magazine clips of him as a teenager, wishing it was her. So when he approached her at the VMAs last month, both of them single, she simply couldn't stay away, even though she knew she should avoid him at all costs, like Sam had urged her.

Faye explains how her foolish act of sleeping with Colton and letting her guard down—thinking he'd never realize she wasn't the same woman he'd been with for years—led him to discover her secret, and what she'd done to Harlow. How he used this as blackmail against her.

"My first mistake was not coming up with a plan fast enough after he'd discovered I wasn't really Harlow," she said. "It didn't take long for the threats to start, telling me he would tell everyone who I was if I didn't do everything he wanted. At first I complied, giving in to his sick sexual fantasies. Part of me liked it. In the very beginning. But then he kept getting weirder and weirder, amping it up. I'll spare you the details, though."

Unfortunately, Naomi is able to imagine the details after learning about the DMs from Meghan. A creeping feeling pricks up her skin at the thought of her sister being involved with someone like him.

She's here in front of you, she's fine, Naomi tells herself.

But is she? She stares at her sister, focusing on the subtle tremor in her leg, the twitch of her hand.

"I couldn't be beholden to him anymore," Faye says, face red. "I needed to find a way to gain control back. So I'd planned to dig up his secrets and blackmail him back. Little did I know, someone had already done the groundwork for me."

"Meghan?" Naomi asks.

Faye frowns in confusion.

Naomi explains how she met with Meghan Rhodes, recapping the horrible things she learned about Colton.

"Well, that was nice of Meghan to share that information with the world, wasn't it?" Faye says sarcastically.

"I wouldn't judge her too harshly. She was scared shitless of his family, had to sign an NDA…" Naomi gives Faye a chastising look, hoping the irony isn't lost on her, of her—of all people—judging Meghan.

Faye rolls her eyes. "Well, no, it wasn't Meghan. It was Harlow."

Now it's Naomi's turn to frown in confusion. "She told you before…?"

Faye shakes her head. "Not exactly, but in a way, yes. Just before she died, she said something like, 'You want my life so badly? Enjoy.' Then she clutched at this large cross necklace hanging off her chest and said, 'Take this. You'll need it.'"

Faye pulls a necklace matching the description out of her bag, holding it up for Naomi, an excited look on her face. "I didn't think anything of it at first. Thought she was being a bitch, saying I needed God or something to help save me because of what I'd done. But she was trying to help me. She didn't want the truth about Colton to die with her."

Naomi narrows her eyes and frowns, not fully understanding.

"Look." Faye twists off the top of the necklace and turns it over. She holds her hand out, revealing a small memory stick. "She'd been gathering evidence against Colton. And hid it in here."

Faye pulls her laptop out of her bag, typing and clicking as she explains what she found.

"So there's lots of files—anonymous emails, social media messages, crime scene photos, and news articles, which I assume are women who Harlow thought were hurt by Colton. Most of these don't actually prove anything—it looks like she was trying to build some sort of case against him, putting together pieces no one else would even be looking for."

She swallows hard, before turning the screen toward Naomi.

"This is the worst of them, but it's her. It's Jade." Faye's voice is filled with sadness and anger. "I didn't know her that well, but we'd bump into each other from time to time, talk about music after gigs."

Naomi fights the urge to vomit as a female corpse fills the screen. She looks so fragile and pale, with hues of blue discoloration on her skin. Faye clicks through the photos, one showing a needle mark in her arm and a few showing the blue bruises covering her neck, with *"Photos deleted from records"* scrawled in the margin. Among the rest of the files is an official autopsy report, citing drug overdose as her death, plus newspaper articles alleging the same. The articles are dated October 2021.

"But look at this," Faye says, opening a photo of a handwritten letter. "This is how I know exactly what happened to Jade…"

Naomi covers her mouth in horror as she reads a witness statement. Written by the real Harlow Hayes.

Stomach roiling with nausea, Naomi forces herself to focus on her breathing as she finishes reading. Turns out her theory about what happened to Jade wasn't far off. In the letter, Harlow summarizes the details leading up to Jade's death. A threesome gone wrong the night before the 2021 VMAs. Colton taking things too far, ignoring Jade struggling below him and Harlow's cries to stop. The morning after, Colton claimed "it" was taken care of.

How fucking cruel, Naomi thinks, heart aching for Jade's sister, Emily. *Not only did Colton kill Jade, but he dumped her body in some shithole to rot and then let her family think she shot herself up with dirty heroin.*

Not that different from what your own sister let you believe, a voice counters.

She huffs out a breath, head spinning. She should feel

vindicated that she pretty much pieced together the true cause of Jade's death, but it doesn't make her feel any better. She feels gross. Disgusted.

"Must've been eating Harlow alive if she was planning to go to the cops with this and implicate herself."

Faye nods, looking down as she picks at her nail beds. Naomi wonders if Faye feels more remorseful for what happened to Harlow after discovering what she was grappling with at the time. How she was actively gathering evidence against Colton to send him to prison, even if it meant she'd go herself. Now, only Naomi and Faye know the truth, while the rest of the world still believes Colton was the victim in all this. She'll have to find a way to fix that. But it will be tricky, since handing this letter into the police will actually implicate Faye, since she's now Harlow.

She exhales. "So you found all this… and then what?"

"I didn't know what to do at first," Faye says, sighing. "If people didn't think I was Harlow, of course I would've turned the documents over. I even thought about sending them to you anonymously, without the letter. But all I could think about was his family getting him off somehow. Using their money and power and connections to simply make it disappear. And the more I thought about it, the more I could only see one option that would truly ensure he never hurt anyone again. One that would also ensure he'd leave me alone. Plus, it felt like a way to honor Jade and Harlow. I know nothing can make up for what I did to her, but maybe finishing what she started would… I don't know… mean something."

Naomi swallows hard, chest tightening at what she knows is coming next.

"I figured an overdose was the best way to do it," Faye says. "Fitting, considering how they covered up Jade's death. Plus, actors and musicians overdose all the time, you know that. So I got in touch with a friend, who got in touch with another friend, who then got in touch with the sketchiest drug dealer in New York. Told them if they didn't ask any questions, they'd be paid double."

Faye runs her tongue over her teeth, shaking her head. "Like I said before, Colton expected me to be on call for his every want and need. So the next time he told me to come over, I was ready. I got him high off good stuff first, and then distracted him with..." Her face reddens as she gestures at her body, looking away from Naomi. "Once I could tell he was in a... trusting... mood, I pulled out the other bag of cocaine, which was heavily laced with fentanyl. He was dead within the hour."

Naomi's breath catches in her throat. It feels as if her blood has run cold. She knows her sister can be vengeful, but premeditated murder? She understands on some level. She didn't want Colton to hurt anyone again either, and his death does feel justified, to her, at least. But still. She stares at her little sister, worried how far gone she is. If she's simply a vigilante or a psychopath. She seems to have remorse, though, for what happened to Harlow, at least...

"So just to clarify," Naomi says. "You didn't poison anyone else with fentanyl, right? Just Colton..."

Faye looks horrified at the suggestion.

"I'm only asking because I need to first rule you out before I make my mind up about something. Harlow and Jade were injected with the same amount of fentanyl, most likely meaning it was from the same source, the same person..."

"Sam," Faye responds, realization dawning on her too.

Naomi nods. "It must've been."

The thought is sickening, but not as sickening as her next thought. The head injury on "Faye's" autopsy report. Was that *really* the cause of death? Or could Harlow have still been alive when Sam injected her with the drugs?

"Do you think Sam got wind of Harlow going to the police?" she asks Faye. "So when she… hit her head… and you called him, he saw it as an opportunity? A way to save both his biggest clients from massive scandals? The perfect chance to silence his problem for good?"

Faye tenses. "I didn't think about it like that, but guess it's possible. The way he would talk about her, especially near the end. Like she was the biggest pain in his ass rather than his golden girl."

Naomi imagines Sam plotting how to get rid of Faye next. "He's really bad news, Faye. You need to get away from him."

"I know," she whispers under her breath.

But again, Naomi realizes there's no way to implicate Sam without also implicating Faye. And even if they managed to find a way to spin it, he'd sure as hell make sure she went down with him if it came to it.

"Maybe you can come to some sort of agreement with him eventually, so you can both part ways… leave everything in the past."

"Mmm." Faye's face is flushed and she's jerking her leg up and down, like she used to do when she was agitated. A wave of uneasiness washes over Naomi in that moment as she studies her sister's blank, distant stare.

Chapter 47

Three Months Later

Leo pushes Naomi's wheelchair into the designated VIP section inside Madison Square Garden. Even after three painful months of bed rest and physical therapy, her leg still isn't fully healed. But she doesn't mind; she'd go through it all again if she had to. She's just grateful to be alive. And even more grateful that her sister is too.

Despite everything Faye has done, waves of pride radiate off Naomi as she looks around the sold-out arena. Packed with twenty-thousand excited fans, all waiting for Harlow Hayes to take to the stage. But only Naomi knows who she really is.

Do you, though? a voice whispers, sending a chill down her spine.

Naomi has had three months to process everything that happened, from discovering her sister is not only alive but is impersonating Harlow Hayes, to learning that she calculated and carried out Colton Scott's murder. They'll never truly know who killed Harlow—Faye by accident or

---

Sam on purpose—but Naomi's gut tells her it was Sam. Or at least that's what she desperately wants to believe.

Over the last few months, there have been moments where it was difficult to accept her new reality, who—and what—Faye had become. Their relationship has been fundamentally changed forever, there's no denying that, but they are sisters, soulmates bound by blood. And Naomi is hardwired to love her no matter what. Together, they'll figure it out.

And to her credit, Faye is trying her best to make up for all the pain she put Naomi through, making sure she has everything she needs during her recovery, helping her heal and covering all the costs, and even buying her a brand-new apartment in Tribeca. They have talked about moving to Nashville or Santa Monica, somewhere where they can start fresh together. But for now, Naomi is enjoying being back in New York. The only reason she left was because of the constant reminder of Faye. But now that she has her back, she's lost her reason to hate the city. Plus, there's Leo.

After he heard about the accident from Amelia, he drove all the way up to Maine with flowers, chocolates, and apologies—even though it was Naomi who had more to be sorry for. But they decided to start over.

"So tell me again how you two became such good friends," Leo says quizzically, staring at a giant photo of "Harlow" on the jumbotron.

They've had this conversation before, but his policeman brain clearly has trouble accepting Naomi's far-fetched explanation. So she tells him again the story she and Faye concocted after the accident to protect "Harlow's" secrets. How she showed up to Harlow's house in Maine, demanding answers. How Harlow shockingly didn't arrest her for trespassing, instead deciding to hear her out. How together, based on Naomi's discoveries and Harlow's own personal experiences, they sadly surmised that Colton was most likely involved in Faye's death.

Leo reaches out to hold Naomi's hand, giving her a sad smile at the mention of her sister. She hates lying to him, but she has no choice for now. Hopefully one day she can tell him the truth and he'll understand why she lied. But for now, Harlow Hayes is just a good friend.

Naomi finishes the rest of the story, explaining how her car hydroplaned off the road into a tree after their encounter, but Harlow managed to see the accident and call for help. It's flimsy, borderline unbelievable, but still a hell of a lot more believable than the truth.

"Well, glad that she wasn't the evil monster you thought she was at one point," Leo says. Naomi cringes at the unwelcome reminder, her rogue article that nearly lost her her job and credibility.

"But I was right about Colton..." Naomi adds. "Before anyone else..."

Leo stiffens. "Can't believe what a scumbag he turned out to be," he says, shaking his head in disbelief. "How all that was happening for years and he still had this good-boy reputation."

Naomi nods. It's something that has unsettled her too, made her question how many other men out there are hiding behind a powerful, charming façade. But at least there's one fewer in the world with Colton gone, his name now tarnished forever thanks to Naomi's recent exposé.

"You still think he overdosed, or do you think someone did it for revenge?"

If only you knew, Naomi thinks. She shrugs, face flushing. "I think someone tipped him off that women were talking, and it was getting to the point where he could no longer control it..."

"I know some of the detectives think maybe his uncle did it. Tried to kill him for sympathy votes but also before Colton could do something that they couldn't keep quiet..."

Naomi chuckles at the new rumor. "Who knows."

While she was recovering, Naomi thought tirelessly about how she could expose Colton without implicating Faye. She initially toyed with the idea of leaking the files, but omitting anything to do with Jade. That way, it wouldn't be traced back to her or her sister, meaning they wouldn't have to worry about Sam's or the Scotts' wrath. But Naomi worried the leak would get buried and simply forgotten about.

So instead she took it upon herself to finish Harlow's investigation, in the hope she could give answers to other families out there, and an avenue for women who were silenced to safely speak up. She chased any leads Harlow had flagged and followed new ones she found along the way, eventually giving her more than enough material to work with—and more importantly, too much for the Scotts to "handle."

Naomi still can't believe Joel let her publish it, especially after he was so adamant about not going after Colton Scott when she mentioned it during the Harlow investigation. But he couldn't ignore the evidence in front of him, especially after various women agreed to speak to Naomi on the record, including Meghan Rhodes.

As for "Harlow," the exposé swayed public opinion back in her favor. She still receives some flak from the usual internet trolls, still convinced she's an evil liar, but for the most part, people seem to feel bad for her being unjustly blamed and have let it go. *Seems the singer was just caught in a very sad, very tragic web*, Naomi wrote.

While she was satisfied with her story, there were two loose ends that bothered her, but neither she could do anything about. One was Jade, of course.

In order to protect Faye, she had to make sure that nothing came back to Harlow Hayes. So she couldn't publish the witness statement or even risk telling Emily and Jade's family that she knew anything concrete. She had to simply imply that Colton killed Jade in a sex act gone wrong, and then he killed himself over the guilt he felt years later.

The next loose end was Sam.

Faye told her they wouldn't have to worry about him for much longer as she had a plan to get out of her agreement with him. She didn't share any details, though, which worried Naomi, since the last time she was keeping secrets she faked her own death...

Joel was the only person to whom Naomi breathed a word about her run-in with Sam. It was awkward, trying to find a way to explain to Joel what happened without actually explaining what happened, but she managed to find a way to confront him. He made it clear that Sam Brixton wasn't a friend, only a source. Apparently, Joel had some damning stuff on him, and they'd made a deal that Joel wouldn't share what he knew so long as Sam gave him good tip-offs from time to time. It was how Joel knew before anyone else that Harlow was arrested in the first place. Joel claimed that after that initial tip, Sam went quiet, so he sent Naomi to New York to investigate, assuming it would be a pretty straightforward case. He never expected it to spiral like it did—for Naomi to spiral like she did.

Naomi isn't naive; she knows that this sort of quid pro quo is part and parcel of the industry—influence, power, and secrets are all their own forms of currency. So she didn't give Joel too hard of a time about it, instead using it to barter with him to let her run the Colton exposé. Once he agreed, though, he started to come around to the idea of C*Leb doing more serious, in-depth investigative pieces.

"I've been wanting to garner a bit more respect for C*Leb... maybe you can lead our new investigative branch," he mused.

Naomi isn't ready to take on another case quite yet, though, but maybe in the future...

After the story was published, Naomi was expecting to hear from Sam, threatening legal action, but she never heard a word. Sam didn't care what they said about Colton, so long as it didn't come back to him. And it hasn't—something Naomi hates, knowing his reign of manipulation will continue. That people with as much power and influence as him seem to always find a way out, never held accountable.

She thinks of her sister then—how she also got away with murder—and a pit of uneasiness settles in her stomach.

To love someone unconditionally can be a dangerous thing. For yourself. And for others. The lengths you'd go to protect them, hide the things they've done. Naomi would do anything not to lose Faye again. Maybe she could bring her back out of the darkness. Get her help. Fix her. Her heart sinks when she remembers the lyrics penned by her sister.

We'd sing it's us against the world. But you couldn't fix me, you tried.

Goosebumps prickle Naomi's arms as the lights dim. She scans the crowd, watching as the fans buzz with glee, their Bluetooth LED bracelets suddenly sparkling like thousands of white stars before abruptly switching to red.

A hushed silence falls across the arena and excitement courses through Naomi as she waits with everyone else for the star of the show to appear. She inhales, wondering if maybe she was too cynical before. That dreams can come true. That it can work out for some people. But a sinister voice counteracts the optimism, warning that only the ruthless survive this "deadly game."

For the glory and fame, I'd do it the same.

Ignoring her sister's unnerving lyrics, Naomi forces her attention to center stage, where "Harlow Hayes" has seemingly appeared out of nowhere. The crowd erupts in applause.

"Can't breathe, can't touch, can't see," she sings. "Violent ends for you and me."

A chill creeps up Naomi's neck as the haunting words travel through the arena. She looks up at the screen, where the singer's face is magnified.

Naomi wonders if the last few months were just a dream as she stares into Harlow Hayes' ice-cold gaze, not recognizing her sister at all.

C*LEB NEWS

FORMER MANAGER OF HARLOW HAYES AND COLTON SCOTT DIES IN CAR CRASH

By Naomi Barnes – *March 20, 2025*

Six months following the death of his close friend and client Colton Scott, Sam Brixton of Sam Brixton Talent Management has died.

One of the most successful managers in the business, Brixton was responsible for handling the careers of stars like Kamryn Hart and Harlow Hayes, who recently parted ways with the mogul.

According to sources, Brixton was facing personal difficulties at the time of the tragedy. A friend who wishes to remain anonymous told us that Sam and his wife, Helena, had separated only months prior, after rumors started swirling of an affair with an aspiring actress. Brixton was also rumored to be the subject of an IRS investigation.

"Sam was going through a lot. His wife left him and the IRS was knocking on his door. He'd lost his two top-earning clients in a matter of months at the end of last year, not to mention dealing with the fallout of the allegations made against Colton Scott, so business wasn't booming like it used to. I'm not saying he crashed on purpose or was drinking, but he'd become reckless."

According to the New York State Police, Brixton was found meters from his 2023 Maserati Ghibli, which had crashed into a wooded area off the Taconic State Parkway.

Police confirm Brixton was not wearing his seatbelt at the time of the crash and that speeding or faulty brakes could have been the cause of the accident.

LYRIC BASE

Last Word
Song by <u>Harlow Hayes</u>

Hit the gas in the daylight, that's what I call a gaslight
Put a hit on my blood, that'll cost you blood
Hit the brakes, but you spin out, that's what I call fallout
Yeah I found you out, karma's what I'm all about
Cruel of me, I know, to say you got what you deserved
But a cold front's moving in, I finally get the last word

I've said it before, I'll say it again
For the glory and fame, I'd do it the same
Yeah, I'd do it the same, revel in the pain
Making a name is a deadly game

Snow covers the tracks, the waves silence the screams
Thought you could control me like her?
Baby only in your dreams
Because the champagne was kerosene
Didn't know you lit the match
Now watch me rise as you crash
Your glittering world turned to ash

Do you understand? I've done bad things, honey
You have to commit, blood is money
I understand, I've done worse things than you
And I'm the one with the last word, violent ends for you
I've said it before, I'll say it again
For the glory and fame, I'd do it the same
The last word is mine, I finished the game

Social Media Post

C*Leb News ✓ @CLebNewsOfficial

New Harlow Hayes song "Last Word" sends fans into a frenzy, claiming it's about her relationship with the now-deceased, ill-famed Colton Scott. Read more here: http://clebnews.com/last-word-by-harlow-hayes

20:47 · July 3, 2025 · **76.3K** Views
976 Reposts **15K** Likes

@LiviaStoneHH: SPILL sis! #songoftheyear

@SheSaidEd: I'm sorry but I hope Colton's family sues her for all the unnecessary stress she's causing. She obviously fabricated all of those documents to get public opinion back on side. She should still be behind bars, we all know it was her! #vilebitch

@HalleSkidmer: "Watch me rise as you crash" didn't her ex manager die in a crash recently? 👀

@ClioNovelist: How in the world is that supposed to be about her manager 💀 obviously it's about CS

@baddiefonts: It's rumored she's a body double and the real Harlow is dead

@StipmoreHH: @baddiefonts it's rumored that we're all aliens

@EmmaAnneDutrond: 😌 OMFG ya'll need to relax. It's just a song, it doesn't mean anything. It's not that deep…

Authors' Note

As we **m**ention in our fi**r**st note at the beginning of the book, in **a**ddition to Harlow's hidden messages, we layered in **s**ome of our own Easter **e**ggs for readers. These were **s**cattered throughout the novel, but if you didn't spot them while you read, other hidde**n** messages reveal where yo**u** can find some of them...

Did you figure it out? Let us know @the_mancaruso_ sisters or @headofzeus on Instagram if so, and we'll tell you if you're right—or give you another clue if you need it! (Hint: We love an **anagram**...)

Acknowledgements

The very first person we want to thank is our incredible agent, Millie Hoskins from United Agents. Thanks for scooping us out of the slush and continuing to believe in us and our crazy ideas. You helped shape *Rumoured* into what it is today and this book simply would not exist without you. Huge thank you also to Amy Mitchell for all your time, invaluable feedback, and support.

To our editor Bethan Jones: It's been nothing short of a joy to work with you. Thank you so much for fighting for *Rumoured* and for helping us take the story to a whole new level. We are so grateful that we get to collaborate with you and the rest of the amazing Head of Zeus team, including Jo Liddiard, Andrew Knowles, Polly Grice, Dan Groenewald, Emily Champion and Peyton Stableford. To copyeditor extraordinaire, Dan Shutt, and proofreading ace, Jenni Davis: Thank you for lending your eagle eyes to the text and flagging those pesky errors! Massive thank you to Simon Michele and the insanely talented Head of Zeus art department for giving us such a fantastic cover!

To our Pitch Wars mentor, Melissa Colasanti: You were the very first person to believe in our work professionally and we are forever grateful for all the time and care you put into helping us hone our craft. Thank you also to Brenda Drake, Irene Reed, and the rest of the Pitch Wars team, as well as mentors Ed Aymar, Lyn Liao Butler, and Ashley Winstead for all your support and advice. To our fellow 2021/22 mentees: Tackling the wild world of publishing would be so much harder without you all to "discord" with, and we're so grateful to have had the opportunity to get to know so many of you and be a part of such a supportive writing community.

Sian Gilbert: Thanks for keeping us (aka Kelly) sane, and for your considered feedback, pep talks (insert Marge here), and friendship (CRY-LAUGH). It's been such a fun, hilarious journey ever since right before the PW showcase and we're so grateful that we (one of us at least) can do all the author things with you in the UK. Sophie Clark: Thanks for virtually holding our hand and cry-laughing with us from post-PW querying until now, and of course, for all your invaluable feedback, pep talks, and friendship as well. We don't know what we would do without you both!

Mom and Dad: Thanks for giving us each other in the first place and always encouraging us to work together! You always told us to be grateful for each other, that a sister was the best friend we'd ever have. You were so right. You also always told us we should "never be bored," and we can confirm that we rarely are with all the book ideas floating around between us. Mom, thanks for encouraging us to dream as big as possible and reach for the moon. And thanks for manifesting—we're now convinced you have some magical powers (thanks to your pet grasshopper as well, obviously). Dad, thanks for always making sure we had a plan B or C while we chased our dreams and followed our hearts. We love you both so much and are so lucky to have you as parents.

To our rocks—our husbands, Mark and Chris: While our books often feature the worst of mankind, you two are truly the best of the best. Your unwavering love, support, and encouragement is what got us through the hundreds of rejections over the years and we hope you know how grateful we are to have you in our lives. Thanks for never doubting us. We love you infinitely and are so happy we get to experience all of life's ups and downs with you.

To baby Elena, who was literally born as I (Auntie Kelly) finished writing these acknowledgments: Our little light, you've given us both a new purpose. Oh, and we can't forget our beloved fur babies, Dany, Adonis, and Bella: Writing wouldn't be the same without you curled up at our feet or nudging us to take a break.

Huge thank you to all our other family and friends who have been so supportive, especially Jayne, Barry, Nancy, Mercedes, John, Aunt Cindy, Grandma, and Uncle Frankie (we love and appreciate you all so much!), and to our colleagues who have cheered us on and answered our millions of questions over many a lunch break and at the coffee machine. Special thanks to Rebecca Peel for being our first beta reader many moons ago!

As mentioned in our author's note, this book was born out of a deep love for writing and music, so we'd also like to shoutout the artists we've had on repeat since we started writing Rumoured in 2022 (and also since we started writing fiction in general thirteen years ago): Taylor Swift, Lana Del Rey, Jack Antonoff, The Beatles, BTS, Halsey, Trent Reznor,

Atticus Ross, Dove Cameron, Ramin Djawadi, Danny Elfman, Blake Neely, Hans Zimmer, Nicholas Britell and Caitlin Sullivan—thanks for the daily dose of inspiration and motivation. Also to the BTS Army and Swifties: Kelly won't share her stan-Twitter usernames she's had since before the pandemic, but thanks for the good vibes and endless content (we hope some of you enjoyed getting lost in the Harlow-verse!). To the Beatlemaniacs and fan blogs out there: Thank you for existing!

Finally, to the two little girls scrawling out two-man shows on A4, the twenty-year-olds writing their first novel together an ocean apart, and the thirty-year-olds still getting rejections: Cheers for never giving up!

About the Authors

KELLY AND KRISTINA MANCARUSO have been crafting stories together since they were children in upstate New York. Now, they collaborate on opposite sides of the Atlantic.

An HR program manager for a Manhattan-based firm, Kristina has a Bachelor's degree from Stony Brook University, where she was named Valedictorian by the College of Business. She still resides in New York with her husband, daughter, and two German Shepherds.

A senior creative copywriter for a software company, former PR manager Kelly now lives in Nottingham, England, with her firefighter husband and beloved dog. She has a Bachelor's degree from The University of North Carolina at Wilmington and a Master's degree from the University of Nottingham.

Rumoured is their debut thriller.